ON THURSDAY, FEBRUARY 1, 1979, THE
HEAD OF EVERY DELEGATION IN THE U.N.
RECEIVED A COPY OF **PROTEUS**, MORRIS
WEST'S NEW NOVEL. THEY KNEW, AS YOU
KNOW, THAT IT IS FICTION . . .
. . . FOR THE MOMENT!

PROTEUS

Morris West

BANTAM BOOKS
TORONTO • NEW YORK • LONDON

For
The Prisoners of Conscience,
of whom
to our shame
there are far too many

PROTEUS
*A Bantam Book | published by arrangement with
William Morrow & Company, Inc.*

PRINTING HISTORY
William Morrow edition published February 1979
4 printings through March 1979
Franklin Library edition October 1978
Literary Guild edition February 1979
Serialized in East | West Network Magazine March 1979
A limited edition of this book has been privately printed
Bantam edition | May 1980

It is becoming more and more obvious that it is not starvation, not microbes, not cancer, but man himself who is mankind's greatest danger because he has no adequate protection against psychic epidemics, which are infinitely more devasting in their effect than the greatest natural catastrophes.

—C. G. Jung,
  Modern Man in Search of a Soul

PROTEUS

1

◇◇◇◇◇◇◇◇◇◇◇◇◇◇◇◇◇◇◇◇◇◇◇◇◇◇◇◇◇◇◇◇◇

He was a man who travelled much and always in singular comfort, so that he had little of the curiosity of the tourist and much of the impatience of the executive who must dispatch his business and be gone again.

However, this Easter Sunday in Rome was different. It was a family feast, a tribal occasion, to which all else—the ancient splendours of the city, the press of pilgrims, the Papal Mass in St. Peter's, even the Pontiff's proclamation to the City and to the World—was backdrop and panoply. It was the one day in his life when he wanted to puff out his chest and shout aloud: "Look at me! Look at John Spada, who today is fifty-five years old and grateful for every hour of it! Look at my Anna, who is still as beautiful as the day I met her! Look at Teresa and the man she has married —a brave one, a good one, who will breed me a grandson to inherit the Spada empire. I am so proud, so happy, I could embrace the whole crazy, wonderful world!"

He said none of it, of course. He was too controlled for that. Even here in the land of his fathers he

1

was half an alien: John Spada from New York, president of a multinational enterprise, a merchant prince among the old nobility and the new restless commons of this city of Emperors and Popes. But Anna knew, without his telling, how happy he was. She clung to him, flushed and excited, as he pushed through the crowds in St. Peter's Square towards the alley behind the Borgo Santo Spirito, where Uncle Andrea's chauffeur was waiting for them.

Teresa and Rodolfo were thrusting ahead, and he watched them with pride and affection. She was small and dark like her mother. He, tall and slim, the scion of an old family of ranchers and horse breeders from the pampas of Argentina. He was ten years older than Teresa, which Spada approved, because a man should have his career made before he settled down to raise a family. Rodolfo Vallenilla, at thirty-eight, was one of the best editors in Buenos Aires, whose opinions on South American politics were read with respect around the world.

Spada's small regret, and Anna's constant complaint, was that the families must live so far apart, the seniors in New York, the juniors in Argentina; but—what the devil!—with jet travel, telephones and telex, distance was a nominal factor anyway. When the children came, arrangements could be made for more regular contact. Besides, speaking for himself—and always in a low voice when Anna was around—he would prefer Teresa to practice a little at being a wife before becoming a mother. He did not want to see her child-bound too early.

Still, that was all in the future. Today was full and good. They would drive out to lunch with Uncle Andrea at his villa in Frascati, talk family and busi-

2

ness and politics, drowsily, in the warm spring sunshine. This was the thing he missed in New York: the sense of proportion, of continuity, of ultimate inconsequence in all but family matters. It was hard to be too concerned about the Dow-Jones index when you walked to the office over the bones of dead legions.

As they crossed the river, Spada asked the driver to take the Appia Antica as far as the Catacombs of San Callisto and then cut across to the Via Ardeatina. Rodolfo should see the remains of the old funerary monuments, while he himself had a small act of piety to perform. As a prelude to the act he asked the driver to stop while he bought a bunch of violets from a flower seller at the curbside. The flowers were small, their fragrance was faint and the price he paid was exorbitant. Teresa protested, but Anna patted her arm and admonished her, smiling.

"It's Papa's birthday. Today he does whatever he wants."

"Doesn't he always?"

"At work, perhaps," said Anna calmly. "At home there are other rules."

"I believe I have heard that before." Rodolfo Vallenilla chuckled. "My mother used to tell my father he was the best horse trainer in the Argentine, but he should not bring the manners of the stable into the house."

"Today," said John Spada, "I am a saint. I've confessed. I've been to Mass. I've had a blessing from the Pope. I demand to be treated with respect—especially by married women!"

"Who's coming to lunch at Uncle Andrea's?"

"Who isn't?" There was a touch of Roman malice in Anna's tone. "The moment they know your father's

3

coming, they start rounding up the guests. There'll be someone from the Quirinal, always one or two from the Vatican, Carlo Magnoli from Turin, certainly Fonseca from the Bank of Rome . . . Count on a dozen, at least, with wives and families as well. Eh! . . . I'm out of practice for this sort of event."

"So, relax, Anna mia!" Spada waved aside her complaint. "Let your daughter take some of the strain. As the newly married one she has to be initiated into the circle of the matriarchs."

"I could cheerfully murder you, Papa!"

"Why? You've been a hard-nosed professional lady long enough. You have dues to pay at the matrons' club. Today will be good practice."

"You talk like a male chauvinist. I'm a physician, not a gossipmonger."

"But if you want to be a successful physician, you need a good bedside manner. The gossip comes in handy for that."

"Rodo, you're supposed to defend your wife."

"Against big John Spada? I'm an editor, not a tank commander!"

"We stop here." Spada pointed out of the window to the black gates that enclosed the somber enclave of the Fosse Ardeatine, the quarry caves where the Germans had machine-gunned three hundred hostages in reprisal for a partisan raid in the Via Rasella.

"I'll wait in the car." Anna Spada shivered and huddled in the corner of the seat.

"I'll stay with Mama," said Teresa.

Spada, carrying the posy of violets, walked into the enclosure with Rodolfo Vallenilla at his side. He explained to Vallenilla the meaning of the memorial

4

and then led him into the dim chamber where the
three hundred sarcophagi were laid row on row. He
said quietly, "I was in Italy when it happened. We
were slogging our way up towards Rome, through the
passes of the Abruzzi. I didn't know then that my uncle Eduardo, who was my father's brother, was one of
the victims. When I made contact with his family and
heard the news, I had to write and tell my father . . .
He was heartbroken. Before he died I promised him
that, whenever I came to Rome, I would make a re-
membrance for him and for me."

He laid the violets on the stone lid of the sarcoph-
agus and stood for a long moment, head bowed in
silent recollection. Then he straightened up, faced his
son-in-law and said soberly, "I get scared, Rodo. I'm
an old navigator and I smell the wind. This could
happen again. Not exactly in the same way, but yes, it
may happen."

"I know." Vallenilla nodded. "It's already started."

"I've wanted to talk to you. There hasn't been
much time—and I didn't want to spoil the women's
holiday."

"We don't really know each other very well, do
we, John?"

"I'd like to change that, Rodo. Next time I come
down to Buenos Aires, let's make some private time,
eh?"

"It will be my pleasure."

"I know you don't entirely approve of me or the
way I operate my business . . ."

"Teresa, I know, loves you very much." Vallenilla
was curiously formal. "I have respect for you, much

respect. That's a good beginning. The understanding should follow. Here, in this place, I have understood a little more."

"You're a thinker," said John Spada. "I'm a doer. I dig minerals out of the ground. I make things and sell things. I trade in money and commodities and political realities. . . . The bigger the scale, the simpler it gets."

"Or does it just look simple? Like pulling the pin out of a grenade—or killing three hundred hostages with a machine gun?"

"Maybe even like that. But don't judge me too quickly, Rodo. Let's be patient with each other, eh?"

"Of course." Vallenilla shrugged and grinned. "Happy birthday, Father-in-law!"

He laid a hand on John Spada's arm and steered him out into the sunlight. Before they reached the gate, Spada halted again and pointed to the mouths of the caves, inside which the bodies of the dead had been found.

"I used to dream about those and what happened inside. Funny thing, though, I was never part of the event. I was always standing up there on the ridge, looking down. I'd see the German trucks arrive, the captives bundled out and pushed towards the entrance. The next moment I'd be standing here, on this spot, looking inside, watching the gunners take aim and shoot, seeing the victims fall . . . I never spoke. I never moved. Nobody ever saw me. I was still there when the caves were sealed and the last German marched away. I always felt ashamed, as if I myself were to blame for the slaughter. I haven't had the dream for a long time now."

"So you've purged your devils, whatever they were?"

Spada gave him a wry grin and an offhand answer. "Or perhaps I've got used to having them around."

"I've seen that happen too." Vallenilla was suddenly tense. There was an undertone of anger in his voice. "It's not pretty. It's like—like blind children playing in a slaughter yard!"

Spada was startled by his vehemence. He gave him a long, searching look and said evenly, "Maybe we should have that talk now."

"There's no time." Vallenilla was very definite. "If we rush into discussion we're bound to quarrel. Besides, you can't spoil the party. Teresa and I fly out in the morning. I'll write to you, try to give you a balanced survey of the situation and the part America is playing in it. If things get bad, I'd like to use the telex facilities at the Spada offices in Buenos Aires."

"Any time. This is family now."

"I know. I should be . . . I am grateful."

There was an apology on the tip of his tongue, but Spada cut him off with brusque good humour.

"In this family you don't always have to be polite. We should go now. The women will be getting impatient."

Forty minutes later they were received with full tribal honours at the villa of Uncle Andrea, who, at seventy-five, was the acknowledged patriarch of the Spada clan, father of ten children, grandfather of twenty-two, a former Minister of Justice, still a member of the Hunt Club, a fancier of orchids and pretty women. He was also a notable negotiator, and the vil-

la, secluded among its vineyards and olive groves,
had been the scene of many a classic maneuver between left and center. In today's exercise the family
was the pivot piece, a solid phalanx of elderly aunts,
junior cousins and their children, all of whom must be
recognized, embraced, complimented, made to feel
loved and honoured by their American relatives. Then
the new son-in-law must be presented and appraised
for bloodlines, manners and virility, while his bride
was covertly inspected for signs of pregnancy. Spada and Uncle Andrea watched the ceremony with
faintly malicious amusement. Finally the old man
grinned and nodded approval.

"Good! He has fire in his belly and brains in
his head. I think you should be happy."

"I am, Uncle. I am also afraid."

"Of him?"

"For him and for Teresa. Do you follow what is
happening in South America?"

"I follow everything, Giovanni. What time is it?"

"Nearly two o'clock. Why?"

"I thought it best to get the family part over first,
so I invited our other guests for two-fifteen. We sit
down at three. Afterwards we can have our talk in the
library."

"Who's coming?"

"Magnoli, Frantisek, Fonseca . . . all the names
you know; but this time there are two new ones." He
hesitated a moment and then added, almost apolo-
getically, "Times change. We have to change too. One
is Castagna of the P.C.I. He is very close to Berlin-
guer."

"And the other?"

8

"Hugo von Kalbach."

"Why him?"

"Because he's one of the great thinkers of our time. He's just finishing a major work which he calls *The Phenomena and Epidemiology of Violence*. I think he may have something of value for us all."

"And Castagna?"

"The Communists took thirty-eight percent of the votes at the last election. We have to cooperate with them to keep the country going. Castagna is a skeptic and afraid of the fanatics. . . . Which reminds me"—he gestured towards Vallenilla, who was spending charm and patience on the most elderly of all the aunts—"have you told him?"

"Not yet."

"Are you sure of him?"

"Yes."

"Bring him in then. We'll soon know what he's made of—and whether he has anything to teach us."

Anna came over to them at that moment, smiling but resolute.

"Come on, you two. No lobbying before lunch! Rejoin the human race! The family wants to talk to you, John. And you, Uncle, should rescue Rodo. I think he's taken enough."

She linked arms with them and forced them to walk with her down the steps and into the terraced garden, where the servants were dispensing lemonade to the children and champagne to their elders.

When Spada approached, the women converged on him like peasants around a peddler in a country square. They wanted news, notice, concern from this Spada who had prospered so hugely. They wanted

9

patronage for their young ones, an assurance of care in the bad times which, they all believed, were just around the corner. Aunt Lisa, seventy-eight years old, seamed and wrinkled like a winter apple, summed it up for him in her harsh Roman accent.

". . . They have lists now, of candidates for kidnapping. They have boys on street corners waiting to put a bullet into a man as he walks to buy a newspaper. . . . Whether they are of the right or the left, what does it matter? The end is the same. Mistrust, disorder, failure of confidence. We are back to the days of the bandits and the condottieri! I know; your uncle Andrea knows. We've lived through two wars and all the time of the Fascisti. . . . All the signs are there again. We are nearly at breaking point . . ."

Spada put his arm around her thin shoulder and tried to calm her.

"Come now, Aunt Lisa! It's not half as bad as that."

"Easy for you to say! You don't live here."

"No, but I have big business here. I know how the system works. The extremists make big noises; the government falls; a new one moves in; but there's still wine and bread on the table. It's a kind of magic, a conjuring trick."

"But the audience is tired of political tricks. They're walking out. They're looking for another kind of theater. They want a play with a hero—and they want to walk through safe streets afterwards. . . ." She looked around at the group. "This is the new generation. Ask them what they think."

Spada smiled and shook his head. "Not before lunch! Not on my birthday! Tell me, what do you think of our Rodo?"

The younger women giggled and exchanged glances. Aunt Lisa gave a high, whinnying laugh.

"For a foreigner, not bad! But you won't tame him too easily."

"I don't want to tame him. I want a man in my household."

"Then let's hope he breeds well—and your Teresa is interested in having a family."

"Why shouldn't she be?"

"Well! These modern women with their careers and their liberated ideas. . . !"

"Teresa's a very good physician."

"She's married now. She has a husband to care for. He won't want to come home to a tired wife who smells of ether and iodine! I've told her that."

"I'm sure she'll manage very well, Aunt Lisa."

"She'll need to; your Anna didn't have an easy time with you."

"Do you hear her complain?"

"No. But you're a Spada—and they last better than most men!"

"You have a dirty mind, Aunt Lisa!"

"That helps too, my boy." She pushed him away gently. "The other guests are arriving. Go join your uncle Andrea!"

Luncheon was served on the sunlit terrace, where Uncle Andrea, the social strategist, had disposed his guests, six to a table, so that the conversation might flow more freely and intimately and the outsiders be spared the boredom of family gossip. Spada found himself placed with Hugo von Kalbach, Luigi Castagna, Aunt Lisa and two of the more intelligent junior wives, to whom Uncle Andrea had given the grudging accolade: "They're not the prettiest of the bunch, but at least they don't chatter and they can read words of three syllables."

Von Kalbach was the most impressive figure in the group, a stooping giant with a mane of white hair and a smile limpid and innocent as a child's. His Italian was stilted; but he was an eager listener, alert to every detail of the talk. Castagna, the P.C.I. man, was a horse of another colour, lean, dark and saturnine, with a cool wit and the uncluttered logic of a man who had all his premises clear and knew all the rules in the book.

Before they had even finished the pasta, Aunt Lisa began testing his defenses: "A Florentine, eh?"

"On my mother's side. My father came from Arezzo."

"And what did your father do?"

"He was a stonemason, signora. He specialized in gravestones."

"And you?"

"I graduated, signora—from epitaphs to political pamphlets."

"You may find the epitaphs last longer."

Castagna laughed a big, happy laugh, surprising from so terse a man. Spada chuckled and patted the old woman's hand.

"I'm sure yours won't be written for a long time yet, Aunt Lisa. Now behave yourself! Come the revolution, you'll need all the friends you can get."

"I am interested." Von Kalbach tried hard to be humourous in his careful, correct Italian. "We are very mixed company—a big American capitalist, a Communist deputy, a Bishop from the Vatican, a banker, a maker of automobiles, a liberal editor, a bankrupt

12

philosopher . . . all invited by a Christian Democrat who lives like a prince!"

"Andrea has a taste for comedy," said Aunt Lisa brusquely.

"And a talent for reasonable compromise," said Castagna evenly. "We need that in these times."

"I agree." Von Kalbach was suddenly eloquent and animated. "It is the absolutists who threaten us now—the terrorist who seeks to reverse history with a bomb blast, the tyrant who wants to perpetuate the present in which he flourishes."

"Is that not too neat a distinction?" Castagna's tone was deceptively mild. "Does it not ignore the organizations which sponsor the terror and those which foster the tyranny to their own profit?"

"Like your own party, for instance?" Aunt Lisa was not easily silenced.

Castagna's answer was polite but pointed. "Or perhaps the Spada companies which helped to put Pinochet in power in Chile and are supporters of similar regimes elsewhere."

All eyes were on Spada as he sat silent, digesting the accusation, knowing that he too was under test. Castagna was too bright a man to be trapped into a quarrel by a shrewd old beldame. He himself ought to be bright enough to avoid the same snare. He reflected a moment longer and then said, calmly enough, "Isn't that, in itself, an absolutist judgment? In business, you live with what is; you try to adapt to what happens. It's like the old caravan masters. They had to make treaties with the tribes on the route and pay the king's tribute at the city gates; otherwise trade came to a standstill."

"Sometimes, too, they paid the plotters to make a new king—or joined the king's men to fight the tribes."

"But can we, who were not there, make true judgments on them?"

"A nice point, my friend." Castagna smiled and made a gesture of deprecation. "I apologize for my bad manners. Perhaps later we can talk about the present."

"With pleasure." Spada turned to Von Kalbach. "Uncle Andrea tells me you've written a new work on the phenomena of violence."

"It is almost finished." The old scholar was curiously subdued. "I am not sure that I know how to finish it—or indeed whether I shall have time to do so."

"Why not, Professor?" The question came from one of the girls.

"Well . . ." Von Kalbach paused, trying to construct the answer in Italian. "We are all familiar with the phenomena, the things that happen: assassination, hijacking, bombing, the violence practiced by police, by security men, by professional torturers . . . . It is our response which is in question. How far can we go? What morality applies?"

"And what is your answer, Professor?" asked John Spada.

"I have none." The old man's tone was somber. "Whichever way I turn I am in dilemma. I can choose, as a Christian, a passive resistance. Am I entitled to stand by while another is brutalized? I have written not an answer but a riddle: 'If I act, I become one of them. If I act not, I become their slave.'"

"I think you must act," said Aunt Lisa stoutly. "It's your right and duty as a man!"

"Is it, dear lady?" Von Kalbach turned to face her. "Then perhaps I should tell you that in my own country I am on the death list of a Baader-Meinhof commando because it is claimed I am a tool of the reactionaries. In Russia a distinguished colleague has been confined to a mental home, reduced by drugs to a vegetal condition, because he protested the invasion of human rights in his own country. Very soon we may both be dead. What will you do about that, signora? Or you, Mr. Spada? Or you, young ladies, what will you teach your children to do?"

"The ladies will do nothing," said Castagna calmly. "Because they are individuals, impotent against the organizations. . . . Spada will do nothing that may damage his goodwill or his profits."

"And you, Castagna?"

"I'm lucky." There was more than a hint of self-mockery in the reply. "I seek a party directive and do as I'm told. It's as comforting as having a father confessor."

"I'd like to believe you." Spada grinned. "I think you itch like the rest of us and scratch as hard. . . . You should get Aunt Lisa to tell you the story of her unknown soldier."

"Please?" Castagna looked puzzled.

Aunt Lisa whinnied again. Spada explained.

"During the German retreat, there was an SS detachment quartered in the villa here. One of them was a drunken brute who constantly terrorized the women of the household. One night he went absent and was never seen again. There used to be an old well at the bottom of the far vineyard. It's bricked over now. He's still at the bottom of it."

"It was very deep," said Aunt Lisa. "And the spring had dried up, so we weren't depriving ourselves of water."

"And it was you, signora, who killed him?"

"That's the legend," said Aunt Lisa placidly. "I never found it necessary either to confirm or deny it."

"So you see"—John Spada added the final footnote—"it's very hard to judge in advance how people will act, or afterwards how right or wrong they were. Let's change the subject, shall we?"

When the meal was over, Uncle Andrea led his privileged guests into the library. A manservant offered coffee and liqueurs, then withdrew. Uncle Andrea made a brief informal announcement.

"For three of you, this is a first visit to my house. As I told you privately before luncheon, you are to be invited to share in a work which has been going on for some time. You have given me your assurance, as gentlemen, that whether you decide to join or not, you will keep secret what passes here today. Is that our understanding?"

There was a murmur of assent from Vallenilla, Castagna and Von Kalbach. Uncle Andrea nodded to John Spada, who fished in his pocket, brought out a black notebook, found the page he wanted, then addressed himself to the small assembly.

"Some of you know that the business I own today started in this room, with a gathering very like this one. Then, as now, Uncle Andrea was host, Carlo Magnoli was here, and Freddie Fonseca. Bishop Frantisek was not here . . . he was still a curate in Philadelphia. Me? I was a kid from New York, with a head

16

full of ideas and five hundred dollars in the bank.
Well, Uncle Andrea and his friends had faith in me
and they helped me to build what we have today
. . . . They did more. They left me free at the end of
it. For that I shall be grateful until the day I die. . . ."

He broke off and with an old-fashioned gesture
took his uncle's hand and pressed it to his lips.

Uncle Andrea said gently, "Tell them the rest of
it."

"As the enterprise got bigger, I found myself
trapped in a prison I had built for myself. Success
makes walls around a man. He gets so used to reading
balance sheets and business reports, he cannot see the
man who has no shoes, the mother who has no milk
for a child. But there is always an automatic absolution for his sins. Without his capital the factory would
not be built and there would be no work for the labour force. Because the factory is there, or the mine or
the oil field, there is a town, a school, a hospital which
otherwise would never have been built. Because he is
a realist, he can keep the politicians halfway honest
and get the bankers to gamble on new ventures. So
it's not all black and white like a propaganda poster.
. . . Though sometimes, as in Chile or Korea or Iran
or Brazil, companies like mine are whores who sleep
in the tyrant's bed and bask under the protection of
his police. . . . Again, it's easy to condemn the whore.
It's not so easy to trace what turns an honest woman
into a harlot . . . or what may happen if she decides to
repent and be virtuous. . . . There are many besides
her bedfellow who profit from what she does." He
laughed and flung out his arms in a gesture of defeat.
"You see! Even here I talk like counsel for the defense! What I am trying to say is that you cannot dis-

17

mantle a vast enterprise to salve your own bad conscience! The best you can do is use the power it gives you to build what Uncle Andrea once called 'bridges of benevolence,' not merely between the rich and the needy, but between those who, without a mediator, might remain enemies, between friends who could not talk to each other because of protocol, between men of goodwill divided by frontiers or ideologies. . . . This group is one such bridge. There are other groups around the world, in Iran, in Korea and many other places. All are secret, all identified by a common symbol. . . . There are three men in this room who do not know the symbol because they have not yet been fully initiated. Before I go further, I have to ask them, do they want to know more, or do they wish to withdraw without commitment?"

There was a long moment of silence, then Rodolfo Vallenilla asked a cold question. "I am married to your daughter, yet you drop me, without warning, into this group. Why?

"Because I do not control it. The members must approve you, as they must approve everything that is proposed."

"Do you fund the groups?"

"Only in part. Other members contribute according to their means. The funds are under joint local control in each area."

"Which is exercised how?"

"By majority vote."

"Each group is, therefore, autonomous?"

"Yes."

"Is each member autonomous? Bishop Frantisek, for instance . . . does he speak for himself or for the Vatican?"

"For myself only," said Frantisek flatly. "I commit myself to act according to my own conscience."

"But if the vote goes against your conscience?"

"I abstain from action. I may withdraw altogether from the group. So far I have not felt obliged to do either."

Luigi Castagna interposed himself into the dialogue. "I am here because I am attracted by the notion that bridges of benevolence can be built. I should feel happier if I knew something of what has been done already."

This time it was Uncle Andrea who answered. "Last week, in Chile, four senior members of the Allende party were released from prison and allowed to leave the country. It was also confirmed that there was a drastic curtailment of the powers of DINA, the security service. My nephew and certain of his colleagues were responsible for that."

"How?"

"By refusing to back any further bank loans to Chile until it was done. It took hard bargaining among the diplomats in Washington and the bankers in New York, but in the end they got the support they needed."

"Yesterday," said Carlo Magnoli, "the leader of the Christian Protest Movement in South Korea arrived in Tokyo. Our group in Seoul got him out of the country one jump ahead of President Park's secret police."

"Three months ago"—Fonseca, the banker, added his own postscript—"a well-known South African editor was placed under house arrest. One of our groups smuggled him out of the country and got him into England."

19

"You might call us body snatchers." Spada grinned at his son-in-law. "Or you might, if you have a taste for history, think of us as ransomers, like the Donkey Men of the Middle Ages who dedicated their lives to the release of captives from the Moors."

"I'd be interested to know," said Castagna quietly, "who gave you the mandate for this work."

"I assumed it," said Spada flatly. "I didn't need a mandate to dig copper out of the ground or start a program of drug research. Why should I need one to save a life or give a man back his liberty?"

"How do you do such things?" asked Vallenilla again.

"We use whatever means are at hand: diplomatic negotiation, commercial bargaining, bribery, blackmail, sometimes . . ."

"Sometimes what?"

"Let's say," said John Spada amiably, "in this kind of exercise one needs to be very flexible. Does the project interest you, Rodo?"

"It might." Vallenilla was cautious and reserved. "However, I'd like to know more. For instance, do you function in the Argentine or Brazil?"

"We do."

"I've never heard of it."

"That's a compliment to our discretion. However, we need more members. Good ones are hard to find, which is why you've been invited to this meeting."

"How do you choose the people you decide to help?"

"Their cases are recommended to us." It was Uncle Andrea who answered. "Professor von Kalbach, for example, has asked us to consider the case of his colleague, Lermontov, who is confined in a psychiatric institution outside Moscow. We're working on that now. Castagna wants us to intervene in the affair of a student who is in police custody in Milan, falsely accused of a bombing six months ago."

Vallenilla was silent. Spada prompted him quietly: "It's the mandate that bothers you, isn't it?"

"In a way, yes."

"Then ask yourself what mandate you have for the editorials you write, the stories you publish . . . You certainly don't get it from a government or a party."

"No, it's a matter of conscience for me."

"And you seek to form the same conscience in your readers?"

"That's right."

"So do we," said Uncle Andrea. "Why should our motives be more suspect than yours?"

Castagna gave a small, dry chuckle and then added a faintly mocking comment. "I found myself in the same dilemma, my friend. It's hard to believe that capital has a social conscience."

"Or the Church a distaste for tyranny," said Bishop Frantisek. "We all carry the guilts of history on our backs."

"And the shame of the present," said Von Kalbach. "The anarchists who threaten me have a very simple premise: there is no remedy for the evils of our system except total destruction and a new beginning. We have to bear witness to the possibility of protest and reform."

"I have one more question for my father-in-law."

"Ask it," said John Spada.

"In this—this work—have you ever killed a man?"

21

"I have. I would again."

"And you, Bishop Frantisek, what do you say to that?"

"Nothing," said the Bishop. "I have never been faced with the exigence of the moment. I cannot say what I would do. John Spada has never opened his conscience to me. I have neither the means nor the right to judge him."

"But you are still prepared to work with him?"

"Yes."

"I am not," said Rodolfo Vallenilla. "I'm sorry, John. I cannot keep company with assassins."

"I respect your decision," said Spada. "I trust you will respect the pledge you have given to this meeting."

"Need you ask?"

"Yes." Spada's tone was harsh. "My life, our lives, are on the line too!"

"You have nothing to fear from me," said Rodolfo Vallenilla. "Excuse me, gentlemen!"

He stood up, gave them a small, stiff bow and walked out of the room. The door closed behind him with a hard, dry snap.

There was a long silence, then Uncle Andrea asked gently: "Was that necessary, Giovanni?"

"It was necessary," said Spada gravely. "Now, Professor Von Kalbach, where do you stand?"

"If I can help, I will." The old scholar consented calmly. "I do not have much time left. I cannot spend it like a child on a seesaw."

"You, Castagna?"

"I've given the best years of my life to the Party. I'm no longer sure it has all the answers. So I'm reserving a little of myself, for myself. Yes . . . count me in."

"Thank you," said John Spada. "Now, let me play a little game with you." He drew a crude sketch in his notebook, tore out the page and held it up for inspection. "This is the symbol of our organization. Can you decipher its meaning?"

The sketch was an incomplete square, enclosing a fish, thus:

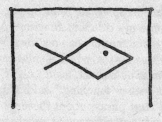

Castagna and Von Kalbach studied it for a long moment and then confessed themselves beaten.

Spada explained with unfamiliar eloquence: "The rectangular shape is one of the oldest forms of the letter *P*. The fish is just a fish. The whole device stands for Proteus, the sea-god, shepherd and guardian of all the creatures who live in the deep: the seals, the dolphins, the tunny and the shoaling minnows. Poseidon endowed him with knowledge of all things, past, present and future, and with the power to change himself at will into a multitude of shapes: a flame of fire, a lion, a flower, a snake, or a snuffling boar . . ." He broke off, smiled a little self-consciously at his own rhetoric and then explained. "You see the relevance of the symbol to what we do. We are guardians of those who live in an alien element, cut off from human concern. We have at our disposal knowledge, intelligence, from all over the world. We can assume many identities, many functions . . . When we are threatened, we can retreat into the sea caves and emerge in a different shape. If one fish is taken, there are always others to take its place. For the present I am Proteus, because I have the means to move and act more freely than most of our collaborators. But if anything happens to John Spada, then a new man will assume my title and function. All our codes are based on the names of sea creatures. We recognize each other by this device, which a child can draw."

"It's an amusing conceit," said Luigi Castagna.

"I find it rather touching," said Hugo von Kalbach. "I liked your phrase about those who are cut off from human concern. How many members do we have altogether?"

"We don't ask," said Uncle Andrea. "When we have need of collaborators in other countries we confer with Giovanni in New York. He provides appropriate contact. It's a safety measure—based on normal intelligence procedures."

"But someone must have the full list?"

"There is such a list," said John Spada carefully. "I am the only person who knows its whereabouts and contents. In the event of my death or incapacity, it will pass to one of two people deputed to carry on the work."

"Interesting," said Luigi Castagna dryly. "To free the captives, we set up a dictatorship."

"There is another point of view," said Fonseca,

the banker. "John Spada was the first to set his hand to the lonely plow. So far he has cut a straight furrow on very stony ground. We have learned to trust him."

"I'm a slow learner," said Luigi Castagna. "I hope you will be patient with me."

"In a dog's world it pays to be cautious." Spada held out his hand to seal the pact. "Now let's get down to business. First, Professor, I wonder if you would consider an invitation to come to New York and . . ."

As they drove back to Rome, in the long fall of the evening, Rodolfo Vallenilla was silent and withdrawn. After a while Teresa demanded, in her forthright fashion: "Something happened between you and Papa today. What was it?"

"A private matter," said John Spada curtly. "None of your business."

"We'll talk about it at the hotel." Anna made a furtive gesture towards the chauffeur. "This is not the time or the place."

"Rodo and I are leaving tomorrow." Teresa was not to be put off. "We don't want to take family problems with us."

"There are no problems." Vallenilla was firm. "Your father made me a proposal. I declined it, as I had a perfect right to do. The matter is closed."

Spada shut his eyes and leaned back against the cushions. "One of the hardest things in marriage is to let your partner be private. So lay off, Teresa mia! Rodo and I understand each other."

"He understands." Vallenilla made a gallant effort to appear amused. "I'm still trying to spell the words! But he's right. Lay off, dear wife!"

"That's what I hate about Italy. All you have to do is ask the time of day and you've got a conspiracy on your hands!"

"Ask it in Manhattan," said Anna, "and people think it's a stickup. I like it when small things are important. . . . When they get big and complicated I pull the sheets over my head and go to sleep."

"I surrender." Teresa sighed wearily. "I'll be a nice, dutiful, boring Latin wife and let the wonderful men get on with their great affairs."

"Great!" Spada gave a theatrical display of relief. "At last, Anna my love, we can relax. Our little daughter has become a woman!"

"Go to hell, Papa!"

"With pleasure, bambina! That's where you find all the pretty girls!"

So the first bad moment passed, but there was one more to endure before the day's end. It was ten in the evening. Anna and Spada had finished supper and were just preparing to go to bed when Vallenilla called from his room and suggested a stroll before retiring. Spada was tired as a miller's mule, but he agreed. They met in the foyer and walked slowly up the Via Bissolati towards the Veneto.

Vallenilla told him baldly, "You offended me very much today, John."

"Why?"

"I'd given you my word to keep your secret. Between gentlemen, that should have been enough."

"You called me an assassin. Wasn't that an ugly judgment?"

"Yes, it was. I apologize."

"I intended no offense when I asked you to affirm

26

your pledge. I'm sorry if I hurt you, but I wanted you to remember that moment very clearly."

"Why?"

"Have you ever thought what may happen when you go back to Buenos Aires and continue writing against the government?"

"Very often. I could disappear like so many others."

"Which would mean what?"

"I'd be killed—which wouldn't be so bad; or imprisoned and tortured—which would be infinitely worse."

"And in the end you would tell what you know."

"Inevitably."

"So whatever would help you to hold out one day, one hour longer would be a gift and not an insult? Yes or no?"

"Yes."

"That's what I was trying to do today: give you a moment to remember."

"I didn't see it that way."

"Just as you never thought of what Frantisek called 'the exigence of the moment'—the moment when you might have to choose to kill a man."

"I've set my face against all killing, all violence. There has to be an end to the social vendetta."

"That's easy. Raise the white flag. Surrender. Hang up your harp by the Waters of Babylon and weep."

"You know that's not the answer."

"Then spell me yours, Rodo! Tell me what I do when Teresa calls and tells me you've disappeared."

"You come down and take her home."

"And what do I answer when she refuses to go and begs me to intervene on your behalf? How far shall I go? At what point do I, too, stand and surrender?"

"You've got eighty million dollars of investment in Buenos Aires and five hundred employees—all hostages to the regime. You cannot endanger them. . . . Besides, it may never happen."

"But if it does?"

"I don't know. I truly don't know."

"Then you'd damn well better make up your mind!" Spada was angry and brutal. "When you sit at your desk and write an editorial, you're not some white-haired scholar penning wisdom for posterity. You're making time bombs, like any bloody terrorist in a back room in Munich. Just like him, you've got a cost to count, an effect to measure, a responsibility to wear! I don't say you should give up and walk away —far from it! But don't kid yourself, sonny! You're in a duel with deadly weapons. So don't be surprised when you see blood on the floor. . . ."

"That's quite a speech," said Vallenilla. "I'd like to print it."

"Print it on the palm of your hand. Read it every day. Read it to your wife in bed."

"She's heard it before, I think."

"For Christ's sake!" Spada's anger went out, suddenly as a quenched fire. "Let's not quarrel. I love Teresa more than my own life—almost as much as my Anna. I think she's got herself a good man. But be careful, eh? And if ever someone comes and gives you the word Proteus, or shows you a drawing of a fish in a box, heed him, eh?"

28

"Proteus and a fish in a box. I'll remember. And thank you for trusting me so far."

"I've broken the rules," said Spada. "But you have to know that I trust you, otherwise we shall end hating each other."

"Thanks for telling me. It helps more than you know. . . . There's something else."

"What?"

"Today I saw another man in John Spada. At first I disliked him because I am always affronted by the use of naked power. Now I realize that sometimes I am jealous of it and, therefore, I could misuse the little I have."

"The power game is like golf," said John Spada mildly. "It takes practice. You make a lot of mistakes. I've learned to live with mine; I don't want to see you die for yours."

"I'll drink to that. Let's have a brandy before we go back."

They linked arms, Latin style, and walked briskly towards the bright booth on the Veneto. It was the closest they had ever come to each other, and for all his misgivings, for all he knew and feared, John Spada was prepared to admit that it had not been a bad Easter Day.

2

The bad days began as soon as he hit New York. They started, as always, with a series of minor annoyances.

Anna was tired and irritable, fretting about her daughter, who must live so far away, and the grandchildren, not even in prospect yet, who would be taken over by "some horsey family in the middle of nowhere." They were stacked up for an hour over Kennedy because of the press of delayed traffic. An officious customs man insisted on opening every one of Anna's bags and held them for another twenty minutes while he laboriously totted up a bill for thirty dollars' excise duties. When they emerged from customs, they stood around fuming for half an hour because the Spada limousine had had a blowout on the expressway. At home, finally, they found Carlos, the houseman, in bed with influenza and his wife in a panic because the maid was late getting back with the shopping.

Spada threw up his hands in despair, left Anna to cope with the domestic crisis, took a hurried shower and retired to the comparative peace of his study. He was not left private for long. A few minutes before five-thirty Kitty Cowan called. Her greeting was a shade more cheerful than the occasion seemed to demand.

"Welcome home, chief! And how is the last tycoon?"

"Bitched and bewildered."

"Sorry about the airport foul-up."

"That was only part of it! Today I'm the forgotten of God! How are things at the store?"

"Well, now!" He could almost see her tensing herself for the explosion. "How would you like it, Mr. Spada, sir? Straight up or on the rocks?"

"Straight up, honey child."

"Maury Feldman's here. I'd better let him tell you. I'll sweep up the mess afterwards."

They had always made jokes, these three. Kitty Cowan was the leggy redhead who had typed the very first invoices for the first Spada company and was now captain of the guard at the top of the glass tower on Central Park West. Maury Feldman, the puckish, urbane attorney who played piano like a minor master and collected cinquecento painters, had graduated from a shoe-box office on Mott Street to one of the biggest corporate practices in Manhattan. Maury came on the line with a world-weary sigh.

"The money's good but the hours are terrible —and the news is worse."

"I've heard the overture, Maury. Now sing me the opera."

"Brace yourself," said Feldman happily. "Remember the reactor we built for Central and Western?"

31

"Sure."

"There's a crack in the shielding of number two pile. It could develop into a major hazard. We've rushed Peters and Dubrowski down from Detroit to cooperate with the local team and send us their report. Kitty's called for copies of the specifications and the acceptance certificates. Best estimate says minor hazard, local protest and nasty publicity. Worst is major damage, major risk and a big negligence suit."

"Do you want me to go down?"

"No way!" Maury Feldman was adamant. "You stay far away. Spada Nucleonics is the contracting company. Their management carries the can. The parent company stands at arm's length. That's the first item . . ."

"Christ! Don't tell me there's more!"

"There's more. Waxman called in from the bank in San Diego. There's a shortfall of half a million in their accounts."

"That's a nice round figure. Where's it gone?"

"The junior accountant was playing computer games—and playing the tables at Las Vegas. As of now, he's crying his eyes out in Waxman's office. What do you want to do about it?"

"Throw the book at him." Spada was curt.

"Waxman says he's got an invalid wife and a handicapped child."

"So now we get violin music and the quality-of-mercy speech! . . . What's the chance of recovering the loot?"

"Zero. Zilch!"

"Have Waxman call me here when we've finished talking. I need time to cool off. Is that the lot?"

"Two more little goodies. You told me you'd settled the strike at the Oxford plant in England."

"I did. The agreements were being drawn when I left."

"Now they're back to square one. The government says the agreements breach the guidelines for pay settlements."

"We're damned if we do and damned if we don't!" Spada exploded. "Meantime, we're bleeding all over the floor!"

"Buckets of blood, lover! Can you bear any more?"

"I feel like Prometheus with the vultures pecking at his liver."

"Carl Channing died while you were away."

"I heard that. We cabled condolences."

"What you didn't hear was the terms of the will. His wife gets half the estate absolutely. The other half—specifically including the Spada stock—is placed in trust for the son and daughter."

"So?"

"So the trustees are Hoffman, Liebowitz."

"God Almighty! And I thought Channing was a friend of mine!"

"You could never see it, lover," said Feldman quietly. "But Carl Channing was a very envious man. He was always jealous of you."

"This means Hoffman, Liebowitz can vote the stock."

"They will vote it, Johnny boy! And they don't love you either because you once called Max Liebowitz a shortsighted bigot. Which leaves you, as of now, two percent short of a majority vote, with a proxy fight looming up on the horizon."

Spada was silent for a long moment.

Feldman prompted him. "Are you still there, John?"

"I'm thinking. How long have we got before the stockholders' meeting?"

"Three months. It's not long."

"I know. Let's meet tomorrow to discuss strategy. Meantime, we'll put in buying orders for every piece of scrip that comes on the market."

"They'll be expecting that. They'll auction you up."

"Then we'll see how good their nerves are. . . . Now, tell me some good news!"

"We can buy Raymond Serum Laboratories."

"How much of it?"

"Seventy percent—and that includes the European subsidiaries."

"What will it cost us?"

"Fifteen dollars a share."

"Conditions?"

"The old man retires. The son gets a five-year contract to head the research division."

"It's too cheap. What's the catch?"

"They're stretched tight on credit. The old man is tired. He's had one heart attack. He wants to go fishing."

"The son?"

"He's a biologist, pure and simple. He hates business. He'd like to carry on research with a nice comfortable personal investment behind him."

"Wise man," said John Spada moodily. "He'll probably die happy at ninety, with the Nobel Prize in his pocket. O.K., Maury, we'll buy. Set it up. See you at ten in the morning."

"Make it ten-thirty," said Maury Feldman cheerfully. "I've got to see a man about a picture. He swears it's an Andrea del Sarto. I fear it's a piece of junk, but I could get lucky."

"How can you afford these little luxuries?"

"I have some generous clients. I'll pay for this one out of the Raymond deal."

"You bastard! Put me back to Kitty. I've got some memos to dictate to her."

"I was just about to take her out to dinner."

"She's on my payroll. Find your own women."

"I love you too, John boy. Get a good night's sleep!"

Kitty Cowan came on the line again. This time she was subdued and solicitous.

"John, let me handle the San Diego business."

"What's your suggestion?"

"Don't press charges—at least not yet. Waxman's got a confession. Let him ask for another document: a voluntary request for psychiatric observation in a recognized institution. I'd also have Waxman continue paying maintenance to the wife and child until we've got the whole picture clear."

"I love it." Spada stifled a laugh. "We get ripped off for half a million, and we respond with free psychiatric treatment and maintenance for the villain's family."

"You won't get the money back, so why not get some free advertising for the human face of Spada Consolidated?"

"And I thought you were pouring out the milk of human kindness!"

"I am—but you're supplying the milk and the pitcher. I thought I'd better sweeten the deal. What do you say, chief?"

"Do it! Now make a note. Put out buying orders for any Spada stock that comes free in the market. Get me full personal and financial information on Max Liebowitz, his associates and his immediate family. Also send a formal invitation to Professor Hugo von Kalbach to make the keynote address at our management conference in New York next month. Call him in Munich and discuss travel arrangements. The fee is fifteen thousand dollars. Find out how and where he'd like it paid. Finally, have an updated list of Spada stockholders on my desk first thing in the morning."

"And I'll also deliver the Hope diamond and a crate of moon rocks! Relax, chief! This is Kitty, remember? The impossible takes an hour or two longer, but we do it in the end. Anything else?"

"Yes. Ask Maury where we can find Henson and the Scarecrow Man."

There was a moment's pause, then Kitty asked quietly, "Going fishing?"

"Could be. Have a nice evening."

"And you take it easy. Give my love to Anna."

"Ciao, Caterina!"

"Shalom, John! Sleep easy."

"Everybody wants me to sleep," said John Spada with sour humour. "So they put thorns in my bed and itching powder in my pajamas. . . !"

Long after Anna was asleep and dreaming, he sat up, tense and wakeful, trying to measure the new threat that was being mounted against him. A big international company was a kind of empire whose stability depended on all sorts of treaties and alliances, some written, many more unratified, but all based on mutual trust, shared interest, a precarious balance of situations and personalities. Every expansion, every new venture, meant the introduction of new funds, fresh interests, an extra strain on the original alliances. Friends died. Family rivalries intruded. Parties fell out of favour with electors. Rivals waxed strong. Old enmities, long covered, flared up like fires in a sawdust pile. Shareholders, avid always for more profit, grew restive and fell easy prey to flimflam men peddling pie in the sky.

John Spada knew—or thought he knew—every gambit in the game. Helped by relatives and friends on the Continent, he had managed to stay in the saddle for twenty-five years, holding in his own two hands the reins of power. Now, suddenly, he was at risk, because a man who, living, would never have dared to oppose him was mocking him from beyond the grave.

When Carl Channing's bank was in trouble Spada had bailed him out with cash and then bought him out with Spada stock. The transaction had turned Channing from a near-bankrupt into a wealthy man. But, apparently, to make a man rich was not to make him a friend. It was not the favour Channing remembered, but the humiliation of having to wed an old WASP name to that of an upstart Italian from Rome. So he had allied himself with Max Liebowitz, who in the old days had written off Spada Consolidated as a fly-by-night enterprise, probably financed by Mafia funds—and had been biting his nails ever since.

Even so, the equation was not yet clear to Spada. Even if Liebowitz could win his proxy fight, he had still to propose a management superior to the present one; and, so far at least, there was no obvious candidate in sight. The right man would have to be diplomat, financier, politician, administrator extraordinary—with a dash of the adventurer as well. Spada himself, having no son to succeed him, was constantly combing the market for such a talent, and finding that it was very thin on the ground.

So it seemed he would have a little breathing space before the big battle was joined. But he would have to use every moment of it, test every ally, watch for any hint of defection from the ranks of his supporters. He would have to tread warily for other reasons as well. He was a man living a double life: openly as president of Spada Consolidated, secretly as Proteus, head of a clandestine organization, involved in the dark and dangerous game of underground politics.

Any hint of his covert activities would damn him utterly in the eyes of the stockholders, who regarded him as the trustee of their financial interests and gave him no mandate at all for a private crusade. They would be happy for him to endow a foundation, found a ballet company, promote cancer research; but to involve himself in moral issues, in political activism—unthinkable!

But he, John Spada, had to think of it every day. What do you do when your man in Frankfurt calls and says: "The police tell me I'm on a Baader-Meinhof list. I need bodyguards for my children when they go to school, alarms in my house, a bulletproof car to drive me to the factory"? What do you say to the man from SAVAK when he says: "You have a hundred technicians working in Teheran and some of them talk too freely about the way the Shah runs his country. Incidentally, we'd like you to replace Baraheni as office manager, because we'll be pulling him in for a chat very soon"? How do you react when your man in Chile is commanded to write political profiles on his staff and report to DINA any union activity on the shop floor? How do you answer the veiled request for contributions to the police fund in Rio when you know the Squadrons of Death are out, riding the highways, and gunning down suspected dissidents? What will you do if the police raid your daughter's house in Buenos Aires because her husband has written an editorial that they find intolerable?

John Spada was no genius; but he spoke six languages and his roots were still planted deep in the Latin culture of Europe. How would Max Liebowitz respond? Max was a great fund raiser, a potent lobbyist for Israel, an eloquent rememberer of the holocausts. But Max still talked about the goyim and the schwartzers and the chicanos. What would he do when they dumped a dead Bantu on the company doorstep in Cape Town and said he fell down drunk in a police cell? Maybe he would do very well. Maybe he would ignore it all, on the principle that you drove down the road you could see, and to hell with the barbarians killing themselves in the wild country on either hand. . . . Maybe, maybe, but whichever way you read him, Max Liebowitz was a hell of a risk.

Suddenly Spada was desperately tired. He switched off the light in the study, made the last round of the apartment, tested the alarms and crept quietly into bed. He reached out to touch Anna. She murmured in sleepy affection and drew close to him. He laid a gentle arm across her body and held her quietly until she slept again. Then he locked his hands under his head and lay a long time, staring into the darkness.

The headquarters of Spada Consolidated Holdings was a tower of concrete and glass on Central Park West. In the forecourt was the emblem of the corporation: a giant crusader sword, plunged into a block of rough-hewn granite. There was an arrogance in the symbol which now, in his later years, he regretted. It was a celebration of personal strength, of corporate might, of the military precision with which John Spada directed a vast variety of enterprises spread around the globe: in Australia, Taiwan, the Philippines, India, Japan, the United Kingdom, South Africa, South America and Europe.

"You name it," the knowing ones said. "Spada is there, in one dress or another: arms, electronics, real estate, hotels, oil, metals, minerals and banking. It's a goddam colossus and he controls it. If he sneezes on a rainy day he can put thousands out of work and cause a run on the stock market. When he started, they wrote him down as just another fast operator who would be winnowed out by the first cold draft. No way! He proved out solid as that chunk of rock in front of his building. He runs his organization like an army and he's a better statesman than half the boys who are warming their backsides in the Senate. . . ."

On the topmost floor of the tower there was a conference room which looked like a battle headquarters with a vast electronic screen on which, at any moment of any hour, the status of every Spada operation could be punched up—the movement of bulk cargoes, the amount of ore at any railhead, the state of the futures market, cash flows, inventories and currency dealings in a dozen capitals.

"We have to know!" Spada's edict was as immutable as the laws of the Medes and Persians. "Good news and bad, we want it all. Never give me a surprise. If we take risks, we take them on known odds. I want daily bookkeeping, not past history. Make one mistake and I'll forgive you. Make the same mistake again and I'll have your head on a dish."

It was no idle threat and his staff knew it. The Man paid well for service and discretion; the Man looked after his own. But his angers were swift and cold—and there were bones bleaching in the undergrowth to prove it.

Yet, for all the stringency of his rule, Spada was a cool and relaxed administrator. With his immediate staff he was considerate and urbane. He never forgot a birthday. There was always a personal gift for high feasts and family occasion. His directives were clear. In discussion he was open and reasonable. Once a decision was made, he himself assumed full responsibility for its consequences.

Among his peers he had another kind of reputation: a witty companion, a generous host, a good friend when the bad times hit. His handshake was as good as a contract; but, come to an adversary situation, then—by God!—you'd best be up early and know the fine print backwards. His business entertainments were lavish; but no one had ever managed to pin a scandal, personal or financial, on his door. As to his family, there was one inviolable rule: John Spada's homelife was private. Entry was by invitation only; don't call us, we'll call you.

In his business life, only two people were privy

to all his secrets. One was Maury Feldman; the other was Kitty Cowan, raw-tongued, protective as a mother hen, loyal as the Light Brigade. With the pair of them in his office he could unbutton and relax, curse and argue happily and come out refreshed for the next encounter. This morning, however, there was an air of urgency and unease about the meeting. Kitty Cowan began with a report from the brokers.

"They say there's very little Spada stock on offer. Most people are hanging on for the half-yearly dividend and the rise in share value."

Spada frowned unhappily and turned to Maury Feldman, who was doodling an erotic miniature of Leda and the Swan on his note pad.

"What's Liebowitz got to sell? We're riding high. In the middle of a recession we're doing better than most corporations on the big board. How can Liebowitz justify a change of management? Who's his candidate?"

"Max isn't saying. I'm just guessing that it's Conan Eisler. He's done a good job with Allman Electronics, and Max thinks he's a financial genius."

"Balls!" said Spada flatly. "I checked him out months ago. He's a systems man, pure and simple. Even his bed sheets are made of graph paper. Politically, he's a babe in arms!"

"We know, John," said Kitty Cowan with a grin. "You're the one who's got to persuade the stockholders."

Spada was still terse and snappish. "So let's talk about persuasion. We can't make a move until Max Liebowitz shows his hand."

"I disagree." Feldman added some fanciful

42

strokes to Leda's anatomy. "Why hang around until the rapist starts unzipping his pants? I say we start lobbying the voters right now. Kitty's got the list. I've marked the ones who could swing either way and therefore need steady personal attention. You'll note, for the record, that most of them represent Jewish capital."

"So now we're involved in a race issue?"

"No, but we're selling a hell of a lot of stuff to the Saudis and the Kuwaitis, and Max Liebowitz is an ardent Zionist . . . Which reminds me—I'm not sure it's a good idea to have Von Kalbach speak at the management conference."

"Why not?" Spada was nettled. "He's an important thinker and an impressive speaker. He'll get a big press coverage."

"Which could make us look like hypocrites," said Maury Feldman. "Von Kalbach talks eloquent sense about repression and violence, while we're shipping weapons systems to Iran and you're photographed skiing with the Shah in Saint Moritz."

"For God's sake, Maury! You know the reason for that."

"I know, but the public doesn't."

"So what am I going to do—blow the whole Proteus network to prove I'm a great humanitarian?"

"Maury's right, John." Kitty Cowan added her own blunt comment. "The President's talking up human rights. Spada Consolidated is making big profits trading under dictatorships. In this town, at this time, that hurts you."

"It would hurt a hell of a lot more if I joined any partisan group."

"Sure, but . . ."

Spada cut her off with a gesture.

"Let's talk Proteus for a moment. Von Kalbach wants us to help get Lermontov released from that nuthouse in Moscow. I've committed to the project. Any ideas?"

"You know," said Maury Feldman, "there's going to be a formal protest at the world conference on mental health next month. The Russians are worried. They've instructed their delegates to walk out if the protest is tabled."

"But they won't let Lermontov out?"

"No. The K.G.B. have dug their heels in. No interference with internal security."

"What about a private deal?"

"You've got something in mind?" Maury Feldman stopped his doodling and looked up.

"I thought I'd talk to Anatoly Kolchak in Washington. He's a first-rate diplomat and in high favour with the Politburo."

"But even Kolchak can't buck the K.G.B."

"No, but he can propose a situation. The Soviet Trade Mission has been negotiating for months to get manufacturing rights on Spada body scanners. So far we've stalled the deal because we think they're good for another one percent royalty. Suppose we agree their bid, and make a free gift of one unit to the Moscow General Hospital—provided Lermontov is released and given an exit visa."

"Then"—Maury Feldman did his famous parody of Earl Warren—"then you are up to your hocks in sewage. You are using shareholders' funds to deal in human bodies."

"Not if I pay for the gift myself."

44

"Then some smart-ass asks whether the royalty contract is the best that could have been secured by open market trading. In other words, how much discount for one beat-up Jewish intellectual?"

Spada grinned and asked amiably, "Who's to know about it except us three?"

"Anatoly Kolchak—and all the boys in the Politburo and the K.G.B."

"But they can't tell—unless they want to admit they're in the ransom business."

"Then there's Liebowitz, who right now will be scrutinizing every goddam document he can lay his hands on."

"What's he going to say? We could have held out for another one percent and let Lermontov die? No, Maury, it's your job to demonstrate the risks. It's mine to accept or reject them. I'll talk to Kolchak."

"By me, that's great," said Kitty Cowan.

"By me," said Maury Feldman, "it's like Leda and the Swan. It's an anatomical impossibility, but it might be fun to try."

Kitty Cowan consulted her notebook and brought up the next item.

"You asked about Henson and the Scarecrow Man. Henson's in Rome, working on a kidnap case for Risk Consultants Limited. The Scarecrow Man is in Teheran, brushing up on his Persian and keeping an eye on Azudi. But if you want him, he'll move."

"Get him to New York," said Spada. "Tell him I want to brief him for twenty-four hours. Then he'll go down to Buenos Aires. Tell Henson not to accept another assignment until he's heard from me."

Maury Feldman began another sketch, this time

of a rampant satyr pursuing an overweight wood
nymph. He asked quietly: "Does that mean you're
worried about Teresa? And her husband?"

"Yes."

"Why not find Rodolfo a job with Spada Consolidated and get him out of the country?"

"He wouldn't take it. He's an old-fashioned patriot. He says his mission as an editor is to bear witness in difficult times."

"Good for him," said Kitty Cowan stoutly.

"Bad for both of them"—Spada's tone was somber—"if the bloody general decides to drop the axe."

"Bad for everybody," said Maury Feldman, "if it
happens in the middle of a proxy fight. You've got a
heavy investment down there and a lot of potential
hostages."

"That's why I want the Scarecrow Man to keep
an eye on the situation."

"And Henson?"

"His Spanish is weak, but he's the best guerrilla
tactician I know. If things get rough I'll move him in
next to the Scarecrow Man."

Maury Feldman frowned and looked at his watch.
"Proteus time you get for free. The rest costs you
money. Now, can we get down to Spada business?"

Spada threw back his head and laughed. "I can
read you like a book, Maury. You've seen the picture.
You're half convinced it's an Andrea del Sarto and
you can't wait to get a second opinion."

"Wrong!" Feldman gave him a sidelong sardonic
grin. "The Sarto's a fake; but the vendor's strapped
for dough and he's willing to sell me a pectoral cross
that I'll swear I've seen on a Farnese portrait. I've
made an appointment to start bargaining at midday."

"The reactor crisis . . ." said Kitty Cowan. "Dubrowski says they can seal the crack in the shielding and add extra cladding at the weak spot. But the pile has to be shut down."

"For how long?"

"No estimate yet."

"Cost?"

"Expensive is all he'll say."

"Hazards?"

"Not too high, given an immediate shutdown, which is now in progress. He recommends we avoid any disputes on costs and responsibilities until he can make a full report. Also, he'd like a good public relations effort in cooperation with the client company."

"Tell him he's got it. I'll talk to Fitch when we've finished here."

"Once again"—Maury Feldman embellished the sexual attributes of the faun and added more fright to the face of the wood nymph—"keep the parent company clear. Let Spada Nucleonics supply the services. The clients will be sweet as sugar until the crisis is over—then they'll turn sour. It always happens. Now, this contract to buy Raymond Serum Laboratories . . ."

And so it went on—the private briefing in the glass tower which was the prelude to his meetings with department heads, the daily schedule of international telephone calls, the six o'clock session in the operations room where the worldwide situation was reviewed. It was a long, punishing day, an exercise in empery, which once he had found exhilarating as a tennis game but now, suddenly, was fraught with irritation and unease.

The threat to his personal authority was a minor

problem compared with the other menaces which he saw building up around the globe: the military tyrannies in South America, the bloody turmoil in the African continent, the buildup of arms in Iran, the wild consumption of energy in the United States, the jealousies of trading nations battling for markets in a contracting world, the disillusion of Europe with its politicians and its pundits, the smouldering enmity between the Chinese and the Russians. The satellites which his companies had helped to build scanned a globe that was spinning out of control towards a zone of cosmic disasters. Man's confidence in his society was being eroded to a point at which, many believed, the brutalities of the tyrant would seem a necessary and saving surgery.

It was against this moment that he had begun to build the Proteus organization, as between the wars Sir William Stephenson had constructed the group called British Security Co-ordination, to prepare for the inevitable confrontation with Hitler's Reich. Now he had come to the point where Spada Consolidated was a vast and profitable cover for a personal crusade. If the cover was broken, if a new management took over, then the Proteus organization could be damaged beyond repair. Its intelligence system would break down. Its potency as a negotiator between diverse interests would be destroyed. In the secret world of international diplomacy, it was not only money that talked, it was the ability to deploy it, to harness resources, provide work, initiate large-scale projects, forge links of interest between rivals and onetime enemies. John Spada, the private man, could live rich and happy to the end of his days, but without Spada Consolidated he would be like Samson shorn of his hair. He was not ready for that. He could not stomach the thought that the testament of a dead man might turn him into a eunuch, an impotent spectator of the power game.

As she was packing his briefcase at the end of the day, Kitty Cowan faced him with the blunt question: "You're really worried, aren't you?"

"Yes, girl. I'm worried."

"I've never asked you before, chief. I'm asking now. Suppose you were faced with an early retirement, would you be prepared for it?"

"No." His answer was flat and definite.

"It will come one day. You're as mortal as the rest of us."

"I've always said I'd die with my boots on."

"You may not be given that choice."

"If you think I'm going to let Liebowitz . . ."

She reached out and laid a cool hand on his cheek. "I'm not talking about Liebowitz."

"What then?"

"You. Big John Spada. How long can you drive yourself the way you're doing now? What happens if you get sick?"

"I'm as strong as an ox—and you know it."

"And as dumb sometimes. Oy vay! What am I going to do with you, chief?"

"You could pour us both a drink."

As she set out glasses and ice and poured the liquor, she said over her shoulder, "Now that Teresa's gone, Anna's going to need more of your time and attention."

"So far she hasn't complained."

"And she won't. But she'll still need you closer than you are now."

She handed him the bourbon. They touched glasses and drank a silent toast. Spada gave her a crooked grin of approval.

"You're a good one, Kitty."

"I know. Old-shoe Kitty! I'm well worn, but I've worn well. But don't change the subject. You've got to start shedding some of the work load. If you don't want Liebowitz, you'd better start grooming your successor. I still say Mike Santos is the best man you've got. Maury agrees with me."

"I'm still not sure of Mike. He's competent, ambitious and very good at his job, but . . ."

"He's better than good. He's the only one with enough brains for you to respect and enough balls to face you down in an argument. I happen to know he's turned down two big offers this month because he believes he owes you a personal loyalty."

"I've been thinking about him."

"Too long," said Kitty Cowan. "It's time to move him next door and let him work with you."

"On Proteus too?"

"Not yet. One step at a time. Let's see how he shapes with the reins in his hands." Suddenly she was very near to tears. She turned away, groped for her handkerchief and blew her nose violently. "Oh hell! Why should I care so much? It's your life, your goddam business!"

Spada reached out and spun her around to face him. He kissed her gently and then held her against his breast, soothing her with strange gentleness.

"Come on, girl! That's not my Kitty. You're family—always have been, always will be. So I'm an old bull and I'm jealous of the young ones in the pastures. O.K.! If it makes you any happier, I'll give Mike

50

Santos a trial. Now dry your eyes and pour us another drink."

"Go home." Kitty Cowan's voice was muffled against his jacket. "Go home to Anna, before I forget where I belong!"

That night after dinner he told Anna of his decision. He was surprised at the ardour of her response. She threw her arms around his neck and kissed him and said, with passionate conviction, "I'm so glad . . . so very glad! This is the best thing you've done for a long time."

"Hey, now! Wait a minute!" He held her like a doll at arm's length. "Why all the emotion? First Kitty, now you. So I'm grooming a successor. What's the big deal?"

"I love you," said Anna simply. "I've been worried for a long time."

"About what?"

"This is the time in a man's life when he needs a son at his side. I was never able to breed you a boy. I've always felt bad about that."

"Anna mia!" Instantly he was tender and solicitous. "You have nothing to regret. Nothing ever! You've made me the happiest man in the world!"

"Please, my love! Please listen to me! A long time ago I knew I had married a great man. I knew that in his world I could not compete—and I didn't want to. I promised myself I would make him a home to which, always, he would be happy to come back. I knew I was not his whole life and I never could be; but he was enough, more than enough, for me. I didn't want to pull him this way and that. I wanted him always to be free, to be himself."

51

"You think I didn't know that—wasn't grateful for it?"

"Yes, you knew, and yes, you held me safe as any woman could be. But you were not safe, my love! Never for one moment in that big, brutal world were you ever quite calm. Once I spoke to Aunt Lisa about it. She told me you had '*Tocchio dello spadaccino*,' the swordsman's eye, always alert, always measuring the danger, always ready to engage an adversary. She said something else too—very much Aunt Lisa! She told me: 'Don't distract him when the duel is on, because a single mistake means death to the swordsman. When he wants to relax, let him do it in his own way, because the vigils he must keep are long and lonely . . .' That wasn't easy for me, because I have always been jealous of your love and attention. But I tried . . . Now, please God, I shan't have to try so hard. Mike Santos is a good man. The more you lean on him, the stronger you will find him."

"Strong is not enough, Anna mia. He has to learn to smell the wind like a jungle animal."

"You can teach him that."

"I can teach him to interpret the scent. I can't give him the nose if he wasn't born with it."

"But you must know by now."

"I think I know, but I can be deceived too. I trusted Carl Channing, and all the time until he died he was preparing to betray me."

"And now you mistrust yourself."

"That's what scares me, Anna. Always, until now, I knew where I was going and why. Now I cannot trust the foundations on which I built. The information that comes to me contradicts itself."

"You're tired, my love. You've been travelling for

weeks and you walk back into a series of disasters.
. . . Come to bed and see what a little loving can
do."

"You're the best of all women, Anna mia!"

"I have to be," said Anna with a smile. "There are
lots of others waiting to pick up big John Spada."

Next morning at nine he was closeted with Mike
Santos, the dark, youthful-looking Californian who
had climbed steadily and quietly up the monkey-
puzzle tree of a giant corporation, until he sat, cool
and patient, one step below the topmost branch,
waiting to be invited upwards. Spada's invitation
was given over the coffee cups. It was couched in the
simplest of words.

"The office next door is vacant, Mike. How would
you like to move in?"

"I'd like it very much, if you think I'm ready for
it."

"Suppose you tell me how you rate yourself."

Santos considered the question for a long moment
and then answered with a series of careful definitions.

"Item one: I'm a good administrator, probably
the best you've got. I know how this outfit works. I
can keep it running smoothly. Item two: I've travelled all the territories. I know the local controllers
and their problems. I believe they trust me. Item
three: I understand money. I've kept us cushioned
against the bad times we're having now. Item four:
I know how to pick men and manage their talents.
Item five: I don't scare easily. . . . That's the credit
side. The debits are equally clear. I know my way
around Washington, but I'm weak on foreign politics.
I need time and opportunity to build diplomatic re-

lationships abroad. I have only English and Spanish, and that's a handicap. Also, I can't match you on international law, so I'm more dependent than you on legal advice and less critical of the opinions we get. All I can say is I'm willing to learn, if you're prepared to give me the time."

"How do you feel about me?"

Santos grinned and spread his hands in a Latin shrug.

"What can I say? We've had some big fights. So far I've managed to stay in the ring. And you've always given me a fair deal and an open hearing."

"Do you want my job?"

"When you're ready to step down, yes."

"How badly do you want it?"

"Let me put it this way," said Santos evenly. "It's lonely at the top. The only company you've got is yourself. You have to be able to live with the guy who stares back from the mirror."

"And you can do that?"

"So far, yes."

"Does anyone have liens on you—man or woman?"

"My wife, my children—and you."

"Could you be blackmailed?"

"I doubt it. My father was a poor man but a great human being. I loved him. I'd like to be able to face him again and see him smile."

"Tell me what the corporation needs now."

"You may not like it."

"That's my affair. Tell me."

"Spada Consolidated is an empire, and you're the man who runs it. Empires are an anachronism. They can't last. Sooner or later they will have to fragment, humanize themselves, give place and opportunity to the tribes who made their wealth for them in the first place. That can't be done overnight, but the structures have to be modified to accomplish it in the end . . ."

"And you think they can be?"

"They must be."

"How?"

"I've prepared a paper I'd like you to study. That is, if you still want to consider my appointment at all after this."

"Why shouldn't I?"

"That monument down there—the sword in the stone. It affronts me every time I look at it."

"It's cost millions in advertising to establish that symbol around the globe."

"I know—and it spells your name."

"What else would you have it spell?"

"Peace," said Mike Santos flatly. "Prosperity shared—not war and weaponry and the gutting of the good earth with nothing put back."

"But you've helped to implement the policy we have now."

"Because that was my contract with you: service to what existed. Now you're offering me a new one: to step into your shoes. You've got a right to know my terms and the policies I would try to set."

"And if they're not acceptable?"

"Then you say so. I offer you my resignation and hope we can still be friends."

"I'd hate to lose you."

"I'd hate to go. I've had fifteen years here—good years; but times are changing and I'd like to plant a tree or two for the future."

"Then stick around." Spada smiled and held out

his hand. "Before you plant the trees you have to prepare the ground. That's a larger job than it looks, and it needs a very patient gardener."

Santos took the proffered hand uncertainly. He seemed torn between relief and incredulity. Finally he asked, "Are you saying you agree with what I've said?"

"It was a very broad statement," said Spada with a grin. "Too broad to debate. I'd rather read the policy document and see how workable it is. You've got some things to learn about me too, Mike Santos. My family's been in business since the time of Lorenzo the Magnificent. You might say we've learned something about the art of the possible."

"My ancestors were peons in the Mission estates. They tasted the earth with their tongues to prove whether it was sweet or sour. That's another kind of lesson that lasts. Thanks for trusting me, John. When do you want me to move up?"

"Now!" said John Spada. "We've got the management conference to prepare for and a proxy fight coming up. I want you to set down a strategy for both events."

Three days after the installation of his deputy, Spada flew down to Washington for a private luncheon with Anatoly Kolchak, the Soviet Ambassador. It was an agreeable occasion for both men. Kolchak had charm, wit, intelligence and the talent of a great navigator for reading the weather of global politics. He was also sharp and durable as blade steel; and woe betide any ambitious Party man who presumed to teach him his business or comment on his manner of transacting it. He knew Washington like the palm of his hand and Wall Street better than the Narodny Bank. His dispatches were meticulously framed, his opinions temperate, his eye for a pretty woman, or a vulnerable opponent, unrivalled in the trade.

Spada, for his part, was relaxed and eager for the meeting. He had digested all the details of the Lermontov affair and every clause in the correspondence with the Trade Mission over the patent rights of the body scanners. It was characteristic of both men that by the time the pre-lunch cocktail was served, they were through the banalities and engaged with the subject in hand.

As Spada put it good-humouredly: "Let's take it for granted, Mr. Ambassador, that we've both done our homework. Let's presume that neither of us wants to turn a good lunch into a fencing match."

"Excellent idea, Mr. Spada. It took me a long time to find a good cook. I hate to see his efforts wasted. What did you want to discuss with me?"

"Trade," said Spada. "One body for a favourable manufacturing contract."

Anatoly Kolchak raised his glass in a silent toast.

"That's a good opening line, Mr. Spada. Did you rehearse it?"

"I always rehearse, Mr. Ambassador."

"Tell me about the body. Whose is it?"

"Lev Lermontov's."

"Ah! That's difficult!" The Ambassador drank and put down his glass. He smiled and took Spada's arm to lead him to the luncheon table. "Lermontov is the usual cause célèbre. His case is a complicated topic and sensitive for my government."

"Human rights are a sensitive topic for any government," said John Spada quietly, "including our

57

own. Let me state, therefore, that my interest is personal and my proposal private. I seek neither advertisement nor gain. I present a business proposition, in which you and your government may see certain advantages."

For the first time Anatoly Kolchak permitted himself an expression of surprise. He said, in a tone of profoundest puzzlement, "I confess that your motives escape me, Mr. Spada."

"I should have thought they were very clear."

"On the surface, yes. But let me put it this way: Your bargain presents itself as a stupidity—and you are not a stupid man. First you want to buy the most perishable and least valuable commodity of all—a sick human body. In return for that you offer a large and continuing asset in the form of patent rights."

"Exactly."

"How do you justify to yourself this one-sided and economically unsound bargain?"

"Do I have to justify it, Mr. Ambassador—provided I am in a position to make it, which I am?"

"No, but if I understood your motives and your reasoning, it might help me to present the proposal to my government."

"Let's approach it from another angle, Mr. Ambassador. You have problems too. You have a huge country, controlling a fusion of minority groups, all jealous of their local identities. You have satellite states, restless under the yoke of Russia. You have China, hostile on your eastern frontier. You have schisms and dissensions in the Party abroad, whose members reject the domination of Moscow. You have dissent among your scholars and intellectuals and a very unpopular K.G.B., whose repressive measures do you no credit abroad. You'd like to show a more human face. You cannot appear to do it at the behest of foreign powers or under pressure of treaty clauses which you read one way and they another. So I offer you a means of making a large liberal gesture, without appearing to submit to outside influence. For my part, I am old enough and rich enough to permit myself the luxury of a moral stance in a world where morality is unfashionable. When I die, I'd like to have a better epitaph than a dollar sign. . . . There you have it, Mr. Ambassador; and—my compliments!— you do have a very good cook!"

Anatoly Kolchak put down his knife and fork and surveyed his visitor with grave and curious eyes. After a moment he said quietly, "I wish I, too, could afford the same luxuries, my friend. Unlike you, I can only mediate a position. I cannot sign a contract."

"But you would be willing to mediate?"

"With the K.G.B.? No. The best I can do is present your proposal and your reasonings to Moscow."

"Thank you."

"May I ask you again, off the record, the real reason for this request?"

"We live on a very fragile planet, Mr. Ambassador. Martyrs can be more dangerous to it than fanatics. Wouldn't you agree?"

Kolchak gave him a sidelong smile of approval.

"No comment, Mr. Spada; but let me try the line on my colleagues in Moscow. There are one or two who may read good sense in it."

"You may also remind them they'll be very grateful for Spada body scanners when they fall sick."

Anatoly Kolchak chuckled and raised his glass in salute.

"That would hardly be wise, Mr. Spada. Have you ever known a politician who did not believe himself immortal? . . . Now, let's talk of other things. You've been travelling recently. What were your impressions of . . . ?"

And that was the other part of the bargain. In diplomacy as in business, there was no such thing as a free lunch, and only a fool would expect it. John Spada paid his score with good grace: a comment on the economic situation in Japan, the excesses of the army in Indonesia, the problem of nuclear waste disposal. When he took his leave, Kolchak was cordial and, he felt, faintly encouraging. Of course, all such things took time and there were many gambits to be played before the game was over. No matter. Proteus was a patient god and Lev Lermontov was only one fish in a very wide sea.

3

◇◇◇◇◇◇◇◇◇◇◇◇◇◇◇◇◇◇◇◇◇◇◇◇◇◇◇◇◇◇◇◇◇◇◇◇

Teresa's first letter from Buenos Aires was brought by the company courier who made the weekly journey to and from New York, carrying confidential correspondence and documents too sensitive to commit to the Argentine mails. It was a long, chatty recital about the new apartment, her meetings with the Vallenilla clan, her first impressions of the bustling life of the capital. The big news she reserved for the last page.

> . . . I have decided to begin work with the Missionary Sisters of the Poor, who run a number of clinics in the depressed areas of the city. They need people with experience in gynecology and pediatrics to consult in the clinics and train their young nurses. It's challenging work and Rodo is happy to have me do it. He calls it a "witness in work" and he feels that it helps him in his own "witness of words." He's working very hard and is under constant pressure to moderate the tone of his editorial comments.
>
> Things are bad here. More than twenty thousand people are listed as *desaparecidos*—

disappeared. The police disclaim all knowledge of their whereabouts or their fate, and this official silence is even more sinister than the brutalities which we know are practiced on victims of the regime. In addition to his editorial work Rodo is preparing a document of protest and indictment, which he proposes to publish in the form of an open letter to the government. It is a bold and dangerous move; but I believe, as he does, that it must be done. I am very proud of him. I love him more than I could ever have dreamed possible; and, busy as our life is, we are happy as children together.

Which brings me, dear ones, to my last big news. I'm going to have a baby—probably in late November. We're both thrilled about it. We know you will be too. I'm hoping for a boy. Rodo is absolutely sure of the sex. He says we'll call him Rodolfo Giovanni Spada Vallenilla. Perhaps, nearer the time, you'll both be able to come down and spend some time with us—and I'd like Mama to be here when the baby is born.

Much, much love from us both. Write soon.

Teresa

Anna wept happy tears over the news and immediately began planning her role as grandmother. John Spada indulged her amiably, passed the news proudly to his friends, and kept the worst of his anxieties to himself, until the day when the Scarecrow Man arrived in New York.

His given name was Pavel Lunarcharsky. His documents—true or false—showed that he was born in Shanghai to Russian émigré parents in the year of the Lord 1930. In 1946 he showed up in England as the adopted child of an elderly British couple with whom he had spent the war years in a Japanese prison camp in Hong Kong. When they died, they left a legacy to educate him, and he had emerged from Oxford with a doctorate in literature, an extraordinary skill as a linguist and a valuable reputation as an eccentric, vagabond scholar.

He was an odd-looking fellow, skinny as a rake, with a curious spastic gait, a shock of straw-coloured hair and a face in which every feature seemed a trifle askew. His gestures were jerky and awkward, like those of a puppet, while his manner was that of a tipsy and slightly mischievous pedant. Spada had met him first in Bangkok where he was engaged in some vague free-lance assignment for the British Embassy. Their first talk, sitting by the pool at the Erewan, had an offbeat, surreal quality.

Spada had asked: "What kind of business are you in, Doctor?"

"Personal service, Mr. Spada. I am first of all a linguist, almost, but not quite, as good as the great Mezzofanti. I speak and write twenty-three languages. In spite of my odd appearance, I have a talent for impersonation and for identification with various national backgrounds. I possess a number of passports in a variety of names: Dr. Pavel, Boris von Paulus, Henry Salmon. I have no family ties and I am an excellent organizer of, shall we say, exotic projects. I have worked all over the world. My fees are high, but I have generally succeeded in satisfying my clients. Did you have something in mind for me, Mr. Spada?"

"Possibly. I run a large multinational business,

which needs accurate local intelligence. Tell me, what are your politics?"

"I have none." Lunarcharsky gave him a lopsided, sardonic grin. "Political systems are as imperfect and corrupt as the men who devise them. Quite simply, I am a mercenary, for sale to the highest bidder; but once I accept a bid, I hold to the bargain—not for any moral reasons, but because it is the best guarantee of survival and continuous revenue."

"Have you ever killed a man?"

"Several. Their deaths were necessary in the circumstances, but they were not premeditated. I am not an assassin. That is a trade for psychopaths, and I am a normal, if somewhat sterile, human being. My only real passion is linguistics, so I have no vices to compromise me or my employers."

"Women?"

"They do not find me attractive. For the most part I am indifferent to them. I use them when I need to do so and leave them without regret."

"Money?"

"I earn well and save enough."

"Personal enemies?"

Lunarcharsky smiled and spread his hands in deprecation.

"I would guess that I have fewer than you, Mr. Spada. I am a tool that people pick up and set down again at will. They may not like me, but they have no cause to envy or to hate me. For my part, I have neither love nor malice. . . . Anything else?"

"What do you charge?"

"Five thousand dollars a week, paid one month in advance, transportation and expenses extra, with an initial down payment of four thousand dollars. I render accurate accounts at the end of each assignment."

"How do I get in touch with you?"

"Through the Travellers Club in London."

"Fine. You'll be hearing from me."

Since that first meeting Spada had used him many times—in Prague, Beirut, Leningrad, Paris and Iran. Now he was on a permanent retainer to Proteus —a strange, shadowy figure, glimpsed one moment, gone the next, with no trace left of his scarecrow presence. An hour after he arrived in New York, he was closeted with John Spada at the top of the glass tower.

Spada's brief was curt and precise: ". . . Rodolfo Vallenilla is a thorn in the hand of the regime. Sooner or later they will try to silence him. I want to preempt that situation if I can. Your job is to protect Vallenilla and my daughter at all costs. Can you establish a feasible identity for yourself?"

"The best of all." Lunarcharsky flapped his big hands. "A real one. I'm a student of languages. I'm interested in dialectal variables in local Spanish— Lunfardo, for example, which is the patois of Buenos Aires. Cultural attachés love that sort of thing. They're only too happy to encourage scholarly visits. It makes the regime look respectable. . . ."

"How soon can you leave?"

"Within a week. The visa I can get immediately. It may take a few days to get the right letters of introduction—but it will be worth the trouble. How far are you prepared to go?"

"To protect my family? Need you ask?"

"Quite," said Lunarcharsky placidly. "Will they know I am coming?"

"That's up to you."

"Then better they don't."

"The company facilities are at your disposal."

"I won't need them—except maybe the telex in an emergency."

"In that case, call Herman Vigo at our office in Buenos Aires. He will respond to the fish name 'Mackerel' and will put you in touch with local members of the Proteus organization if you need to use them. If you want me, I'll come instantly."

"I hope it won't come to that," said the Scarecrow Man. "But it's a wild world down there. Anything is possible."

"If you have to go into action, I'll send Henson down to help you."

"He's a good man. We work well together. Anything else I should know?"

"My daughter is pregnant," said Spada flatly.

"A complication. I shall take account of it."

"She admires her husband and is desperately in love with him."

"How do you feel about him?"

"I prize him."

"Does he belong to Proteus?"

"No. He declined to join, but he knows the symbol and will respond to it."

"That's all, then." Lunarcharsky stood up to leave. "Unless you want to hear about Azudi in Teheran. The man's a beast. For him the SAVAK torture room is a playground. Personally, I'd like to eliminate him."

"Not yet. I'll deal with him when I'm ready."

"Then I'll call you before I leave for Buenos Aires."

"Go with God," said John Spada.

"I'd like to do that," said the Scarecrow Man. "If only I knew who He was or where to find Him."

He left without a backwards glance, bumping against the desk, shambling through the doorway, an oddity of nature, a survivor from the age of Lilith before the Almighty had complicated man with a soul.

The arrival of Meister Hugo von Kalbach, philosopher, theologian, Nobel Laureate, was a more cheerful event. Spada and Anna met him at the airport and drove him down to the Bay House so that he could rest for the weekend before the management conference opened on the Monday.

In spite of his age and the fatigue of the journey, the old scholar was as exuberant as a child. He kissed Anna on both cheeks, clasped Spada in a bear-hug embrace and talked volubly all through the journey.

He had given much thought to the address he was to deliver. He had written it in German. Fräulein Helga, his secretary, had made the first translation into English, which had then been polished by a member of the British Consular Staff in Munich. After that he had rehearsed it with a very pretty English soprano at the Munich opera—a good preparation, eh? But then the audience would be critical. . . . There would be discussion, no? Good! He had come to participate, not to make sermons. It was important to hear the voices in response. . . . Lermontov? It was good news that a beginning had been made. Always with the Russians one had to be patient; but this Kolchak sounded like a good man. . . . Himself? God be thanked, his health was still good. Fräulein Helga bullied him to take care, not to eat too much, wrap

himself warmly, drink English whiskey instead of
German beer. Ach! He might just as well be married!
. . . The threats against him? Well . . . The police
still guarded his house at Tegernsee. They insisted he
take an escort whenever he went into Munich.
There were times when he felt like a museum piece,
always dusted and guarded. Still, he supposed a philosopher had to be more valuable than a politician. . . .

He was scarcely installed in the Bay House when
he demanded to be taken for a walk in the garden,
then along the beach. He was so obviously happy, so
innocently greedy for every small joy, that it was
impossible to entertain a mournful thought in his
presence. However, when Spada mentioned the subject of his new book, and the possibility of an English
translation, the old man seemed uneasy.

". . . I know you read German, so I brought a
copy of the manuscript with me. I shall give it to you
tonight. I need a second opinion on the last chapter;
and you, with your large experience of practical life,
may be the right man to give it to me. I seem to have
written myself into a corner. Worse! If my fears are
justified, then, as a philosopher, I am bankrupt."

Spada, thinking to soothe him, said firmly, "I
don't believe for one moment that is possible."

"My dear friend!" Von Kalbach was emphatic.
"Life is so full of surprises, anything is possible. But
at seventy-five, to write oneself into absolute negation
. . . there is a real horror in the thought! It has both-
ered me so much, I went up to Tübingen last week to
talk to my old friend Hans Koenig. Now there is a
man you should meet! His new book is going like an
avalanche. Think of it—a document on Modern Chris-

tology, and it is selling like a pornographic novel! The Vatican summoned him to Rome last April; kept him there for two months, grilling him as if he were an old-fashioned heretic. However, he subdued even the inquisitors of the Borgo Santo Spirito. Now he's back again, still smiling, still teaching and preaching. But, my dear John, even he is stubbing his toes on the same big stone as I am ..."

"And what is the stumbling stone, Meister?"

"It is the problem we talked about in your uncle's house: our personal response to the violence enacted around us and upon us. It is no new question—God knows!" The old man threw out his arms in a gesture of defeat. "Even the most rigid moralists have been forced to compromise their answers. We may kill in a just war—whatever that is! We may kill to defend our lives or our properties. We may terminate fetal lives, stop fleeing thieves with a bullet. Kill, kill, kill! For a soldier it is a mandate; for you and me, a permissible exercise, provided we can prove a major threat. . . . Is that the end of it? Is that the sole fruit of all our accumulated wisdom, our spiritual experience, our sacred revelations?"

The old man was shaken by his own vehemence. Spada led him inside and poured a pair of drinks.

Still Von Kalbach would not let the subject drop. More calmly he went on: "Forgive me. I am full of this terror. I have to talk about it to your people, answer their questions . . ."

Spada prompted him gently. "You said you went to see Koenig. What did he have to say?"

"He takes an even darker view than I do. He is prepared—however unwillingly—to contemplate a theology in which violence may not only be tolerable, but justifiable and even obligatory for a religious man. It makes a kind of dark sense. It is possible to read the Crucifixion as an act of self-immolation, deliberately courted by the victim. Christ purged the temple with whips—an undeniably violent act. Dietrich Bonhoeffer could seriously contemplate the assassination of Hitler as a Christian duty. . . . Koenig sums it up in a strange way. He says there are certain situations from which God seems to absent himself, concrete circumstances of violent action and response, from which there is no retreat, and in which man is left alone and in darkness to make his own life-or-death decision. . . ."

"I would accept that." Spada chewed on the thought for a moment. "In a way, I have to make such consequential decisions every day. There's no Bible, no Talmud, no Koran that codifies the moralities of the modern world. The things I make have constructive uses as well as lethal ones. I make deals with bad men that benefit good people. I can't sit still and wait for a heavenly judgment. I have to act in what your friend Koenig calls 'the concrete circumstance.' . . . Another drink?"

"Wait for the wine," said Anna firmly. "We're ready to sit down to dinner, and seeing I cooked it, I won't have it spoiled!"

"That's the concrete circumstance!" Spada laughed and led the way to the dinner table. "Nothing must spoil my wife's chicken cacciatore!"

"Exactly like Fräulein Helga!" Meister Hugo beamed happily at Anna. "She says good food and philosophy don't mix. Tell me, dear lady, how is your beautiful daughter?"

70

Spada smiled and addressed himself to the pasta, while Anna launched into her own lyrical discourse on being a prospective grandmother. As a philosopher, Hugo von Kalbach might have his problems. As a dinner-table diplomat, he was better than Talleyrand.

The management conference of Spada Consolidated Holdings opened traditionally with a formal dinner at the Waldorf, where John Spada and his colleagues hosted overseas delegates, diplomats from the countries in which the corporation operated, the U.S. Secretary of State and the financial editors of major dailies and magazines.

It was a day for political courtesies, and the protocols which Spada laid down were simple and rigid. No wives were invited. The only women present were those who held diplomatic appointments or offices within the company. Security precautions were massive; a fleet of limousines delivered the guests and collected them after the function. There was no display of company emblems or products. The only symbols were the flags of the countries in which the Spada corporation functioned.

All guests were announced by name and title. Spada and his senior officers received them. There was a carefully brief prelude for cocktails and introductions, then dinner was served. Spada himself gave the address of welcome and introduced the keynote speaker. The responses were made by two delegates from abroad. Afterwards, over the coffee and liqueurs, there was an interval for informal discussion between the speaker and the guests. The whole affair was timed to finish at eleven-thirty, since the delegates were expected to begin work in the operations room in the glass tower by ten the next morning.

There were those in the corporation who questioned the value of so stiff and elitist an occasion, but Spada's reasoning was always the same: "It says what it is meant to say. We are a worldwide organization, operating in, and to the benefit of, many countries. We observe their laws and submit to their fiscal rulings. We offer their representatives a diplomatic hospitality in the United States. We offer them the best food and the best wine in the land and the opportunity to hear an address by a speaker of note. After that, finish! We are about our own business."

Spada's speech of welcome carried the same message, in terms less formal and more cordial. Normally he added a few remarks on the theme of the keynote address, but tonight the subject was so sensitive that he decided to let Hugo von Kalbach carry the full weight of the argument and the debate that would follow.

The old man made a patriarchal figure as he stood to the lectern, adjusted his pince-nez and began to speak. He opened quietly, but the mounting passion in his voice stirred them all.

". . . Violence, we are told, is an irrational act, an animal response. This is true only in the most limited context, in the crime of passion, for instance, the affray in a beer hall, the brawl at a football match . . .

"I invite you, my friends, to consider a much more sinister proposition: that violence, cruelty and murder are completely rational acts, devised as deliberately as a theater piece, to further the aims—

political, financial or personal—of those who perpetrate them . . .

"The hijack of a train or an airplane, the murder of a busload of children, the bomb exploded in a hotel foyer—these are events in a political campaign. They are designed to bring about other events, some immediate, like the release of prisoners, others more distant, like the overthrow of a regime or the destruction of confidence in legitimate governments . . .

"But guerrillas and terrorists have no monopoly of this brutal game. Governments play it too—and on a much grander scale. The concentration camps, the detention centers, the torture rooms are all contrived, rationally and scientifically, as an apparatus of oppression, to stifle dissent and strike fear into the mass of the people who have no recourse against the tyranny . . .

"Where will it end? I am an old man now. I have lived through the monstrous years of the Third Reich, the years of the holocausts. I tell you they will return unless there is an end—and soon!—to this vicious social vendetta."

He broke off for a moment to polish his glasses and turn the page of his script. His audience was deathly silent, wondering where he would lead them next.

"It may surprise you to know that I, who stand before you now, have been marked for death by assassination, because I, who belong to no party, who have spent my whole life in the pursuit of truth, am deemed to be a tool of the reactionaries. I hear you say to yourselves: 'This is a madness.' It is not. It is a piece of black theater devised by those who believe

73

that anarchy is the first necessary step on the road to a new order.

"The terrible thing is they may be right. Anarchy will inevitably produce tyranny. Tyranny is the seed-bed of revolution. And the whole bloody cycle will complete itself, unless we can find a remedy for the lunacy that afflicts us.

"It is a lunacy, my friends! Should you wonder at the desperation of guerrillas when torturers are paid from the public purse, and governments, like gangsters, hire assassins? Should you wonder at the brutality of police when, as in my country recently, masked youths parade in mockery at the grave of a terrorist victim? . . .

"Have we rejected reason and humanity alto-gether? Are we so accustomed to living under the mushroom cloud that we no longer believe that a just and peaceful society is possible or even desirable? If we have come to that, we have committed the sin against the Holy Spirit, and we are damned irrevoca-bly to a hell on our own planet!"

He gathered up his papers and sat down. There was a moment of dead silence, and then the whole assembly stood up and applauded. They were still clapping when a bellboy hurried in with a message for John Spada. The message read: "Please come to telex room, urgent."

Spada hesitated a moment, then tapped Mike Santos on the shoulder and whispered, "I have to leave for a few minutes. Cover for me."

As he moved away, Santos was already on his feet and announcing: ". . . Our friend from Iran, Riza Baraheni, who will move the vote of thanks to the speaker."

In the telex room the operator pointed to the first dialogue on the printout:

WALDORF HOTEL?

THIS IS WALDORF.

BEWLEY . . . U.S. AMBASSADOR TO ARGENTINA. UNDERSTAND MR. JOHN SPADA IS PRESENTLY AT COMPANY BANQUET YOUR HOTEL. PLEASE GET HIM. MOST URGENT.

WILL DO. PLEASE WAIT.

Spada stood beside the operator and began the dialogue.

SPADA HERE. GO AHEAD.

THIS IS BEWLEY. CALLED YOUR HOUSE. YOUR WIFE TOLD ME WHERE TO FIND YOU. BAD NEWS. YOUR SON-IN-LAW TELEPHONED AT 21.00 HOURS. INFORMED ME YOUR DAUGHTER TERESA ARRESTED BY SECURITY POLICE AT 18.00 HOURS WHILE WORKING AT CLINIC IN OLD TOWN. HE IS UNABLE ASCERTAIN PRESENT WHEREABOUTS BUT IS USING ALL EFFORTS AND CONTACTS. HIS HOME AND BUSINESS LINES TAPPED, THEREFORE HE MAY NOT BE ABLE MAKE PERSONAL CONTACT FOR SOME TIME. PROBABLY SPADA LINES ALSO.

WHY TERESA ARRESTED?

WAS CALLED BY NUNS LAST NIGHT TO
PERFORM EMERGENCY OPERATION ON
GUNSHOT CASE. VICTIM IMMEDIATELY
REMOVED FROM CLINIC BY FRIENDS.
TERESA RETURNED HOME. POLICE AP-
PARENTLY STATE HE WAS REVOLUTION-
ARY TERRORIST. YOUR SON-IN-LAW
BELIEVES POLICE ACT DESIGNED
FRIGHTEN HIM.

WHAT ACTION ARE YOU TAKING?

PROTEST AND PRESSURE FOR IMMEDI-
ATE CONSULAR CONTACT WITH TERESA.
AM PERSONALLY SEEKING AUDIENCE
WITH MINISTER INTERIOR AND PRESI-
DENT BUT HE IS ABSENT ON UP-COUN-
TRY TOUR. ANY PRESSURE YOU CAN
BRING FROM STATE OR WHITE HOUSE
WILL BE GREAT ASSIST.

SECRETARY HENDRICK IS OUR GUEST
TONIGHT. WILL CONFER IMMEDIATELY.
MOST IMPORTANT YOU AND POLICE KNOW
TERESA IS PREGNANT.

NOTED JOHN.

WHAT IS SITUATION RODOLFO VAL-
LENILLA?

SO FAR AT LIBERTY BUT UNDER CON-
STANT THREAT. HAVE OFFERED ASSIS-
TANCE IF REQUIRED. HE FEELS DUTY
KEEP PRESS LINES OPEN. FOREIGN
CORRESPONDENTS ALL FILING DIS-
PATCHES TONIGHT.

I WILL COME DOWN EARLIEST. MY
THANKS YOUR EFFORTS. PLEASE KEEP
TELEX LINES OPEN, IN CASE HENDRICK
WANTS CALL BACK.

WILL DO.

DID YOU TELL MY WIFE ANYTHING?

NO. JUST THAT I WANTED YOU.

THANKS AGAIN. SPADA OFF.

He tore the printout from the machine and read
it again, trembling with impotent rage. Then he
folded it carefully, concentrating on each movement
as if it were an affirmation that he was still in a real
world. He walked slowly back into the banquet room,
where Toshi Hatanaka was seconding the vote of
thanks. Secretary of State Hendrick was seated in the
place of honour at the right of Spada's chair. Spada
passed him the telex. He read it slowly, refolded it
and passed it back.

He whispered, "I'll go talk to Bewley now. We'll
do everything we can. Where will you be afterwards?"

"At my apartment. You've got the number."

"I'll call you."

"I think I'm going to announce this."

The Secretary reflected a moment and then
nodded. "Why the hell not? But let me get out first.
I'll take the Argentine Ambassador with me. No point
in submitting him to embarrassment. He's a decent
enough guy and he could be helpful."

The two men left the room just as the Japanese
finished his speech. John Spada rose and stilled the

applause with a gesture. He paused for a moment, composing himself, and then announced quietly: "At this time there is a period for free discussion between our guests and the speaker. First, I beg your indulgence to make a personal statement. I have just received some news which perhaps will confirm everything that Meister Hugo von Kalbach has said to you. My daughter, Teresa, was recently married to Rodolfo Vallenilla, whom some of you will know as one of the most liberal and outspoken editors in South America. Since her return to Buenos Aires she has been working as a physician in a clinic run by the Missionary Sisters of the Poor. Yesterday she was called to do an emergency operation on a man suffering from gunshot wounds. Tonight she was arrested by the security police and is being held in an undisclosed location. Her husband is still at liberty but, according to official information, is under constant threat. I leave you to draw your own conclusions. . . . Please excuse me now. Mr. Mike Santos will take the chair for the rest of the proceedings."

Mike Santos moved swiftly to the microphone, put a protective hand on his shoulder and steered him away from the table towards the door. Kitty Cowan and Maury Feldman, seated halfway down the room, made a move to join him, but he motioned them to stay. He tried to hold himself straight and firm, but he felt as though something had broken inside him.

The trials of the evening were not yet over. He was five minutes back in his apartment, holding a sobbing Anna in his arms, when the telephone rang and a Spanish-speaking operator came on the line.

"Mr. John Spada?"

"Yes?"

"One moment, please. I have a call for you from Montevideo."

For a second he was nonplussed. He knew no one in that city. Then he remembered that Montevideo, the capital of Uruguay, was only a short plane ride across the gulf from Buenos Aires. He waited through an interminable series of bleeps and clicks, and then Lunarcharsky came on the line. His report was delivered in terse, crackling Italian.

"I presume you've heard the news?"

"Yes. Where the hell were you?"

"I arrived in Buenos Aires this morning. I checked in at the Palace Hotel. In the afternoon I went around the locations: the residence, the newspaper office, the clinic. I went back to the hotel and called Mackerel. By then it was too late. I hopped a late plane over here to report to you. I'm going back in the morning."

"What does Mackerel say?"

"About the lady? It's bad and it's good. The arrest is public and official. Therefore they have to respond to diplomatic inquiries, though they'll stall as long as they can. If they move against the man, it won't be official, and that could be very bad. I'll mount surveillance; but I've also got to assemble some help, so he won't be fully covered for a while."

"I understand. Do your best. I'll get Henson down as soon as I can."

"That would help."

"I'm coming myself in the next forty-eight hours."

"You're going to need some high-handed diplomacy."

"It's in train."

"Good. If I'm not at the hotel when you arrive, leave a fish message. *Hasta la vista.*"

He had just set down the telephone when there was another call, this time from Secretary Hendrick.

"John? . . . Hendrick. Things are in motion. I've called the White House. The Man is sympathetic and will make representations, once I can assure him that there is nothing in the case that can compromise him."

"That's fair. I'll drop him a note of thanks. What next?"

"Bewley has instructions to work vigorously at the ministerial level. The Ambassador here is shocked and sympathetic, and he'll get a strong note from us in the morning. However, you'd better understand the situation. The boys down there will hang tough as long as they can. They'll stick to the rules: no consular contact before three days, which they can stretch to seven. They'll try to get some kind of deposition from your daughter that will justify the arrest and then make the release look like an act of clemency."

"There's no doubt she will be released?"

"There's every probability."

"I see. Will they let me see her?"

"I doubt it. Not until they've got their depositions."

"If that means what I think it does . . ."

"We're taking a very strong line for that reason."

"Christ!"

"One more thing, John. If you go down . . ."

"I'm going."

"Then stay very quiet and don't make a single

80

move without Ambassador Bewley. If you put a foot wrong, you'll blow everything we're trying to do."

"I understand. If there's anything I can do . . ."

"Sit tight and pray. Good night."

He set down the receiver and turned to face Anna. She was dry-eyed now but pale and shocked. He told her, "That was Secretary Hendrick. Good news. The President will intervene if necessary. All the machinery at State is working for us."

"What was the first call?"

"The Scarecrow Man. He's down in Argentina starting private inquiries. You know how good he is. Contacts everywhere."

He crossed to the bar, poured two stiff drinks and handed one to Anna. She gagged on the first mouthful. He wiped her lips and her hands and then held the glass to her mouth until she got down a big swallow. Then he made her sit down while he tried to reassure her.

"We knew something like this could happen. Now that it's come, we have to be very calm and very wise. Everyone, from the President down, wants to help—and that's a lot of power, Anna, a real steamroller! We'll have Teresa out in no time!"

"But she can't stay down there! The next time it will be Rodo. They'll never have any peace!"

"That's why I'm going down. I want to have a long talk with Rodo."

"I'm coming with you."

"No way, my love! No way in the world! You sit tight. I'll be in touch by phone or telex every day. I'll have Kitty Cowan come and stay with you."

"I don't want Kitty!" Her tone was high and angry. "I don't want anyone!"

"Fine! Fine!" He stroked her forehead and her hair. "Whatever you say. But if you get lonely or depressed . . ."

Her head came up proudly and she gave him a pale, tremulous smile.

"I'm Anna Spada. If my daughter can endure a prison cell, I can surely sit in the comfort of my own home and wait for her!"

"That's my girl! I'm John Spada, and if I can't raise enough hell to . . ."

The doorbell rang. Carlos, the houseman, went to answer it. A moment later Maury Feldman, Kitty Cowan and Mike Santos came in.

When the flurry of greetings had subsided and they all sat with drinks in their hands, Maury Feldman said, "We stopped off at my apartment. I called the attorney we use in Buenos Aires. He'll move in as Teresa's legal representative first thing in the morning."

"Thanks, Maury. What does he say?"

Feldman gave him a small warning lift of the eyebrow.

"He never says much. He's a good man with high connections. He'll give the best service."

"Thanks, Maury. What happened after I left the dinner?"

Mike Santos answered for them all. "Question time was a washout. Nobody could top your announcement. The press boys rushed for the phones. The others hung around chatting in little groups until I ordered the bar closed. Everybody was shocked. The

82

chancelleries will be buzzing in the morning. Some of our people were asking whether economic reprisals were contemplated. I chopped that one off very fast."

"Good. What about Von Kalbach?"

"We took him back to his hotel," said Kitty Cowan. "I told him you'd come around for breakfast in the morning. . . . What's the next move, chief?"

"The State Department is pulling out all the stops. The White House will intervene later, if necessary. I'm going down to Buenos Aires tomorrow. I'll take the company jet. It's a ten-hour flight. Tell them to be fuelled and ready for takeoff by midday. Telex the Embassy. Have our people get in touch with Rodo and bring him to meet me at the airport. Book me the usual suite. I won't be there much, but I'll need an official address. Which reminds me . . ."

He crossed to the telephone and dialled a New York number.

"Is Mr. George Kunz there, please? John Spada calling . . . Hello, George. Sorry to call so late, but I'm needing a great favour. My daughter has been arrested in Buenos Aires . . . It's a political thing, too long to go into over the phone. Point is, I'm flying down there tomorrow and I'm damn sure all our company lines are bugged and there'll be a tap on my hotel line as well. I know you have a company apartment. If it's free, I'd like to use it as a hidey-hole . . . That's great. A thousand thanks. Have them send the key over to Herman Vigo . . . You're a real friend. I won't forget it."

"So!" As he walked back, Anna sat bolt upright and challenged him. "It is that kind of affair now."

"It may be, my love. I like to be prepared. An-

other thing, Kitty. Get Henson in as soon as possible.
Tell him our other friend is at the Palace Hotel."

"Right."

"I've never heard of Henson." Mike Santos cut
in. "I've never heard of his friend at the Palace Hotel.
If it's company business, I should know about it, yes?"

There was a brief, strained silence. Kitty and
Anna looked at each other. Maury Feldman studied
the backs of his long, soft hands. Mike Santos waited
impassively.

Finally Spada answered. "It affects my daughter,
but it's not company business."

"But company people are involved in it—Kitty
here, for one."

"So?"

"So you trust me to run a billion-dollar enterprise and protect your personal stake therein. It seems
to me you shouldn't ask me to walk anywhere—and I
mean anywhere!—in the dark."

"The man's got a point," said Maury Feldman.

"The man's got a good point," said Kitty Cowan.

"I would like to ask you a question, Mike," said
Anna Spada, "since I also pressed my husband to
promote you."

"Ask anything you want, ma'am." Mike Santos
was calm and deferential.

"You have seen what can happen, even to
people who sit in high places. Can you imagine what
it is like when the same things happen to people
who have no protection, no redress?"

"Yes, I can, ma'am. I made reference to the
matter in a paper which I prepared for your husband,

although I know he hasn't had too much time to read it."

"I've read it," said John Spada. "Kitty's read it, and so has Maury. There are things we don't agree with, but the general line makes sense."

"You took a big risk when you wrote it," said Feldman with a grin.

"I wonder if you'd take a bigger one?" asked John Spada.

"Like what?"

"Gamble your career for something you believe in."

"I don't understand."

"I'll try to explain. We had all intended to invite you to join us. We simply wanted to wait until you'd digested the new appointment. Now we've been outrun by events. The three of us here—and I exclude Anna because she is part of me and not part of the corporation—do another job, private, unpaid, subject to certain risks. Our work for Spada Consolidated is a cover, a necessary cover, for that private work. In my case, for example, if it became known, I should certainly lose the proxy fight with Liebowitz. Now if you involve yourself in it, you're at greater risk, because you're an executive employee who can be fired at will by paying out his contract. So here's the bottom line. You walk out of here knowing nothing and, whether I go or stay, your career's in no jeopardy. Once I tell you, you're in a cleft stick. If you can't live with what you hear, you'll resign. If you can, you'll be doing what we've all done for a long time: living a double life. Clear?"

"So far, yes. Let me ask you something. Is this political—left and right, that sort of thing?"

"It's a human thing," said Kitty Cowan. "I still vote Democrat."

"You can still swear the oath of allegiance," said Maury Feldman. "And look your God in the eye on Sunday."

"But," said Spada, "you could get a hell of a roasting at a stockholders' meeting—and in extreme circumstances you might get a bullet in the back."

"Stop it, Giovanni!" Anna was outraged. "There is no call for all this."

"I asked for it, ma'am," said Mike Santos. "O.K., boys and girls. I'm duly warned. Now let's have it!"

"There's a final warning," said John Spada firmly. "Once you know, you carry human lives in your hands."

"I still want to have my father smile at me when we meet."

"Fine!" said John Spada. "We start with a little puzzle that looks like a fish in a box . . ."

It was one in the morning when he finished his story of Proteus and the sea creatures. At the end of it Mike Santos sat, chin cupped in his hands, staring at the carpet. Kitty Cowan reached out and touched him.

"That's all there is; there ain't no more."

Mike Santos shook his head like a man waking from a long nap. He straightened up and faced John Spada. "It's a lot to swallow at one gulp."

"Do you want more time?"

"No."

"What's your answer?"

"A few days ago you asked me how badly I wanted this job. I told you I had to be able to live with the man I saw in the mirror."

"Yes?"

"I figure this is one way I can do it."

"Welcome!" said John Spada. "Maury and Kitty will brief you. Now, all of you, get the hell out of here. I want to go to bed with my wife!"

As they kissed good-bye at the front door Kitty asked softly, "Are you coming to the office in the morning?"

"Sure. I'll be there at nine. I'll stop by and have breakfast with Von Kalbach first."

"How bad is it for Teresa?"

"Very bad. Hold Anna's hand while I'm gone."

"Anything you say, chief. Courage, eh?"

Mike Santos clasped his hand and said with rare emotion, "Thanks for asking me in. I've always admired you, John, but this is the first time I've really liked you."

To which Maury Feldman added his own tart postscript: "Tonight, enjoy! Tomorrow you'll be eating Dead Sea fruit—dust and ashes in the mouth. Good night, John boy. When you get to Buenos Aires, walk close to the wall."

Next morning, as Spada drank his last cup of coffee in Hugo von Kalbach's hotel room, the old man said with poignant conviction, "Last night was horrible; but in the end I saw it plain. There is no way to bargain with evil. You have to fight it—even to death."

"Are you sure of that, Meister?"

"Yes. At long last I am sure. When I went to bed, I had, again, a warning—what do they call it in English?—a fibrillation of the heart. I lay very quiet until it passed and the rhythm was regular again. I was not really afraid. I understand now that death is a very small event, soon over, soon forgotten; but to be a man is a big event, full of possibilities, even when one is old. When I go back to Germany I shall try to find good people for you—Proteus people. When I have them I shall send you their names."

"Thank you, Meister."

"And you, when you can, please come to visit me. You should meet Fräulein Helga. A good woman, who needed a good marriage; but I was too old and too occupied to prepare her for it. Eh! The passing years!"

"I'll come. Maybe sooner than you expect."

"It cannot be too soon. I shall pray for your daughter and her husband. There is little else I can do."

"There is something."

"Anything."

"One day I may need a new identity, therefore a new passport. My German is good. I am told I could pass for a Swabian."

"Near enough." The old scholar brightened. "Let me think about it, see what I can do."

"But quickly, please."

"How else, my friend? When you hear the knocking on the gate, everything becomes very urgent."

They embraced in the old way. At the door Spada turned back. The old man smiled and waved, but his face was wet with tears.

As she set down the last page of directives to cover his absence, Kitty Cowan said, "Chief . . ."

"What?"

"We've been together a long time. When you hurt, I hurt too."

"I know, girl. I'm grateful. The rest of it is hard to put into words, but . . ."

"But you love Anna and you love Teresa and it's all clean and none of it comes together. Just remember, I sure as hell care what happens. So be honest with me, eh?"

"That's a promise."

"You say that, but I know you. I see that killer's look in your eye and I start to sweat."

"Ladies perspire."

"I'm not a lady. Never have been. Never will be. You need me, you call. Promise?"

"Every day. Even if I don't need you. How's Mike Santos this morning?"

"You'll see. Fire in the eyes, fire in the guts, ready to go crusading. He's fine, though."

"Keep an eye on him, girl. He's still under test."

"There's something else."

"What?"

"Maury and I talked about it last night. We're both Jewish, so we understand. When things turn bad, like they have down there, like they did in Germany before the war, there's only two things you can do—go underground, or leave and fight from outside. If you stand up in the public square they pick you off. Your Teresa and her Rodo, they've got to understand that. You have to make them see it."

"I'm sure as hell going to try."

"It won't be easy. Teresa's like you, a hardhead."

"And Rodo's full of pride and Spanish vinegar, I know. All I can do is try to persuade them."

"But if you can't?"

"We wear their decision."

"You say that, but will Anna wear it?"

"I'll have to help her."

"Right . . . But you can't do it and you won't do it with that goddam Spada gall in your guts. You won't break, you'll just turn tough and sour. But Anna will break, unless you teach her to bend to the wind. You read me, big John?"

"I read you, Kitty girl. Wish me luck, eh?"

"All the luck in the world." She took his face in her hands and kissed him. "Say hullo to Mike on the way out. I've learned to live without you. He hasn't yet."

When he landed in Buenos Aires, twenty minutes before midnight, he found that his luck had run out. Herman Vigo met him at the entrance to the customs hall and told him that Rodolfo Vallenilla had been arrested.

"How? When?"

"Wait till we're in the car, please!"

"Who's driving?"

"I am."

As they drove towards the city, Vigo gave him the sparse details.

"As soon as I got your telex I called Vallenilla's apartment. Believing the phones were bugged, I made it a normal family message. You were coming in. He might like to drive out with me to the airport.

90

We arranged to meet for coffee in a bar near the Plaza de Mayo. He didn't turn up. I went to his apartment. The place was a shambles, every drawer turned out, clothes and books and papers all over the place. I went to his office. They said he didn't usually come in until three o'clock, when it was time to start setting up the midnight edition. I left a message for him to call me when he came in. At five, his assistant telephoned and said he hadn't showed up. Then your man Lunarcharsky telephoned and asked me to have a drink with him before dinner. He told me he'd been watching Vallenilla's apartment since early morning from a car parked across the street. He saw Vallenilla leave and start walking towards the Plaza. Three men got out of a parked car, stopped him, bundled him inside and drove off. Lunarcharsky followed them for a dozen blocks, then lost them in traffic. He said he'd been poking around all day trying to get a lead. So far nothing."

"Where's Lunarcharsky now?"

"He's waiting for us at the bus stop outside the General Hospital."

"Any word of Teresa?"

"Your lawyer and the Embassy people have been in touch with the police. They've filed formal requests for access. The police say they'll be dealt with in due course."

"Shit!"

"I've put the word out to all our Proteus people. They're digging around for information."

"How do you read it, Herman?"

"It's bad—but easy to read. They've always wanted to silence Vallenilla. When he married your

91

daughter they were in trouble, because you control a lot of investment down here. This way they figure they've got you tied. Your daughter's up on a criminal charge—conspiracy to aid and abet a criminal. They'll assemble enough documents to prove it. Then they'll release her and extradite her. They figure she'll stay quiet and you'll sit still because of what may happen to Vallenilla."

"The bastards! Has his family been told?"

"Yes. The father will come in to Buenos Aires to see you. But first he wants to make his own inquiries."

"Can he do anything?"

"I doubt it. He's got lots of friends in high places, but most people are scared to talk too loudly."

"Anything for order in the streets, eh?"

"That's the way it is down here," said Herman Vigo. "There's the hospital ahead. Get ready to open the rear door. We don't want to stop, just slow down."

Spada reached back and held the door slightly ajar. As they rolled past the bus stop, he thrust it open and the Scarecrow Man scrambled, with surprising agility, into the back seat of the limousine. Vigo gunned the motor and they moved off at speed.

Spada demanded abruptly, "Any news?"

"A little. There's no record of your son-in-law's arrest by the police. That means the security boys have got him."

"Where?"

"Headquarters, probably. The place they call the 'Fun Palace.' I'm sorry. I saw it happen, but I couldn't intervene—not with your daughter in custody."

"What's the next move?"

"For you, only one. Work with the Embassy and the lawyers to get your daughter out. Leave Vallenilla to me. That's another kind of job altogether. Let me out at the next traffic light, please. I'll walk the rest of the way."

"Keep in touch," said John Spada.

"Of course," said the Scarecrow Man. "But don't expect miracles; and send your aircraft back to New York. You're likely to be here for some time."

He had dealt with bureaucracy before, but always as a man of power who could walk away, jingling his dollars in his jeans, until the clerks and jacks-in-office had a fire lit under their backsides. Now everything was different, brutally different. He was the petitioner, forced to be courteous, driven to be humble, because there were lives at stake, and here the writ of habeas corpus ran no longer.

The lawyer whom Maury Feldman had hired spelled it out for him on the first day: "There is more happening in Argentina than you see on the surface: a power struggle between the diehards and the moderates in the military junta, a lesson for foreign investors that whoever wants to do business here plays by army rules, a warning to the liberals that, now that they are saved from revolution, they had better be content with an orderly tyranny. . . . To you, and to your daughter, they will dole out their favours in droplets, so that in the end you will accept her conviction and her banishment as a mercy. Personally, I should advise you not to stay, but to come and go often."

"How long will it take to get Teresa out?"

"Not less than a month, possibly longer."

"When will they let me see her?"

"I don't know. Certainly not soon. Even I cannot get near her and I am her legal representative."

The reason was made plain enough after the Consul General's visit, ten days later. He made his report to Spada and Ambassador Bewley in a closed session at the Embassy.

"I was taken to see her at the women's prison. I was not permitted to be alone with her. There was a woman warder and a security man present. I told her you were here and that we were making all efforts to have her released. She herself spoke very cautiously."

"How is she?"

"In her own words, 'Well enough, considering . . .' She said she had suffered a miscarriage but was now recovered from it."

"How did it happen?"

"Mr. Spada"—the Consul was obviously distressed—"you may as well face it now. Your daughter has obviously been questioned under duress."

"You mean tortured?"

"I'm afraid so."

"Did she tell you that?"

"Obviously she could not, since her ultimate release will depend on her signing a document that she has been well treated. She did, however, manage to pass me the clue. Speaking of the miscarriage, she said she attributed it medically to her state of shock after the arrest. One of the standard methods of interrogation is the application of electric shock."

"God Almighty!"

Spada was murderously angry. The Consul tried to calm him.

"If it is any help, the interrogations are obviously finished, since she is now confined in the political wing of the women's prison."

"But they could begin again."

"It is not usual. The first session is usually exhaustive."

Spada heaved himself out of his chair and paced the room like a caged lion, raging impotently.

"In God's name, something's got to be done! We can't just sit here and . . ."

"We're not just sitting here, John!" There was a ring of steel in Bewley's tone. "Now that we've made contact, know what's happened to her, we're much stronger. I'm ordered to make personal representations to the President. I'm seeing him at ten tomorrow morning. By then he'll have had a personal communication from the White House."

"Representations, for Christ's sake! My daughter is . . ."

"Your daughter is one of many thousands who have suffered in this way. Her husband is a far worse case and may, for all we know, be dead! You ask what representations mean. I'll tell you. I'll talk to the President at ten. He'll tell me that, being a very busy man, he's not familiar with the case, but he'll certainly call for an urgent report on it and let me know within a week. Then he'll pass the word down the line that it's time to stage act two, which means prepare the papers that will prove your daughter is a criminal. Then he'll summon me and we'll get to dealing for her release. How tough we can be depends on how much public opinion we can muster outside— the press, television, the threat of economic sanctions."

"Meantime, Teresa's sitting in a goddam prison cell and her husband's dropped off the face of the earth." A sudden thought struck him and he swung around to face the Consul. "Did she say anything about Rodo?"

"Yes. She asked if there was any news of him. The way she said it, I think she knew he was gone. They probably told her anyway to break her down more during the interrogation. I assured her we were making all possible efforts to trace him."

"What did she say to that?"

"Something very simple: 'At least I'm not the only one. Say thank you to Papa.'"

Suddenly Spada's control snapped and he found himself weeping—salt bitter tears that gave him no relief at all. When finally the tears were spent and he turned to face them, they saw a grey mask, bleak eyed and pitiless. The voice that spoke from the mask was like a voice from the dead.

"I am not usually so emotional. You will not see me this way again. Thank you both for what you are doing. I'll cooperate as far as I can. But I will swear you an oath. If the President refuses to release Teresa, I shall personally pay the assassins who will kill him!"

4

◇◇◇◇◇◇◇◇◇◇◇◇◇◇◇◇◇◇◇◇◇◇◇◇◇◇◇◇◇◇◇◇◇◇◇

At five that same afternoon, John Spada walked out of his hotel to keep a rendezvous with the Scarecrow Man.

His route lay along the Calle Florída, and in spite of his preoccupations he forced himself to observe the colourful crowd, tune his ears to the scraps of talk, Criollo, Spanish, German, French, Italian. The air was warm and languid, a potpourri of pampas dust, petrol fumes and the exhalations of the silt beds on which the great city sprawled itself like an uneasy giant.

Spada was in no hurry. His appointment was made on a Latin time scale, between five-thirty and six in a wineshop. He was grateful for the leisure to set his thoughts in order, get his tangled emotions under control. He was at war now, his hand against every man who stood between him and his objective. He could no longer afford the luxuries of regret and penitence or even the distraction of loving. He must become what he had been in his youth: a fighting machine, precise, passionless and devoid of pity.

Halfway along the Calle Florída he turned left into a narrow thoroughfare, where wheeled traffic was forbidden and ambling citizens might hold quiet commerce with butcher, baker, tailor, a vendor of pearls, milady's milliner, milord's wine seller, a binder of books in fine leather. The wineshop was a dark cellar, ten steps below the pavement, with banquettes built out from the walls like choir stalls. The tables were wine casks covered with red cloths and crowned with wax candles, big as a man's fist. In one corner four cronies were playing cards. In the opposite angle a short, tubby fellow in a grimy sweat shirt was nursing a glass of brandy. Behind the zinc-covered bar a burly, pockmarked *padrón* studied the football scores. The Scarecrow Man sat opposite with a notebook in front of him and at his elbow a glass of wine and a bottle of mineral water.

Spada sat down beside him, ordered a coffee and a cognac and waited for the Scarecrow Man to make the opening gambit. Before he had time to initiate any move there was a diversion: sirens, a distant scream of brakes, shouts, a flurry of running feet, then an ominous silence.

The cardplayers continued their game, unheeding. The barman folded his paper carefully, took down a ledger from the shelf and began a painful pantomime of totting up his accounts. The tubby man in the corner stooped, as if to pick up a dropped coin, then burrowed into the dark belly of the barrel and drew the tablecloth over the aperture. The Scarecrow Man took a sip of wine, a mouthful of mineral water, and continued his note-taking.

A moment later, two men in sports trousers and

98

leather jackets thrust open the door, clattered down the stairs and stood silently surveying the drinkers. The barman shrugged and made a gesture that said: "What you see is what is here." The four cardplayers delved into their breast pockets, brought out documents, laid them on the barrel top and continued playing. The Scarecrow Man still wrote assiduously in his notebook. Spada watched with the wary puzzlement of a stranger.

The two men made a perfunctory check of the cardplayers' documents, then walked slowly to Lunarcharsky's table and stood over him. One of them said curtly, "You! Pay attention!"

The Scarecrow Man looked up, mildly surprised, almost obsequious. He said in Spanish, "Yes, gentlemen. What can I do for you?"

"Documents!"

"Of course. Documents." He put his hand into his breast pocket, brought out his passport and handed it to the interrogator. "I am, as you see, a visitor to your country."

First one, then the other, examined the passport; then the questioning began.

"When did you arrive in Buenos Aires?"

"The date is indicated by the entry stamp, there."

"The purpose of your visit?"

"Excuse me." He fished again in his pocket and brought out a large, official envelope. "This is a letter from your Embassy in London to the appropriate ministries in Argentina. It explains, better than I can, the purpose of my visit."

After they had read the letter they were suddenly respectful.

"Excuse us, sir. This is a security operation. We had no wish to disturb you."

"Of course not."

"How long have you been here?"

"About fifteen minutes. Why?"

"Did you see anyone else come in or go out?"

"No one."

"Why did you come here?"

"As you see, to have a drink. I'd been for a walk. I was tired and thirsty."

"Where are you registered?"

"The Plaza Hotel."

"These studies of yours—what precisely are they?"

"May I offer you gentlemen a drink?"

"No, thank you. We have work to do. Please answer the question."

"Well . . . How shall I put it? I study the development of language under environmental influences. You two for example, you both speak Spanish. Yet I would guess that you, sir, are from the north near Uruguay, and your friend comes from much farther south, perhaps from the sheep country near Tierra del Fuego. Am I right?"

"How do you know?"

"Oh, the intonations, the quality of the vowels, the slurring of certain consonants."

"Well, you could be right."

"May I have my documents, please? I'd be lost without them."

With obvious reluctance the interrogator handed back the documents.

"How long do you intend to stay in Argentina?"

"I'm not sure. But the visa is valid for three months, yes?"

"Yes. After that you must leave—or apply for renewal."

"Thank you, gentlemen."

"You're sure you saw no one else here?"

"I saw no one else; but, as you observe, I have been writing up notes. Anyone could have come and gone without my knowing. I'm sorry I can't be more helpful."

"It doesn't matter." They dismissed him with a shrug and turned their attention to John Spada. He handed them his passport without a word. They examined it minutely, then asked: "What is your business in Buenos Aires?"

"I own a large company here. Impresa Spada de Argentina."

He had expected an immediate reaction. When none came he was puzzled. Then he remembered that Teresa would be known under her married name: Vallenilla.

The interrogator closed the passport and handed it back. "How long have you been in this place?"

Spada pointed to his coffee and the brandy glass, both untouched. "I have just sat down."

"Then enjoy your drink!"

"A good idea." Spada raised his glass in an ironic toast. "Salud!"

Abruptly as they had come, they were gone. Like a figure from a Boccaccio novella, the tubby fellow emerged from under the tablecloth, with the glass of liquor still in his hand. The cardplayers continued their game. The Scarecrow Man bent again to his

101

notes. Spada said nothing. After a moment the barman approached and refilled their glasses.

"With the compliments of the house, gentlemen."

"Thank you," said the Scarecrow Man placidly. "You are very kind."

"On the contrary," said the barman. "You are welcome here at any time, either of you."

"The shits are everywhere these days." One of the cardplayers spoke over his shoulder. "It's nice to meet a pair of gentlemen." He slapped down a card and raked the money towards him. "How come you speak such good Spanish?"

"It's a knack." The Scarecrow Man chuckled, heh-heh, in his rasping fashion. "Like dealing cards. Either you can or you can't."

The tubby fellow tossed off his drink at a gulp and made to leave. He paused a moment by their tables and said softly, "I am called Sancho. If either of you needs a service, ask for me here, anytime. Someone will call you. Oh, and watch out at the Plaza. The girls on the switchboard listen to the calls. *Hasta la vista, amigos*."

"*Hasta la vista*," said the Scarecrow Man.

"Go with God," said John Spada.

"Believe me," said the barman, "Sancho is a good friend and a bad enemy."

"I'll remember it," said the Scarecrow Man. He raised his glass to John Spada. "Damnation to all bastards."

"I'll drink to that." Then, more quietly, he asked: "What news?"

"Vallenilla's alive, but in bad shape. They've moved him out of the Fun Palace."

"Where are they holding him now?"

"Martín García. It's a prison island at the mouth of the Río de la Plata."

"Are you sure of that information?"

"I am always sure," said the Scarecrow Man reproachfully.

"Plans?"

"When does Henson get here?"

"Tomorrow, from Madrid. He's booked into your hotel."

"First move, Henson looks at the prison and the approaches. Second, I've got to get information about what goes on inside and, if possible, a set of plans. I'll need help with that."

"What sort of help?"

"Contacts among the underground groups. They're closed tighter than oysters. The only way in is by recommendation from outside."

"What do you mean, outside?"

"The South American Revolutionary Junta in Paris. They have emissaries coming in and out all the time. Of course, you may not want to compromise yourself by dealing with them."

"My daughter and her husband are in the hands of the butchers. I'll deal with the devil himself to get them out. I've a friend in Rome who might help. He's a member of Proteus—and of the Italian Communist Party."

"You'd better move fast," said the Scarecrow Man. "There's a high casualty rate in Martín García."

"My Ambassador is talking with the President in the morning. I'll wait for his report. Then I'll decide whether I can safely leave for a few days. I'll come back via Munich and Rome."

"Have you ever thought," asked the Scarecrow

Man, "that once your daughter is extradited she can never come back?"

"I should have thought that was obvious."

"Have you thought they might extend the ban to you too?"

"I've thought of it," said Spada grimly. "That's why I've got to go to Germany. . . . Finish your drink and let's go for a walk. There's someone I want you to meet."

He signalled to the barman to bring the check. As he was sorting out the change, the barman said in English, "It is not wise to come here too often. We get a lot of unwelcome visitors. . . . You were talking about Martín García." Spada and the Scarecrow Man looked at each other. The barman pointed at the ceiling. "In a cellar the sound travels. At the bar I hear everything. Fortunately, the others do not understand English."

"Thanks," said John Spada.

"That Sancho." The barman lowered his voice to a whisper. "He was a prisoner for twelve months inside Martín García. Maybe he could help."

"Maybe he could," said the Scarecrow Man. "Ask him if he'd be willing to meet me—and where. I'll call you for the answer tomorrow."

"Make it the day after," said the barman. "He's a busy man. Always on the move. ¡Hasta la vista, señores!"

The shop of Salvador Gonzalez, Dealer in Rare Books and Prints, was a narrow building with a single dusty window protected by wrought-iron grillwork. The window revealed nothing except a few yellowed prints and nondescript volumes bound in leather. Inside, it was orderly and immaculate: the examples of the old cartographers' art beautifully framed and illuminated, the folios of prints laid out on a vast refectory table, the antique volumes meticulously dusted, their leather bindings dressed by tender hands.

Salvador Gonzalez himself was a singular specimen of a singular race—the antiquarians who somehow managed to survive wars, earthquakes and political change and emerge, unharmed, still clutching their precious relics as a talisman against misfortune. He was a tiny, gnomelike man with a mane of white hair and a grandee's beard, always neatly trimmed. His suits were of antique cut. He still wore buttoned boots and spats, and sported a monocle, hung from a ribbon of black silk, and a gold watch chain with a seal, draped across his waistcoat.

A bell tinkled over the doorway as John Spada entered with the Scarecrow Man. The tiny grandee advanced to greet them.

"Good day, sirs! You are welcome. I am Salvador Gonzalez. You wish to see something special . . . prints, maps . . . I do not think I have had the pleasure of meeting you before?"

"The loss is mine," said John Spada gravely. He held out a visiting card on which was the symbol of the fish in a box. "You are Dolphin. I believe that you may be able to find me a rather rare map."

The little man screwed the monocle into his eye, studied the card for a moment and then passed it back to Spada.

"Ah, yes! Mackerel told me to expect you. And what map are you looking for?"

"Martín García," said the Scarecrow Man crisply.

"The river approaches, the island and its installations, the interior and exterior of the fortress itself. Warning systems and electrical circuits. How long?"

The bell over the shop door sounded, and Salvador Gonzalez launched himself, like an actor, into an elaborate monologue: ". . . A very rare copy of the *Tratados* of Bartolomé de las Casas, edition of 1552. The condition is not as good as one would wish, but the rarity of this edition fully justifies the asking price. I do not have the volumes myself, but I could . . . Oh, my dear Señora Moreno! A pleasure to see you, as always. Your picture is framed. Permit me to show you . . . Excuse me a moment, señores. This way, please . . ."

He followed his visitor, a young and attractive matron, through the rear door of the room and up the stairs. They were gone about five minutes, and when they returned the young woman was carrying a flat package about a third of a meter square. When he had ushered her out of the shop, the little man became brisk and businesslike.

"What you need . . . it's quite a lot. I'm not sure how much information is assembled on Martín García. I'll need at least three days to see what's available and put it together."

"This hour three days hence," said John Spada. "One of us will be here."

"Better you telephone first. I have an odd selection of clients. That one, the Moreno woman, for example. She's the second wife of one of our prominent generals. He likes antique pornography. She collects it for him. I sell her whatever comes my way. *¡Ay de mi!* It's a shame I'm too old to enjoy it myself. When you call, mention the *Tratados* and the edition of

106

1552. Tell me you'd be interested if the price could be revised. Oh, and talking of price . . ."

"Let's not talk money," said John Spada politely. "We need the map and your service. We are prepared to pay for them."

"Please!" The grandee was eager to avoid any misunderstanding. "For the friends of Proteus the price is minimal; but there are always some incidentals, small items . . ."

"Always," said John Spada. "I'm sure we can agree them without contention. Now I'd like to forget business for a moment and let us see some of your treasures."

"This, for instance . . ." The Scarecrow Man pointed to a large parchment map, carefully laid under glass. The little man looked at him with new respect.

"Ah, I see you have the connoisseur's eye. That is one of my best pieces. Its provenance is well established. It is one of the charts of the Río de la Plata, prepared by the cartographer of Pedro de Mendoza in 1536 . . ."

"I've seen another like it in London," said the Scarecrow Man.

"You must travel a great deal."

"Regrettably, yes. I envy you this scholar's life, with all these beautiful pieces."

The little man frowned and shifted uncomfortably on his buttoned boots.

"Please! Call no man happy. It's bad luck. In these times one is grateful to stay alive. My grandson, a boy of eighteen, was shot by the military six months ago."

"I'm sorry," said John Spada. "My daughter is in

the hands of the police. Her husband, Rodolfo Vallenilla, is a prisoner in Martín García."

"I know. His father is an old and dear friend. I have been selling him sporting prints for many years. I shall do my best to help. You should go now. And don't forget . . ."

"I won't. Three days from now, we'll talk about the price of the *Tratados*, edition of 1552. By the way, who does have that edition?"

"It's in the President's library. Not that he ever reads it; but I'm sure he wouldn't sell it to the likes of you or me. Go with God, my friends."

"Do you still believe in God, Señor Gonzalez?" asked John Spada.

"It gets harder every year," said the tiny grandee. "But if you can open up Martín García, I'll go to the Archbishop's Mass on Sunday!"

As they walked out of the shop into the glow of a dusty sunset, the Scarecrow Man said, "Permit me to say you are a surprising man, Mr. Spada."

"Permit me to say, Doctor, that I want to be able to open that goddam prison like a can of sardines— and I don't want the key breaking off in my hand!"

"Amen," said the Scarecrow Man.

The man behind the desk looked like an actor typecast for the role of military dictator. He was lean, dark and saturnine. His uniform fitted him like a skin. His gestures were restrained. His Argentine accent was hidden under a high Castilian gloss. His hostility was masked by a punctiliously formal address.

". . . As President of Argentina, I intervene rarely in the affairs of my ministries. However, as a gesture of fraternal goodwill to the President of the United States, I made a personal study of the case of Teresa Spada. There is no doubt in my mind that she is guilty, as charged, of aiding and abetting the enemies of the state and of obstructing police investigators. Confronted with all the evidence, she wrote and signed a full and free confession. She has also signed a statement that, at all times during her imprisonment, she was treated with due respect for her sex and for her legal and personal rights. All of this is noted in the protocol and confirmed by the photostat documents which I shall deliver into your hands. Now, Mr. Ambassador . . ." He leaned back in his chair and joined his hands fingertip to fingertip, like an inquisitor considering a nice point of theology. "Now, Mr. Ambassador, you see my dilemma. This young woman is an American citizen, who was granted the privilege of residence and work in this country. She has committed grave crimes, for which the penalty is long-term imprisonment. I am bound by oath to maintain law and order and the due process of justice. What would you do if you were in my position?"

Ambassador Charles Bewley permitted himself a thin, bleak smile.

"I was a banker before I became a diplomat, Mr. President. I think in terms of costs and profits. An act of clemency would cost you nothing and would certainly pay good dividends."

"What sort of dividends, Mr. Ambassador?"

"Better relations with the White House. A degree of personal absolution from the excesses of your subordinates."

"Do you think I need absolution?" There was a faint overtone of anger in the question. "You talk like a banker. I think like a historian and a soldier. Revolutions are not made with rose water!"

"Sébastien Chamfort to Marmontel. I've read some history too, Mr. President. I know recent history very well. The horse that rode you into the palace was saddled by American and other business interests in this country. If you want to stay in the saddle you need markets for your agricultural products, you need industrial investment to employ your workless. Fifteen percent of your exports are absorbed by companies controlled by John Spada. Ten percent of the dollar investment in Argentina passes through his hands. And you want to hold his daughter in prison?"

"No. I want to know what I get if I let her go."

"Then talk to Spada yourself. He's waiting outside. But take my advice, Mr. President, let me meet him first, with the act of amnesty in my pocket."

There was a long silence in the chamber, a silence broken only by the ticking of the ormolu clock on the mantel. Finally, with an odd, finical care, the President tied the pink ribbon around the folder on his desk and thrust it towards Bewley.

"It's all there: the protocol, the documents, the act of amnesty. The girl will be delivered to your Embassy at midday tomorrow. I want her out of the country in twelve hours."

"Thank you, Mr. President." Charles Bewley stood up and smoothed the front of his jacket. "I'll call the White House and my people at State. I'm sure they'll be pleased and grateful for your decision. May I now know what decision has been made in the matter of the lady's husband—Rodolfo Vallenilla?"

"No decision at all," said the President calmly. "For the simple reason that nobody knows where he is. He was not arrested as you suggest. Neither the police nor the security forces have any idea of his whereabouts."

Bewley digested the answer in silence. The President added a cold comment.

". . . However, even if he were in custody, his case would be dealt with as a domestic matter. It would be, shall we say, an indiscretion for the United States to intrude."

"So I am to inform Mr. Spada that his daughter will be released but that there is no record of her husband's whereabouts."

"Exactly, Mr. Ambassador. You will also inform him that his daughter will not be permitted to reenter Argentina, and we should be obliged if he himself would restrict his own visits to the minimum necessary to conduct his business affairs here."

"With great respect, Mr. President . . ."

"Yes, Mr. Ambassador?"

"You consented to receive Mr. Spada at the conclusion of this talk. May I suggest that a more humane attitude on your part may be, in the end, more profitable to your country. Mr. Spada is a man of much influence."

"I am grateful for your advice." The President was brusque. "Does Mr. Spada speak Spanish?"

"Spanish, French, Italian, German—and I believe Russian."

"A formidable accomplishment."

"He's a formidable fellow altogether . . . By your leave, Mr. President."

"Until we meet, Mr. Ambassador."

In the anteroom Bewley gave Spada a final, terse counsel.

"Teresa will be out tomorrow. The President denies all knowledge of Vallenilla's whereabouts. He'll see you now. Hang on to yourself, for God's sake! I'll wait for you in the car."

Spada nodded but said nothing. Bewley hesitated a moment and then left him, rigid as a marble statue under the eye of the guard. A muted bell sounded. The sentry opened the door to the presidential suite, motioned Spada inside, saluted as he passed and then closed the door silently behind him.

He had expected a long ritual walk to the feet of the potentate. Instead, he found the President standing in the middle of the room, a grave and penitent host. His first greeting was a bow. His second an apology.

"I do not offer you my hand, Mr. Spada. I am sure you would not wish to take it. Were I in your shoes, I should feel the same. . . . However, I hope you will endure my presence for a few moments."

John Spada said nothing. The President motioned him to a chair and then stood looking down at him. He said calmly, "I know what is in your mind, Mr. Spada. Your daughter is still in the hands of the police. You will do or say nothing that may compromise her safety. Let me tell you, therefore, that whatever passes between us in this room, your daughter will be released at midday tomorrow. I have informed your Ambassador that she must leave the country within twelve hours."

"My aircraft is already on standby here. We

shall embark as soon as my daughter is released. I had hoped her husband would be able to accompany her."

"Nothing would have given me greater pleasure, Mr. Spada. Unfortunately, he seems to have absented himself—which, in the circumstances, does him small credit."

"He was abducted, Mr. President; and I have witnesses to prove it."

"Then you should make their testimony available to the police."

"And put the witnesses in jeopardy too? No, thank you."

A faint smile twitched at the corners of the President's mouth. He said, "You are a man like me, Mr. Spada. You understand the usages and the exactions of power. Your daughter has been tortured and violated by professional interrogators under my command. Had I known at the outset who she was, such things would never have been done. I have three daughters of my own; I shudder to think of them in the hands of my own minions. But in this unstable country I am forced to use such methods and such people. Is there not a proverb which says: 'Fear keeps the garden more safely than the gardener'? If you feel the need for personal revenge, I will give you the names and addresses of the officials responsible. I will even send them to New York, where you can deal with them at your pleasure. But what good would that do? I would find others to take their place, just as you replace the guard dogs in your factories once they become tame or lazy. So I offer you a sweeter vengeance. I abase myself to you. I ask what effect this unfortunate affair will have upon your business dealings with my country."

"To hell with business! Let's talk about my daughter. She was arrested and tortured because she performed an act of mercy—took a bullet out of a man wounded in a police raid."

"I have already told you how much I regret what has happened, Mr. Spada. I am now concerned with a larger matter: the economic well-being of my people."

"Business is like prostitution," said John Spada flatly. "The brothels were still open while they were washing Caesar's blood off the stones of the Forum. My enterprises will still be here when you are dead—unless you want to expropriate them, which you can't afford to do."

"And your personal attitude to my government?"

"Is private to me; but I'll tell you anyway. You have no government. You have a tyranny."

"But you still profit from it, Mr. Spada—and your profits have doubled since I took over the presidency."

"I know. What should I do about that? Hang myself for a Judas or kill you for a butcher?"

"You'd be dead before you pulled the trigger, Mr. Spada."

"I wonder. Do you read much, Mr. President?"

"Very little now—except official papers."

"A pity. You seem to have a taste for proverbs. Try this one from Cervantes: 'To every pig comes his Martinmas.' I bid you good day, sir."

"Good day, Mr. Spada," said the President bleakly. "I trust you find your daughter in good health."

That night, in the apartment loaned to him by George Kunz, Spada held a council of war. Those present were the Scarecrow Man, Major Henson, a swarthy, taciturn fellow with a West Country accent and a leery eye for the civilians who surrounded him, Salvador Gonzalez, who dealt in rare books and prints, and a lean, leather-skinned man in his late fifties who was the father of Rodolfo Vallenilla. Spada's briefing was precise and detailed.

"Teresa will be delivered to the U.S. Embassy at noon tomorrow. I'll fly back with her to New York. I'll spend enough time there to see her settled and tidy some business matters; then I'm going to Europe to make contact with the South American Revolutionary Junta and find myself a new identity. I'll be back as soon as I can."

"How long will you be gone?" asked the Scarecrow Man.

"Ten days, I hope. Two weeks at most. Meantime, I'm relying on you to come up with a plan to break Rodo out of Martín García. What progress so far?"

"You have a headquarters," said the elder Vallenilla. "I own fifty acres of orange groves on the river flats. There is a large house and the staff is loyal. It's only a twenty-minute drive to the waterfront opposite Martín García."

"Plans of the prison . . ." The little antiquarian was eager. "I have an old drawing of the fortress itself, and an up-to-date pilot chart of the river approaches. There's a small company that makes aerial surveys upriver. We're trying to find a man who could make photographs from the air."

"I've spoken to Sancho," said the Scarecrow Man. "That's the fellow we met in the wineshop. He's making sketches of the interior layout and any strategic points he can remember. He's also giving us details of prison routine. . . . I think he'll do more if you can come back with a clearance from the Revolutionary Junta."

"I can supply vehicles," said the elder Vallenilla. "Two jeeps and a couple of farm trucks. Also sporting guns and pistols."

"Manpower?" The question came from Spada.

The rancher shook his head. "No! I can't compromise my staff."

"Again we come back to Sancho," said the Scarecrow Man. "He's an organizer in the underground; but he won't risk his groups unless there's official approval from the Revolutionary Junta. Once we've got that, however, Henson can start a training program."

"Training for what?" It was the first time Henson had spoken. "I've taken a look at Martín García, cruised up there with a local boatman. There's no way you're going to assault it, short of bombardment from a cruiser. Even if we did get in, there's no place to go when you get out. It's just a bloody great lobster trap. If you want your man out, you have to get the prison authorities to hand him over."

"And how do you propose to do that?" asked Salvador Gonzalez.

"I don't know yet. The information we have is still too sketchy. I do know we can't stage any sort of operation without adequate intelligence: geography, timetables, details of prison personnel, local communications. A job like this can take weeks to set up."

116

"My son may not survive that long," said the elder Vallenilla.

"A lot more people will die if we botch the operation."

"There's a problem," said the Scarecrow Man. "Rodolfo Vallenilla is a liberal. He was never a member of the Revolutionary movement. Why should they risk their own people to liberate him?"

"That's why I'm going to Europe," said John Spada. "I want to make a deal with the Revolutionary Junta. If they'll help us with Rodo, we'll help them with any one of their people they care to nominate."

"So now we're talking about two people, at least." Henson was a very persistent fellow. "We're also talking about double jeopardy—the security boys on one side and the revolutionary groups on the other. I'd hate to get caught in that nutcracker."

"Let me say something." The elder Vallenilla was suddenly a commanding figure in the group. "I know my son. He would never consent to save himself at the expense of other men's lives."

"We need him," said Spada flatly. "We need his voice in witness against the tyranny that exists in this country."

"His wife, who is also your daughter, may have something to say."

"Nothing!" John Spada was grim. "What we do henceforth is for our own reasons, at our own risk. Now, let's try to set down what information we need and where we're likely to get it. . . ."

Punctually at noon the next day, Teresa Spada was delivered, under military escort, to the U.S. Embassy. When he saw her limping up the Embassy

117

steps, refusing the arm of the escort, John Spada swore with impotent rage. She was twenty-eight years old, but her dark hair was streaked with grey and her skin was golden and transparent, like honey in a jar. She might have been blood sister to the Madonna Annunziata in Palermo, with the same big, somber eyes, the same sad irony in the mouth. Although there was no visible deformity, she supported herself with a cane, and when John Spada clasped her to his breast she winced and whispered, "Handle me gently, Papa. I still hurt."

There was a brief, strained ceremony of welcome at the Embassy, a hectic drive through the noonday city, a swift diplomatic clearance at the airport, and then they were driving across the tarmac to the big Boeing with the Spada emblem on the fuselage. The rear of the aircraft was converted into an emergency surgery, with a doctor and a nurse in attendance. The girl protested weakly, but Spada was adamant.

"It's a long haul back to New York and we don't want any nasty surprises on the way. Doc Timmins will examine you and see what attention you need when you arrive. Please let us coddle you now."

"First, you promised to tell me about Rodol"

"We know he's alive—in Martín García. I've got a whole team down there making plans to get him out. I'm going back as soon as you're settled. Trust me, bambina!"

"I have to, Papa!"

She began to cry then, soft, grateful tears; and as they took off, she held his hand and leaned her head on his shoulder and gave a great shuddering sigh of relief, like a child wakened out of a nightmare. The

118

full horror of the nightmare was made clear an hour later when Dr. Timmins came to make his first report.

"I've given her a sedative, John. She'll sleep for two or three hours."

"How is she, Doctor?"

"You know she's lost the baby?"

"Yes. Give me the rest of it."

Timmins hesitated a moment and then began to check off his notes in a dry, clinical fashion.

"There is extensive evidence of trauma, both internal and external. The lower dorsal region is scarred as if from beating. There is damage to the fifth lumbar disk and inflammation of the sciatic nerve—which accounts for the limp. Both breasts show burn marks, either from cigarettes or cigars. The nipples are cauterized and would have to be opened surgically to permit lactation after childbirth. She's been repeatedly raped, both by male congress and by instruments, so there is much damage to membrane tissue. There are cardiac irregularities, probably due to the repeated application of electric shocks. There is bruising of kidneys and spleen. There are rales in both lungs, and she herself diagnosed pneumonia after water torture."

"The bastards! The bloody sadistic bastards! . . . What will happen to her now?"

"She'll recover physically from most of it, though there will be sequelae, and she'll need regular observation for a long time."

"How is she mentally?"

"Well, she's lucid, calm and apparently stable. The best sign is that her concerns are centered not

119

on herself but on her husband and the fellow prisoners she left behind. She's a very brave woman,
John. You should be proud of her."

"Can she have any more children?"

"I doubt it."

"Does she know that?"

"She's a physician. She has to suspect it."

"Christ! Join me in a drink?"

"Sure."

The pretty stewardess, with the Spada emblem
on her breast, served the drinks, hovered uncertainly
for his smile of thanks and then drifted away, disappointed. Spada took a long swallow and then sat
staring into the glass.

Finally he asked: "Would you do me a favour,
Doctor?"

"Of course."

"Write up your notes in a form that can be published. I want them circulated to the press and every
medical journal."

Timmins shook his head.

"I can't do that without the consent of my patient. I don't think now is the time to ask for it."

"Forget it then."

"There's something else, John."

"What?"

"The press—keep them away from her. No point
in making her relive the outrage all over again."

"I've thought of that. There's an ambulance waiting at Kennedy. We'll take her straight to your clinic.
Her mother can stay there with her."

"She'll need you too, John."

"She needs her husband more."

"What are his chances?"

"Slim. You saw what they did to Teresa even when they knew they were going to release her. Imagine what they've done to one of their own nationals—and their bitterest critic! We're living in Bedlam, Doctor. A madhouse run by psychopathic butchers!" He slewed around suddenly in his seat to face the doctor. "Is she still asleep?"

"She'll be out for a while yet. Why?"

"I've got to see her. I've got to remember what they've done to her."

"John, please!"

"Show me!"

Timmins shrugged, unbuckled his seat belt and led the way back to the rear compartment. He made a sign to the nurse, who walked forward to talk to the stewardess. Timmins asked once more: "Are you sure you want this?"

"I'm sure."

Timmins laid back the sheet and lifted the surgical gown so that Teresa's whole body was exposed. Spada looked at her a long time, then he bent and kissed the scars and covered her again like a sleeping child.

He said simply, "Thanks. I know now what I have to do." Then he turned on his heel, walked back to his seat and ordered another drink.

It was midnight when they touched down in New York, and two in the morning before Teresa was settled in the clinic with a special nurse in attendance and Anna lodged in the room next door. Spada was amazed at how calm Anna was, how determined to lend strength and reassurance to her daughter. She was brutally fatigued. Her eyes were bright with unshed tears; but she sat, quiet, composed and tender, until Teresa fell asleep. Then she took Spada's hand and led him into the next room.

She put her arms around his neck and kissed him and then held him at arm's length while she told him, "You're a good man, Giovanni. We are both lucky to have you. You should go home now. Carlos has left a supper for you."

"Will you be all right here?"

"I'll be fine."

"I have to go away again, very soon, Anna."

"I understand. That is what I want to tell you: leave Teresa to me. This is women's business now. When she's better, I'll take her down to the Bay House. Where will you be going?"

"Better you don't know, Anna. I will say one place and be in another. I promised Teresa . . ."

"I know what you promised her: you will bring Rodo back. But I want you back too. Remember that, amore."

"Always, Anna mia. Always. But I have to be free for a while to come and go, appear and disappear without questions. What I do has to be my business —only mine, understand?"

"You don't have to spell things for me, amore. I read them in your eyes."

"Do you blame me?"

"No. You are the head of this family. You have always protected us. Whatever you do, there will be no reproaches from me. Go home now, amore. Go home and sleep."

They embraced again, and he wished, for one

wild moment, that she would ask him to stay. But she pushed him gently to the door and went to take a last look at Teresa, drugged and tranquil, in the next room. As he walked down the dim corridors and out into the chill morning air, he felt as though a stranger had stepped into his skin: some dark and sinister duellist, eager for his hour on the killing ground.

Next morning, when he passed by the clinic on the way to his office, he heard for the first time Teresa's own account of her arrest and imprisonment. At first he tried to dissuade her from the telling, but she would have none of his objections.

She told him fretfully, "Please, Papa! I have to talk. I learned that from the others. Some of them had been through far worse things than I; but they all agreed it was best to talk things out, even the beastliest acts. If you didn't, you felt so mean and dirty and cowardly that you could go crazy. To stay sane, you had to keep things in a human proportion. So let me talk, Papa! Part of it's a confession, and I need that too."

"No one in the world has a right to judge you, bambina!"

"Just let me tell it, Papa. You're risking so much for Rodo; you have to know what these people are like. . . ." She began in a fashion so clinical and dispassionate that she might have been detailing a case for the house surgeon on his morning rounds. ". . . I was at home after a long day at the clinic. Just before midnight I had a telephone call from one of the Sisters, asking me to go to an address in one of the low quarters of the city. I went. I found a group of people, some of whom I knew, with a young man

123

who had been wounded during a police roundup. I took a bullet out of him and patched him up enough so that he could be moved to safety. Then I went home. The next night I was arrested. They blindfolded me and took me to a place which, I was told later, was called the Fun Palace. It was the headquarters of the secret security police. I waited three hours in a cell. Then they took me to the office of one Major Ilario Sanchez O'Higgins. He was a man in his late thirties, very handsome, very polite. He read me a fairly accurate account of my actions on the previous night. He pointed out that I had committed a criminal act—although he was not yet prepared to press the charge. He understood that my motives were pure, merciful and non-political. However, I had unwittingly become involved with political and criminal elements. Therefore, he required me to give him full information on all the persons concerned in the night's affair. That done, I should be free to go and resume my normal life as a welcome guest in Buenos Aires.

"I told him I could not do that. He asked why. I explained that I was bound by the Hippocratic oath, which forbade me to disclose anything which I might learn in the practice of the healing art. He accepted that. He even paid me a compliment on what he called my 'professional fidelity.' Then, very persuasively, he began to argue another case: that in abnormal conditions, conditions of crisis for a community, of mortal danger to its citizens, other considerations must prevail. He even quoted the classic argument of Aquinas for situations of moral dilemma: 'the greatest good of the greatest number.' I told him that in the forum of my own conscience I alone must judge. He accepted that too; he hoped I would grant

124

him the same liberty of conscience in the performance of his duty. I agreed that I must.

"Then he said—and I remember the words very clearly: 'I regret, dear lady, that I must now consign you to a season in hell. If you wish to be released from it at any time, call for me and answer my questions. Unless and until you do that, there is no hope for you. . . .' His meaning was plain. If I did not cooperate, I should be handed over to the torturers. An hour later I was in their hands. I remained there for seven days. . . . In the end I had told them everything they wanted to know. I betrayed Rodo, our friends, everybody and everything."

"Seven days is an eternity," said John Spada quietly. "In the war, even with our best men, the most we could bet on was forty-eight hours. So you mustn't blame yourself—even for Rodo. If they hadn't got him this way, they'd have found another."

"I know that in my mind. My heart tells me something else. If we hadn't fallen in love, if we hadn't married, if I hadn't been carrying his child, Rodo would have had a better chance. . . . This is the horror they make. Even love is a weapon in their hands."

Suddenly she began to tremble, as if in the onset of fever. She lay back on the pillows and closed her eyes. Spada wiped the clammy sweat from her forehead and her hands. He bent and kissed her.

"Sleep now, bambina. I'll bring your Rodo back."

Even as he whispered the promise, he wondered how fearful its fulfillment might be—and whether a certificate of death might not be a gentler gift than one of the grotesque victims of the Fun Palace.

5

<>⬦⬦⬦⬦⬦⬦⬦⬦⬦⬦⬦⬦⬦⬦⬦⬦⬦⬦⬦⬦⬦⬦⬦><

He was hardly settled at his desk when Kitty
Cowan came in to tell him that Max Liebowitz had
arrived, unannounced, and demanded to see him immediately. For a single, angry moment Spada was
tempted to refuse; then a saner thought presented itself: Max Liebowitz was too prickly a man to risk
a snub without good reason; better to receive him and
be done with it.

Liebowitz was a small man, dapper, brusque and
snappish, as if he suffered from a chronic dyspepsia.
This morning, however, he was subdued, almost amia-
ble. His first words were an apology.

"I do not mean to intrude; but after what I read
in the papers, I had to stop by and tell you I am very
grieved for what has happened to your daughter."

"That's kind of you, Max."

"I understand these things. I lost many relatives
in the camps. Some of the men responsible are
now respected citizens in South America."

"It's a dirty world down there." Spada found himself at a loss with this unfamiliar adversary.

"It's a dirty world everywhere," said Max Liebowitz. "I have been thinking we should not make it dirtier for each other."

"What's on your mind, Max?"

"It's not easy to say. So let me walk you around it, eh?"

"As you wish."

"Sol . . ." Liebowitz fished a silk handkerchief from his pocket and began to polish his spectacles. "I have the Channing votes in my pocket—enough to fight with, enough, maybe, to win with at a stockholders' meeting. I have more than the votes. I have a sentiment, shared by many, that one-man rule is not to last forever. You are not—excuse the expression—a dynasty like the Fords or the Mellons or the Rockefellers. So the future for the corporation is not clear. It could even be risky. We need better insurance than we have for a continuity of management. For that we are prepared to fight. . . ."

Spada said nothing. Liebowitz gave him an odd, strained smile.

"Do you think maybe we could have coffee? I missed breakfast this morning."

"Sure." Spada buzzed Kitty Cowan. "Send in some coffee and cookies."

"I prefer a doughnut," said Max Liebowitz.

"Doughnuts," said Kitty Cowan on the intercom. "Coming right up."

"You were talking about a fight," said John Spada.

"I was," said Max Liebowitz. "But now, not. I hear things that I did not know before. Your friend Feldman serves with me on a committee that tries to help our people in the Soviet Union. He tells me you have personally intervened in the affair of Lev Lermontov. Also, there is the business of the bank in San Diego. We are caught for half a million. I call Waxman. He tells me we are supporting the family of the man who steals from us."

"And you agree with that, of course?"

"I don't. I think it a stupidity, but I respect the man who commits it. Also, I think he has more trouble than he needs at this moment."

"What are you trying to tell me, Max?"

"Please!" Liebowitz waved the question away. "You have moved Mike Santos upstairs. That, too, I like. I don't know if he's as good as Conan Eisler, but . . ."

"Better, Max! Much better!"

"Maybe, maybe. At least I am prepared to wait for results."

"How long?"

"One year from the day you resign."

"And when do you figure that will be?"

Before he had time to answer, the door opened and Kitty Cowan came in with the tray of coffee and doughnuts. She lingered long enough to ask: "Have you seen the *Wall Street Journal*, chief?"

"Not yet," said John Spada. "I came straight from the hospital. Why?"

"There's a piece about Spada Consolidated."

"I have it with me," said Max Liebowitz.

He fished in his breast pocket, brought out a clipping and laid it in front of Spada. Kitty gave Spada a warning wink and left the room. Spada picked up the clipping and read:

. . . An ominous silence broods over the glass tower of Spada Consolidated. John Spada has never suffered fools gladly. It seems unlikely that he will wear, without rancour, the injuries inflicted on his daughter and the suspicious disappearance of her husband in Buenos Aires. Senior Spada executive Mike Santos insists that the "business-as-usual" sign means what it says; but old hands in the market predict dramatic moves in the near future. Spada has a notable reputation as a strategist, and this correspondent would advise his readers to watch the stock carefully . . . and keep an eye on the news columns as well.

John Spada folded the clipping and handed it back to Liebowitz with a shrugging comment: "So, the newshounds are baying the moon. They'll soon get tired of it."

"But they may wake the wolves as well," said Max Liebowitz quietly. "I told you we needed more insurance."

"And the premium is my resignation?" Spada's tone was cold.

"Not quite." Max Liebowitz broke a doughnut in half and dipped it in his coffee. "I figure there's a deal we could make. I vote the Channing stock in your favour at the next meeting. You are confirmed as president. You then arrange that you will continue for one year only, after which a successor will be appointed. You will move upstairs as Chairman of the Board."

"And the successor would be. . . ?"

"If he measures up, Mike Santos. If he doesn't, it's Conan Eisler."

"So you take over without a proxy fight." John Spada gave him a thin smile of admiration. "I hand you my head on a golden dish, and there's not even a drop of blood on the floor. Very neat, Max!"

"I think so." Liebowitz dabbed at his mouth with a napkin. "It takes the strain off you. It defuses a nasty political situation for the company. It gives the stockholders the continuity they need."

"Tell me something, Max. What do you really expect me to say?"

"Only that you'll think about it," said Max Liebowitz placidly.

"I'll do better than that," said John Spada. "You wipe Conan Eisler off your slate. You agree to confirm Santos as president with a five-year contract. You accept Maury Feldman as Chairman of the Board. You go in as Vice-Chairman. And I'll move out immediately."

Liebowitz gaped at him in amazement.

"You mean. . . ?"

"Exactly what I say, Max."

"I'm not sure it's a good idea."

"Why?"

"It's too sudden. It could depress the stock. We need more time to prepare the market, guarantee a smooth transition . . ."

"Take it or leave it, Max! But if you leave it, I'll give you the bloodiest proxy fight this town has seen in ten years. Right now I'm just in the mood for it."

"I don't see what you stand to gain by a hasty move."

"Nothing, Max—at least nothing you would understand. . . . Well?"

"I need time to . . ."

"No time, Max! Now or never."

Liebowitz shifted uneasily in his chair. Spada

sat silent, watching him with hooded, hostile eyes. Finally Liebowitz made a shrugging gesture of defeat.

"You play rough . . . but O.K.! How do we arrange things?"

"I'll talk to Maury Feldman. He'll be in touch with you. By the way, if you breathe a word outside, the deal is off."

"There's no call to make threats."

"It's not a threat, Max. It's friendly advice. Be content that you've got what you wanted. Don't try to finesse me! There's an old Italian proverb: 'Never stir the fire with a sword.'"

The moment Max Liebowitz was gone, he picked up the red phone on his desk and spoke for twenty minutes with Maury Feldman.

At midday he called Hugo von Kalbach in Bavaria and asked, "The arrangements we talked about, Meister. Any progress?"

The old man's reply was guarded. "In principle it is possible. In fact, it would be best to meet, face to face, with my friend. You will find he shares your interest in fishing."

"Good. I'll be coming to Munich in a few days."

"Then you must stay with me."

"Delighted."

"How is your daughter?"

"Recovering."

"And her husband?"

"No contact yet. We are working on his case."

"I pray for your success. Please cable or telephone your flight number. I shall send a car to meet you at the airport."

"Thank you, Meister. *Auf Wiedersehen.*"

His next call was to a number in Turin. Castagna answered it. Their conversation was brief.

"You've heard the news about my daughter and her husband?"

"Yes."

"I need help. I want to meet the man who runs the South American Revolutionary Junta. I understand he works from Paris."

"When do you want to meet him?"

"The earliest."

"Can I give him a reason?"

"My son-in-law is in Martín García Prison."

"That will not interest him too much."

"I am prepared to interest myself in any other prisoner he may care to nominate."

"That may interest him. I'll do my best."

"How soon?"

"Give me twenty-four hours. Call me back at this number."

"Thank you."

Kitty Cowan came in just as he was setting down the receiver. She stood off from his desk, surveyed him like a museum exhibit and then pronounced her verdict.

"You look like a hole in the ground that nobody wants to fill. I've called the hospital. Teresa's resting well and Anna's decided to go back to the apartment. We've got lunch in fifteen minutes with Maury Feldman and Mike Santos. . . . Now take ten and talk to Kitty, eh?"

"What can I say, girl? It was rough. It'll get rougher."

"I wasn't thinking about Teresa. What's the

meaning of this deal with Max Liebowitz? I thought we were going to fight him?"

"We don't have to now. We've got Mike Santos in on a five-year contract. Maury will be Chairman of the Board."

"So Mike will be running the corporation. What will you be doing—bowling with the geriatrics? And what's going to happen to me? I've wet-nursed you all these years. I'm too old to repeat the performance for Mike Santos."

"Sit down!" Spada grinned at her. "You look like Medusa with snakes in her hair."

"Who the hell is Medusa?"

"Skip it!"

"I'm serious, chief. You've helped me make enough money so I can go play for the rest of my life —except there's no one I specially want to play with. I love this job; but it won't be the same when you're not here. So come clean with me, O.K.?"

"I'm not hiding anything, Kitty. It's just that after what's happened to Teresa and to Rodo, everything I've done seems suddenly futile. Look! Ever since the military took over in Argentina there's been one of the most savage reigns of terror in South American history—fifteen thousand people vanished without trace, ten thousand detainees, four thousand known dead, bodies picked up every week from rivers and lakes and beaches! It's not only there. You can walk yourself around the map and fill in a whole catalogue of horrors. . . . In a special way, I'm part of that catalogue. That bloody upstart in Buenos Aires bargained with me for Teresa. For him it was just a business deal; and I'm mixed up in similar situations all over the world. The way I am now, my hands are tied, because I'm bound in law and conscience to represent the interests of our investors. Once I quit, I'm free to dispose of my own life, my own money, any way I please. I can't take it anymore. I'm getting out. From now on I'm not Spada Consolidated, I'm Proteus. . . . Before I die, I'm going to fight one decent battle with the bastards of the world. If you want to join me, you're welcome; but I've got no right to ask you, because out there it's a battlefield. People get maimed and killed. They live dangerous, secret lives that they can't share with ordinary people. You've seen some of it—but very, very little. . . . So truly, it's up to you. I daren't persuade you one way or the other. I can't even show you a plan, because I don't have one yet. I'm simply reacting to events. All I know is that I have to stand up and say: 'Enough. I'm going to fight the evil, whatever face it wears . . .'"

He broke off, surprised at his own vehemence. Kitty Cowan sat looking at him with a strange, sad tenderness.

Finally she asked quietly, "What does Anna say about this?"

"I haven't told her all of it. She sees only as far as Teresa and Rodo. She's in full agreement with whatever I do for them."

"And afterwards?"

"I don't know. It all depends how Rodo is when we get him out—if we get him out. Anna may have two invalids on her hands."

"And a husband who's walking a very dangerous road."

"There's always a price tag on the wedding cake."

134

"I guess so. The question is, who picks up the tab? . . . Anyway, thanks for being honest with me."

"Have I ever been anything else?"

"No. So here's my side of it. I'll hold Mike's hand until he's settled, then I'll move out. If there's a place for me in what you're doing, I'll take it gladly."

"It's always been reserved—priority one."

"Thanks, John. What does Maury think of this arrangement?"

"As my lawyer, he's happy. No one can compromise me with the stockholders. I go out clean. On a personal level, Maury's worried. He thinks the Proteus organization is still too fragile to stand the strain. However, now that I have time and freedom I can strengthen and perfect it."

"And Mike Santos?"

"He doesn't know yet. We'll give him the news at lunch and drink to his success."

"I'd rather drink to yours."

"Don't!" said John Spada sharply. "In this game there's nothing to win but the right to die free."

Luncheon was an uneasy meal. Far from being elated by his appointment, Mike Santos was distinctly unhappy about it. He agreed with Max Liebowitz. The timing was wrong; it emphasized Spada's political involvements. There would be an immediate negative reaction in the stock market. Why not wait until the annual meeting and make the change then?

Maury Feldman had already defaced two napkins with unsuccessful erotic renderings of Pasiphaë and the Bull. Now he was grumbling at the quality of the coffee and urging immediate reform in the president's catering service. On the question of the changeover, while he agreed with Mike Santos in principle, he saw greater dangers in having a president who was engaged in criminal activity—which was exactly what Spada was planning in Argentina. Also, in plain fact and among friends, he wouldn't venture a plugged nickel on any business decision John Spada made in his present frame of mind.

It was a real piece of ironic advocacy, and in the end Santos was convinced by it. If Maury would handle the details with the Board and Spada himself would prepare a personal statement for the press, and Kitty would agree to stay at least six months longer, he would accept the appointment. Finally it was agreed that the announcement should be made during Spada's absence in Europe, so that the severance of his control would be defined physically as well as legally.

At the end, Kitty Cowan made a tart comment. "It's like a bloody conjuring trick. Now you see John Spada. Now he disappears in a puff of blue smoke! But I suppose the suckers will buy it."

"They always do," said Maury Feldman. "Otherwise I'd be out of a job. Half the law is magic—paper tigers guarding the temple of a blindfold goddess."

"I don't believe it," said Mike Santos.

"I do," said John Spada. "When the law permits you to rape a woman with a cattle prod, and pay the torturer from the public purse, it's time to take to the barricades. . . . Thanks for what you're doing, Mike. You too, Maury."

"Don't thank me," said Maury Feldman with a grin. "Not until you've seen the bill. . . . There's a

136

Mantegna for sale in Paris. As Chairman of the Board, I figure I can afford it."

"And what do I get?" Mike Santos relaxed enough to join in the joke.

"Ulcers in ten languages," said Kitty Cowan. "Pour me another glass of wine, Mr. President."

Two days later, after a second telephone conversation with Castagna, John Spada flew to the city of Basel in Switzerland. In the jargon of the underground trade, Basel and its environs had a special name: the Iron Thumb, a projection of neutral land that touched France on the west and Germany on the east, with so many exits and entrances that even the most zealous border patrols could not police them all.

If you were on the run from the French or the Germans, an obliging barge skipper could drop you north in Little Basel or south in Great Basel. You could come by rail from Stockholm, Rome, Madrid, Istanbul, Athens and the Channel ports. You could fly into Blotzheim and, twelve kilometers later, be back in France. You could, if you needed a rendezvous, meet by Erasmus' tomb in the Munster, wander together through the Holbeins in the Kunstmuseum, or sit whispering among a million volumes in the University library on Peters Platz. If you were a more leisurely conspirator you could do as you damn well pleased, provided you didn't do it in the streets and frighten the burghers, who believed in clean money, clean streets and the eternity of the Swiss Confederation.

It was in this grey enclave that a man who called himself El Tigre, leader in exile of the South American

Revolutionary Junta, had consented to meet with John Spada to discuss the fate of a man named Rodolfo Vallenilla, a prisoner in Argentina. Their meeting was scheduled for eight-thirty in a small inn called The Golden Stag on the outskirts of the city.

It was two minutes after eight-thirty when El Tigre presented himself: a tall, swarthy man in a suit of Italian cut. He was immaculately groomed, the hands manicured, the shoes brightly polished, the grey hair freshly barbered. He smiled and said in Spanish, "Mr. Spada? El Tigre at your service."

"Thank you for coming."

"Your friend, Castagna, was very persuasive."

The waiter presented the menu with a flourish and then retired. John Spada asked, "Shall we order first?"

"Fish . . . an almond trout. Then a mousse. I have a passion for sweet things."

"I'll join you. Wine?"

"A chablis, if you please."

Spada signalled the waiter, and when the order was given, plunged straight into business.

"Let me tell you what I want."

"I know already. You want to spring Rodolfo Vallenilla from Martín García prison."

"Are you prepared to help?"

"For Vallenilla alone—no. He is of no interest to us. He is a brave man, yes; a notable journalist, yes; but he is not, never has been, one of us. He is a liberal, a moralist, always thinking like Thomas Aquinas about right and wrong, the nature of the state, the duties of a citizen. . . . To us that's irrelevant shit, not worth the risks we have to take to get him out. He'll still be doing his balancing act on Judgment Day! However, we've got one of our own inside Martín García whom I'd specially like to spring. He's an old hand in the E.R.P., total believer, totally dedicated. Whatever works for the cause is right; everything else is variable and dispensable. Mind you, he's not worth a big operation, which would bring more raids, more pressures; but in combination, yes, we'd go for him. Clear?"

"Quite clear," said John Spada. "What's his name?"

"Chavez."

"O.K. Chavez and Vallenilla in the same delivery."

"What do you need from me, Mr. Spada?"

"A note, a signal to your people in Buenos Aires, telling them I can be trusted and that I pay for services rendered."

"That's simple enough. However, you must know I can't force them to join your operation."

"I need volunteers, not conscripts."

"And we need money, Mr. Spada." El Tigre smiled amiably. "Bank robbery and kidnapping aren't as profitable as they used to be."

"How much?"

"Let's try to do the arithmetic. Let's say Chavez and Vallenilla balance each other. I would not insult you by bargaining for your son-in-law's body. However, without our help you cannot move—or at least you cannot move as fast or as securely. So shall we say two hundred thousand dollars, paid here in Switzerland? It's less than we'd charge for a middle-class kidnapping."

"One hundred."

139

"Much too low, Mr. Spada."

"Is it? Your man Chavez is still in prison. So far as I'm concerned, your organization is untested."

"But you still need us."

"So I'll add another hundred as a bonus—if we succeed."

"You have a deal, Mr. Spada."

"Whom do I see in Buenos Aires?"

"You've already met him, Mr. Spada. In a wine-shop, I believe. His name is Sancho."

"I could have had him for nothing."

"Don't believe it, Mr. Spada." El Tigre was suddenly grim. "You are a dangerous man to treat with, a lone wolf and a very rich one—with a name that is known in every continent. You could be sold for ten times the money you are paying us."

"It would be a bad bargain," said Spada easily. "I've just retired from business and my trustees have written instructions that, in the event of a kidnap, no ransom is to be paid."

"Don't count on reason in today's world," said El Tigre gravely. "With drugs and sensory deprivation you can turn any man into a puppet. . . . However, so long as we are allies, you have nothing to fear from us."

"Can you give me any other contacts in Buenos Aires?"

"No." El Tigre was blunt. "Everything goes through Sancho. He decides what contacts you may make. Oh . . . there's another condition. If you want a hit man—you bring in your own. We take care of party scores, not private ones."

"Any recommendations?"

El Tigre considered the question for a moment, then gave a shrugging answer.

"There's a fellow we've used recently. He's a German, one of the Baader-Meinhof bunch. Holes up in Amsterdam, makes half a living as a painter, the rest as a hit man. Very good at close-quarters work, I'm told—crowded streets, public transport, that sort of thing. His real name is Gebhardt Semmler."

"How do I get in touch with him?"

"Call this number in Amsterdam." El Tigre scribbled it on the corner of a paper napkin. "Ask him if he'd like to buy a case of Tiger Beer. That will tell him you come from me."

"And what's his price?"

"Ten thousand U.S.—and not a cent more, or you'll spoil the market for the rest of us."

Spada grinned and made a sour joke.

"I thought all revolutionaries were idealists!"

"We are!" said El Tigre good-humouredly. "But the day dawns slowly. It helps to have a little comfort in exile. Now let me tell you how our money is to be paid. . . ."

Once their bargain was struck, El Tigre lost interest in the proceedings. He ate hurriedly and left without ceremony. Spada sat alone nursing a brandy and watching the small, sober comedy of manners in the restaurant. It was a new experience. Suddenly he was the spectator in absolute, remote, indifferent, a being from another dimension. All his scales and measures fell askew. His primal identity was gone. He was no longer John Spada, pillar of capitalist society, but the *spadaccino nero,* the dark duellist, lurking in the alleys of an international underworld.

As he strolled back to his hotel through the darkened streets of the old city, he felt an odd perverse elation. For the first time since his youth, he was

141

totally free—a nameless particle adrift in an alien element. As he undressed and made ready for bed, he had an impulse to call Amsterdam and talk with Gebhardt Semmler, the hit man.

He lifted the receiver and then stopped short. What should he say? How should he identify himself? Was he truly interested in hiring a killer? In the end he yielded to the impulse of curiosity. He sat on the edge of the bed and dialled the number. It rang once, twice and again, then a man's voice answered: "*Ja, bitte?*"

Spada answered in German. "I am told you might be interested in a consignment of Tiger Beer."

"Oh! . . . From where are you calling?"

"Outside Holland. Are you interested?"

"I could be—but not for a few days."

"I would be happy to come to Amsterdam to discuss the matter."

"What did you say your name was?"

"I didn't—but the beer is Tiger Beer."

"Yes, well . . . I'll be away for a few days, as I told you. Why don't you call me on—let me look at the calendar—yes, on the seventeenth, about this time. Then we can arrange a meeting."

"I'll do that."

"You know about the price?"

"Ten—and expenses."

"Where's the merchandise located?"

"I'll tell you that when we meet."

"That's fine. *Wiedersehen.*"

"*Wiedersehen!*"

John Spada put down the receiver and wiped the sweat from his palms. Suddenly he found himself laughing. It was all so simple. You could order death like a drink at a bar. All you needed was the nerve and the money. Besides—a new thought struck him—with luck he now had something to bargain with in Munich.

As he left the passport control booth at Munich airport, a tall, youngish man fell into step beside him.

"Mr. John Spada?"

Spada swung around, startled. "Yes?"

The tall fellow smiled and held out his hand. "Deskau . . . Kurt Deskau. I am a friend of Meister Hugo von Kalbach. I shall drive you out to Tegernsee."

"That's very kind."

"You have luggage?"

"One valise."

"If you will point it out to me, please."

It was on the tip of Spada's tongue to ask how a chauffeur was permitted to enter the customs area, but he refrained. When his valise came through on the carousel, Deskau picked it up and walked ahead of him through the barrier. His car was parked in a prohibited zone, just in front of the taxi rank. A man in police uniform stood beside it. The policeman saluted, took the valise and stowed it in the trunk. Deskau motioned Spada into the front seat and took the wheel. Spada was puzzled.

"A police car?"

"Divisional Inspector Deskau, at your service."

"This is an honour, Inspector."

"I am in charge of anti-terrorist operations in this area. Meister Hugo is closely protected. He comes under my jurisdiction—as you will during your stay." He took out his wallet and extracted a personal card which he handed to Spada. On the back of the card was a pencil sketch of the Proteus symbol. "I was curious to meet you for other reasons as well."

"I am happy to know you, Inspector," said John Spada.

"Meister Hugo has informed me of your family problems—and your need for a new document of identity. I am curious to know why you need a German one."

"First, I speak the language. Second, there are, as you know, many Germans in South America. It is, therefore, an easy role to sustain."

"Provided the document is genuine and that it can be proved back to its source."

"Quite."

"And that's the difficulty. However, it is not insuperable. If it could be shown, for example, that you were providing certain services . . ."

He left the rest of the sentence unspoken. Spada completed it for him.

"In areas of common interest?"

"Precisely."

"I'll think about that," said John Spada. "This threat to Hugo. How real is it?"

"Very real, Mr. Spada. The techniques of urban terror are developing every day. Certain personages —and Meister Hugo is one of them—have an exploitable value which goes far beyond that of normal victims. They are symbols, whose kidnap or assassination has a special theatrical impact. You yourself are a similar case . . . which is another reason for my interest in you while you are a guest in my country."

"I wonder if I am a similar case," asked Spada moodily. "My daughter and her husband are the victims of another kind of terror, the terror of governments and institutions which abrogate human rights to hold themselves in power."

"So now you see both sides of the medal! Our post-war liberty and prosperity have produced the *Spontis*—spontaneous radicals—who have no other program than the destruction of existing order, good and bad together. They're well organized, well financed, well armed—educated too, most of them. Yet their dedication is to a mindless terror. In the end . . ."

"You get civil disorder," said Spada. "Then the professionals take over again, with their own brand of terror. Cold comfort in that!"

"I've got men out in Schwabing now," said Kurt Deskau somberly. "Do you know what the student talk is: 'Pity if it has to be Von Kalbach, but he'll die soon anyway—and the name is important on the list!' "

"Christ. It's obscene!"

"In Geiselgasteig you'll hear another kind of obscenity, the same which you have experienced in Argentina: 'Let's open up Dachau again and give these bastards a taste of real discipline.' My problem as a policeman is that I understand both points of view. Which is why I responded with interest to Meister Hugo's invitation to join your group. There has to be a middle road somewhere. Maybe Proteus points the way to it . . . I understand you have come by way of Basel. An interesting city."

"I didn't have much time to explore it. I had one meeting last night. I left first thing this morning. Tell me, have you ever heard of a man called Gebhardt Semmler?"

A sudden gleam of interest showed in Deskau's dark eyes.

"Was that the man you met?"

"No. His name was mentioned."

"In what connection?"

"As a *Meuchelmörder*—a hit man."

"I would give a lot to know where to find him."

"A passport, for instance?" Spada gave him a cool, sidelong grin.

"A special kind of passport, Mr. Spada. One which is used by our agents. The true identity of the bearer is known only to the issuing officer—who can also withdraw it at will. Interested?"

"Very," said John Spada.

"Did you propose to use Semmler?"

"No. He was offered to me in case I needed such an operator."

"You keep strange company, Mr. Spada."

"What would you do, Inspector, if you were in my shoes?"

"Take warning from a friend, Mr. Spada. To sup with the devil, you need a very long spoon!"

The house of Meister Hugo von Kalbach was set on the shore of Tegernsee. It was one of the older dwellings in the area: a large, two-storied chalet, in traditional Bavarian style, with a garden running down to the strand and a wooden jetty with a motorboat moored to the piling. The house was almost hidden by trees. The window boxes were ablaze with flowers.

Meister Hugo himself received his guests at the door. He gave Spada a bear hug of welcome, then steered the two men immediately to his study, talking volubly all the time.

"Welcome, my friends! Welcome! You had a good journey, John? You look strong and healthy. Good! Now, let me remember: you drink bourbon whiskey with ice and water . . . Splendid! Fräulein Helga told me I wouldn't get it right; but I did, you see! Prost, my dear John. Prost, Kurt. We drink to a happier future for all of us!"

They drank the toast; then the old man asked eagerly, "You two—you have talked. You have come to an understanding?"

"We are getting there—I think," said Kurt Deskau.

"Let's agree the principle first," said John Spada. "I give you your man, you give me the passport, right?"

"Right."

"The question is how we make the exchange. I can't compromise the operation in Buenos Aires."

"Why should it be compromised?"

"It can be if you misuse the information I give you."

"I have trusted you, Mr. Spada. I have even joined the Proteus group, at the instance of Meister Hugo."

"Forgive me." Spada was instantly apologetic. "I didn't mean it the way it sounded. . . . Last night I talked with a man called El Tigre, who runs the European operation of the South American Revolutionary junta. He's promised, for a large amount of money, to recommend me to his people in Argentina. I need their help to get Vallenilla out of jail. He mentioned Semmler in case I needed a gunman. Later I called Semmler. I have an arrangement to telephone him in four days' time—on the seventeenth."

"Why, Mr. Spada? I thought you told me you had no idea of using him."

"I was curious," said Spada. "Just that I wanted to know how such deals were made."

"I think you made a mistake, Mr. Spada." Deskau's response was cold. "A bad one! Your cover is thin. There is a direct connection now between you and El Tigre and Semmler."

"I realize that. Therefore we should discuss how to repair the mistake and leave my operation clean."

"That may not be possible, Mr. Spada."

"Everything is possible." Hugo von Kalbach cut in hastily and poured another round of drinks. "We are intelligent men. We have a common interest. Let us use a little patience. Drink up, my friends! Even the eagle needs two wings to fly—and tomorrow we may be dead, with the girls crying over our coffins."

The tension relaxed then. Deskau shrugged off his irritation and said, lightly enough, "Forgive me, Mr. Spada. I forget that you are still new to this game."

"I'm learning." Spada raised his glass in a small salute. "Semmler is in Amsterdam. He earns his living as a painter. I have his telephone number. He said he was going to be away for a few days."

Deskau digested the new information and then said, "That probably means a new job. I'll cast around and see what I can dig up. . . . With luck we may take him in the act. If not, it may pay for you to keep your appointment."

"You see!" The old scholar beamed with satisfaction. "Now you use your brains. We should eat now—otherwise Fräulein Helga will make my life impossible!"

All through lunch he played with gusto the role of the aging scholar dominated by his strong-willed secretary. Fräulein Helga, grey-haired and blushing, loved every moment of it. She told little tales of his foibles and forgetfulness. She chided him for his indulgent appetites, his extravagance with money, his rages when wrestling with a difficult passage. It was all very tender and touching—a late-blooming love affair between a fifty-one-year-old virgin and an elder savant who still preserved the capricious innocence of a child.

At two-thirty precisely Hugo consulted his gold hunter—a present from Adenauer on the occasion of the Nobel award—and announced that he was going to take his afternoon nap. Deskau and Spada should relax and discuss their business in private. They might like to take the boat out on the lake. Oh—and tomorrow he had arranged a treat. He had two seats for the opera in Munich, where the new diva, Minna Gottmer, was to make her debut in *Rosenkavalier*.

Spada felt trapped. He was in no mood for entertainment. Inspector Deskau frowned. He had to make proper security arrangements; therefore he should know about such things in advance. How long had the bookings been made? What were the transport arrangements? Fräulein Helga promised that before he left he would have a typewritten list. Hugo fussed and fumed about the restraints on his liberty. Truly, he might just as well be in prison! Helga shepherded him from the room, clucking like a mother hen.

Kurt Deskau chuckled and said, "It's like a fairy tale, isn't it? Now, Mr. Spada, let's see what sense you and I can make of our affairs."

They walked down to the jetty, climbed into the boat and rode out to the middle of the lake, where they sat rocking gently to the wash of the passing pleasure craft. Deskau had Hugo's old panama hat tipped over his eyes and a fishing line looped over his hand. Spada at first was faintly irritated by the childish pastime, but after a while he felt relaxed and in tune with Deskau's mood, which seemed to be one of philosophic detachment.

"I am the law, Mr. Spada. I know the law is inadequate, but if I corrupt it, I endorse my own damnation."

"I am outside the law," said John Spada. "Because, for my family, the law has proved an instrument of injustice."

"Let me tell you about Gebhardt Semmler." Deskau gave a few desultory twitches on the empty line. "I know he is a killer, but I have no proof. In Germany I can arrest him for complicity in various Baader-Meinhof affairs, but to extradite him from Holland—that's another matter. The Dutch have problems of their own and they'll want a plateful of hard evidence before they will proceed against him and issue an extradition order. The moment they put him on trial they invite new terrorist attacks."

"So in effect the bandits call the tune."

"As you, my friend, hope to do in Buenos Aires."

"Check," said Spada. "So let's make a deal. You give me the passport. I'll undertake to deliver Gebhardt Semmler."

"I want him alive."

"I'll do my best," said John Spada. "I can't promise more."

"How does it feel?" asked Deskau with apparent irrelevance.

"How does what feel?"

"When you step over the fence onto the killing ground?"

"No different from you, Inspector, when you shove a man into Stammheim prison for twenty years. It's an empirical act." He used the German phrase: *"auf Erfahrung gegründet."* "The necessary end to a chain of unavoidable circumstances. No moral judgment is possible. You'll go mad if you try to make one. . . . Do we have a deal?"

"Come to my office at eleven tomorrow. Bring me three photographs, passport size, and five thousand Deutschmarks to open a bank account for you, because you'll need a check book and credit cards as well. But remember one thing: I'm the issuing officer. Any trouble you make lands—plop!—on my desk. I need that as much as I need an attack of influenza."

"I'll try to spare you," said Spada with a grin. "A man without a passport is like the living dead."

The next day in Munich was a rush. He was photographed. He delivered the prints to Kurt Deskau. He bought a cheap but passable dinner suit for the opera. He spent an hour in a gun shop choosing a pistol and arranging for its legal export on his outgoing flight. On the way back to Tegernsee he was caught in a press of city traffic.

When he reached the house a little before five, he

found Fräulein Helga in a fuss. He was late. He must hurry and dress. The limousine would be arriving in thirty minutes. Could he be ready, please, please? He could and would and, thank God, the dinner suit didn't look too bad, because Meister Hugo was punctilious about his public appearances. He had no patience with what he called "scurf and dandruff scholarship." Wisdom, he claimed, should be honoured in her lovers.

Spada hurried through his toilet and was ready, if a trifle breathless, when the master descended the stairs, resplendent in tails and opera cloak, sporting white gloves and a gold-headed cane. Helga surveyed the old man critically, twitched at his tie, brushed an imaginary dust mote from his shoulder and then pronounced him ready for his public. He gave her a fatherly peck on the cheek and strode out like a prince, with John Spada at his heels.

There were two automobiles outside—a hired limousine for Meister Hugo and a police car for the escorting detectives. It was a tart reminder that, however much Von Kalbach discounted the threats to his life, the police took them very seriously indeed. As they drove through the rolling uplands, Hugo was as excited as a child on the way to a carnival.

"Tonight, my friend, we forget the ugliness of the world and divert ourselves. We look at fairy-tale women. We hear great music from a new talent. We eat raspberries and ice cream in the galleries and remember the sweets of yesterday."

"The best news I've heard in weeks!" Spada tried hard to match the master's mood. "The first time I saw *Rosenkavalier* was when Schwarzkopf sang the Marschallin in San Francisco."

"And I, my young friend, remember my mother dressing for the first performance in Dresden in 1911. She was more beautiful than any Marschallin I have ever seen. Alas for the passing years . . . !"

Spada waited for him to say more, but he closed his eyes, leaned back on the cushions and began to whistle a high, reedy version of *"Mein schöner Schatz, will Sie sich traurig machen . . ."* Spada permitted himself a small private chuckle. For all his monumental learning, there was a streak of the mountebank in the old man, a flourish of happy vanity that was infinitely attractive.

When they turned into the Maximilianstrasse and drew level with the Hotel Vier Jahreszeiten, Hugo commanded the driver to stop. They were thirty minutes early. He must consult with the headwaiter about supper; then they would proceed to the Opera House on foot. The chauffeur should park the car. As for the detectives, they might just as well go and drink beer in the Hofbrauhaus. What could possibly happen to any man in the two hundred meters between the hotel and the Opera House? . . . At least they should stay at a respectful distance and not disturb his promenade.

John Spada smiled again. It was all so happily contrived: the master making his grand entrance into the Walterspiel, consulting publicly and at length about the table and the wine and the supper, then strolling along the boulevard, acknowledging the salutes of the men and the smiles of the women, challenging the curiosity of the callow students who were too young to know what a great scholar looked like.

As a piece of theater, it all worked beautifully. The headwaiter fawned and scribbled furiously and snapped his fingers at his underlings. The doorman saluted like a drill sergeant. A party of American tourists drew back to let him pass first through the driveway, and their women whispered excitedly at his back.

There were more salutes and more whispers as he strode slowly along the sidewalk, pausing to admire the old Dresden in the corner shop and deprecate the lithographs in the modern art gallery, and point out a minor treasure in the antique store next to it. A small knot of people gathered about him as he studied the photographs in the Opera House booking office and told a spicy anecdote about the basso and the tenor and the overweight contralto. The gossips on the steps watched him as he pointed with his cane at the massive pediment and read John Spada a brief lecture on the sculptures, their history and their significance.

Then, the lecture over, he grinned like a mischievous boy, laid a hand on Spada's arm and said, "Now we've entertained them, let's entertain ourselves."

As they reached the top of the steps, where the theatergoers were thickest, a young man in evening dress stepped from behind one of the massive pillars of the portico and jostled them. He turned as if to apologize. Spada heard two muted sounds like the popping of champagne corks. The next moment Meister Hugo was lying on the pavement with blood spreading over his shirtfront, and the man was gone, lost in the panic press of the crowd.

Kurt Deskau was a man in cold and murderous rage, but he worked with the efficiency of a robot. Five minutes after the murder he was on the steps of the Opera House, directing the first operations, culling witnesses, ordering the disposition of roadblocks on the city arteries. When the hectic work was over he drove Spada to the hospital and afterwards, when Meister Hugo was pronounced legally dead, to headquarters, where he sat him down at a desk with three volumes of police photographs and the harsh order: "The bastard's in there somewhere. Call me when you've found him—and don't forget, it could be a woman in drag!"

"I know it was a man!"

"Don't argue! Find the face! I've got work to do."

There were no identifications on the photographs, only index numbers. Spada was halfway through the second volume when he found a shot of a group of students taken during a demonstration in Frankfurt. One of the heads was ringed in red ink. Beside it was a blowup, grainy but distinct. He stared at it for a few moments, then signalled Deskau.

"That's the one, I'm almost sure."

Deskau lifted the telephone and snapped an order.

"Get Fischer in here—on the double!"

A few moments later the police artist came in carrying a sketch pad. Deskau pointed at the photograph.

"That one! Take the stubble off, groom the hair and put him in evening dress, white tie and waistcoat." The artist sat down at the desk and began to work.

Spada asked wearily, "Any luck at your end?"

"The usual crowd reaction. Conflicting accounts, contradictory descriptions. We're looking for a bearded dwarf, seven feet high, carrying a butcher's knife!"

155

"How did they know Hugo was going to be at the opera?"

"Oh, that! The old man's had the same seats for twenty years. He went to every first night of every season. If they hadn't got him before, they'd have got him afterwards; but he helped them by putting on that big show for you."

"Oh Christ!"

"Another thing: Hugo's always used the same limousine service in Tegernsee. They have only one big vehicle, which you used tonight. Someone telephoned asking to hire it. They were told it was already booked for a regular client."

"They were very thorough."

"They get better all the time."

The artist put the last strokes to his drawing and pushed it across the desk to Spada. Deskau watched him closely. Spada nodded emphatically.

"That's him."

"You'd swear it?" There was a high rasp of warning in Deskau's voice. "You're convinced enough to send him to Stammheim for twenty years?"

Spada hesitated. "Well, if you put it like that, I'm not sure."

Deskau swung back to the artist. "Bring me the index sheet."

The artist hurried from the room. He was back in three minutes with a buff-coloured dossier card.

Deskau studied it in silence for a few moments, then said to the artist, "That's all, thank you. Leave us now." The artist gathered up his gear and went out.

Deskau said quietly, "Now that we are alone, I ask you again: Is that the man?"

"Yes."

Deskau handed the card to Spada. The name on the top was Gebhardt Semmler. Spada stared at it, dumbfounded. Then a new horror struck him. He turned, white-faced, to Deskau.

"I was photographed by the press outside the Opera House."

"I know," said Kurt Deskau somberly.

"So if you take Semmler, I'm involved. El Tigre will know I identified him, and my whole operation in Argentina is broken wide open. I'll never get near Vallenilla."

"Only if we publish the fact that an identification has been made."

"Even if you don't, I'm still your principal witness. You can't keep me out of the documents."

"We can defer them—but not for long."

"How long?"

"Until we ask the Dutch police to arrest and extradite him."

"Not good enough. I've got a whole team trapped in Buenos Aires. If El Tigre blows the whistle, they're dead."

Deskau said nothing. He opened the drawer of his desk and took out two envelopes which he handed to Spada.

"Your passport in the name of Erwin Hengst, German driver's license, checkbook, credit cards, account number at the Deutsche Bank. Your new biography. You're a consulting engineer from Frankfurt am Main. Study the details carefully. . . . There's a KLM flight to Amsterdam at 14.35 tomorrow. Be on it."

"And what I do in Amsterdam is my own business?"

"Precisely." Deskau had already dismissed the subject. "Now I'm going to call in a stenographer to take your deposition on tonight's events. You'll sign it before you go. There's no way I can bury it, so be careful what you say about your reasons for being in Munich and be very vague about your identification of the murderer."

"Thanks, Kurt."

"Don't thank me!" Deskau's control was wearing very thin. "A great German is dead. I think you've got a better chance than I have to nail the bastard who killed him."

"How do you want him?"

"He's your pigeon," said Deskau with studied indifference. "Just call me here when the job's done. Now let's get this deposition written. Then I'll have a police car take you back to Tegernsee. You're elected to break the news to Fräulein Helga."

When he reached Tegernsee he found that the news had outrun him. Helga and the housekeeper had seen the first accounts on television. Neighbours had come running, in the fashion of country folk, and the house was mercifully busy with mourners and comforters, sitting deathwatch with the bereaved.

Helga rushed to greet him, wept on his shoulder and then begged to know every last detail of the grisly evening. He would gladly have dispensed himself from the role of narrator, but there was no escape. The reliving of the drama was a curative act, a purgation of the terror that, else, could poison them all.

Yet even as he spoke, Spada became aware that each word took him a pace further away from his audience. It was not that they were hostile; it was simply that they sensed him as a fateful person. Had he not come, Hugo von Kalbach might still be alive; therefore . . . but no! Logic had nothing to do with their attitude. Rather it was a primitive, instinctive withdrawal from the shadow of so portentous a stranger. So as soon as he could decently do so, he excused himself to the company, kissed Helga good night and went to his bedroom, carrying with him the cardboard box containing the manuscript of Meister Hugo's last work.

He had promised to read it in New York, but the news of Teresa's arrest had banished it from his mind. He should at least dip into it, as a compliment to the old scholar; in the same instant he saw it as a futile exercise. Hugo von Kalbach was dead—a victim of the epidemic violence whose course he tried to chart. Once they got rid of the last medic, the plague would take its course unhindered; the city would be given over to the pillagers and the grave robbers. It was a bleak thought to end a brutal day. He left the manuscript unopened on the table and ten minutes later was asleep and dreaming.

6

◇◇◇◇◇◇◇◇◇◇◇◇◇◇◇◇◇◇◇◇◇◇◇◇◇◇◇◇◇◇◇◇◇◇◇◇

In a small, smoky bar on the Leidesplein in Amsterdam, the man who had killed Meister Hugo von Kalbach drank schnapps with lager chasers and waited for the man who wanted to discuss a consignment of Tiger Beer. He sounded a good prospect—recommended by former clients, and apparently not scared of the price. The money would be useful. This last job paid nothing but expenses, because it was done on behalf of his own commando. Outside work paid well—and was much less dangerous, because there was no routine to it.

Gebhardt Semmler was a man who liked to keep his head down. Because he was no bad painter anyway, he had been able to establish a pattern of legitimate activity: sketching and copying in the galleries, peddling his folios to the winter tourists in the night spots. The police presented no problem. His name was not listed among those of the other Baader-Meinhof groups in Holland. The sketch of Von Kalbach's assassin, published by the Munich police, was so inaccurate as to be laughable. His only real worry was loneliness, a sense of unease and displacement, a need for reassurance that he was still loved and respected by his comrades-in-arms. That was another good reason for taking on a new job. He needed it to hold his confidence.

Some of the other comrades, he knew, were already posted around Amsterdam; but the word was out: "Stay away from that lot. They're special and sensitive." Which was somewhat of an understatement, since the group in question was known to be the custodian of two SAM missiles and to be seeking a suitable emplacement near the flight paths into Schiphol Airport.

However, Gebhardt Semmler did not envy them too much. He preferred to work alone, devising his own tactic for his own target. He was absorbed in his reverie and his second glass of schnapps when a fellow wearing a soiled trench coat, tinted glasses and two days' growth of stubble eased himself onto the bench beside him and asked politely in German: "Mind if I sit here?"

"Suit yourself."

The waitress came; the visitor ordered rum and hot water. Then he said casually, "Usually I drink Tiger Beer, but it's cold outside."

"Talk," said Gebhardt Semmler. "But not too loud!"

Spada pulled a folded newspaper out of his pocket and spread it, half open, on the table. The headline was a report of the arrest of four terrorists in an apartment near Schiphol Airport and the discovery of a large stock of arms, including a rocket launcher. Spada refolded the paper and stuffed it back in his pocket.

"That happened in the early hours of this morning. So the comrades have been under interrogation all day. We figure the dragnets will be out soon. Now would be a good time to move out of Holland."

"I'm not worried. Nobody can prove anything against me—nobody!"

"All the better—for us and for you."

"Where do you want me to go?"

"Switzerland."

"What's the job?"

"The same as you did on Hugo von Kalbach: one man in a crowded public place. You're in and out before anyone knows what's happened."

"How the hell did you know about Hugo von Kalbach?"

Spada shrugged and gave him a sidelong grin.

"We kept tabs on you, sonny. You didn't think we'd buy smoke in a bag, did you?"

"Haven't I seen you someplace before?"

"I doubt it."

Semmler puzzled for a moment and then said abruptly, "Name the price."

"Ten thousand dollars."

"When do I collect?"

"Five now, five on completion."

"Who pays?"

Spada took out his wallet and extracted a card on which was engraved the Proteus symbol. He handed it to Semmler.

"Put that in your wallet. When the job's done, you go to an address I'll give you in Paris, present that card and collect the rest of the fee. . . . Well, are you in or out?"

"I'd like to see the cash first."

"Here, in this dive? You must be joking. We'd

be knocked on the head before we were twenty paces down the street. If you like to come to my hotel . . ."

"We'll go to my place," said Semmler. "It's only a block from here, on the canal."

"Fine! Let's get the hell out of here."

Spada paid the check and they walked out into a freezing wind and slush trodden into the pavements. He asked casually, "What sort of a gun did you use on Von Kalbach?"

"A Walther PK. Why?"

"Have you still got it?"

"Sure. I always carry it."

"Change it!" said Spada curtly. "We don't want two killings with the same gun. That's the sort of thing that puts a noose around your neck."

"If I change, I've got to run around half the city looking for a new gun. And that could be hot too."

"Can you handle a Luger?"

"Sure."

"When we get to your apartment we'll swop."

"The money first," said Semmler firmly. "In here. I'm on the third floor."

On the landing Spada wiped his feet carefully, took off his galoshes and set them beside the door. Semmler laughed.

"For God's sake! You needn't be that particular. Come inside."

The room was a large mansard apartment, half artist's studio, half living quarters, all of it untidy and grubby from bachelor neglect. Spada surveyed the litter with distaste.

"My God! You don't live very well, do you?"

"That's my business. Now let's see the colour of your money."

Spada plunged a gloved hand into his breast pocket and brought out two manila envelopes, one of which he handed to Semmler.

"Count it."

Semmler counted carefully through the bills, then slapped them against his palm.

"Good! Now tell me about the job."

Spada handed him the second envelope.

"It's all in there. Read it, memorize it, destroy it. While you're reading it, let's have a look at that Walther of yours."

The young man hesitated. Spada took out his own pistol and laid it on the table beside the money. Semmler handed him the Walther, which was fitted with a silencer.

"Be careful, it's loaded."

Spada took it in his gloved hands and slipped off the safety catch. He cocked it and sighted it at the window.

Semmler shoved his thumb in the flap of the envelope and slit it open. He looked up and said, "With the silencer, it throws a fraction to the left; but for close work it's fine."

"That's handy to know," said Spada, and shot him in the head.

He gathered up the papers and the money, shoved his own pistol into his pocket, then pressed the Walther into the palm of the dead man. Stepping delicately as Agag through the mess, he went out, closing the door softly behind him. He was in no hurry. All he needed was a shave before his next appointment. At the first dark spot he tossed the pistol into the canal and walked on, whistling.

In the master list of the Proteus organization, Jan Pieter Maartens was listed under the code name Herring. He was a big, ruddy-faced fellow whose appetite for good food and pretty women was almost as large as his private fortune and his collection of Dutch Masters. He called himself, in the old-fashioned way, a shipmaster, and his vessels tramped the coasts from Caracas to Callao, from Bandung to Botany Bay. He had long-term contracts with Spada Consolidated and a long and intimate friendship with John Spada himself.

Half an hour after the execution of Gebhardt Semmler, Spada was seated in Maartens' study, with a glass of bourbon in his hand and one of Rembrandt's burghers as the sole witness to their colloquy.

Maartens said in his usual bluff fashion, "Man, you look ragged. What have you been doing to yourself?"

"One of our people was killed in Munich. Hugo von Kalbach."

"I saw the news. A pity. I didn't know he was one of us."

"He was also a dear friend of mine."

"So what brings you to Amsterdam?"

"I've just shot the man who killed him."

"Oh!" Maartens was studiously unsurprised. "Need any help?"

"For that, no. It was a clean job. And the police won't break their necks in the inquiry. However, there is another problem. You know what's happened to my daughter and her husband?"

"Yes. What can I do?"

"I'm trying to spring Rodolfo Vallenilla from jail

165

in Argentina. If I can—and that's a big 'if'—I've still got to get him out of the country. He's probably sick, which makes a bigger problem."

"So you need a ship."

"More, Jan. I need it standing by, ready to weigh anchor as soon as we're aboard."

"So . . . !" Maartens thought for a moment, puffing on his cigar. "It should be swinging out in the roads, not at the docks where you have to pass the port police and the customs boys."

"Can you help?"

"I'm just thinking. There's the *Freya*. She's in Caracas now, waiting for casual cargo. We could send her down to Buenos Aires. She's an old tub, but we're still screwing a small profit out of her."

"Could you hold her there for a while?"

"Sure! Best thing would be to stage a breakdown. That way the harbour authorities don't ask questions."

"What's the skipper like?"

"Young. *Freya*'s his first command." Maartens chuckled. "We like to let them cut their teeth on rusty boiler plate. . . . Yes, *Freya* would probably do."

"Is she fast?"

"Hell, no! Twelve knots and she's popping her rivets. But that's no matter. A couple of hours' steaming and you're safe."

"O.K. *Freya* it is. Who are your local agents?"

"Guzman Brothers; but I'd rather not involve them. Just leave a note for the skipper in their office. I'll tell him to expect it."

"The note will be from Erwin Hengst."

"Let me write it down." Maartens scribbled the name on his telephone pad.

"You'll be out of pocket, Jan. We'll pick up the tab afterwards."

"For Proteus, no charges." Maartens was indignant. "A personal handout to the skipper and the crew. That's all."

"You're a good friend, Jan."

"Have another drink. . . . I read in the New York press that you've resigned as president?"

"Yes."

"Want some advice?"

"From you? Sure."

"When this is over, go play a little. It's a dogs' world. Even Proteus can't mend it in one man's lifetime."

"So what do we do, old friend? Let the dogs take it over?"

"We finish our drinks. I take you out to supper."

"I couldn't eat a mouthful."

"You'll eat!" said Jan Pieter Maartens firmly. "You'll drink. You'll be nice to a couple of very pretty women, and tomorrow . . ."

"Tomorrow I leave for Buenos Aires. Make sure you get me on the plane!"

As the aircraft lifted off from the tarmac, he felt suddenly empty and intolerably lonely. The last links that bound him to normality were broken. He was a new man, with a new name, whose very identity depended upon the goodwill of a policeman in Munich. In Amsterdam he had killed a man; and although he felt no compunction for the act, it set him apart from the commonality of men. It was an experience, unique, unshareable and utterly joyless.

In the place to which he was going he would lead

the life of a criminal, sidelong and wary always. He must speak an alien tongue, play, to the letter, every line of a complicated fiction, knowing that any slip meant torture and death. And for what? That was the real desolation: for what? He remembered what Anatoly Kolchak had said to him about Lev Lermontov. "Your bargain presents itself as a stupidity. . . . You want to buy the most perishable and least valuable commodity of all—a sick human body! . . ." Now he was risking his life to procure that poor commodity and hand it back to his daughter to love and to cherish until death liberated her from it. He himself had demonstrated how trivial the gift really was. He had killed a man in cold blood and then gone out carousing with Jan Pieter Maartens.

For one wild moment he felt his skull would burst with the madness. Then, slowly, the old pragmatic John Spada took control again. You can't go back; go forwards. Don't dream; act! Don't change the categories; otherwise the logic will become an absurdity.

So, he began, *da capo*, the exercise of the questionnaire. Name? Erwin Hengst. Nationality? West German. Age? 55. Place of birth? Frankfurt am Main. Profession? Consulting engineer. What sort of engineering? Mining. Purpose of visit to Argentina? Tourism. Address in Argentina? Plaza Hotel, Buenos Aires. Languages? German, Spanish, Italian. He must speak no English at all, except in the company of his colleagues. Points of references? He should register immediately with the German Consul General. Any contact with the Spada Office must be made, in secret, with Herman Vigo. For secrecy he could use the Kunz apartment. Money? He had twenty thousand

168

Deutschmarks to declare. Herman Vigo would supply all his other funds. Habits? He must give up bourbon and drink wine, beer or Scotch whisky. He must ask for German newspapers, buy a couple of German novels and a German language guidebook to Argentina. Father's name? Franz Erwin Hengst. Father's profession? Schoolteacher. Mother's maiden name? Ludmilla Dürer. . . .

The rehearsal and the cocktail service carried him through the first short leg to Zurich. During the long night haul from Zurich to Monrovia to Rio he ate and drank and slept fitfully, haunted always by the threshold fear that he might start talking in his sleep. In the transit lounge at Rio he shaved, changed his shirt and underthings and composed himself to enjoy the last four hours' run to Montevideo and Buenos Aires.

There was only one moment of tension, while the blank-faced official at the immigration desk studied his passport and searched laboriously in his file of undesirables. Finally he closed the passport with a snap and handed it back. Two paces more and John Spada, alias Erwin Hengst, stepped onto the killing ground.

"We have a plan," said the Scarecrow Man.

"I don't like it," said Major Henson.

"But you have not come up with anything better," said Sancho. "You exaggerate the risks because you think like a British soldier, not like a *guerrillero!*"

"Time is against us," said the elder Vallenilla. "The news is that my son is very sick. He dies a little every day."

They were seated on the patio of the farmhouse,

sipping ice-cold beer and looking out across the serried ranks of orange trees that marched across the flatlands to the river's edge. They were frayed and tense, all except the Scarecrow Man, who still preserved his air of sardonic detachment.

Spada said calmly, "Let's take the good news first. There's a vessel on her way down from Caracas. When we break the boys out, she'll take us aboard and head home."

"She'll take your man home," said Sancho. "Chavez stays here with us. We need him."

"Fine!" said Spada amiably. "Now, what's the plan for the breakout?"

"It's not a breakout." Sancho was obviously eager to justify himself. "It's a hand-over. . . . Let me explain. When the security boys have finished with a subject, they either kill him or put him in detention in case they need him again. If and when they want him, they send an order to the prison commandant, who hands over the prisoner. Clear?"

"So far."

"The order is on an official form signed by a senior officer of security, normally the chief interrogator, Major O'Higgins."

"That's the bastard who committed my daughter." Spada was eager. "I want him crucified!"

"One thing at a time," said the Scarecrow Man. "We are all involved in this. Go on, Sancho."

"So we have to procure both the form and the signature," Sancho continued. "Next, our people have to present themselves at the prison, pick up the bodies and sign a receipt."

"Can we get the official forms?"

"Yes," said Sancho with a grin. "There's a girl who

works at headquarters—ugly as sin, but I keep her from getting lonely."

"The signature?"

"Same girl, same reason. We can make a passable forgery."

"So where's the catch?"

"The catch," said Major Henson, "is in the routine of the prison itself. Sancho here knows it, because he's been inside and worked as an orderly in the office. Normally the security boys telephone first. They say they want prisoner X and they're sending down a detachment, with a written order to collect him."

"Can't we do that?"

"Sure," said Henson. "But suppose the real security boys call and someone mentions the first order. We walk ourselves into a trap."

"I covered that," said Sancho irritably. "We telephone and then cut the line."

"But Martín García still has an army radio link. We can't cut that."

"But they work regular schedules. We can find out what they are."

"If the telephone is out, they'll work outside the schedule. It's a hell of a risk."

"How can we avoid it?" asked Spada. "Or at least minimize it?"

"Martín García is an island," said Henson. "The prison has its own ferry link to the mainland. If we can have the prisoners delivered to the mainland, then at least we've got a line of retreat if anything goes wrong. The other way we're trapped on the island itself."

"Sancho?"

"In theory, it's possible. In fact, it's a break in

routine. That's already suspicious. The duty officer at the prison might check back to security for confirmation."

"What sort of traffic is there between the prison and the mainland?"

"Quite a lot. Supplies going in. Prison personnel coming out on leave. The commandant comes up to town regularly."

"Have we got any sort of a timetable for these things?"

"We're preparing one." Sancho was defensive. "Remember we didn't get clearance on you until a few days ago. These things take time."

Major Henson shrugged, as if to say, "You see what I mean? How can you run an operation like that?"

The Scarecrow Man spoke for the first time. "I see the Major's point. I see Sancho's also. Let's consider it from the point of view of the security men themselves. They have their own emergencies. They're interrogating a man and suddenly—boom!—they want to cross-check with a previous subject. They telephone the prison. They want quick action. Get the prisoner to the mainland. We'll pick him up on the run. It's possible, isn't it?"

"Possible," said Sancho sharply. "But not probable. These people work in their own closed circuit. Why should they hurry when they've got their victims on ice? I've been there, remember?"

"So," said the Scarecrow Man placidly, "they don't have emergencies. We could always create one for them, couldn't we?"

"We could." Sancho was immediately wary. "Provided you don't put too much heat on my people.

You go away, but we have to live here. Remember that—remember it always!"

"Sancho is right," said the elder Vallenilla. "The last thing we want is a new wave of repression. However, our friend Lunarcharsky has at least produced a new idea, which we must consider carefully. Now may I please say something? . . . We get news from the prison. It is garbled and fragmentary. Sometimes it is deliberately falsified. But all that we hear points to the fact that Rodo is being treated in a particularly brutal fashion—as if they wanted to make an example by debasing an intellectual. He was badly damaged by the torture. Now it would seem . . ."

They had finished with him long ago, in the Fun Palace. They had scooped him out like an orange, pulp and pips and fiber, until there was nothing left but a hollow yellow rind. They had been careful to see that he missed nothing in the catalogue of cruelties: the parrot's perch, the electric shocks, the near-drowning in a tank of sewage, the beatings, the days and nights in the kennel, where he must squat on a bed of sharp stones, unable to stand or lie down, the evulsion of toenails, the weights that stretched him as he hung by his wrists from the ceiling.

Many times he had been only a heartbeat from dying, but always they had denied him the last merciful exit into darkness. When he had begged them to let him go, to toss him into the river like the hundreds of others, dead and near dead, they had laughed. Never, they said. Martín García needed a clown to brighten the prison days, a mascot to grace the parade of the damned. So now, while the other inmates shuffled around the exercise yard, they chained him, like a dog, to one of the execution posts, so that he could only sit or crawl in a two-meter circle, to exercise his atrophying muscles and his calcifying joints.

Sometimes one of the guards would stop and pat him, half in pity, half in contempt. Every day without fail Colonel Ildefonso Juarez would come limping towards him, lift his head with the crook of his cane and mock him.

"So! How is the great Rodolfo Vallenilla today? Still working, I hope. You mustn't disappoint your public. They expect great things from you, testimonies for our difficult times. But of course, I'd forgotten. It's a book you're writing, isn't it? Have you found a title yet? How about *The Book of Revelations?* Or *The Confessions of Rodolfo Vallenilla*, with selected photographs? Nothing yet? Well, never mind! There's plenty of time—years and years! . . ."

Then he would slap him with the cane, playfully but painfully, on his skinny rump and hobble away, while Rodolfo Vallenilla sat, bowed and shrunken, against the post where others, more fortunate, had been shot.

The Colonel thought himself a comedian, but he had missed the point of the comedy; because Rodolfo Vallenilla was indeed writing: not on paper—because he had none, because his fingers were crooked beyond repair, because, even had there been a light in his cell, his sight was beginning to fail—but in his head. He was writing a litany which he recited over and over in a tuneless monotone—a litany of the living and of the dead, who like himself had been snatched out of human ken, erased from the record as if they had never existed. Each day, each week, he added to it: names whispered in the parade ground, shouted by the guards, scrawled among the graffiti in the shower block. One day—were it only Judgment Day!—he would chant the litany aloud and exact for every name a darker damnation on the tyrants.

He dreamed other works too: a vast, visionary epic of the land that had absorbed so many strains of mankind, folklore celebrated in Lunfardo, a garland of love lyrics for Teresa. But these he could not hold long in his head. They came, they went. Only the scraps remained, like tatters of cloth clinging to a thornbush on the pampas. . . . Sometimes the rag on the thornbush was himself, dusty, windblown, pierced with a miscellany of pains, alone, so terribly alone. . . .

And yet—he had learned to count blessings too! —he was not always alone. When exercise time was over, the guard would unlock his shackles, and two of the prisoners would hoist him to his feet, put his arms around their shoulders and half walk, half drag him back to the cell block. One was Ferrer, who had been a country priest and had protested the brutalities of a local landlord in Sunday sermons. The other was Chavez, onetime schoolteacher, old-line activist, who had survived a hundred police raids and led a score of bomb operations, and had finally been arrested for singing bawdy protest songs while half drunk in a bar. They managed to walk him slowly enough to pass on whispered news and perhaps press into his hand a sticky sweetmeat or a scrap of fruit. Even their touch and their nearness made him want to weep with gratitude. On Saturdays old Corporal Pascarelli took over the rounds of the cell block while his juniors drank late in the canteen. He was always good for two minutes of talk and some tiny gift—a vitamin pill or a cigarette. More rarely, when there was blood in his sputum and they permitted him to visit the infirmary, the junior aide, a pale, melancholy fellow, would massage his back and try to relieve the pain of his distorted spine. For all his effeminate manners he had much courage and he would face down the prison physician, Dr. Wolfschmidt, whose only preoccupations seemed to be the bottle and the torture rooms.

Yes, even in hell there were mercies, pitifully small, yet large enough to hold a man sane and nourish the lone guttering taper of hope. But hope for what?

Ferrer, robust and spartan in the ancient faith, urged constantly: "Christ is with you, Rodolfo. The worse it gets, the more you are like Him. Believe Him. Hold to Him. He will never abandon you."

Chavez put it in other words, no less heartening: "Hang on to your skull, man! Everything's in there. Shut your eyes, shut your mouth. Close your ears. Curl up inside your skull and forget 'em. It works. Believe me, it works!"

Old Pascarelli grunted and broke wind and scratched his armpits and talked like a gangster out of the side of his mouth: "The big boys, they're all scared. They want to kill you like they killed all the others, but they're scared they may have to produce you one day. Don't try to fight 'em; they'll only hurt you more. Just look stupid, punch-drunk, and they'll leave you alone. That's the good word. Look stupid. Act dumb!"

So for want of better remedies he tried them all. He, who had not been to a church since confirmation day, tried to pray. He, the communicator, nursed his visions—or were they his madness?—in solitude.

He, the defiant, bobbed and shambled and grinned like a tame ape before his tormentors. . . .

When the others had gone their separate ways back to the city, John Spada stayed on to dine and talk family matters with the elder Vallenilla. It was the first time that they had ever been truly private together—the first time Spada had ever been invited to use his host's given name, Francisco.

"Strange, isn't it?" Spada commented. "Our children have married, yet you and I hardly know each other."

"Strange still," said Francisco Vallenilla, "my son is a prisoner in my country, and you, the foreigner, come to rescue him. It makes me feel inadequate and ashamed."

"It shouldn't. The rest of your family are here, still hostages to the system."

"Which I myself helped to create—if not by co-operation, at least by political indifference. So long as I was free to do what I wanted—and believe me, John, I do breed the best bloodstock in the country—I was happy. I also had an easy absolution. I was the man with one talent. I was doing no harm—even a certain amount of good. I thought, I truly believed, my son made unnecessary disturbance about matters which would right themselves in time."

"We've all fallen into the same trap," said John Spada soberly. "We've all made deals with the devil, because he's a very prompt paymaster. Polite, too—until you cross him."

"Tell me honestly, John, what do you think of our chances?"

"As of now, fifty-fifty."

"Can we better the odds?"

"With more accurate information, yes. Beyond that, it's dangerous to speculate. It can be demoralizing. We have to make rational judgments on the basis of hard intelligence. . . . There is a problem, though. Assume we're successful, what happens to you and your family?"

"Not too much, I think. We'll be questioned, of course; harassed probably. But in the end they'll leave us alone. We're country folk. The security boys are not at home on the pampas. They're rat catchers, trained for the city sewers. . . . I think, in the end, you will be in more danger than I."

"Please God, I'll be far away—back in New York with Rodo."

"We live in the age of the assassins," said Francisco Vallenilla. "If Rodo lives to write again, and you are known as the man who beat the system here, you will both be targets."

"One thing at a time," said John Spada. "One day at a time."

"They may try to expropriate your business here."

"They'd be fools to try. Their bankers would go sour overnight. Besides, it's now public news that I've retired. Spada Consolidated is a public corporation with a lot of powerful shareholders. The rules of the game dictate that men are mortal but giant corporations are sacred to eternity."

Francisco Vallenilla poured more wine.

"Do you think, John, there will be violence in this affair?"

"We'll try to avoid it, of course; but, yes, it's possible."

"I want to come with you on the operation."

178

"No!" Spada was emphatic. "You stay away. You could compromise too many people. You could, in the end, be forced to pay tribute to the E.R.P."

"I see that, but . . ."

"But sink your pride and stay away. Which reminds me, I need a good handgun."

"I'll get you one," said Francisco Vallenilla. "But for God's sake, don't keep it on your person or in the hotel. A lot of the staff are in the pay of security."

"I'll keep it in the Kunz apartment."

"Would you be prepared to kill a man?"

"Yes."

"Then I ask you—no, I beg you!—if anything goes wrong, if there is danger that Rodo will be taken again—kill him!"

"Mother of God!" John Spada swore softly. "What kind of a man do you think I am?"

Colonel Ildefonso Juarez was a very methodical man, which was not the least of his qualifications as commandant of a prison island. His records were beautifully kept—except where the security people dictated that no records should be kept at all. His accounts always balanced, which meant that peculation of prison funds was always kept at an acceptable figure. His reports were spare and illuminating: accidents and casualties nil, infectious diseases minimal, escapes nil, major disciplinary infractions nil, prisoners' complaints nil, staff problems nil.

His office was a model of neatness, not a paper out of place, no trace of dust on the files, the pencils freshly sharpened each day, the wastebasket emptied at noon and at the close of each day's business. His shoes shone like glass; his hair was trimmed twice a

week by the prison barber, who also shaved him before each morning's rounds. To his superiors he
showed a military respect; to his inferiors a peremptory tyranny, lightened at times by a sardonic humour which never failed to elicit an appreciative
chuckle from the troops.

His quarters outside the prison compound con-
sisted of a neat cottage with a flower garden and a
vegetable plot, cultivated by a former sergeant, dis-
charged and imprisoned twenty years ago for the
murder of his mistress, a male orderly and an elderly
criolla from Mesopotamia who cleaned and cooked
for him.

Even his diversions were methodical. On the last
four days of every fortnight he took leave of his command, always after a formal hand-over to Major Gutierrez, and was driven to Buenos Aires, where a suite
was reserved for him at the Hotel Formosa. There
the same maidservant received him and showed him
that his civilian suits were pressed, his linen and un-
derwear laid out in the cabinet, his supply of liquor
and cigars untouched since his last visit. She waited
while he undressed, helped him into his dressing
gown, poured him a drink and then retired, taking
his soiled clothes to be laundered and his uniform to
be pressed.

Then the routine of diversion began. Bathed and
dressed in civilian clothes, he went to the Staff Officers
Club to renew the acquaintance of his peers in the
service. They were cordial enough—though he wondered sometimes whether the jail smell still hung
about him; but their cordiality was less important
than the service talk: who was posted where, who
had moved into the political sector, what visitors were

in town from frontier areas, what colleagues from Uruguay or Chile or Paraguay. It was information like this that kept a man safe, enabled him to do private favours and build up a credit in the hierarchy.

If the company were sparse, he would leave early; if the club were full, he would dine in and afterwards limp from group to group in the coffee room to exchange salutations. With new people the limp was as useful as a visiting card. He could always be prevailed upon to explain—albeit with casual modesty—that he had taken a bullet in a revolutionary ambush up-country, but that the bastards had fared much worse, with three dead and two who survived to tell a very long story in the Fun Palace.

After dinner, declining any lonely fellow who might offer to accompany him, he left the club and was driven to another kind of resort half a mile from the Plaza de la República. Here an officer and a gentleman could divert himself to his heart's content, knowing that the girls were guaranteed safe by army medical inspectors and the house carefully guarded by the security people. Downstairs was a bar, with music and dancing, upstairs a whole complex of rooms which could be hired, like their occupants, by the hour or the night. The tariff was high, but the risks were low; and Rosita, a smiling, bouncy matron from Mar de la Plata, always looked after her regulars.

Colonel Ildefonso Juarez was a very regular client—loyal, too, in his way. He had been known to favour one girl for three visits in succession—until, as he put it, "she turned old overnight, looked more like eighteen than fourteen." So, on this warm night of October, he had ordered a new one, trusting that Rosita would never disappoint him. When the car drew up at the entrance he instructed his driver, as always: "Pick me up at ten in the morning. Until then, enjoy yourself." To which, as always, the driver responded with gratitude: "The Colonel is too kind. I have to watch my pocket." To which he added in an undertone: "But I still get more tail than you do, you old fart!" Then he drove away towards the beach, where his cousin Luis kept a cantina and where, by three in the morning, nobody gave a damn about the pox or the police or the politicians.

It was in this happy, noisy cellar that he had the good fortune to sit at the same bench with two pretty girls, a freakish-looking fellow who called himself Pavel or Paul something or other and a big spender called Sancho, whose pockets seemed to be lined with money. . . .

"Our friend in there"—Sancho jerked his thumb at the bedroom where the driver of Colonel Ildefonso Juarez was snoring happily between two girls—"we should give him a medal! Think how much he's told us for the price of a couple of bottles of bad brandy. Eight days a month he's in town with Colonel Juarez. Always Juarez goes the same route to the same places —Hotel Formosa, the Staff Officers Club, Rosita's for two nights, then back again to the Hotel Formosa and home to Martín García. You see how stupid these fellows are! We could knock him off any time we wanted. We could plastic his car, kill him in his hotel room, slip a pill into his bedtime drink at Rosita's, follow him out of town and ambush him on the way . . . Beautiful, beautiful!"

"Even more beautiful," said the Scarecrow Man amiably, "we don't touch him. We leave him ignorant

182

and happy like a grasshopper in a jar full of greenery, until we're ready to use him."

"Let's think how we can use him." Sancho was eager now. "Every time he comes to town he goes to Rosita's—always between eleven and midnight. He never comes out until ten in the morning. So we pick him up as he goes in."

"He presumes we're security men?"

"Right. They're always in civilian clothes. They drive unmarked cars. So if we flash a document at him, he's not going to be too suspicious. We take him out to a safe house where he telephones the prison and tells them to make an emergency delivery of the two prisoners to the mainland. He confirms that he will be present for the delivery."

"That call will also tell us whether there have been any real calls from security."

"I like it!" said Sancho happily. "It makes better sense every minute."

"Question," said the Scarecrow Man. "What do we do with the Colonel afterwards?"

"You? Nothing." Sancho was instantly cagey. "He's our bonus. You don't have to think about him."

"Spada will want to know."

"Then I'll tell him," said Sancho. "We're not in bed together—just working out a contract. That's why I don't want him meddling in the local situation. He goes away. We're stuck with our own bloody mess. And after this there'll be a lot more heat."

"Spada's a bright fellow," said the Scarecrow Man. "He'll understand."

"I've been in the game a long time," said Sancho quietly. "But Spada scares even me. He's too quiet, too controlled. It's like juggling with a hand grenade—all that power inside."

"I should be getting home," said the Scarecrow Man. "This has been a very instructive evening. I want to think about it quietly."

"You'll need transport. This is a bad area in the small hours, and you could be picked up by a police patrol. Hang on for five minutes and I'll get you a taxi."

"No trouble. I can find one."

"I need the right one," said Sancho flatly. "This is a safe house, and I'd like to keep it that way."

"What about our drunken friend in there?"

"Him? Oh, no problem. He'll be moved out. He'll wake up in the Colonel's car and wonder how the hell he got there. But a foreigner stepping out of here at four in the morning—that's news for the police bulletins!"

For three days after each return from Buenos Aires, Colonel Ildefonso Juarez indulged an insufferable good humour. As old Pascarelli put it: "He's like an old hound; slobbers all over you and pisses on every chair leg, just to let you know he can still sniff a bitch in heat." His officers he regaled with service gossip from the club and spicy tales from Rosita's. His troops he teased with hints of unimaginable bawdry, available only to officers and gentlemen but to which one day, given good conduct and regular promotion, they might hope to aspire. For his prisoners he invented small cruelties, like tales of new security checks or dropping the names of female relatives in their hearing, and then bursting into laughter as if at some obscene comedy. Always, in this post-coital period, the tension in the cell blocks rose to breaking point, and the guards became edgy and apprehensive.

This time, however, the Colonel's customary exuberance was dampened by a report from Major Gutierrez. There was an outbreak of dysentery in D block and Dr. Wolfschmidt, sober for once, had diagnosed it as *Endamoeba histolytica,* highly infectious, extremely dangerous to staff and inmates alike.

The medical measures he demanded were drastic: a massive requisition of drugs, and a drastic revision of prison hygiene. The requisition must be supported by a personal explanation from the commandant; and the hygienic measures must include an expert check on the prison water supply and extra staff to cope with the treatment of the patients. All of a sudden Colonel Ildefonso Juarez saw his comfortable little kingdom fragmenting under his feet and its carefully constructed history exposed as a fiction. More dangerous still was the prospect of riot and disorder among a prison population grossly overcrowded, more than averagely intelligent and isolated in a potential pesthouse.

So when he strode out into the exercise yard to inspect the shuffling parade, he was in a foul temper, snappish and cruel. Rodolfo Vallenilla, chained and squatting against the execution post, was his first and most obvious victim. Slapping his cane against his thigh, he limped across the yard, hooked his cane under Vallenilla's chin and jerked his head up.

"Well! And how is our little dog today? Getting lazy, I'm afraid. Dozing in the sun and dreaming of the bitches. We can't have that, can we? This is exercise time! We're supposed to move about, get the circulation going, tighten up those muscles! Up now, little dog! Hands and knees, right! Now, move! ..."

He slapped him twice on the rump and forced him to crawl around and around the pole, prodding and slapping and urging him to go faster and faster until he collapsed, face-down on the ground, retching blood over the Colonel's polished boots. This enraged Colonel Ildefonso Juarez, and he began to belabour the prostrate man until a sudden hoarse bellow stayed his hand. He looked up, sweating, to see that the prisoners had stopped their shuffle and were ranged about him in a closed circle, hating and hostile. He shouted at them to get moving. They ignored him. He threatened that if they did not move, the guards would open fire. They stood their ground, dumb accusers, while Colonel Ildefonso Juarez swiftly weighed the consequences of a yard full of bodies as well as a lazarette full of dysentery cases. The guards held their breath, noting with relief that the first rush would carry the prisoners inward and over the body of the Colonel. Seconds ticked away: one, two, three, four ... and then he recovered his sanity. He snapped at the nearest guard.

"You! Unchain this man!"

Then he pointed to Chavez and Ferrer.

"You and you! Carry him into the infirmary."

The guard hurried forward and, kneeling beside Vallenilla, unlocked the shackles. Then he looked up, witless and afraid.

"He's dead, Colonel!"

"Are you a doctor?"

"No, sir, but ..."

"Then don't make medical decisions! Get him inside!"

Chavez and Ferrer bent over Vallenilla. Chavez felt his pulse and laid his head against the shrunken, skeletal chest. Then he stood up, confronting the Colonel. Loud and clear as a judge, he announced: "He's alive, only just. But if he dies, you're the killer, Colonel. We are all witnesses."

Then he bent, lifted Vallenilla in his arms and carried him inside like a child. Colonel Ildefonso Juarez followed, limping behind him, while the guards moved in, shouting and shoving, to get the shuffling parade moving again. Half an hour later Colonel Ildefonso Juarez summoned Dr. Wolfschmidt to his office, poured him half a tumbler of brandy and questioned him.

"How is Vallenilla?"

Wolfschmidt shrugged indifferently. "Hanging on. We've stopped the hemorrhage, I've pumped him up with stimulants, but there's not much of him left."

"Keep him alive!" Colonel Ildefonso Juarez was emphatic. "If you don't, we're all in trouble. There's an ugly atmosphere among the inmates."

"If you want him alive, you have to feed and house him like a human being."

"Very well. Keep him in the infirmary. Nurse him until he's well enough to go back to the cells."

"I'll try, but you've left it rather late. I can't promise anything. . . . Why the hell should you care about this trash anyway?"

"Because the security people may want him again, and because I don't want to be accused of murder, now or later."

"Well, you've been lucky so far. This is very good brandy."

"Help yourself."

"There's another problem. How soon do I get my drugs and the hygiene team? This dysentery is spreading like a grass fire."

"Can't you confine it by quarantine?"

"Not if the water supply is polluted. Not until we've got adequate disposal of sewage, disinfected clothing and halfway cleanliness in the cookhouse."

"I've talked to headquarters. They've promised urgent action. . . . Also, it would help if you stayed sober for longer hours each day!"

"It helps me to stay drunk." Wolfschmidt tossed off his brandy at a gulp and stood up. "Don't push me, my dear Colonel. I've buried a lot of your mistakes. Now you're asking me to bring this one back from the dead. I have to be very drunk to make a miracle like that."

"For the love of God!" said Colonel Ildefonso Juarez. "Keep the bottle!"

7

In the grey dawn of a drizzly day, the *Freya*, an old-fashioned freighter of eight thousand tons, limped into the estuary and dropped anchor in the roadstead of Buenos Aires harbour. When the port officials boarded her for the usual pratique, her papers showed that she was bound for Callao and that she was temporarily disabled by a cracked shaft bearing, which must be replaced before she could proceed. The replacement parts were being flown out from Holland. The formalities were quickly completed. Temporary landing permits were granted to officers and crew, and an hour later the captain went ashore to visit the company's agents, Guzman Brothers. At midday he was sitting in a small waterside restaurant with John Spada, alias Erwin Hengst.

The instructions he received were simple. For five days he would follow the normal routine of a vessel under repair. The deck crew would clean ship, chip and paint, take shore leave in the evenings. In the engine room they would fake the clutter of a repair job, with tools and spare parts spread about in sufficient confusion to distract any casual official. On the sixth day, as late as possible, they would make ship and get clearance papers, so that they could be ready to move between midnight and dawn, as soon as the escapees were on board.

The captain raised an immediate problem. He could take the ship out, sure. But by regulation he must have a pilot on board until he cleared the estuary channel. Therefore the escapees must come on board before the pilot and remain belowdecks until he was dropped at the channel mouth. If they tried to run without a pilot, they could be boarded and arrested by the harbour police. Either way there was a risk, but the pilot was a lesser one.

"So be it then." Spada nodded agreement. "Now, there's another problem. My son-in-law is a sick man. He'll need medical attention. Where's the first port we can get it?"

The captain looked dubious.

"Montevideo is out. Uruguay and Argentina co-operate in anti-subversive measures. We could call into Rio, but I don't like that either. If we've got a sick man, with no papers, on our manifest, the police will get very suspicious. The best thing would be to get a doctor on board and let us head straight back to the Dutch Antilles. From there you can fly your patient back to New York."

"What sort of medical kit do you have?"

"The usual captain's medicine chest, but that's not too sophisticated: oxygen, penicillin, sulfa drugs, pills for bellyache, burn salves, heart stimulants, splints, a few scalpels . . . it's first-aid stuff really."

"O.K. We need a doctor and a medical kit. Let me see what I can do. You're clear on the timetable?"

190

"Absolutely."

"Good. Then unless there's any change, you won't hear from me again. Just check with the Guzman office every day in case I have to leave a message. How much will you have to tell the crew?"

"Nothing. The engineer knows, of course, because he had to fake the breakdown. The others will know nothing until the last moment; then I'll hand around some cash to keep them quiet until we've dropped the pilot."

"Then I guess that's all—except to say thank you, skipper."

"My pleasure," said the captain with a grin. "It's better than a cargo of hides and tallow, which is what we usually ship from here. Good luck, my friend!"

Spada's next call was at a convent of the Missionary Sisters of the Poor, in one of the older quarters of the city. It was ten o'clock in the evening when he arrived, and the Sister who answered the door protested his presence at so late an hour. The community was preparing for bed. The Mother Superior had had a long and tiring day. Tomorrow perhaps? Please, Sister, now! It was most important. Well ... !

In the small parlour, smelling of beeswax, under the blank gaze of a plaster Madonna, John Spada explained himself and his mission to the Mother Superior, a surprisingly young woman with a strong Nebraska twang.

". . . My daughter, Teresa, worked with you, so I felt you'd be willing to help if you could."

"I want to, of course. Teresa did great work here and suffered terribly because of it. How is she now?"

191

"Recovering. But it's a slow job. Now our information is that her husband is in bad shape. I'll need medical help if I'm to get him back alive."

"There are difficulties, Mr. Spada. Any doctor who goes with you goes into virtual exile because he would have great difficulty in reentering the country, since he could not demonstrate how or when he left it. While he was away his friends and relatives would be in danger."

"Perhaps, then, there is someone who would like to get out and stay out. There would be no difficulty about funds or help in reestablishing himself."

"In which case we deprive our poor people of help which they can ill afford to lose. However, let me think . . ." She reflected for a few moments and then went on. "Sister Martha will be leaving us very soon. She's applied for release from her vows. She's a fully trained physician and an American citizen. If she's willing to take the risk, I'll release her to go with you . . ."

"Could we speak with her now?"

"I'm afraid not. She's up-country at our mission in Mendoza. She flies back in three days' time."

"That's running it very fine."

"I know. But it's the best I can do; and if she consents, she's the best possible person: no local ties, no immediate connection with us in Buenos Aires. How shall I get in touch with you?"

"I'll call you—and remember, I'm Erwin Hengst. Next question. Can you assemble a medical kit for me: drugs, surgical instruments, that sort of thing?" He fished out his wallet and laid a stack of bills on the table. "Pay for it out of that and keep the rest for the mission."

The Mother Superior left the money untouched on the table. She asked gravely, "I have to ask this, Mr. Spada. What are the risks for Sister Martha?"

"Minimal." Spada was very definite. "Once we're on board the worst is over. Tell me, what kind of a woman is Sister Martha?"

"As a physician, first-rate. As a woman"—the Mother Superior gave a faint, ironic smile—"let's say she gets on better with men than with women. In a convent, that does create certain problems. . . ."

"If that were our biggest problem," said John Spada, "we'd be very fortunate people."

In the dining room of the Kunz apartment, Major Henson clipped a series of hand-drawn charts to the tabletop and outlined his battle plan.

". . . From Buenos Aires to the mouth of the Paraná River and the ferry terminal for Martín García is about eighty miles by road. I've driven it by day and night. In traffic you have to allow two and a half hours. If there's a jam in the city, it can take longer. However, at night we should do it in two. . . . Now, here's the island of Martín García; and here, on the mainland, is the ferry jetty. As you see, there is a parking spot in front of the jetty, and then a quarter of a mile of narrow road leading back to the highway. On either side there are citrus groves, good for concealment. However, the approach to the jetty can easily be blocked, and our vehicles could be bottled up. So it's a good place to hide but a bad place to fight. . . . Now follow the main highway back about eight miles and you'll see this other turning down to the river. There's a quiet beach there where we can bring in the motorboat from the *Freya.*

The *Freya* will be lying here, just on the edge of the channel. . . . All clear so far?"

There was a murmur of agreement around the table. Henson laid another, smaller chart over the free space on the table.

"Now let's look at dispositions and timetables. We're divided into two parties. I have my detachment in the truck, with the driver Sancho has found for us. We park by the jetty, with our boys dispersed on the edges of the orange groves. There's no ferry traffic after midnight, so it should be nothing more than a quiet waiting game. . . .

"Back in the city, Colonel Juarez has dinner at the Staff Officers Club. Sometime between eleven and midnight he goes to Rosita's, here, on this other map. He dismisses his driver at this corner and then walks ten paces down the colonnade to the entrance of Rosita's. That's where he's accosted by Sancho, Dr. Lunarcharsky and Spada. They show him their security cards. They walk him back to the car, then he is driven out of town to Sancho's safe house, which is about twenty minutes from the jetty. From there the Colonel makes his telephone call to the prison. Then you all continue to the jetty to form part of the reception committee. . . ."

"With the Colonel?" Spada was dubious.

"I advise it," said Sancho curtly. "It adds urgency and authenticity to the scene when the prisoners are brought from the prison under escort and handed over. If he makes a false move, we cut him down."

"What's the next move?" Again it was Spada's question.

"You and your people drive with Vallenilla to the embarkation point and head out to the *Freya*. The

194

rest of us go back to town. Finish . . . done! Simple as that."

"It sounds simple, but what are the principal risks?"

"Tell him," said Major Henson to Sancho.

"First, that a police patrol comes by the jetty. They prowl that stretch of highway, and sometimes they turn off to the water for a smoke or ten minutes with a girl they've picked up. In that case we turn very formal. We show them our security cards, tell them there's an operation in progress and hustle them off. Even the police don't meddle with the goons from security. The second and bigger risk is that someone at the prison has checked back to security headquarters, and they've decided to mount a raid. That means the boys in the orange grove have to decide whether to open fire or disengage on foot. We'll have one advantage. We'll arrive last, with the Colonel. We'll cruise past the turnoff and double back. That way we should be able to spot an ambush. . . . The only other risk is that either of the vehicles runs into a routine highway check, coming or going. Again, the only answer is to flourish the security cards and bluff our way through. Any other questions?"

"Only one," said the Scarecrow Man. "How good are your troops, Major? For instance, will they stay cool enough to sweat out a police check?"

"They'd damned well better. I've told them that I'll kill the first son of a bitch who even breaks wind without an order."

"Did you say that in Spanish?" asked Spada with a grin.

"No. Sancho said it for me. And they seemed to believe him."

"One more question," said John Spada. "What happens to the Colonel?"

"He's ours," said Sancho flatly.

"What will you do with him?"

"Why the hell should you care?"

"Because I'm a party to all this—and afterwards that fact will be known."

"That's the risk you took at the beginning."

"So I repeat the question. What are you going to do with the Colonel?"

"Sweat him for information; then kill him. Objections?"

"None," said Spada. "Just so you don't plant the body on my doorstep—or try to charge me undertaker's fees."

"How could you possibly think that?" said Sancho with sour humour. "A deal's a deal, isn't it?"

"Provided you can read the small print," said John Spada.

In the infirmary of Martín García they were trying to keep Rodolfo Vallenilla alive. Dr. Wolfschmidt prescribed the regimen; the junior aide administered it with a constancy and a tenderness touching to see— except that there was no one to see it save the doctor, who had a profound contempt for anything remotely resembling humanity. He had a whole repertory of epithets for his junior: "my mother superior," "sister sweet-lips," "our young gelding," "the commandant's choirboy." Yet there was a limit line which, drunk or sober, the good doctor never dared to cross.

Whatever he did in the torture rooms, inside the infirmary he never laid violent hands on a patient. He might neglect his charges, but he might never insult them. Once, and once only, he had tried it and had been reduced to gibbering terror by the cold, murderous fury of his assistant, who had backed him into a corner of the surgery and demonstrated how many, how subtle and how painful ways there were to kill him, and how, waking or sleeping, inside the prison or abroad, there was always an executioner in attendance.

The fact that Wolfschmidt submitted to the blackmail was a matter of wonder to the inmates, but to his junior it was an exquisite, if dangerous, calculation, because Dr. Wolfschmidt was wanted by the Israelis and by the underground and was, moreover, avid for dominance and punishment which no one but this pale youth had the courage to inflict on him. So the strange relationship persisted, and the dark angel of Wolfschmidt's gehenna became the minister of mercy to his victims.

For Vallenilla he had developed an almost filial affection, a protective gentleness, from which all sexual emotion had long since purged itself. He washed Vallenilla's bent and emaciated body. He fed him, patiently, as one might feed an infant, spoonful by spoonful. He coaxed back the courage upon which Vallenilla's slim hope of survival depended.

"Listen to me, Rodolfo! Don't give up! I need you alive. We all do. What you have in your head, what you will one day tell the world, is important to us all— even to a nothing man like me. Oh yes, you must believe that. I feed you like this, but you feed me too. One day I will be able to stand up and say: 'You see that great man? I gave him back to the world. The words he says are the words I wish I

197

could say.' . . . That's my boy! Eat another spoonful. It's good broth. I made it myself on the burner. . . . Not like the prison slop, is it? . . . That's splendid! Now lie quiet while I make up your injection. . . . I know it hurts, but that's because you're too skinny. When I fatten you up, you won't feel it half as much. . . ."

But the battle was not easily won. Often Vallenilla would slip away into the black pit of depression, where he cowered, fearful and fretful, suspicious even of his benefactor.

"Why are they treating me like this? They never cared before. The security boys want me back, don't they? They're just trying to get me better so they can put me through it all over again. They've done it to others . . ."

"No, Rodolfo! No! I keep telling you, the commandant is scared. If you die, he'll be blamed, because everybody saw what happened in the exercise yard. He can't afford that. He's a bastard, but even among the bastards there are rules. . . . Come on now! You know I'm your friend, don't you?"

"Yes, I know that. But promise me something."

"Anything, Rodolfo. Anything in my power."

"Then swear to me!" The bony hands clutched at his stained jacket. "Swear that if you even hear they're taking me back, you'll kill me! You can do it . . . a pill, an injection—anything! On your mother's grave, swear it!"

"I can't swear it on my mother's grave. She's still alive and sleeping with an artillery sergeant. But sure, I promise. They'll never get you back. . . . There now, don't cry! Wolfschmidt will be back in a minute. You've got to look strong and defiant!"

It was a promise easily given and, at the final test, not too hard to fulfill. He had finished off more than one poor devil too broken to survive and yet not so far gone that they could not inflict a few more agonies on him. It was not too hard to accomplish —a bubble of air in the syringe, while the butchers were relaxed and waiting for the next session. There were no postmortems to worry about, and collapses were all too commonplace. . . . He drew the blanket over his patient, made him close his eyes and crooned over him until he lapsed into a restless, wheezing doze. Poor devil! All that brain, all that fire, in such a frail carcass.

The door of the infirmary creaked open and old Corporal Pascarelli came in, bleeding all over the floor. He had been trying to take out a broken pane from the window in his quarters. He had slipped and gashed his palm. He needed stitches and a large shot of brandy from Wolfschmidt's cupboard. The son of a bitch would never notice! While the operation was being performed, he talked compulsively in a conspirator's whisper.

"I've got a couple of messages from outside. One's for your boy over there." He jerked his head in the direction of Vallenilla's bed. "Tell him somebody's sending him a fish in a box."

"Is that all—a fish in a box?"

"That's all."

"What does it mean?"

"I never ask, sonny boy. It's safer that way. People outside pay me to deliver messages and then forget. If they want an answer, I try to get one back."

"How do they know the message has been delivered?"

"They know me. They trust me." There was a glimmer of pride in the rheumy, bloodshot eyes. "It's a good reputation to have. Not ever prisoner stays in this dump forever. When they get out, they remember old Pascarelli. A lot of the other guards are idiots. They forget that, when they're transferred, there'll be someone waiting to stick a knife in their ribs or kick 'em to death in a dark alley. Not me! Live and let live, I say. Better to have money in your pocket than six inches of steel in your gut. So pass the message like a good boy, eh?"

"Sure, sure! Hold still now while I get the dressing on. . . . Who's the other message for?"

"Chavez—but he's been in solitary for six days. Gets out tomorrow if he's lucky."

"Which means he'll probably end up here first. What do you want me to tell him?"

"The tiger's sniffing around. Got that?"

"Got it! . . . There, you're wrapped up like a wounded hero. All you need is a medal to go with it."

"For our kind of war," Pascarelli grunted contemptuously, "there won't be any medals, just curses scratched on our tombstones. Well, thanks! See you, sonny boy. Keep your back to the wall!"

On the morning of his departure for Buenos Aires, Colonel Juarez made his customary rounds with Major Gutierrez. As always, the Colonel was elated by the prospect of four days' freedom in the capital. When he came to the infirmary and saw Rodolfo Vallenilla huddled under the soiled blankets, his spirits rose. He twitched back the covers with the tip of his cane and surveyed his victim with tolerant contempt.

"Good! My little dog looks better. They must be feeding you well. Enjoy it while you can. It won't last forever. I'm going up to the city today. I'll let the security boys know you're almost ready for another interrogation. Did you think they'd forgotten you? Never! They have a passion for detail and there are still a lot of unanswered questions. But don't let it worry you! After this vacation you'll be able to stand quite a long session! Go back to sleep now, little dog. Sweet dreams!"

When he had gone, Rodolfo Vallenilla lay curled into a fetal position, trembling and chattering as if in an ague. The junior aide sat on the edge of the bunk and tried to comfort him.

"Relax, Rodolfo! He's gone now. He'll be gone the whole weekend—Monday and Tuesday as well. I'll make you some coffee with lots of sugar. You'd like that, wouldn't you?"

"No! I don't want anything." The intensity of the protest was like a convulsion racking his withered frame. "I can't take any more! I can't!"

"He's playing a game. Can't you see that? Ignore him! Pull the shutters down and blot him out of your mind."

"He means it. Why else does he let me stay here? He wants me dead; but he doesn't want to kill me himself. He knows the security boys will do it for him. Please, my friend. You made me a promise. Kill me, I beg of you, kill me!"

As suddenly as it had flared, the fire died in him and he lay whimpering like a small animal. The junior aide sponged the sweat from his face with a wad of cotton wool and crooned over him softly.

"Come on! I've got a message for you from outside."

"What sort of message?"

"Someone's sending you a fish in a box."

"Say that again." The frail, bony hands clutched at his sleeve.

"A fish in a box."

"Then I'll try to hang on."

"You do that."

"But promise me you'll never let them take me back to the Fun Palace?"

"I promise! I'll give you something to make you sleep now."

"Thank you." A grateful whisper. "You're a kind boy."

"When you get wherever you're going, Rodolfo, say a good word for me, eh?"

"The best I know," said Rodolfo Vallenilla. "The very best. . . . Will you sit with me awhile? I . . . I'd like to feel you near until I go to sleep."

"It's still early." Sancho parked the car in a shadowy angle at the end of the colonnade. "You two stay here. I'll stroll down past Rosita's and make sure everything's quiet."

He got out of the car and strolled casually through the shadows of the vaulted passageway. Spada turned to the Scarecrow Man.

"Everything's O.K.?"

"Everything. Henson left on time with his troops in the truck. The woman doctor's on board the *Freya*. The boat is already at the rendezvous point. We're in good shape."

"So far," said John Spada. "Sancho's coming back."

Sancho slid into the seat beside Spada and gave a last hurried direction.

"We should get ready now. There's a doorway on either side of the entrance to Rosita's. You two take up positions there. As soon as the Colonel moves into the colonnade, close in on him. Make sure he doesn't ring the bell, because the fellow who opens the door is a security man. Just flash your cards at the Colonel and say you'd like a few words with him. I'll make sure his driver has moved off; then I'll come in from the rear. We walk him back here, put him in the middle of the back seat and then shove a gun in his ribs.... Clear?"

"Clear."

"Let's go!"

They waited five, ten, twelve agonizing minutes in the shadows until they saw the military vehicle draw up a few yards down from the entrance and the driver hurry around to open the door for his passenger. They heard the ritual exchange: "Pick me up at ten in the morning. Until then, enjoy yourself."

"The Colonel is too kind. I have to watch my pocket."

They saw the Colonel pause on the sidewalk, straightening his jacket, twitching at his tie, setting his cap square on his head, while the driver engaged the gears and moved off with decorous precision. Then Spada and the Scarecrow Man stepped out of the doorway to accost Juarez. It was the Scarecrow Man who spoke the first words in a very passable Buenos Aires accent.

"Colonel Ildefonso Juarez?"

"Yes!" The colonel stiffened into a defensive formality.

"Security! Our identification . . . We'd like a few words with you. We won't detain you long."

"Oh! Let's go inside then."

"Our car is just up there. If you please, Colonel."

The Colonel hesitated a moment, but when he saw Sancho moving out of the shadows he shrugged and said irritably, "Very well. But I hope you understand that . . ."

"Perfectly, Colonel!" The Scarecrow Man was politeness itself. "But the matter is urgent, as we shall explain."

"What matter?"

"Inside the car, please. We don't want to talk our business up and down the street."

They squeezed him into the middle of the back seat with Spada on one side and the Scarecrow Man on the other. The Scarecrow Man held a gun at his belly.

Sancho sat in the driver's seat and announced calmly: "Now, Colonel, sit quiet and you'll be fine. Make one silly move or a single noise and you're dead."

He gunned the motor and they moved off, threading a careful course through the alleys towards the northern highway. It was at least a minute before Colonel Juarez found voice or words.

"What is all this? Where are you taking me?"

"This is a security operation," said the Scarecrow Man. "Please cooperate."

"Then why do you have to threaten me?"

204

"People do silly things in the heat of the moment; we can't afford to take chances, even with reliable folk like you, Colonel. Now just relax. If we're stopped at any point, say nothing."

"You still haven't said where you're taking me."

"Back to Martín García."

"I'm on leave."

"We know, Colonel; but a good soldier is always on call, isn't he? Now listen carefully. We're taking in two of your prisoners for further questioning. Their names are Pablo Maria Chavez and Rodolfo Vallenilla. You're going to telephone the prison and instruct your deputy to have the prisoners delivered to us at the ferry dock upriver."

"I could have done that from Rosita's. Anyway, Vallenilla's sick."

"We'd like it done our way, Colonel."

"I need documents, authorizations."

"We have them, as you will see."

"Then what?"

"We'll drive you back with the prisoners."

"This is most irregular."

"We live in irregular times," said the Scarecrow Man mildly.

"You're not from security!"

"No? Our documents say we are. Why don't you just play along? Much safer, I promise you."

"Mother of God!"

"Lean back, Colonel. Put your hands on your knees. That's better. Now tell me, who is the officer-in-charge during your absence?"

"Major Gutierrez. But he'll be asleep now. There's a night duty officer."

"You'll have the Major wakened and pass your instructions direct."

"He'll want identification and confirmation."

"We'll provide it. The number of the documents. The originals will be handed over at the landing stage. . . ."

"I don't believe you."

"Oh man of little faith!" The Scarecrow Man admonished him amiably. "Please try to believe. Otherwise you'll never see the girls at Rosita's again. Now, you said Vallenilla is sick. How bad is he?"

"He's in the infirmary."

"That means he's damned near dying," said Sancho from the front seat. "We heard you kept him chained in the exercise yard and beat him like a dog."

"That's a lie."

"We'll soon know, won't we?"

During all the talk Spada remained silent, trying to read the body chemistry of the man pressed against his flank. The Colonel was tense, but he was far from panic. He was still functioning logically, weighing the contradictory information that was being fed to him, observing the route they were driving, alert to any possible chance of escape. Spada decided to push him harder.

"Save yourself some labour, Colonel. The route is perfectly straightforward. You're not gagged or blindfolded. You can even memorize our faces. That must tell you something, surely?"

"I don't understand any of this."

"You've been under observation for some time, Colonel."

"Observation? For what?"

"You have a nice comfortable job. We'd like to be sure you haven't abused its privileges."

"Abused. . . ? I have no idea what you're talking about! My record demonstrates . . ."

"Ah yes! The record! Who writes the record, Colonel? Who files the reports?"

"I do."

"Quite. Of course, if the facts conform with the record, there's nothing to worry about, is there? The army protects its own. Tell me about Vallenilla."

"The man was a recalcitrant, a troublemaker. He had to be disciplined. . . ."

"By you, personally?"

"In exemplary situations, sometimes . . ."

"Not now, Colonel. Later you can explain these 'exemplary situations.' Tell me, have you ever thought about defection?"

"Defection? To whom? Where? The idea's preposterous."

"Strange! We've talked to your driver. He seemed to think you maintain a very expensive lifestyle on a colonel's pay. A private room at the Formosa . . . and Rosita's girls aren't cheap. Of course, we know you don't have high living expenses on Martín García; but still . . . you do see there are questions to be answered."

"Then I'll answer them at the proper tribunal."

"After you've made your depositions to us."

"Look! I've nothing to hide. I'm perfectly happy to cooperate."

He was confused now. The first smell of fear began to exude from him. Spada drew away and looked out of the window at the traffic and the sprawling lights of the suburbs. The habitations had thinned out now, and they were passing from the outer suburbs into the first fringes of the small holdings and the truck farmers. Suddenly Sancho swung the car hard left onto a rutted track, at the end of which was a large, barn-like structure, with fruit crates and vegetable boxes stacked in front of it. He switched off the engine and the lights and turned his head to address the Colonel.

"Now listen carefully. There's a telephone inside. You'll call the prison and have Major Gutierrez brought to the phone. You'll instruct him to send the two prisoners, Vallenilla and Chavez, immediately to the ferry dock on the mainland. You'll quote him the numbers of the documents we'll give you. Tell him you'll be there with us to take delivery. Clear so far?"

"Clear."

"How many escorts would he send normally?"

"Three. A boatman and two officers."

"Is your radio working?"

"Not at this hour. We close down at ten, unless there's an emergency."

"Which this is not. Now, when you've given your instructions, pass the phone to me."

"Very well."

"One last word, Colonel. Say only what I've told you. Otherwise you end up like a Martinmas pig with an apple in your mouth."

"I don't understand why you have to threaten me like this. I've told you I'll cooperate."

"But you're bluffing, Colonel," said the Scarecrow Man gently. "You think we're not security, so you're playing the game they taught you in Staff School.

208

Be calm. Placate the captors. Try to establish a
personal relationship. . . . This time it won't work,
because we've got different rules. There are only two.
Get clever and you die inside that shed. Cooperate
and you stay alive awhile longer. . . . That's all.
Let's go inside."

The barn was a single large hangar with a tiny
cubbyhole office at one end. They sat Colonel Juarez
at the table and stood up about him with pistols
drawn. Sancho laid the security document in front of
him and pointed to the serial number. Then he
handed him the telephone.

"Make sure you get it right, Colonel."

Juarez dialed the number with an unsteady hand.
On the first round his finger slipped and he had to
begin the series again. Spada winked at the Scarecrow Man, who nodded assent: Colonel Juarez was no
hero. They heard the ringing of the telephone, then
the voice of the prison operator, distant and crackly.
Sancho bent close to listen. The Colonel spoke, a trifle
unsteadily.

"This is Colonel Juarez. I want to speak to Major
Gutierrez. . . . Of course, you fool, I know he's in
bed. Wake him up!"

There was a long pause, the sound of a switchboard transfer and then a grumpish, slurred voice.

"Gutierrez!"

"Major! Rub the sleep out of your eyes. This is
Colonel Juarez."

"Yes, sir! Yes, Colonel!"

"Listen to me and listen carefully. I am with the
security people. They want immediate delivery of two
prisoners: Chavez and Vallenilla. Get them ready

as quickly as you can. . . . Tonight? Of course tonight! We'll be waiting at the ferry dock. Yes, I know
Vallenilla's sick. Put him on a stretcher! . . . No,
don't go yet! Make a note of the custody order number. Write it in the log. You'll get the original document at the hand-over. Here it is: OS 759 stroke 8635
stroke 4126. Got it? . . . Hold on a moment."

Sancho took the receiver out of his hand and
continued the call.

"Major Gutierrez, this is Major Borja, security.
Have you got any civilian clothes for these men? . . .
Good, so long as they're halfway decent. They're not
going to a dinner party. Oh . . . and no chains. We've
got enough troops to keep 'em quiet. How long will it
take to have them at the mainland? . . . Forty
minutes? Christ, that's running it fine. This is part of a
bigger operation. If you can do it in thirty minutes,
you'd help us a lot. . . . One more thing. As of now we
want complete radio silence. No transmissions at all
from Martín García. If you want to contact me or
the Colonel, don't go through Central Office; use this
number: 758-9563. We're working out of town and
we're busy as hell. . . . So if we're engaged, just keep
trying; but don't hold up the dispatch of the prisoners.
That's absolutely vital. Any more questions for the
Colonel? . . . No, he won't be coming to the prison.
He'll be returning to town with us. . . . Thank you,
Major. Good night!"

He put down the receiver and patted Colonel
Juarez on the shoulder. "Nicely done, my friend! Just
keep going like that and you'll live to lay a lot more
girls." He lifted the receiver off the hook and laid it
on the table. Then he laid the barrel of his pistol
along the Colonel's cheek. "And remember, from here

on you're walking through a minefield. One false step and . . . boom-boom! *Vamos, amigo!*"

The truck was parked in the open space by the ferry dock. The driver sat at the wheel, smoking one cigarette after another. The mercenaries were dispersed along the edges of the orange grove, sweating in the still, dank air of the river flats. Henson himself made the rounds continuously, checking the entrance to the highway, passing from tree to tree, whispering commands in bad Spanish supplemented by hand signs, a pointing finger, a touch on the shoulder, a signal indicating the line of fire if the police should come.

The river itself was empty, grey under the pallid moon, with yellow lights pricking out from the estuary islands. The only sounds were the distant drone of the traffic along the highway, the occasional cry of a night bird and the slurring sigh of the river around the piles of the jetty. When he reached the truck, Henson snatched the cigarette from the driver's mouth and ground it out under his heel. The fellow protested in voluble Spanish, but Henson drew a hand across his throat in a meaning gesture and walked away towards the jetty. He looked at his watch and cursed quietly. Spada was ten minutes late. If the boat arrived before the reception committee . . . Then he heard the car, swung around and saw the headlights shining down the lane. The headlights went out and the car rolled into the parking space, turned to face back to the road and stopped. Sancho got out, opened the rear door and shepherded three men onto the circle of gravel. Henson hurried across to offer an anxious greeting.

"Thank Christ you're here. I was beginning to get worried."

"No sweat," said John Spada. "There's plenty of time."

Sancho, the stage manager, asked a single question.

"Where are your men posted?"

"Two at the entrance to the highway. Two half-way down. Two at the edge of the parking area."

"Good." He turned back to the Colonel and the Scarecrow Man. "When the boat arrives, we three walk along the jetty to meet it. You, Colonel, will present the documents. You, Major, and you, Mr. Spada, follow behind. We don't want Vallenilla to recognize you immediately. The prison guards will hand the prisoners onto the jetty. Then you, Colonel, send them back. Understood?"

"I understand."

"Major, as soon as you hear the boat, move your men out into the open. We want a show of strength."

"Right."

"And, Colonel . . ."

"Yes?"

"Think like a soldier now. We are ten on the land against three guards in a boat. That's bad odds— and you'll be the first man dead."

"Mother of God, do you think I'm stupid?"

"You have been," said the Scarecrow Man. "This is your last chance to use your brains."

From far across the river they heard the sound of the engine; then, a few moments later, they saw the lights, red and green, heading towards the landing stage. Sancho and the Scarecrow Man pushed the Colonel ahead of them and strode along the jetty.

Major Henson gave a low whistle, and six men emerged from the orange grove and came running to join him. He ranged them in a circle, four facing the jetty, two facing back to the roadway; then, with Spada at his side, he stood watching the small, tense drama at the landing stage. First the boatman tied up, then one of the guards addressed the Colonel.

"Two prisoners as requested. Chavez and Vallenilla. This one . . ." He pointed to Vallenilla lying on the stretcher. "He's unconscious. They gave him a sedative before he left."

"Lift him onto the jetty," said Sancho curtly.

The two guards hoisted the stretcher out of the boat, climbed the steps from the landing stage to the deck of the pier, laid down the stretcher, then looked to the Colonel for instructions.

Sancho intervened again. He called to the other prisoner, "You, Chavez!"

"Yes?"

"Come up here."

Chavez mounted the steps and stood facing Sancho. A faint flicker of recognition showed in his eyes, but he said nothing. The guard turned to the Colonel.

"Are you coming back with us, Colonel?"

"No . . . I have business here. Tell Major Gutierrez . . ."

"Tell him nothing! This is security business," said Sancho sharply. "You can telephone later, Colonel, when this operation is over. Dismiss your men, please."

"Dismiss!" said Colonel Ildefonso Juarez.

The guard stood his ground. "We need the order, sir, and a receipt for the bodies."

"Oh, of course."

Sancho stood close as the documents were exchanged. Then, with obvious relief, the guards saluted and climbed back into the boat. The handler cast off, started the motor and headed back at full speed towards the island. Sancho threw his arms around Chavez and embraced him.

"Welcome back, comrade!"

John Spada came at a run and turned back the greasy blanket from Vallenilla's face. He looked so tiny and waxen that for a moment Spada thought he was dead.

Chavez said harshly, "You'd better get him some good medical attention. He's damn near dead—and this bastard did it." He spat in the Colonel's face.

"Enough!" said Spada harshly. "Get Vallenilla into the truck."

Sancho and Chavez picked up the stretcher. Spada and the Scarecrow Man followed, with the Colonel two paces in front of them. As the small procession moved along the jetty to the vehicles, the Colonel turned and asked plaintively: "Who are you? What are you going to do with me?"

Spada was silent. The Scarecrow Man answered for him.

"We? Nothing. You don't belong to us. Your own people will take care of you. But don't worry. They're very careful about protocol. When they bury you, there'll always be someone to spit on your grave."

It was an hour after dawn when they dropped the pilot and headed, north by east, across the gulf into the long Atlantic swell. Spada and his companions emerged from the hold; and while the others climbed on deck to refresh themselves in the cool morning air, Spada went to the mate's cabin to see

Vallenilla. He was still comatose. Sister Martha had rigged a drip bottle and an oxygen mask and was taking his pulse count.

Spada asked, "How is he, Sister?"

"He's holding; that's all I can say just now. I've pumped him full of penicillin and I'm drip-feeding him. His pulse is weak but steady." She handed Spada a gauze mask. "Wear this whenever you come to see him. All the symptoms indicate he's got TB: nummular sputum, bloody at times, the chest full of rales and rhonchi. The rest of him . . . God. knows— he must have suffered terribly."

"Can you keep him alive until we get him home?"

"With luck, yes."

"I'll help you nurse him," said Spada. "Just show me what to do."

"It's simple enough. Regular injections, change the drip bottle, keep him clean and comfortable. Most important, make him want to stay alive."

"I want to thank you for agreeing to come, Sister."

"Not Sister anymore. Just plain Martha—Martha Moorhouse. I'm happy to help."

Vallenilla stirred and groaned and opened his eyes. They were glazed and unfocussed. Spada bent towards him. Martha held him back.

"The mask first."

Spada slipped the gauze pad over his mouth and nostrils. His voice came out muffled and strange.

"Rodo, this is John . . . John Spada. Can you hear me? If you can, squeeze my hand."

He felt a faint answering pressure from the thin, clammy fingers. He talked on soothingly: "Don't try to answer. You're safe now. Understand that. You're safe. We're taking you home to Teresa."

"Teresa!" Through the transparent plastic of the oxygen mask they saw his lips form the word; then he closed his eyes again and his hand went slack in Spada's grip.

"That's enough," said Martha. "Let him rest."

"I have to see the captain," said John Spada. "I'll relieve you in an hour. Where will you sleep?"

"The second officer has lent me his cabin. It's just across the companionway. Oh, Mr. Spada ..."

"Yes?"

"I presume you'll be getting in touch with your family?"

"Of course. I'll use the ship's radio as soon as we're out of Argentine waters. Why do you ask?"

"Don't let them expect too much, especially your daughter. You're taking home an invalid—a permanent invalid; and he'll never be able to mate with a woman again."

8

In the old walled garden of the Bay House, summer was in early flush with a profusion of rose blooms and lavender, a bourdon of questing bees, pears ripening against the warm stones of the wall, the spaces between the mullioned windows hung with clematis. The sky was blue above the mirror pool, where golden carp swam lazily among the lily pads; the shadow of the gnomon lay sharp and clear across the antique brass of the sundial.

In the center of the eastern wall, sheltered from the search of the sea cold, there was a large, semicircular alcove, roofed with red tiles and set with rustic furniture, where on the good days the master of the house might divert himself with his friends and delight in the sweet contrivance of his domain. This day Rodolfo Vallenilla was there, a small humped figure in a wheelchair, dozing sometimes, then, in brief bursts of energy, writing in a child's exercise book, while Teresa watched, smiled approvingly and bent again to her needlepoint. For John Spada and Anna, watching from the window, there was an odd pastoral pathos in the scene.

217

". . . As if they were the old ones," said Anna sadly. "And we were the young, with all our lives in front of us."

Spada put a protective arm around her shoulders and drew her to him.

"Don't brood on it, Anna. They're counting their own blessings."

"I don't brood." Anna denied it stoutly. "But Teresa talks to me sometimes. She says she doesn't miss the sex part; after what they did to her she has no want for it. But she worries about Rodo. He feels broken and useless. She had to encourage him all the time to write, because he has important things to say; but when he gets tired, he frets like a baby."

"You can't blame the poor devil. Part of him wants to record what he's been through; the other part wants to forget it. Teresa has the same problem. For the present, the best we can offer them is here: a quiet place and cherishing when they need it."

"And what about you, amore?" Anna laid a soft hand on his cheek. "What do you need?"

"What I have, I suppose." Spada was suddenly moody and withdrawn. "You—and a lot of work to keep me busy."

"I haven't been much help to you lately."

"Have I complained?"

"No; but it happens to us women—the children always seem to need us more than the husband, especially when he's a strong one like you. It's not good for us, you being so much in town and me out here with Teresa and Rodo. But they still need me around."

"I know." Spada bent and kissed her dark hair. "We'll work it out."

"It's a pity you stepped out of the business. You need to be busy now."

"No!" Spada was a shade too emphatic about it. "Make no mistake, Anna! Since I bought out the Poseidon Press I've been busy as hell reorganizing. We're setting up foreign-language subsidiaries, and a computer system for storage and retrieval of data. Give us three months more and we'll be pumping out some really sensational material."

"What sort of material?"

"I told you . . ."

"I know you told me." Anna was penitent. "I listened, but I didn't hear half of it—and the rest I didn't understand. Don't be angry with me, amore. It's just that Teresa and Rodo were more important."

"Sure they were! But now we have to use their experiences to help others, thousands of others, all over the world. The greatest weapons of tyranny are silence and false report. We're going to break the silence and publish true records of what goes on around the world: lists of political prisoners, factual accounts of what has happened to them and their families, names, addresses, personal histories of those who engage in the trades of torture and terror. Our Proteus people will gather the information. We'll record it, cross-check it, publish it in regular bulletins, until one day, please God, the villains will be afraid to show their faces in civilized society. It's a big job, a long job, but it could be the most important I've ever attempted."

"The most dangerous too." Anna shivered and

clung to him. "I hate the way we're living now, with guards at the gate and on the beach—people following us wherever we go."

"It's necessary, Anna. Dictators have long arms."

"But now you're creating more danger, inviting new threats."

"What should I do? Stay silent? Let the evil men flourish?"

"There's no need to get angry. I have a right to say what I feel."

"Look out there!" Spada pointed towards the summerhouse, where Teresa was settling the covers around a dozing Rodo. "The men who put them through the mincer still walk free and respectable in the sunlight. Some of them seem to be quite ordinary people. They wash the blood off their hands after a day's session, put on clean clothes and go home to caress their wives and fondle their children. Because their trade is invisible, they're ignored, like embalmers or sewage men. They flourish by tacit consent of ordinary folk, who want to see the streets clean and the trains run on time and their houses safe from thieves in the night. The taxpayers pay their wages. They are promoted in civil and military lists. They walk safe in the open while their victims rot in cells a hundred yards from the city square. . . . That's why they have to be stopped. That's why . . ."

"You're prepared to risk us all again?" Anna broke away from his embrace and challenged him in tearful anger. "Haven't you done enough? Will we never again have a moment's peace?"

The next moment she was gone, running up the stairs to their bedroom. He heard the door slam and the key turn in the lock. He stood like a stone man, staring out at the summer garden. Never in his life had he felt so empty, so utterly desolate.

He was normally too proud to bandy complaints around his family; but this time he found himself not only distressed but totally disoriented, as if he were half drunk and committing a foolishness that made others embarrassed. He walked out into the garden and beckoned to Teresa to stroll with him on the lawn while Rodo still dozed in his wheelchair. When he told her of Anna's outburst, she seemed oddly defensive.

". . . You don't see it, Papa, because you're always on the move, always in action. Mama's in the bad years now. She needs tenderness, stability—the special feeling of growing safely into middle age with the man she loves. What happened to me and to Rodo was a terrible shock for her. You weren't here to see it all, but . . ."

"For Christ's sake!" Spada was suddenly ablaze with anger. "How could I see anything? I was down in Buenos Aires, risking a dozen lives to get your husband out."

"Please, Papa! That's not what I mean."

"Then say what you mean! I've got a right to hear it, straight and plain. Yes or no?"

"Yes, Papa! Yes! Yes! But don't you understand? I'm the wrong one to ask."

"Why?"

"Because Rodo and I are casualties. They broke us! . . . Oh yes, we're putting ourselves together again, one piece every day; but we'll never be front-line fighters again. Every day we look at the newspapers and see some terror story that brings back the nightmares. We're scared, because we know we're conditioned like Pavlov's dogs and we're incompetent to handle any more risks."

"So I've stepped in to fight in your stead. What's wrong with that?"

"We're afraid of you too!"

Her vehemence shocked him. He recovered after a moment and then asked calmly enough, "Would you feel happier if I pulled out? Surrendered?"

"Happier, no! Safer, yes. But we have no right to ask it."

"I'm damn sure you haven't." Anger took hold of him again. "I've been a good husband, a good father. Neither you nor your mother has a right to turn me into a eunuch!"

"Papa, please. . . !"

"Shut up and listen! I don't want to live like a slave, grovelling to a goddam jack-in-office, scared to go to the can because some half-assed anarchist may have planted a bomb under the seat! If I'm a threat to you or your mother, or Rodo, I'll go away, draw the fire somewhere else. But there's no way I'll sit here, doing nothing, while the bullyboys take over the world! I'm going to fight, bambina—and to hell with . . ."

"Papa, for the last time, listen to me!"

"I'm listening."

"Enough!" Rodolfo Vallenilla wheeled himself between them like a charioteer. "Be quiet, Teresa! John, I was once a man like you. Now I would not last ten minutes with the interrogators. But I tell you, go your own way. Fight your own battle! We will support you with the little strength we have!"

"And what about Mother?" Teresa rounded on him furiously. "Doesn't she have any rights?"

"Yes, she does," said Rodolfo Vallenilla. "But she claims them from her husband, not from her daughter. Can't you see what's happening, Teresa? You're doing exactly what the villains hope. They want us scared, quarrelling, hating one another."

"I want some peace!" The words came out in a plaintive cry.

"In Martín García I begged a man to kill me," said Rodo bitterly. "Because I wanted peace, just as you do now."

"Maybe it would have been better if we'd both died!"

"Never say that again," said Spada softly. "Good men risked their lives for you and Rodo. Murder was done because of you, and now you spit in our faces! Rodo, try to talk some decency into your wife!"

He turned on his heel and left them, striding across the lawn like an angry giant. Then, minutes later, he was gone, driving furiously up the parkway, choked with the bitterness of rejection.

"What did you expect, lover?" Maury Feldman sketched a muscly Narcissus admiring his sex in a lily pond. "You've stepped through the looking glass into a different dimension. There's no way your family can understand you anymore. . . . Come to that, I don't understand you very well myself!"

"Christ! How simple do I have to make it? What did you do in the holocausts, Daddy?"

"You son of a bitch!"

"That I can understand." Spada snatched the pencil from his hand and snapped it in two. "My family's been violated. An old friend has been murdered. I

223

want to fight the butchers. So I'm a son of a bitch! Fine! Suppose I sit down and swallow it and say, 'Thank you, Doctor. That medicine makes me feel good.' What am I then, eh?"

"You're a wise man who doesn't push his luck too far. You're a good husband who protects his wife and family."

"And that's enough?"

"For me, yes—but I don't have a wife or a family."

"It's not enough for me," said John Spada.

"What do you want then—justice or vengeance?"

"Justice!"

"No way you'll get it." Maury Feldman picked out another pencil from his tray and turned back to his sketching. "I'm a servant of the law and I tell you justice is an illusion—unless the Almighty keeps better accounts than He seems to."

"Let's say, then, I'm looking for punitive damages."

"It's a hard suit to win."

"Because there's no court of jurisdiction."

"Right."

"But there's still the court of public opinion—which is why I've gone into the publishing business."

"I've thought about that." Maury Feldman put down his pencil, clasped his hands behind his head and stretched his legs under the desk. "I've thought about it very carefully, because you're a good client and you pay well on the due date. You're going to publish a series of dossiers on terror—institutional terror, revolutionary terror. You're going to collect evidence: names, dates, places, personal histories of victims and tormentors alike. . . . You're going to circulate this information around the world."

"You're damn right I am!"

"And you'll personally guarantee every item you publish is the truth?"

"As far as I can, yes."

"How far is that, lover?"

"With the systems I'm installing, a bloody long way."

"But it's still not a hundred percent guarantee. . . . No! Don't pounce on me! Sit still and listen! There's an elementary fact about terrorists and political criminals. They use false names, fictitious identities, as you yourself did in Argentina. What happens if you name the wrong man and someone tosses a bomb into his living room and kills his wife and kids? What happens if you lay a false charge against a guilty man and he sues you for libel or defamation—and goes scot-free at the end of it? What happens if an intelligence service feeds you false information and destroys your credibility at the outset? What happens if you publish the right information and they put out a contract on your life and the lives of your family or your employees. . . ?"

"All good questions, Maury. Now here's one from me. What happens if I do nothing?"

"You'll die quietly in bed," said Maury Feldman wearily. "And I'll sit Shivah—which won't help you, but it'll make me feel better, because you're a great dumb goy and I love you! . . . Do you want me to call Anna?"

"No. She'll come around."

"Teresa?"

"I'll let that one ride, too, for a day or so. . . . How are things at the store?"

"Fine. Mike Santos is doing a good job. We've almost tied up the purchase of the Raymond Serum Laboratories. Spada Nucleonics has solved the cladding problem, and there's a reasonable compromise with the clients on costs. Liebowitz is quiet for the time being. . . . Kitty's getting restless, though. She wants to quit and join your publishing venture."

"I could use her right now."

"Talk to Mike first." Maury shrugged off the subject and then frowned unhappily over a new thought. "I wanted to suggest something . . ."

"What?"

"A visit to Washington, a quiet chat with Hendrick at State. You're not very popular there at the moment, and the company lobby's not very welcome either."

"What's the complaint?"

"Oh, lots of little things." Maury was theatrically casual. "Rumors and gossip that are very embarrassing to Secretary Hendrick."

"Like what?"

"Like that you're a big contributor to Marxist funds in Europe. That you worked with the E.R.P. in Argentina. That you're an accessory with them to the murder of a prison commandant. . . . The Argentines are doing a beautiful hatchet job on you."

"Okay. I'll go down to Washington soon and say my party piece. Also, I want to talk to Ambassador Kolchak. The Lermontov affair is hanging fire too long."

"Now that you're a friend of the Party, the Russians may be more amenable!" Maury's grin was deliberately provocative. "You're quite a notorious figure, one way and another. I shouldn't be surprised if you were getting a little attention from the C.I.A. and the F.B.I."

"Any evidence to that effect?"

"Some. Mike Santos has been asked to send in an updated list of security clearances. The timing's a bit unusual. If I were you, I'd have your apartment checked for bugs."

"Oh, brother! That sort of harassment I need like the measles."

Maury Feldman shrugged and bent again to his sketching.

"I told you, lover. You've stepped through the looking glass. You'd better be prepared for some curious encounters—dangerous ones too, perhaps."

"The family's protected night and day. I'm covered as well as I can be; but there's no protection on a city sidewalk."

"I guess not. . . . But take care, eh? If you die, I lose an awful lot of revenue."

He had known Maury Feldman too long to take the warning lightly. They had climbed together from back-alley business to the heady crags of big money and high politics. Up there, foothold and handhold were precarious. One slip, one jostle, was enough to send the unwary toppling back into the dark alley. So when he reached his apartment, he placed a personal call to Secretary of State Hendrick, in Washington. After a significant delay he was informed that the Secretary was in conference but might possibly be reached at his home after seven o'clock. So far, so good—or bad. Secretary Hendrick did not want a call from John Spada entered on his office log.

His next call was to Mike Santos, who, if he kept to the traditional schedule, would have fifteen minutes to spare before the six o'clock session in the operations room. On this line, too, there was a delay; but Kitty Cowan explained it.

"Visitors, chief. A couple of buttoned-down boys from the Defense Investigative Service."

"What's the subject?"

"Security of defense projects, they say. They want an update on custody measures for documents and precautions for access to high-security areas in our plants. . . . At least that's the documentation I've been passing through."

"How long have they been there?"

"About an hour. They should be going in a minute. Mike was very firm that they had to be out by five forty-five. . . . How are things with you, chief?"

"So-so. Teresa and Rodo are mending slowly, but Anna's feeling the strain. So am I."

"We miss you around here. Why don't you pass by and say hullo?"

"Not my style, Miz Cowan. You know that. Why don't you pass by and have dinner with me . . . say this evening?"

"It's a date. I'll be around about eight, after the briefing conference. . . . Hold on, the buttoned-down boys are just leaving. I'll put you through to Mike."

Mike Santos sounded frayed and out of humour with the world, but he made a brave attempt to be cordial.

". . . These boys are a real pain in the ass, John. They're always so dead serious you'd think they had a private line to God."

"Any problems?"

"Not really. Our security systems check out pretty well. They've got minor complaints on the custody of fissionable material; but their principal interest seemed to be in you."

"Oh?" Spada was alert and cautious. "What sort of questions were they asking?"

"Recent activities abroad—which I told them were none of my business. Possible future services for the company—I told them you had agreed to be on call for counsel and advice at any time. They asked in what areas. I told them right across the board—but, specifically and as of now, I needed your help on the reorganization of Raymond Serum Laboratories. Which, by the way, I do."

"What was their reaction?"

"They hemmed and hawed and asked whether we still wanted top secret clearance for you. I told them yes, most definitely, and we wanted it current at all times."

"Thanks, Mike."

"¡De nada! . . . And while we're talking, would you make time to talk about the Raymond Laboratories? I've been screening candidates to take over when old man Raymond moves out, but mostly they're second-rate material."

"If you like, I'll move in for a while and reorganize the place for you."

"I'd be grateful—but it's a hell of a lot to ask of an ex-president."

"Not at all. It's a new field for me." Spada laughed. "And you can make a little sermon on it at the next executive conference. All for one, one for all, that sort of thing. Besides, I bought the outfit; the

229

least I can do is hand it to you in good shape. . . .
What about lunch next Monday?"

"Can do."

"Any other problems?"

"None that won't keep. Thanks, John. See you
Monday."

As he put down the phone, Spada was frowning.
He had no illusions about the activities of America's
Hounds of God and their sidelong sniffing through the
undergrowth of business and politics. As Maury Feldman had once put it: they raised a lot of false
scents, but they also found a lot of truffles. Once
they had established his connection with a revolutionary group, his file would be upgraded to active.
He would be subject to constant surveillance, and
the Proteus network might very easily be compromised.

He poured himself a drink and waited, with growing impatience, until it was time to call Secretary
Hendrick. It was nearly eight before he was able
to make the connection. The Secretary was agreeable
but a shade more formal than usual.

"What can I do for you, John?"

"I hear there's some flak flying around. I'd like to
come down and talk to you about it."

"I wouldn't recommend that, at least not at this
time. You've put me in a rather embarrassing situation."

"Can you specify, Mr. Secretary?"

"Yes. The Argentines are pressing for your extradition to stand trial on charges of conspiracy to
commit armed violence, to effect a jailbreak, and
complicity in the murder of an army officer. We asked
them to submit evidence. Fortunately for you, it's circumstantial and some of it was exacted under duress.

We've advised them that it would not stand up under American legal process. However, they filed a lot of information with the local bureau of the C.I.A., most of which ended up on my desk and was passed, as a matter of routine, to the F.B.I. It doesn't show you in a very good light, John."

"Can I ask you what you would have done in my place?"

"Fortunately, I haven't had to answer that question, but I'm sure you understand I can't let personal feelings confuse my political judgment."

"Naturally. May I ask another question?"

"Go ahead."

"This one is very personal. It touches me and my family. Am I being set up?"

"By this department, no. By your own company, possibly. By the boys in Buenos Aires, very probably."

"And I couldn't count on any official intervention?"

"None at all—unless you could demonstrate a clear threat or were prepared to offer, shall we say, a great deal of viable intelligence material."

"I doubt that would be possible."

"I thought as much."

"But I'll give you a personal assurance: I am not engaged in subversive activity against the United States."

"I never believed you were." There was a faint note of humour in the Secretary's tone. "But that doesn't help either of us very much, does it?"

"I guess not. Anyway, I'm grateful—very grateful —for your frankness."

"Just so you don't ask for a repeat performance. I've got more hot potatoes than I can handle. Take care, eh?"

"I'll take care," said John Spada flatly. "Thanks, Mr. Secretary."

It was a cold and comfortless farewell to an old friend; but he had no time to brood on it, because he wanted to call Anna at the Bay House, and there would scarcely be time to shave and change before Kitty Cowan arrived for dinner.

"It smells, chief! It smells like rotten fish!" Kitty Cowan was perched on the bar stool, flipping olive stones at his best Matisse. "The Argentines hate your guts, that's natural; but someone inside the company, that makes me want to puke!"

"Hendrick wouldn't have said it without a reason. Remember, he's seen the documents."

"But what can anybody inside the company say? The only people who really know your private affairs are Maury Feldman and myself. Even Mike Santos doesn't know as much as we do."

"They don't have to know, Kitty. All they need to do is suggest that there may be grounds for a security investigation. The F.B.I. and the Defense Investigative Service do the rest. They're not mounting a court case, remember. They're just compiling information—at this stage anyway."

"But what's the point, if they can't use the information?"

"Oh, they can use it all right!" Spada busied himself with another batch of drinks. "It's the oldest technique in the book, and it's still the most effective. First you isolate the victim, then you pull the switches on him, cut off his power supply, spread reports that he's under investigation. Then it's as if he's got the plague or the pox. Nobody wants to know him anymore."

"But why? How can anyone hurt you? You've stepped out of the presidency. With your fortune, you can buy and sell half the people in this country."

"It's not money, Kitty. It's power, influence, the ability to create and direct situations—and that's a question of personal credit and credibility. Try this for size. I stepped down in favour of Mike Santos. But I still hold enough stock—almost enough—to fight my way back if I wanted to do it. . . . When I brought Rodo out from Argentina, the press, who are Rodo's colleagues, made me into a folk hero, a kind of Scarlet Pimpernel. It wasn't a role I wanted, but the media created it for me. So in business I was alive again. In politics, too, if I wanted to throw my hat in the ring. It was Wild West stuff, the old frontier. There was a new hero in town . . . and a lot of people got scared or jealous or both."

"Like who?"

"Like Max Liebowitz perhaps?"

"Oh, brother! Do you think he'd stoop to this? It's a kind of murder, isn't it?"

"It could be real murder, girl. This isn't duck shooting. You don't have to put up posters to say it's open season. . . . Besides, there's this new publishing thing. There are a lot of people who don't want it to happen."

"Do you have to go ahead with it?"

"Anna asked me the same question. The answer's yes."

"Why?" She looked at him with grave, troubled eyes. "Why does it have to be you?"

"Because if I don't do it, I'll be ashamed every day of my life. Simple as that."

"Simple for you. What about the people who love you—and that includes me, John Spada?"

"Teresa answered that one, though she's probably forgotten what she said: 'This is the horror they make. Even love is a weapon in their hands.' Don't you see, girl . . . ?" He reached across the bar and laid a gentle hand on her cheek. "That's an intolerable brutality! I'd rather die than submit to it. You're a good Jewish girl. You, of all people, ought to understand."

She put his hand to her lips and kissed it.

"You're a very rough man, John Spada . . . And don't kid yourself about Jewish girls. We scare just as easily as the goyim."

"Dinner is served, sir," said Carlos from the door.

For the rest of the week he was busy, day and night, with the affairs of Poseidon Press, which he had installed on two floors of a new office development on Third Avenue. As director, he had appointed a Canadian-Scot, Andrew Maclean, who had had twenty years of experience in the publication of trade directories, biographical indexes, almanacs and encyclopedias. He was a longtime member of Proteus and had established the first cells of the organization in Ottawa and Montreal. The second key person was a Hungarian, Lajos Forman, whom he had lured away from I.B.M. to install the computer hardware and design the programming operation. Forman also had the responsibility for screening and training the operators, while Maclean would organize the gathering and sifting of intelligence and the hiring of translators and editorial staff.

Even in its embryo stage, it was a costly operation and the variety of planning details was daunting. Maclean, however, was a stubborn and meticulous general, who knew exactly what he wanted.

". . . Let's get it right from day one, John, because afterwards there'll be very little margin for error. First there's the source material, journals, bulletins, magazines, newspapers in all languages. There'll be reports from organizations like Amnesty, Red Cross, religious aid groups. That means a big staff. Then there's the material from our Proteus people—secret and highly sensitive. They'll have to get it out of their own countries and then here to us in New York. How do you propose to cope with that?"

"Let's express it by example," said John Spada. "Take a risky area like Russia, where there's heavy surveillance, strict censorship and high risk to our members. At this moment we've got about a hundred Proteus people scattered through the Soviet Union. We've got one man in the Politburo. About a dozen of the others are diplomats, and three or four are connected with foreign construction projects. These people are our exit channels. They receive information from their local groups and pass it to their nearest outside contact. From Leningrad, for example, the stuff goes to Tallinn and then, by tourist ferry, to Helsinki. From Helsinki it comes to the U.S.—but not to New York. Helsinki's correspondent is in Boston."

"It's a long way round," said Maclean dubiously.

"It's a safe way," said John Spada. "Remember, we're not running a newspaper. We're building records. Time is far less important than accuracy."

"Let's accept that for the moment. The information arrives in the U.S.—Florida, Boston, San Francisco, wherever. Now it has to come to New York. Where is it delivered? I hate the idea of all that explosive data landing in one place in a postbag."

"It doesn't. There's a courier service. It comes in by hand."

"Christ! You'll be spending a mint of money."

"I've got enough for three lifetimes, Mac. I can't take it with me."

"Aye." Maclean sighed unhappily. "But let's see if we can put it to better use, eh? Now, who's holding all the contacts together?"

"Heads of local groups, who report to an area chief, who ultimately reports to me."

"And how do you know it's he reporting, and not some police agent?"

"There's a built-in recognition sign."

"What happens if—God forbid!—you drop dead in the street?"

"My deputy takes over."

"And how will we know him?"

Spada undid the buttons of his shirt and showed him a gold chain hung around his neck. Suspended from the chain was a religious medallion and a gold-plated key. On the thumb grip was engraved the symbol of the fish in the box.

"He'll show you the mate of this," said John Spada. "It's the key to the safe-deposit where the Proteus records are kept."

"That's a lot of trust you're giving me," said Maclean gravely.

"In this job you'll earn it," said Spada. "Once we

236

start to publish, your life will be on the line every day. . . . Now, let's talk some more about security. Who's going to screen your staff?"

"Denman Calder. They're expensive but reliable. They also have pretty good relations with government agencies."

"Which is more than we have; and as a private intelligence group, we're not going to get any more popular."

"I wouldn't be so sure of that." Maclean was more optimistic than he had expected. "Once they find that our stuff is accurate, they'll be very happy to have it. . . . Oh, you realize we're going to need microfilm as well as computer storage? I never like relying on a single system . . . and I'd also recommend we keep a vault somewhere with duplicate records."

"I've already rented one from Union and Chemical."

"With our own locking system, I hope?"

"That, too, Mac."

"It's a pleasure to work with a thorough man. . . . This is a specimen of the record cards we'll keep on each subject. This is how Lajos will program it for the computer. You'll note that all the information is graded for reliability, and the sources are coded for internal reference only. Now, here's a mock-up of three publications: a monthly bulletin, a quarterly summary, classified by countries, and two yearly black books, one on prisoners of conscience, the other on known practitioners of terror and institutional brutality. This is our initial circulation list . . ."

It was all first-rate work and he was immensely heartened by it; but there was still something missing.

There was a flaw in the grand design that he knew existed but still could not identify, until, during his weekend sojourn at the Bay House, Rodolfo Vallenilla pointed it out to him.

It was the tag end of a bright, warm day and he was sitting in the pavilion with Rodo, while Anna and Teresa picked lavender and rose blooms for the pomanders which Anna made as presents to her friends. Rodo was brighter now, though he still looked pitifully pale and shrunken. He had written four or five pages and seemed pleased with what he had done.

He said, "You know, John, I believe I have discovered the key to open my mind again. All this time I have been trying to write an indictment . . . a bill of terrible particulars on what is going on in my country and around the world. Today I set it aside. I was too weary to continue the argument. Instead, I tried to remember the good things that had happened in prison. It was strange how many there were: old Pascarelli with his cigarettes and his vitamin pills, Chavez with his strong arms supporting me back to the cell, that strange boy in the infirmary who fed me soup that he made himself . . . my comrades in the prison yard defying the guns to protect me. . . . It was a relief to think about them. I could write without feeling tired. Then a new thought came to me. Evil is so monotonous and charity is such a sweet surprise . . ."

"I know what you mean," said John Spada.

"I wonder if you do, John." The challenge took Spada by surprise. "I was very like you in some ways. For me the typewriter was always a weapon—a

238

sword against the ungodly. Now I am not sure whether I flourished it bravely or brazenly. . . . Oh, I gave good witness, I know that, necessary witness too, just as you are trying to do now with your new press. But I asked myself today if perhaps even good people are so hardened to obscenity that it does not touch them anymore, and whether the only thing that will open their minds is innocence: the smile of a sleeping child, an old grandmother dozing in the sun. You are publishing documents of indictment. Should you not publish the good things too, light small candles in the dark . . . ?"

"Why don't you write them for me, Rodo?"

Vallenilla shook his head sadly.

"You know, and I know, John, that whatever I do now will be very small. But there are others, many others. Let it be known that you are looking for them. They will come to you. . . . How did you attract your Proteus people in the first place? You told them you wanted to build bridges of benevolence. Those are your words, John, not mine."

"If you'll point the way, Rodo, I'll walk it, as far as I can. But don't forget, the evil is still there."

"I know—and part of what I say is an excuse for my own weakness, but not all of it. Believe that, John! Believe it!"

He wanted to believe. Rodo's sober admonition had touched him almost to tears. It was a testament from two loved ones who had been to hell and back. He did not want to gainsay it. He would try to put it into practice; but there was in him now a hard core of skepticism. In the walled garden of the Bay House a man could see visions and dream dreams;

but outside, in the big, wide, wonderful world of ordinary folk, there were snipers on the rooftops and butchers in the rooms of the Fun Palace.

On Monday he lunched with Mike Santos and afterwards drove to Wilton to take a first look at the headquarters of Raymond Serum Laboratories—a sprawl of outdated buildings grouped around a central administration block which looked more like an army barracks than a modern serological institute.

The history of the corporation was a common one: a steady expansion from a narrow base of family-held capital, a good production record, but an old-fashioned and wasteful administration, an aging founder with a son who was a brilliant researcher, an executive body hamstrung by years of regimentation. It was the kind of situation which Spada liked. He could buy in cheaply, inject liquid capital, reform the management, raise the stock value and then either sell out or stay in at will.

This time, however, there were added attractions. He was eager for activity. The field of serum research and production was new to him. He had the chance to set out a copybook operation, without the burdens and distractions of high corporate responsibility. Besides, with a good research staff there was always the possibility of a breakthrough that would make medical history.

Old man Raymond was a genial guide—eager to quit, but still enthusiastic about the work itself and happily proud of his son's talent. The younger man was at first withdrawn and cautious; but Spada drew him out with promises of new research facilities and capital enough to buy new talent for the team.

The young man was frank about his own short-comings. He knew nothing of finance, but he could direct research. He had recently identified a variant of the Boise Type A botulinus, which had remained stable through a whole series of cultures. He was still trying to determine whether the variant was an existing strain or whether it had mutated under specific laboratory conditions.

Spada was intrigued. The botulinus bacillus was one of those designated in military handbooks for possible use in biological warfare. Its toxic effect was high. The mortality rate was more than 50 percent and the incubation period minimal. The antitoxin was available but could normally be produced only in the later or less severe cases of an outbreak.

This discussion led naturally to a question of major policy. Raymond Laboratories had always refused to accept any government contracts associated with biological warfare. Young Raymond himself was a resolute defender of this position. Did Spada intend to change it?

Spada assured him he did not. There was enough horror in the world without that one. However, he was interested to know what precautions were taken against the dissemination of the bacillus, the theft of cultures from a laboratory or from a consignment in transit. They were, it seemed, rather elementary. Laboratory rules were strict, of course. There were the usual burglar alarms and a security patrol. Dispatches were made in padded and sealed boxes, and there were shipping agents who specialized in the handling of laboratory specimens. Apart from that, young Raymond shrugged off the issue. The market was too restricted to encourage thieves. Research documents were much more vulnerable than the cultures themselves. . . .

It was almost seven in the evening before Spada had finished his inspection. He accepted an invitation to take coffee with the old man, then drove back to New York with a pocket full of notes and the conviction that Spada Consolidated had made a very good buy indeed.

When he reached the apartment he was surprised to find Anna waiting for him. She was bored at the Bay House. She thought Teresa and Rodo would be better alone for a while. Besides, she missed her man and needed to be with him. Spada was delighted. He too was bored with his own company, suddenly aware of the swift passage of time and the waste of gentle hours.

As he walked into the lounge with his arm around Anna's shoulder, he noticed a package on the hall table. He picked it up. It was a large manila envelope, addressed to Mr. John Spada, marked PERSONAL DOCUMENT—URGENT. He put it down again and asked, "When did this come?"

"Just after seven," Anna told him. "The hall porter brought it up."

Spada felt a faint prickle of unease. Corporation documents were not normally delivered through the doorman. A Spada messenger brought them to the apartment and required a signed receipt. Spada went to the telephone and dialled Kitty Cowan's home number.

"Kitty? John. Did you send me any documents this evening?"

"No." Kitty was obviously puzzled. "Mike didn't

either. I cleared all his mail personally before I left. What sort of documents are they?"

"I haven't opened the envelope yet."

"It didn't come from us."

"O.K. That's all. I'll check around in the morning. Have a pleasant evening." He cut the connection abruptly.

Anna asked, "Is something wrong, John?"

"I don't know, Anna." He was silent for a moment, then he said quietly, "Ring for Carlos, please."

"But, John . . ."

"Do as I ask, Anna!"

When Carlos presented himself, Spada gave him curt, precise directions.

"I want you to take the staff and Mrs. Spada and buy them all dinner at the Restaurant du Midi. I'll call the restaurant and tell you when I want you back."

"But, sir, the dinner is ready to be served here."

"I know; but just do as I ask. Turn off the cookers and get the staff ready."

"Yes, sir." He went out puzzled and unhappy.

Anna demanded: "John, please! What is all this?"

"That envelope. It didn't come from Kitty or Mike Santos. I want the police to have a look at it—and I want you all out of the apartment. I'll wait till the police get here."

"Oh God!" Anna was suddenly ashen. "Will this madness never end?"

"Hurry!" said John Spada.

When they were gone, he picked up the telephone and called the police.

". . . This is Mr. John Spada of Spada Consolidated Holdings. A package has just been delivered to my apartment. I have reason to believe it may contain explosives. Can you send someone over to this address, please . . . ?"

There was a pause while the police operator copied the address, then a faintly skeptical question: "Can you give me the reason for your suspicions, sir?"

"Yes. I'm a well-known businessman, with political connections which cannot be discussed on a telephone."

"Thank you, sir. I'll have someone there within minutes. Don't touch the package. Close the room and get as far away as possible."

Five minutes later two men from the Bomb Squad presented themselves at the apartment. They were brusque and taciturn. Depositions could wait. They took possession of the package and went away, admonishing him to wait by the telephone. Half an hour later one of them called back.

"Mallard here . . . Bomb Squad. That package was a live one, Mr. Spada. Half a pound of plastic, with two detonators primed to explode as soon as the envelope was opened."

"Any idea where it came from?"

"Not yet. We're checking for fingerprints. We'll probably find the only ones we get are from innocent handlers. We'll need a statement from you, of course."

"Could it wait till morning?"

"It's your life, Mr. Spada." He sounded as though he did not value it very highly.

"You've already got all the facts. The rest is speculation. I can tell you, however, that the matter will probably fall under the jurisdiction of the F.B.I."

"That's for us to decide after we have your deposition. We'll expect you here at ten tomorrow."

"I'll be there. And thanks."

"Our pleasure, Mr. Spada. Oh, if you're going out tonight, be careful. Whoever delivered that bomb may be waiting around for the bang!"

The line went dead. He debated a moment whether to call Teresa at the Bay House, then decided against it. The night guards were on duty; the most he could do was counsel extra vigilance. He called the restaurant and spoke briefly with Anna, telling her to finish her meal at leisure. No, he would not join them. There were details to be dealt with. Details! When he put down the telephone he found that he was shaking, as if with malaria. He crossed to the bar, poured himself a slug of neat liquor, drank half of it in a gulp and then sat, hunched over the counter, cupping the glass in his hands until the trembling stopped.

There was no escape now from the bleak reality. The contract on his life had been issued. The assassins were abroad. And they cared not at all whom they cut down with him.

9

◇◇◇◇◇◇◇◇◇◇◇◇◇◇◇◇◇◇◇◇◇◇◇◇◇◇◇◇◇◇◇◇

The new Director of the F.B.I. was, unlike some of his predecessors, a man of mild manners and faintly academic charm. He apologized for calling Spada to Washington, but he believed that there were certain aspects of the case best discussed, as it were, between principals. Spada was happy to agree the proposition. The Director suggested that they check, together, matters of fact in the files. Spada thought that, too, might be a good idea.

"First," said the Director, "we accept, as a prime possibility, that the contract on your life was let in Argentina. There is a secondary possibility which we can examine later. So if you will permit me to lead to you . . ."

"By all means."

"Did you, at any time, have connections with the South American Revolutionary Junta, and specifically with a man called El Tigre?"

"Yes. I paid him two hundred thousand dollars for the cooperation of one of his groups in Buenos Aires. I am not prepared to disclose the names of any members of that group."

"But with their assistance you planned the release of your son-in-law and of a man called Chavez."

"Yes."

"Were you party to the death of the prison commandant, Colonel Ildefonso Juarez?"

"No. When I last saw him, he was very much alive."

"Did you import any help of your own into Argentina?"

"Yes. Again I will not specify names or numbers."

"How did you enter the country?"

"Illegally."

"Quite." The Director permitted himself a faint scholarly smile. "So there is ample motive for your elimination by agents of the regime?"

"Yes."

"Are you aware that, after the jailbreak, members of the prison staff were questioned intensively by the security forces?"

"I wasn't aware of it; but yes, it would be normal procedure."

"One of the persons questioned was a prison orderly called Corporal Pascarelli."

"I've never heard of him."

"He confessed to passing a message to Rodolfo Vallenilla. The message said, in Spanish: 'A fish in a box.' Does that mean anything to you?"

"Nothing."

"That's very curious."

"Why?"

"Something very like it cropped up in a C.I.A. report from Amsterdam. Our people there maintain close liaison with the Dutch authorities on terrorist activities."

247

"I imagine they do."

"You yourself were in Amsterdam, were you not?"

"Yes. I flew there from Munich to see one of our shipping contractors, Jan Pieter Maartens."

"Shortly after your visit, the body of a German terrorist, Gebhardt Semmler, was discovered in an artist's studio in Amsterdam. The evidence pointed to suicide. In his wallet the police found a card embossed with a symbol that looks like a fish in a box." The Director picked out of the file a photostat of the Proteus card and laid it in front of Spada. "Does that suggest anything to you?"

"I'm afraid not."

"Perhaps we could ask your son-in-law about the fish message."

"You stay the hell away from him." Spada's control snapped. "He's had enough for two lifetimes!"

The Director shrugged and turned again to his file.

"There's another curious coincidence. The same Corporal Pascarelli admitted to passing a different message to the prisoner Chavez. This message said: 'The tiger is sniffing around.' You do see my point, Mr. Spada? Why the fish for one and the tiger for the other?"

"I see it very clearly. I'm afraid I can't help you to elucidate it."

"Then let me put before you another possibility: that the people who want to kill you may not be from Argentina at all but may be connected in some way with El Tigre."

"I can't see why. I honoured the deal I had made with him."

"Well . . ." The Director let the word hang in the

air for a moment. Then he changed direction altogether. "What identity did you use in Argentina?"

"A fictitious one."

"Supported, of course, by documents?"

"Of course."

"How did you procure the documents?"

"I paid a very high price for them."

"Mr. Spada. We are trying to protect your life and the lives of your family."

"Correction! You are doing nothing of the kind. You're fishing for information to fill out files originating from the C.I.A., which has no jurisdiction over internal security in the United States. I admit freely to committing illegal acts in the confines of another sovereign state, which itself had committed abominations against my daughter and her husband. I'd do it all again—and worse, if I had to! So would you! Let's stop playing games. What protection can you offer me?"

"Very little, I'm afraid," said the Director coolly. "We're light on personnel, light on information. I suggest you hire your own bodyguards. There are people who supply such services. Some of them are very good . . . . Oh, there's one more question. Were you not a witness to the killing of the philosopher Hugo von Kalbach in Munich?"

"I was. I was going to the opera with him."

"But you did not stay for the funeral."

"The German police asked me to leave—for my own safety."

"You'll be interested, then, to know that the man who killed him was Gebhardt Semmler, who later suicided in Amsterdam."

"Then I hope he's rotting in hell," said John Spada.

"If you'll forgive me, Director, I think we're wasting each other's time."

He had one more call to make before he went to pick up Anna at the hotel. This time his reception was cordial. He might have called it effusive—except that Anatoly Kolchak tempered it with his habitual irony.

Closeted with Spada in his private study, he said, "My friend, I was deeply distressed to hear what happened to your daughter and her husband. Will you please convey my sympathies to your wife."

"Thank you, Mr. Ambassador."

"And I offer you, if I may, an expression of personal respect for what you have done. When I read the details, I confess I felt a very undiplomatic excitement. I was also glad you were operating in Buenos Aires and not in Moscow."

"We were lucky. We were also too late."

"You will not easily be forgiven."

"They want my life," said Spada flatly. "They sent me a letter bomb a couple of days ago."

"And they will keep trying, of course. Governments are very sensitive about insults to their majesty. I am happy that our comrades were able to be of service to you."

"You heard about that?"

"We hear almost everything, my friend. I am prompted to ask whether you need any help now. This time there will be no charge. You did us a service too."

"I still want Lermontov," said John Spada.

"Oh yes, Lermontov." The Ambassador polished his spectacles assiduously with a silk handkerchief and set them back on his nose. "I regret—I sincerely regret—to tell you that question is now closed, irrevocably. The news is not yet public, but Lermontov died last week."

"Still in confinement?"

"Unhappily, yes."

"Then, as you say, the question is closed."

"Not quite, Mr. Spada. I am directed—and I use the word deliberately so as not to involve our personal relationship, which I value highly—I am directed to say that, in return for your personal assistance in certain business transactions still pending, other Jewish intellectuals would be considered for early emigration. . . . There now, my duty is done. All I need to do is minute your reply."

"*Nyet!*" said Spada with a grin. "*Nyet. Nyet.*"

"I'm delighted." Anatoly Kolchak relaxed. "I am forced to deal with idiots. But there is some method in their insanity. In this trade everyone gets corrupted—even if it is only a little."

"Tell me something, Mr. Ambassador."

"Anything." Kolchak gave him a boyish, mischievous grin. "Except the Soviet order of battle and the date of Judgment Day!"

"What's the thing you're most afraid of?"

"Politically or personally?"

"Both."

Kolchak considered the question for a long, silent moment, then pieced out his answer, phrase by phrase.

"It is a thing which has already happened, whose consequences are already upon us. We have so debased human language that it is impossible any longer to believe what we hear or read. I tell you 'yes'; the echo answers 'no.' We state one position and negotiate another. You talk 'food'; I hear 'bombs.' We

have created a language of the mad. You show on
television bodies broken in a railway accident. The
next instant some impossibly beautiful wench is dem-
onstrating how to make floors shine like glass. The illusion is complete. There are no bodies. There never
could be blood on so bright a surface. . . ."

"And the consequence, Mr. Ambassador?"

"That which you have experienced, my friend.
Reason is out the window. There is left only the black
magic of violence, and even then the language of the
mad foments it . . . 'brushfire war,' 'limited actions,'
'clean atom bombs'! We are all guilty because we
all cooperate with the illusionists. . . . Oh, I know!
If they heard me talk like this in Moscow they would
want my head; but it is still the truth. . . ." He broke
off, as if embarrassed, and continued on another
train of thought altogether. "Tell me, my friend, now
that you know your life is in danger, what do you
propose to do?"

"Ask you one more question, Mr. Ambassador. It
arises out of a statement made to me half an hour
ago by the Director of the F.B.I. Is there, in your
view, any possibility that my assassins are not from
Argentina at all but from the South American Revolutionary Junta?"

The Ambassador considered the question for a
moment and then smiled grimly.

"He's very clever, your Director. The Americans
are much more comfortable in bed with dictators than
with revolutionary governments. It pays your Director to suggest a scapegoat from the left. . . . My first
answer is no. You are not in danger from the Revolutionary Junta. On the other hand, we are no more
one big happy family of comrades. We pursue a

dozen different roads. So don't take my verdict as gospel. Let me ask you: is there any reason why the Revolutionary Junta should want your head?"

"None that I know," said Spada. "Unless the security boys in Argentina invented one and fed it back."

"Always possible," said Kolchak. "That is the madness of which I speak. Let me make some inquiries and get back to you."

"Thank you, Mr. Ambassador."

"I am sorry about Lermontov."

"At least he's out of the madhouse!"

"While you and I, my friend, have to try to stay sane inside it. Good luck!"

"Amore?"

"Che c'è?"

"Do we have to go out to dinner?"

"No. What do you want to do?"

"Stay in bed with you."

It was the time after the act of love, and they were lying, folded drowsily in one another, in a hotel bed in Washington, D.C.

Spada turned his face to her breasts and said softly, *"Sto tanto contento, tanto tranquillo."*

"Anch'io amore . . . tanto tranquilla. . . ." When we booked in, I hated the room. Now I don't want to leave it."

"It's good to be alone together."

"Dolce come zucchero!"

"Femmina! Sei tutta femmina, Anna mia."

"I like talking Italian with you."

"You always used to—in bed."

"Eh! When you gave me time to talk! . . ."

253

"We have to talk soon, Anna."

"About what?"

"How we're going to arrange our lives."

"There's nothing to talk about." She anchored him close to her with arms and legs. "I've thought about it over and over. We go on living the way we always did. I don't want guards and cameras and alarm bells by our bedside. I know! I was scared before, but not now. Life's too short for all that. Let's enjoy it—just like we're doing now. . . ."

"Hey! This is something new. What's happened?"

"While you were out I called Uncle Andrea in Rome. I told him all the things that were happening and how worried I was. First he scolded me. He said no woman had the right to rob her husband of his manhood. Then he told me how things were in Italy right now, with the shootings and the kidnappings— more than one a week. He said: 'Anna, remember something. A parasite in the blood, a clot in an artery, can kill you quicker than a bullet. But the worst enemy of all is fear. . . .' Waiting for you here, I thought about that. I remembered that my being afraid stopped us making love, made me into a woman I hated, and in the end you would have hated her too. . . . So we go on, amore! You do what you want. We have our good times together. We go to the theater, the concerts, the opera like always. Teresa and Rodo will arrange themselves. We cannot always be their nurses. . . . *Capisci, amore? C'è il mio cuore che parla.*"

"*Son tanto grato.*"

"*Come grato? Ti lo debo, marito mio.*"

"There are no debts between us. Just love."

"Like this?"

"Oh yes, yes . . . !"

But even in the long, sweet aftermath he could not tell her that the Scarecrow Man sat watch in the lobby, while Major Henson, swarthy and taciturn, prowled the corridors with the house detectives.

Oddly enough, it was the Scarecrow Man—that least domesticated of humans—who showed him how he must profit from the change in his family situation. In a brief, furtive conference before they left Washington he explained: ". . . Now you must rid yourself of the siege mentality. You have taken all possible precautions. Go about your business in the normal fashion. Stop looking over your shoulder, because, truly, you will see nothing. You must learn to trust Henson and myself, even when we are not visibly present. This is our trade, remember, and you will agree that we are good at it. . . . But once you accept that there are no guarantees, you will live much more calmly. . . ."

Spada nodded a sober agreement, then asked: "How do you assess the risk to my family?"

"Small." The Scarecrow Man was definite. "In Europe we should have to be concerned with kidnapping. But here it is less fashionable and the end less profitable. There is, in my view, more danger for your wife than for your daughter and son-in-law. They are in a sense already disposed of, out of the battle. To attack them again would be counterproductive—bad propaganda. No! You are still the prime target!"

"For how long?"

The Scarecrow Man shrugged. "Who knows?

Years perhaps. Think how long Stalin waited to have Trotsky killed. I'm afraid you have to wear this sort of thing like a peptic ulcer . . . bland food, bland thoughts and as much good humour as you can command."

"You're a real Job's comforter," said Spada with a grin.

"Comfort's another business. I'm paid to keep you alive."

"I may want you to start travelling again soon . . . contact with the Proteus groups. I'll want them to start feeding us information on a regular basis."

"How soon?"

"A month, six weeks."

"The later the better," said the Scarecrow Man. "I need time to build a screen around you—and I have to have people I can trust. Henson's a good organizer, but he thinks like an Anglo-Saxon."

"And you?"

"I told you when we first met, Mr. Spada. I am a mathematical man. I understand everything and feel nothing at all."

It was a chilling thought—but there was still a grain of hope in it. Anatoly Kolchak had spoken of a world controlled by illusionists. The Scarecrow Man had no illusions at all; yet, wondrously, he still had the courage to endure the bleak damnation of existence.

Immediately after their return to New York, Anna set about reviving their social life: a cocktail party for friends neglected too long, a series of theater nights and concerts at Lincoln Center. Teresa and

Rodo, they decided, should take over the Bay House. They needed the quiet and a separate place in which to work out a life together. Spada divided his week between the Poseidon Press and the Raymond Laboratories and an occasional discreet visit to the club, just to affirm that the plague was not really catching after all.

He found an ironic amusement in the confusion of his colleagues, who, having dismissed him either as a spent force or a tainted contact, were reminded of just how much equity he held in the market and how easily he could upset it if he chose. It was on one of these visits, with Maury Feldman and Mike Santos, that he had his first contact in months with Max Liebowitz. They had just sat down when Max passed by with a plate of salad in his hand, to take his place at the long table. Spada invited him to join them. He was obviously embarrassed, but he covered well and took the vacant seat. Maury Feldman made a joke of the event.

"It's good for the market, Max. All big voters of Spada Consolidated munching away in harmony. We'll be up three points before the close of business."

"I like us the way we are." Liebowitz decided to ignore the humour. "A little undervalued. That way none of our floaters are likely to dump stock for profit."

"I'm always a buyer, Max." Spada teased him quietly. "We've got a nice thing going for us with Raymond Laboratories."

"How nice?" Max stiffened like a pointer waiting for the game to fall.

"Well, we bought at fifteen. . . . Give me a few

more months, I'd say we'll be worth twenty-five. . . . Of course, my services come high."

"How much are we paying him?" Liebowitz turned to Maury Feldman, who laughed him down.

"Relax! Where's your sense of humour, Max?"

"I mislaid it." Liebowitz was irritated. He addressed himself to Mike Santos. "I hear we're not nearly as popular at the Pentagon as we used to be."

"Let me explain that," said Spada in the same mild fashion. "I talked to Secretary Hendrick and to the F.B.I. The suggestion was made that someone in the corporation was setting me up. You know, a call here and there, a discreet suggestion that I might be keeping the wrong company."

"Madness!" said Max Liebowitz irritably. "What bird is so stupid as to shit in its own nest?"

"But you see what happens, Max." Feldman laid a restraining hand on his wrist. "Once you make a man politically unpopular, you set him up like a target in a shooting gallery. You make it sound as though nobody cares what happens to him. . . . There's a contract out on Spada's life. Already he's had a letter bomb delivered to his home!"

Max Liebowitz was shaken. He set down his knife and fork and reached for a glass of water.

"And you say that this is arranged from inside the company?"

"No, Max." Spada explained patiently. "The two things are separate. The threat to me comes from outside, but it helps if I'm unpopular in my own hometown. You know this better than anyone. You support the Zionist lobby because you know that Mister Nice

Guy always gets a better shake than Mister Sour-puss."

"So you wonder who makes trouble for you in Washington?"

"Right."

"Not I," said Max Liebowitz. "In the board room, yes. That's business. But outside, no! I have said nothing to anyone. I swear it on my mother's grave."

"If you tell me that, I believe you, Max."

"I tell you."

"Then who's the enemy in the house?" asked Mike Santos.

"We don't know," said Maury Feldman. "Rumour is always a nameless child."

"We have to know." Max Liebowitz was excited again. "Someone spreads dirt at our door, it hurts us all! For instance, my information is we may lose out on our bid for the new Minotaur Guidance System."

"I didn't know that." John Spada was shocked. "I thought it was in the bag. Well, Mike?"

"Max exaggerates," said Mike Santos easily. "There are still two more committees to pass the bids."

"But we're in trouble in the first one, no?"

"Not trouble, John, a little heat, that's all."

"Another thing." Liebowitz was launched now into his bill of complaints. "The Norden Trust unloaded fifty thousand shares of Spada Consolidated this morning."

"Then I presume I bought 'em," said John Spada. "I've got firm orders out for any stock that comes on the market. Unless you beat me to it, Max."

"No, I didn't," said Max Liebowitz. "The deal

259

wasn't made on the floor. It was a private transaction with Morgan Guaranty as nominee for the
buyer."

"Norden Trust are supposed to be friends of ours."
Spada was puzzled and angry. "Why didn't they offer
to us first?"

"Or to me," said Max Liebowitz. "I do a lot of
business with them too."

"It seems to me"—Maury Feldman crumbled a
bread roll between his fingers—"with all respect, Mike,
we need a little more information than you're giving
us."

"I don't have it," said Mike Santos flatly. "I told
you, we're not too popular in Washington and I'm
trying to rebuild some bridges. As for the share transfer—hell!—it only happened this morning."

"My point," Maury Feldman persisted, "is that it
shouldn't have happened at all. You're paid to stay
on top of things like that."

"There are only twenty-four hours in the day,
Maury."

"Then delegate!" said Spada. "Let someone else
lick the stamps."

"Now hold it!" Santos flushed. "We've had certain
crises, remember? I didn't create them, but the mess
landed on my desk. I've been clearing it up as best
I can, but it all takes time and some pretty devious
diplomacy."

"Tell us about the Minotaur contract." Max
Liebowitz shovelled salad into his mouth. "What's the
holdup?"

"Security," said Mike Santos reluctantly. "They
want John's clearance lifted before they'll go to the

next committee stage. I've been fighting to keep it current."

"But you didn't tell me that," objected John Spada. "You gave me the impression that the matter was settled."

"And that's what I still hope will be the case."

"Hope is a cardinal virtue," said Maury Feldman dryly. "But it doesn't put butter on toast."

"You should have told me straight," said Spada. "I'm a big boy. I can spell the words on the wall of the john!"

"Me," said Max Liebowitz, "I'd like to know who's spreading the dirt and who's trading us out of our shares in a private market."

"If you'll excuse me," said Mike Santos curtly, "I don't like having my ears pinned back in the club! Thanks for the lunch, gentlemen!"

He crumpled his napkin on the table and walked away. The three men looked at each other. Max Liebowitz shook his head in mock sadness.

"Oy vay! Conan Eisler may not have so many brains, but he does know the rules of the game."

"I'm sure Mike knows them," said Maury Feldman. "I wonder if he's not trying to shade them a little."

"In whose favour?" asked John Spada.

"Fifty thousand shares." Max Liebowitz disposed of the last of his salad and mopped the dressing from his mouth. "It's a very nice packet to build on. I truly would like to know who's holding them."

As he rode uptown with Maury Feldman, Spada put his anxieties into words: "It's a hell of a note, Maury, but do you think Mike could be going sour on us?"

Feldman shrugged unhappily. "Men get drunk in high places. Sometimes they get illusions of grandeur."

"He lied to me about the security clearance."

"It's a bad word to use in law. I'd agree he gilded the proposition."

"And what about the shares? He should have known . . ."

"I'm wondering if he bought them himself."

"Fifty thousand at thirty-five dollars apiece. That's a million seven. No way he could raise it—besides, that's insider trading. We could send him up the river."

"If you could prove it—and in a nominee situation it's damn near impossible. Besides, as you say, a million seven is very, very rich . . . Unless someone else is footing the bill."

"I don't see it, Maury. What's he got to sell—or pledge for that matter?"

"You," said Maury Feldman softly. "You and Proteus. We know there's a market, don't we?"

"God Almighty! . . . But no! I can't believe it. We've never had a traitor yet."

"That's inflation for you. A really good Judas gets a lot more than thirty pieces of silver."

It helped sometimes to be flippant; it was a useful shorthand in which to deal with the complexities of a huge power structure like Spada Consolidated. But neither Spada nor Maury Feldman was prepared to discount the risks of a traitor—or even a too ambitious servant within the organization. The base was so broad, the information so valuable, the opportunities for action so diverse, that a venal executive could make millions out of a carefully planned malfeasance.

The danger to the Proteus organization was even

more acute. Mike Santos had not yet been called upon to participate in its activities, but the mere knowledge of its existence and its structure was a weapon in his hand. Spada and Feldman debated the problem for two hours while Maury's doodlings became more erotic and more fantastical.

Finally Spada summed up wearily: ". . . Item one: we may be doing Mike a grave injustice. Item two: he's gone rotten and we have to get rid of him. Item three: we don't need judicial proof—just enough to nail the indictment on his door and frighten him into telling us what game he's playing and with whom."

"So we investigate him."

"Leave that to me," said John Spada grimly. "Before I've finished, I'll know what goddam soap he uses in the bathtub!"

"And if he doesn't check out clean, we blow him out of the water."

"Better if he hangs himself," said John Spada. "I'll happily bury him in the potter's field."

The precarious calm which he had enjoyed since his return from Washington was shattered now. He was out of the eye of the hurricane and back in the boiling darkness of the storm. When he left Maury Feldman's office he walked the thirty blocks to his apartment, forcing himself to reason, steadying himself for the domestic encounters of the evening.

He would not tell Anna. There was no point in upsetting her with news that he still could not explain to himself. He thought of calling Kitty Cowan, the most obvious monitor of events in Spada Consolidated. Once again he decided on silence. Kitty's loyalties were long; but her temper was very short, and he could not risk a premature explosion in the glass tower. He needed cool counsel and a conspirator's finesse. So he stepped into a bar, called a Manhattan number and left a message for the Scarecrow Man.

When he reached the apartment, Anna was out. She had left a message saying that she was at the hairdresser and that she had arranged with Carlos to pick her up and drive her back. On his desk in the study there was a registered letter. The stamp and the postmark were Swiss, but the letter was handwritten by Kurt Deskau in Munich. Deskau's handwriting was tight and crabbed, the style prosaic and stilted, so that it took Spada some time to decipher the whole text. It was not an encouraging document.

My dear friend,

I break a good habit and put sensitive matters on paper. When you have read this, destroy it. I am paid as a policeman and not as a political journalist.

I have followed, in the European press, the accounts of your doings in Argentina. I rejoice that you were able to secure your son-in-law's release, though I am well aware of the risk you incurred and the dangers that must still threaten you. It is these dangers which prompt me to write.

I do not have to explain to you that police work has now become an international trade. All national forces communicate with one another, even though they do not expose all that they know. However, to the degree that we have common concerns, as with hijacking, terrorist

activities, drug-running, fugitive murderers or
grand thieves, we do cooperate.

I have been recently in Italy to confer with
the police on the Moro affair and the possible
involvement of German elements in the kidnap.
I have also been to Stockholm, Amsterdam,
Vienna and to a three-day international police
seminar in Paris. So I have picked up some important information. As a good clerk, I list it by
numbers.

First: you yourself have become notorious.
Everybody agrees that the Argentines were fools
to attack your family, but many are frightened
by the idea of an enormously wealthy man
meddling in the political underground. You will
smile when I say it, but criminals and police
have a very private life together, and they don't
like outsiders.

Second: you must know that you are in
personal danger from government agents. Nowhere in South America do they want freelance
subversion—especially not from someone they
call a renegade capitalist.

Third: you are also a target for the extremists of the left; not, I think, because they
suspect any connection between you and Gebhardt Semmler, but simply because they are
now turning their attention to the disruption of
international business and may well extend their
activities to the United States. We have seen
target lists of institutions and high executives.
Your name appears on most of them.

Fourth: the Proteus card which was found
in Semmler's wallet has excited much curiosity
among my European colleagues because it is in-
terpreted as the symbol of some new terror
group. I have always thought it was an indiscre-

tion on your part to leave the card. It was a theatrical act which I understood but would never myself have committed.

So far, no one has any idea of its real meaning, but the official interest will persist. Policemen are trained to be inquisitive about unexplained details. I myself see another danger. The symbol intrigues people. I ask myself what happens if an extremist group does adopt it and we of Proteus are blamed for their crimes. I know you command much loyalty, but no organization is wholly secure against indiscretion or defection. I beg you to think on this. If possible, we should meet and talk about it.

Finally, I am presuming you still retain the documents of Erwin Hengst. If you do not intend to use them again, I should like them returned. If you do, please be sure to inform me in advance, so that I can cover the situation here.

I wish I could tell you better news. Instead I report that, with Italy in such a mess, the prospect of a big swing to the right in Germany remains a constant possibility. I talked with a Russian at the seminar. He said: "You think we are too tough on dissenters. Wait till you try to sit on the lid of your own cook pot!" What could I say? Already our tails are burning.

I wish we may see each other soon. With friendliest greetings,

Kurt

Spada read the letter twice, then tore it into shreds and burned it in an ashtray. He wished to God the Scarecrow Man would call. There was now one hell of a lot to talk about.

The investigation of Mike Santos was planned and executed as finically as a piece of cerebral surgery. The margin of error was minimal, the risks enormous. A botched operation could damage irrevocably the reputation of an innocent man. An indiscreet revelation could send shock waves around the markets of the world. If the subject himself became aware of his situation, he could put the whole Proteus network in jeopardy. So, for the first time in years, the message was circulated through the North American network: "Proteus to the fishes . . . please supply all available information on Michael Santos. . . ."

A fish name in Morgan Guaranty set up a trace on nominee transactions in Spada stock. Another in Nassau began an elaborate search for trust deeds and new company registrations. An electronics expert came into the glass tower with the cleaners and installed an elaborate bugging system in Santos' office. His social engagements were plotted and monitored. His bank statements were copied. His domestic routine was scrutinized; his visits to doctor, dentist and hairdresser were logged.

Since Mike Santos was a very active man, it was an intelligence exercise of large dimension. Without Spada's money and the resources of the Proteus organization it would have been impossible to complete it within the two weeks Spada had prescribed. Finally, however, it was done; and while Anna went down to the Bay House to spend the weekend with Teresa and Rodo, Spada stayed in New York to discuss the report with Maury Feldman and the Scarecrow Man.

". . . It's an odd situation." Maury Feldman frowned over the close-typed pages. "Upside and downside, he's clean. All his financial records, including his tax returns, show prudent management of his known income. He doesn't gamble. He has only monthly debts. His family life appears to be stable. His telephone calls and correspondence fit the context of the business as we know it. . . ."

"Except for two things," said the Scarecrow Man. "Every Wednesday he stays in town. He has a permanent booking at the Regency. He plays squash at the Racquet Club—which is his excuse for the night away from home—then goes to an apartment on the East Side—you've got the address there—which is occupied by one Marina Altamira. He stays for an hour, then returns to the hotel, has a couple of drinks in the bar and goes to bed. The curious fact is that the lady is on the wrong side of sixty. . . ."

"What do we know about her?"

"Nothing, except what's in the report. She's the window of an Argentine businessman who died twenty years ago. She lives on investment income, administered by Morgan Guaranty. She's a naturalized citizen of the United States, and she works a couple of days a week in a small gallery selling primitive artifacts."

"And her connection with Santos?"

"We don't know yet. However, the next item is more revealing. Those fifty thousand shares of Spada stock . . . Here's the chain. They were marked out from Norden Trust to Morgan Guaranty, account client. The client in this case is Altamira Investments Limited, a company registered in Nassau, Bahamas. The shares in this company are owned by a trust, set up two months ago by Madame Marina Altamira for the benefit of one Michael Santos. We got a D and B report on the company. It is good for transactions up to two million dollars."

"And what was the origin of the funds?" The question came from John Spada.

The Scarecrow Man shrugged and spread his hands in a gesture of surrender.

"Anybody's guess! Mine is that they came to Nassau in a suitcase."

"So sometime in the last two months an Argentine widow makes Mike Santos richer by two million dollars. What's the consideration?"

"Sex?" asked Maury Feldman with a grin.

"No stud in the world is worth two million dollars." Spada was in no mood for jokes. "So what's the conclusion?"

"Maybe it is in the law of trusts itself," said the Scarecrow Man. "Mr. Feldman, you're the expert. Is it not correct that the trustee administers the funds at his or her own discretion? The beneficiary cannot legally direct the trust?"

"That's right."

"So may we not have a position where Mr. Santos can benefit only if and when he performs appropriate service?"

"Oh brother!" John Spada let out a long whistle of amazement. "What a sweet, sweet setup! We're paying our own assassin!"

"We haven't proved it yet," said Maury Feldman judicially.

"We won't," said the Scarecrow Man, "until we can put a bug in the lady's apartment—which is not as easy as it sounds. The place is locked and wired like a fortress. You know how it is in this city, especially with elderly ladies living alone. However, I've got Henson working on the project."

"Meantime, what do we do about Mike Santos?"

"Nothing." Spada was cold as a hanging judge. "It's tradition, isn't it? Even Judas was invited to the Last Supper before he picked up his thirty pieces of silver. We can hardly do less for Mr. Mike Santos."

"I have a dirty taste in my mouth," said Maury Feldman. "I'd like to be diverted. Two seats for *Trovatore* at the Met ... anybody interested?"

"I'll come," said John Spada. "I used to be very tender in '*Ai nostri monti.*'"

"Count me out," said the Scarecrow Man. "I'm afraid I find opera rather ridiculous. Besides, Henson is taking me to a restaurant called Sign of the Dove, where Madame Altamira always eats dinner on Saturday evenings. You'll be covered at the opera of course, Mr. Spada."

"And Mike Santos?"

"You'll find his routine in the report," said the Scarecrow Man. "Always on Saturday he plays golf, dines at the club with his wife and makes love to her afterwards. Would you like to hear the tapes?"

"If you find opera ridiculous," asked John Spada incredulously, "what about Mike Santos in heat?"

The curtain came down at a quarter to twelve. At midnight Spada and Feldman were strolling arm in arm across town, two middle-aged gentlemen regaling the passersby with a shaky rendition of '*Ai nostri monti.*' At one in the morning Spada was playing duets with the pianist in the Regency Bar, while Maury Feldman held earnest converse with a fashion buyer from Bonwit Teller. At two-thirty John Spada walked unsteadily into the foyer of his apartment building.

As he waved good night to the porter, two men converged on him.

"Mr. Spada?"

"The same. What can I do for you, gentlemen?"

"Police officers, Mr. Spada. I'm afraid we've got bad news for you."

The Bay House was gutted, a black and smouldering ruin in the light of the false dawn. The three bodies, charred beyond recognition, were laid on the terrace, enclosed in green plastic sacks. Beside them were six gasoline cans, half melted in the blaze.

It had happened, they told him, just after midnight. All the lights were out; the family had retired early. There were two security men on duty. One, working from the gatehouse, patrolled the road. The other walked the perimeter on the beach side. It was the man on the beach who first saw the flames. By the time he reached the house, the whole ground floor was ablaze and flames were licking up the creeper on the outside walls. There was no hope of rescue. The occupants—strange, neutral word!—the occupants had died in their beds. The place had been drenched with gasoline, and the arsonists—they had found traces of two intruders—had made an easy escape through the woodland on either side of the house. The detective in charge of the investigation insisted on explaining that death by fire was quicker than it seemed. The fire ate up the oxygen. Most people died quickly of suffocation. Spada turned away and vomited on the grass.

In their brusque, professional fashion they were kind to Spada. They sat him on the bench in the pavilion house and talked earnestly while the plastic

271

sacks were loaded into the ambulance. The medical examiner fished in his little bag and offered capsules to make him sleep. He was driven back to the city in a police car, and the officers waited until Carlos had settled him, passive as a child, in his bed and fed him the capsules. They called Maury Feldman as he asked; but before he arrived, John Spada was dead to the world.

It was the very excess of the horror that kept him sane. Reason recoiled from the effort to compass or explain it. No tears, no tirades, could purge it from the memory. So those who had business with John Spada in the immediate aftermath—the police, the coroner and his jury, journalists, colleagues, Kitty Cowan, the Scarecrow Man, Mike Santos—all marvelled at his granite calm. He accepted their condolences with grave courtesy. He answered questions with icy precision. He dispatched efficiently all the business that was laid before him, estate documents, letters to Anna's family, his own and Vallenilla's, preparations for the Requiem and the funeral, the daily affairs of Poseidon Press and Raymond Laboratories.

He did not weep. He showed no rage. He uttered no reproach. Whatever he felt—if indeed he felt anything at all—was hidden behind a grey, unsmiling mask, so that even Kitty and Maury Feldman found themselves shut out from his confidence.

At night he dined alone in his apartment. Then, when Carlos had retired, he went out and, in a small hotel on the West Side, closeted himself with the Scarecrow Man, poring over maps and gazetteers until the early hours of the morning. They were like blood brothers now, spawned from some cold planet far from the sun, absorbed in an intricate mathematic of retribution.

Yet however late the vigil, he presented himself, promptly at nine-thirty, at the offices of Poseidon Press. By one he was in Wilton, immersed in the problems of finding markets for the serums and the cultures developed by the younger Raymond.

Wherever he went, he carried, pinned in his breast pocket, a linen envelope in which was a strip of microfilm consigned to him by the fish man in Nassau. The microfilm was a copy of a document signed and witnessed two days after the fire at the Bay House. The document was entitled "Determination of a Deed of Trust," and it stated that Marina Altamira had vacated her office of trust and devolved to the beneficiary, Michael Santos, all the materia of the trust, to wit, the shares of Altamira Investments Limited. . . .

The tiny strip of film was the one warm thing in the icebound world of John Spada. It was as if what was left of his life reposed in it, as if, should he lose it, he must surrender himself to nothingness.

The day of the obsequies dawned warm and clear. Maury Feldman and Kitty Cowan rode with him in the limousine to St. Patrick's Cathedral, sat with him in the first pew, and felt his first reaction of shock at the sight of the three coffins, ranged side by side, in the sanctuary. Kitty wept quietly. Maury Feldman blew his nose violently and then bowed his head in his hands. Behind them, a whisper of pity rustled through the congregation of mourners who had come from all over the country to pay their respects to the dead and to memorialize John Spada's lost hopes of love and continuity. The Cardinal Archbishop intoned the antiphon: "Eternal rest grant to them, O Lord, and let perpetual light shine upon them."

John Spada tried to join in the response, but the words stuck in his throat. He tried to focus on the celebrant, but he could not take his eyes away from the three caskets on their brass stands. After a while they melted into a misty blur, while the chant of the ritual rose and fell with the monotony of waves on a winter beach.

The Cardinal's eulogy was eloquent but sterile: a careful, syncretic sermon, acceptable to folk of all beliefs and none, on the faith that failed not, the hope that made the only sense possible out of man's barbaric propensities, the charity that embraced even the evildoer. All the sting, which His Eminence meant for sweetness, was in the final peroration.

". . . And we pray for our brother, John Spada, that, in this his hour of desolation, he may be given the grace to bear his grief with courage, and the generosity to forgive those who have so brutally robbed him of his loved ones. We should not mourn for Anna, Teresa or Rodolfo. They are at peace now. Our care should be for John Spada, who has so much need of our fraternal support. . . . In the name of the Father, the Son and the Holy Spirit. Amen."

As they stood for the Creed, John Spada swayed on his feet. Maury Feldman put an arm around his shoulder to steady him. Kitty Cowan clasped his hand and whispered, "Hold on, John. It will soon be over."

But it was not soon; it was a whole eternity of irrelevant events: the blessing of the remains, the procession to the hearse, he helping to carry Anna's casket, and wondering that she felt so light, the long drive to the Gate of Heaven Cemetery in Westchester, the last envois, the first clods of earth tossed into the sepulchers. There was one moment of exquisite agony, when he saw Mike Santos facing him across Anna's grave and felt a fierce demonic urge to leap at him, kill him with bare hands and toss him into the gaping hole in the ground.

Then, at long last, it was over. Maury Feldman helped him into the limousine with Kitty and perched himself on the jump seat in front of them. As they drove out of the city of the dead, back into the land of the living, Maury said firmly: "Enough is enough, lover. We're not leaving you alone tonight."

"You're eating at my place," said Kitty Cowan. "I think we should all get drunk."

"It sounds like a good idea." John Spada nodded vaguely. "I can't seem to think straight anymore."

Then the dam burst. He leaned his head on her shoulder and cried helplessly all the way back to Manhattan.

10

◇◇◇◇◇◇◇◇◇◇◇◇◇◇◇◇◇◇◇◇◇◇◇◇◇◇◇◇◇◇◇◇◇◇◇

On a Monday morning, four weeks after the funeral, Kitty Cowan resigned from Spada Consolidated. Mike Santos made formal noises of regret, wished her well and asked whether she wanted to dispose of her holdings in Spada stock. Kitty declined. She also declined to participate in any ceremonies of farewell. A very practical lady, she preferred to take the money and run. What were her plans? A long holiday in Europe. After that? She wasn't sure. With any luck she might discover a rich suitor or a talent for idleness. She wasn't joining Spada at the Poseidon Press? For the present, no. . . . If Mike didn't mind, she would clear out her desk, hand over the files and be gone by the end of the week. Mike Santos agreed that a clean break would be better for everyone.

On the afternoon of the same day, John Spada introduced at Raymond Serum Laboratories a European client, Dr. von Paulus, who conducted, from Paris, a multilingual service, disseminating scientific information. He was particularly interested in Mr. Raymond's work on aberrant strains of bacilli and would like to publish some of his material. . . . In this connection also, the good doctor could offer an active export market for microscopic slides, for cultures and toxins. He was interested to establish in France the counterpart of the American National Collection of Type Cultures—a unique library from which any reputable bacteriologist could draw his specimens. When Dr. von Paulus left, late in the afternoon, to drive back to town with Spada, he took with him a folder of documents, a package of slides and a box containing six sealed vials of anaerobic soup full of live botulinus cultures.

The next evening Spada entertained Max Liebowitz at cocktails in his apartment. It was a small, somber occasion, which Max honoured with lugubrious dignity.

". . . It is good of you to tell me first, John. We have never been close, I know; but this—this monstrosity should happen to no man. I bleed for you!"

"I have to pull out, Max. I simply can't take any more. I need to go into smoke for a while, get myself together again."

"Best thing you could do. We'll keep a close eye on the store."

"I wanted to talk to you about that, Max. I may not be back for a long time. Maury Feldman will vote my stock. You can work with him, I think."

"Easier than with you." Max Liebowitz permitted himself a wintry smile. "But—if you'll excuse the expression—I like you better now. You're a real mensch!"

"I'm glad, Max, because I need you to trust me. No questions, no explanations."

"So I trust you. Now tell me."

"Mike Santos has to go."

"So! . . ." Max nodded his head up and down like

277

a porcelain Buddha. "I agree and I don't ask why. I've always thought he was too big for his shoes. But what does Mike Santos have to say about it?"

"He doesn't know yet. He will before I leave. How soon can you move in Conan Eisler?"

"Two months, three at the outside. His old contract's expired. There's a new one under negotiation. He'd be free to come to us fairly quickly. . . . More important, how soon can you get Santos out? He's got a five-year contract."

"I doubt he'll invoke it."

"What makes you so sure?"

"No questions, Max. Believe me, it's better. When it happens, you can swear you know nothing."

"Meantime, what do I tell Conan Eisler?"

"The job's falling vacant, but he'll blow it if he opens his mouth."

"He'll get the point! But tell me, are we going to have a scandal on our hands?"

"There is a scandal, Max, bigger than you can imagine; but I believe I can keep the lid on it."

"Does Maury know what it is?"

"Yes. He agrees that you should stay well clear of the whole situation."

"I hear Kitty Cowan resigned."

"I suggested it, Max. I didn't want her around, either, when Santos gets the news."

"Does she know about the scandal?"

"No."

"I like Kitty," said Max Liebowitz judicially. "She's a lot of woman—and she's always carried a big torch for you."

"We've been friends a long time, Max."

"It's none of my business, John. But you know

what they say: after a good marriage, it's doubly hard to be alone."

"Turning matchmaker, Max?"

"Better I should stick my head in a gas oven! But a man could marry a lot worse than Kitty Cowan."

"She can do a lot better for herself—and I may not be around too long."

"You mean . . . ?"

"They still want me dead, Max. They also want to make my dying as painful as possible."

"Who are they?"

"That's my secret, Max."

"But you can't just sit around waiting for a bullet!"

"That's why I'm going away."

"Sometimes," said Max Liebowitz wearily, "sometimes I wonder if the animals aren't taking over the zoo. . . . What else do you want from me?"

"Nothing but silence," said John Spada. "You've heard nothing. You know nothing."

"All these secrets! They give me nightmares. But, sure, I'm blind and dumb!" He raised his glass in a toast. "I wish you good tomorrows, John!"

The following morning Mike Santos received a handwritten note from John Spada.

My dear Mike,

I have decided to travel for a while and try to put the pieces of my life together again. I don't know how long I shall be gone, nor indeed where I shall go. I guess the simplest thing to do is stick a pin in a map and then head for the hole!

Raymond Laboratories is now in good running order, and I shall send you all my notes and recommendations before I leave.

On Wednesday evening next week I am having a small, informal gathering at the apartment to say good-bye to very special friends and colleagues. The time is eight o'clock, the dress informal. There will be drinks and a buffet supper. I do hope you'll come. It may be a long time before I pass this way again.

Just give me a call to confirm. If I'm out, Carlos will take the message.

Until we meet,

John

Mike Santos was a very methodical man. He called Spada's apartment and spoke with Carlos. He noted the date in his diary, then scribbled on the corner of the note: "Rec'd. 10.15 A.M. Accepted by telephone. 10.20 A.M.," and tossed the paper into his out tray. Immediately afterwards, on his private line, he spoke with the sixty-year-old lady who had endowed him with his first two million. The tape of their conversation was delivered into John Spada's hands at midday.

Now that he had no family, Sunday in New York was the worst of all days. The apartment was empty. Carlos and his wife and the housemaid were all away. There was no Anna to walk him down to the Church of Faith, Hope and Charity, put the Mass book in his hands and urge him fiercely through the liturgy and the sermon. Whatever God resided there was silent now and faceless, abashed by the botch of His own creation. The streets were empty until midday. Those who slept together slept late. Those who slept alone went jogging or read the Sunday funnies or padded through the morning until the bars and the stores opened.

Still, he had no grounds for complaint. He could be a welcome guest anywhere across the continent. He could host a dozen luncheons. He could summon a harem of women, fly to Haiti or Honolulu or Honduras at the flash of a credit card. He could also call Kitty Cowan, who more than once had sworn blue murder at him over the telephone.

"For Chrissake, John! One of us is nuts—and it isn't me! You can't waste your life away like this. Go to a theater! Go to a cathouse! Take off for Vegas! Buy a baseball team! Anything . . . ! I can't bear to think of you in that great empty apartment! Come around here and I'll make you lunch; or, if you don't like my cooking, take me out. I'll even buy the wine if you're strapped for dough. . . ."

Always he had refused. The ennui of grief pressed on him like a leaden cope. Fight he would. Plot he could—ah yes, the plot was even better than the fight, an intricate inverted joy, half pleasure and half pain. But today was different. He woke early to a new and poignant solitude. He was plagued by a sudden desire for a woman, someone who could at least prove to him that he was still a man in a wilderness of apes. He took in the newspapers, made himself toast and coffee, showered, shaved and dressed himself in his best sports clothes, gazed out the window at the emptiness of Park Avenue and then, after much hesitation, dialled Kitty Cowan's number.

"Kitty? John. What are you doing right now?"

"I'm dripping water all over the carpet. What did you have in mind?"

"Brunch at the Plaza?"

"With all those palm trees? No way!"

"Let's get out into the country. It's a beautiful day."

"And by noon we'll be bumper to bumper on the turnpike. Tell you what. Why don't you come around about eleven-thirty? We'll have some drinks and I'll cook you a meal. If we feel like it later, we can go window-shopping down Fifth Avenue."

"Sounds great. Want me to bring anything?"

"Two bottles of your best burgundy. I've got steaks in the freezer."

"I'll be there."

"I'll be waiting. Now get off the line. The carpet's soaked already."

It was the first meal he could remember tasting in weeks, the first talk that had no taint of money or of malice in it. They recalled old times sweetly. They laughed at old comedies, forgotten for too long. While Kitty washed the dishes, he stretched himself on the divan, kicked off his shoes and talked drowsily until sleep carried him away. When he woke, the room was dark, and Kitty was sitting on the floor beside him, smoothing his rumpled hair.

He blinked at her and murmured, "Hullo, young Kitty."

"Hullo, big John. That was a long sleep."

"What time is it?"

"Does it matter?"

"I guess not."

"You looked so peaceful, I didn't dare to wake you."

"Thanks. For the first time in weeks I feel rested."

282

"You don't have to move. Stay there."

"I thought you wanted to go window-shopping."

"Who needs it? I can buy what I want in Paris."

"Paris? Oh yes, I forgot. You're going to Paris."

"That's where you recommended I should go first."

"Did I?"

"I leave tomorrow."

"I forgot that too. I'm sorry."

"Don't be. I'm almost packed."

"Kitty girl . . ."

"What?"

"I'm going away myself."

"I know. You told me."

"Don't you want to know where or why?"

"I know why. You've got to find the pieces of Humpty-Dumpty and put them all together again. I guess the place doesn't matter very much."

"I suppose you wouldn't think of coming with me?"

"I might."

"You'd have to go on ahead. I'd pick you up somewhere along the way."

"Why?"

"Otherwise it could be dangerous for you. They're still gunning for me. You know that."

"I know."

"Maybe it isn't such a good idea. I told you to quit your job so you wouldn't be in danger."

"I don't care about danger. I care about you."

He cupped her face in his hands and kissed her gently on the lips. She drew away, sat back on her heels and challenged him.

"So where do we go from here, Mr. Spada?"

"A long way, Miz Cowan. Tokyo, Bangkok, Delhi, Moscow . . . You name it, I'll be touching down there sometime. It could be quite a picnic—for a while."

"And afterwards?"

"I leave you," said John Spada brusquely. "That's the catch. I leave you. I have an appointment in Samarra—and I keep it alone."

"Where's Samarra?"

"It's a different place for every man."

"And that's the deal you're offering me—a picnic and a parting?"

"It's not a deal, Kitty love. It's a crazy dream. Forget it! . . . By the way, there's something you'd better know. I've made a new will. As the legal boys say: you're a substantial legatee. I've arranged things so that you won't have to give too much to the tax man. You can buy a lot of bagels with the rest."

"Don't talk like that! I don't want a nickel from you. I want you alive and smiling again, John Spada."

"Ay-ay-ay! Why do I always say the wrong words?"

"Keep your legacy! You offered me a picnic. I'll take it."

"And a parting?"

"I'll take that too."

"Are you sure?"

"I'm sure. But I haven't had a picnic in a long time. You'd better tell me how we spread the rugs. I mean . . ."

"I know what you mean, Kitty love. Here's what we do. You fly out to Paris tomorrow. Do your shopping, see the sights, just the way you planned. Then

284

go down to Rome. There'll be a booking in your name at the Grand Hotel. Wait till I come. We'll take it together from there."

"Promise me there'll be no ghosts in the bedroom?"

"There are no ghosts, girl—just memories."

"I'm scared now."

"Why?"

"I'm not a young girl anymore, John, and I've lived alone a long time."

"I'm not a boy either—and I don't like the man who lives in my skin."

"I'm cold," said Kitty Cowan.

"So am I," said John Spada. "Let's keep each other warm."

As he lifted her in his arms and carried her to the bedroom, the still, small voice inside him added the cautionary cadenza: "As long as we can, as long as we may."

They were sitting in Maclean's office at Poseidon Press, drinking coffee and working through a final checklist. Spada announced: "Immediately after the party on Wednesday evening I leave on a night flight to Europe. I'll be gone a long time, because I want to make contact with all the Proteus groups and start the flow of information back here to you . . ."

Maclean asked, "How long are we funded for, John?"

"Indefinitely. There's a trust fund that will turn you in an income of two million a year. The articles specify Poseidon as a non-profit organization and permit the raising of extra funds by way of dona-

285

tion and grant. Any questions in that area Maury Feldman can answer for you."

"Priorities next." Lajos Forman flipped through his notes. "Already it's clear that the information will be heavily loaded with records of political prisoners. All the organizations we've contacted have responded with lists and histories of detainees. The other information—on institutions and persons engaged in gross and inhuman acts of oppression—is, for obvious reasons, much more sparse and requires most careful checking before we publish."

"We were prepared for that, I think," said Andrew Maclean.

John Spada nodded agreement.

"The prisoners should come first anyway. It's the right order of things—compassion before indictment; Rodo told me that and he was right. . . . Now, something very important. No later than the last week in August, I must have in my hands comprehensive lists of all political detainees, country by country. Where lists are not possible, you will supply the most authoritative figures and quote the sources. You will specify the known places of detention and indicate the transport facilities by which they are linked to major cities. I'll need a master copy, typed on white paper with no identifying marks at all. At the same time I'll require a thousand copies printed, bound and held ready for distribution. You will be instructed later where to send them—if not by me, then someone with a fish name. Clear?"

"What's the significance of the date?" asked Lajos Forman.

"The General Assembly of the United Nations

goes into session on the third Tuesday in September."

"We'll be ready." Maclean was confident. "It's a basic document with a lot of uses. I'd suggest a first print run of twenty thousand. . . ."

"That's your decision," said John Spada. "I'm concerned only with the first thousand. . . . What I have to tell you next is vitally important. From the moment I step out that door, I have no further legal connection with Poseidon. It's an autonomous organization and you two will run it as such. Whatever happens to me, whatever is said or written about me, touches you not at all. The funds are out of my control. The future policy you will determine in the light of world events. I've helped to forge a weapon. Now it's in your hands. . . ."

"That sounds very final." Lajos Forman sounded dubious.

"Final as dying," said John Spada.

Maclean looked at him with grave, troubled eyes.

"I thought you wanted this to be your new life-work?"

"I did, Mac. I do. But after what's happened, I am, in a sense, incompetent. I'm marked, tainted if you like. I am no longer a help but a danger. So . . . it's all yours, gentlemen! I wish you a long and honourable service."

"We wish you well too, John," said Andrew Maclean. "Keep in touch when you can."

"If you don't hear from me," said John Spada, "you'll hear from Proteus."

"Safe journey," said Lajos Forman. "And peace at the end of it."

The hardest session he had to face was that with Maury Feldman. They had been friends so long, their relationship was so simple and yet so complex, it was brutal to have to end with half-truths and evasions. And yet this was the ground rule to which they had played all their lives. Maury Feldman had formulated it a millennium ago in the shoe box on Mott Street.

"Two things don't change with me. I'm a son of the law and a servant of the law. All the rest is pretty much negotiable. So if I'm to be your attorney, there are two conditions: never tell me a lie; but never give me a truth I can't handle. . . . If you're in doubt, read me a parable and I'll interpret it as Joseph did with Pharaoh's dream. But never tell me you've committed murder one or uttered a document with intent to defraud. So far as I'm concerned, you're innocent until a jury of your peers pronounces you guilty. Clear?"

It was clear then. It was clearer than ever now. So when he came to Maury's apartment, he brought a gift: a bezel ring, seventeenth century, of impeccable provenance, which had once belonged to a Grand Duke of Tuscany. The stone was a cabochon emerald, engraved with a figure of Eros.

Maury Feldman examined it with reverence and said quietly, "It's beautiful. But what have I done to deserve it?"

"Nothing," said Spada with a grin. "I thought you'd enjoy it more, knowing you hadn't earned it. Call it a going-away gift."

"What can I say? You were born a prince, John. I'm touched. Don't stay away too long. I'll miss you."

"Let's not kid each other, Maury. Come Wednesday midnight, I'm over the hills and gone. When I come back, if I come back, stand well away from me ... I'll be a dangerous man to know."

"John, whatever you're planning, drop it. I say that because you're my friend and I love you. I don't want to see you outlaw yourself. It doesn't take much, you know. It's very few steps from the village to the jungle."

"My whole family is dead, Maury! There has to be an accounting for that!"

"'Vengeance is mine,' saith the Lord ..."

"You think I'm looking for vengeance? Hell, no! You're a million miles off the mark! I always thought vendetta was a wasteful cult anyway. But I want an accounting for my dead! And, by the living God, I'm going to get it! And it isn't only with the hired killers, it's with every goddam group and system that makes such horrors possible! ... I'm a civilized man, for Christ's sake, and in half a year they've stripped me naked, back to barbarism. Now they'll contend with the beast they've made! ..."

"What are you going to do, John?"

Spada shook his head.

"I remember our deal, Maury. No lies between us —and no truth you can't handle. You'd never be able to handle this one."

"What can I say?" Maury Feldman shrugged helplessly. "Whatever happens, I'm your friend. Whenever you want me, I'm still your attorney."

"This case I plead alone, Maury; and win or lose, I promise you the world will never forget my day in court."

"I could use a drink," said Maury Feldman. "Brandy?"

"Thanks."

Feldman poured the liquor with an unsteady hand. They raised the glasses to each other and drank the first mouthful in silence.

Spada asked, more calmly: "You've read the transcripts on Mike Santos?"

"Yes."

"What's your opinion?"

"The same as yours. What are you going to do about him?"

"Present him with the evidence—and fire him."

"You can't just leave it like that. The man's a criminal. He's conspired in the murder of your family! There's enough evidence there to put him behind bars for life."

"But I won't be here to give it. I have more important things to do. . . . So I'm leaving Mike Santos to God."

"I don't believe you, lover."

"You'll be at the farewell party tomorrow. You'll see for yourself. I'm going straight from the apartment to Kennedy. I'd like you to drive me if you would."

"Sure. . . . Kitty told me you'd be meeting her in Rome. You have my blessing. It's a good thing for both of you. Take good care of her, eh?"

"You and Kitty are the only family I've got in America."

"That's what I mean," said Maury Feldman. "We've been together a long time. We've seen a lot of bastards come and go . . . I hate the thought of breaking up now."

"I'll send her back to you safely."

"She won't want to come."

"I'll see that she does."

"When I'm miserable, I feel hungry. Are you going to buy me dinner?"

"Spaghetti and wine at Gino's—for old times' sake. How does that grab you?"

"Right where it hurts," said Maury Feldman unhappily. "Let's go."

At five o'clock on the evening of Spada's farewell party, a man called Ruiz Patino walked out of a massage parlour on Seventh Avenue. A gangling, lopsided fellow, who looked as though he had been tied together with string, fell into step beside him and said, in Lunfardo: "Keep walking. I want to talk to you."

"Who the hell are you?" Ruiz Patino was trained to be leery of casual contacts.

"I'm from headquarters," said the lopsided one. "You don't know me. I know you. Your name is Ruiz Patino. You have been employed by Marina Altamira. Your last job was at a place called the Bay House. Your assistant was Vespucci. You don't have to say anything. Just keep walking. The woman Altamira has gone sour on us. She's selling us out—and that means you and Vespucci as well. She and the American Santos are setting up a deal with the F.B.I."

"Mother of God! How can I believe that?"

"If you don't," said the lopsided one, "you end up in jail. . . . I'm going to give you an envelope. Take it and stick it in your pocket. Don't open it until you get back to your room. It contains ten thousand dollars. Five for you and five for Vespucci. It also contains a photograph of Santos and an address on Park Avenue. Tonight, sometime after nine-thirty,

Santos will leave a party he's attending at that address. One of you can deal with him. The other will eliminate Altamira at her apartment. Then you both get out of New York for a week or two. Where's Vespucci?"

"At his own place. We're meeting at seven."

"You've got plenty of time then. With silencers, it's a simple job. No problems. Here's the envelope. And make sure you split the cash down the middle. It's headquarters money. They're fussy about clean pay-offs. On your way now."

He peeled off and went hurrying across town towards Fifth Avenue. Ruiz Patino stared after him in momentary puzzlement and then shrugged resignedly. In this business it didn't pay to be too nosy. And ten thousand dollars was more than they'd got for the Bay House job.

John Spada's farewell party was a subdued affair, very unlike the gatherings of the old days when Anna had presided, warm and affectionate, over her own domain. Then the drinks had flowed freely, the talk was high, the laughter open and free. The men had paid court to Anna, while Spada played gallant to the women.

Tonight the whole tone was elegiac, a memorial rather than a celebration. Spada kept moving about the room, not lingering with any one group lest his presence interrupt the flow of courteous irrelevances or revive the brutal memory of recent events. Once again he felt, as he had felt in Von Kalbach's house, a fateful personage, an alien presence. He wished Kitty were there. Her brusque and bawdy good humour would at least have taken the chill off the occasion.

When Mike Santos arrived, Spada was amazed at his self-assurance. He apologized for his lateness. The squash game had been tougher than usual. He offered greetings from his absent wife. He made the rounds of the guests, smiling and confident, the very image of a reigning prince of industry.

With Spada he was cordial and full of solicitous counsel. He should not worry about a thing. He should simply enjoy his vacation. Anything Spada needed, anywhere in the world, Mike Santos would supply it for him. He had even brought a gift—a pair of gold cufflinks with Spada's monogram in high relief. Spada thanked him with sober courtesy—and wondered at the man's effrontery.

Noting the incident, Maury Feldman moved in and drew Spada away to a safe spot near the bar. He asked in a whisper: "What's going to happen?"

"Nothing yet," said John Spada. "Enjoy your supper."

"It's damn near choking me." Maury was outraged. "The nerve of the guy!"

"To every pig comes his Martinmas!" It was the same proverb he had used to the President in Buenos Aires.

"I've heard you say that before. In twenty years I've never known what it meant."

"Old Spanish proverb. In Spain pigs are killed on Saint Martin's Day."

"You live and learn," said Maury Feldman, and he drifted back into the crowd.

Alison Hirchfeld, happily vague, as always, ever

so slightly crocked, tugged at his sleeve and said, "You've got more guts than I have, John. It's turning out quite a nice evening—in a sad sort of way."

"I'm glad you're enjoying it, Alison."

"Your Mr. Santos is something again! All that charm and dazzle. Is he good at his job?"

"Very good." Spada was carefully patient. Alison slurred everything and forgot nothing. "Spada Consolidated will be in very good hands."

"That's good. That's very good! . . . Do you think Carlos could make me another martini? I hate wine."

"I'll make it myself, sweetheart."

At least it was a relief from the tension of the masquerade. He was just mixing the drink when Mike Santos clapped his hands and demanded silence. As the murmurs died around the room he announced: "Ladies and gentlemen. I want to propose a toast! . . ."

Spada rammed his fists into the counter of the bar and battled to control himself.

". . . It's a very simple one. No grace notes, no embellishments. To a gallant gentleman, John Spada! Godspeed and come safely home!"

They clapped. They cried "Hear, hear." They raised their glasses and drank. They called "Speech! Speech!"

John Spada raised his hands for silence and responded: "Thank you, Mike. Thank you, dear friends! I know it isn't like the old days. It never will be again. . . . But I'm glad and grateful that you came. You shared the good times with me; you are still here in the bad ones. God knows when I'll be back, but I trust to find all you girls just as beautiful and you fellows half as fat and twice as prosperous. God bless you all! . . ."

It was the right note to end on. They gave a little cheer. The women came to kiss him. The men shook his hand and clapped him on the shoulder and wished him all the good luck in the world. When the exodus began shortly afterwards, Spada held Santos back.

"Hang around, Mike. I'd like a last drink with you and Maury."

"Sure John. Sure!"

When the door closed on the last of the stragglers, Spada said "Let Carlos clear up in here. Bring your drinks into the library."

"It's a quarter of ten, lover," said Maury Feldman. "We shouldn't hang around too long."

"I'm all packed, Maury. We'll leave in fifteen minutes."

He sat them in the big leather armchairs while he himself perched on the edge of the desk. He picked up a sheet of Spada notepaper and a ballpoint pen and held them out to Santos.

"One last document, Mike. I need a signature."

"What is it, John?"

"Your resignation. effective immediately. Sign it."

"I don't understand." Santos looked from one to the other in puzzlement. "I've got a five-year contract."

"It's cancelled." said John Spada.

"You can't do that!"

"He's just done it," said Maury Feldman. "Sign the paper. Mike."

"No!" Santos heaved himself to his feet.

"Then you're fired," said Spada.

295

"I don't accept that either. I've got a right to hear reasons."

"I'll give you four," said Maury Feldman. "Anna Spada; Teresa and Rodo Vallenilla; two million dollars' worth of investment in Nassau, Bahamas, which was your price for setting up a murder."

Mike Santos went white. He stood speechless, rocking back and forth on his feet.

John Spada said, "Take a look at yourself in the hall mirror, Mike. I hope you can live with what you see. I hope your father will still smile at you when you meet him."

"This . . . this is madness!" Santos found voice at last. "You're bluffing. If you're so sure, why don't you call the cops and have me arrested right now?"

"We have the evidence," said Maury Feldman wearily. "Copies of the trust deed from Nassau, identification of Marina Altamira as a longtime Argentine agent in New York, transcripts of some of your conversations with her, an identification of the two men who burned down the Bay House—their names are Patino and Vespucci. . . . Satisfied?"

"Why did you do it, Mike?" asked Spada coldly. "I can't believe it was for the money."

"I admit nothing." Santos stood up. "So you've got two choices: either you make a citizen's arrest, which I won't resist, or I walk out of here free."

"Our man has spirit," said Maury Feldman.

"Our man is a Judas," said John Spada. "A greedy, ambitious hypocrite . . . a killer for gain—two million lousy dollars!"

"It's still a bluff," said Mike Santos. "I haven't seen a document yet—not a goddam line!"

"Here's your copy."

John Spada tossed a bulky envelope at his feet. Santos picked it up and weighed it contemptuously in his hands then he laughed.

"So that's the game! You don't dare file charges because I know about Proteus and I can spread that story across the world and compromise a lot of your people. Instead. you want me to cut and run or blow my brains out like some right honourable Victorian hero. No way! You pull me down and I'll pull Spada Consolidated and the Proteus organization down with me." He tossed the envelope back to Spada. "I'll be at my desk in the morning. Maury. I'll expect you for coffee. Have a nice trip, John. Send us a card from time to time. Good night. gentlemen!" He turned on his heel and walked out, jaunty as an actor with a juicy exit line.

As the door closed behind him, Maury Feldman said, "I wonder what he'll do now."

"I have no idea," said John Spada. "But let's you and me have the record straight. We three had a final drink together. Mike left. He didn't say where he was going. That's the truth. isn't it?"

"It's a truth I can handle," said Maury Feldman.

As the aircraft headed north. still climbing to cruising altitude over Martha's Vineyard, the Scarecrow Man slid into the seat beside him.

"The job's done."

"Confirmed?"

"Yes. Henson was watching the house. I followed Santos from your apartment. He stopped to make a telephone call from a booth on Seventy-first Street. Patino shot him inside it. Henson was watching Altamira's apartment. Vespucci went in and came out

297

four minutes later. Henson and I drove out to the airport and waited. So far as we could see there was no surveillance on you."

"Where's Henson now?"

"He's on the British Airways flight. We'll meet in London and work out the European operation from there. Then I'll go down and organize the South American setup. I'll be in New York when you get back."

"The merchandise?"

"Henson's got some. I've got some. This is yours." He handed Spada a leather cigar case containing four cigars. "The vials are inside the cigars. Each one is wrapped in a paper on which are written the directions for reproducing the cultures. It's very simple. It can be done in a household kitchen. . . . Any change in your plans?"

"None," said John Spada. "You'll hear from me when I'm ready to move. The important thing is that everybody understands what is to happen if my communications are blacked out."

"Our people will understand. I can't speak for the others."

"That's the purpose of the exercise. The others must answer for themselves."

"I wonder," said the Scarecrow Man, "I wonder if you understand what is in store for you. Every city needs a rat catcher to go down the sewers, but none of the citizens will invite him to dinner."

"I know what you mean. I find myself quite calm about it."

He spoke the simple truth. He was quite calm; in the real sense of the archaic phrase, he was at peace—even though the peace was the quietude of despair.

The murder of his family had thrust him into a new dimension, beyond law, beyond reason, beyond guilt, beyond all philosophic or religious speculation. He was, simply and absolutely, there. No one could recall him. He could not retreat, even of his own volition, because his intellect was held, like iron to a magnet, his will frozen, like that of the dead, in the disposition of the last living moment. Without so imperative a certainty, the act which he was planning now would have proved impossible.

The rats were too many and too savage. The sewers in which they lived were too dark and too complicated. Besides, the city and the citizens thereof were, in a strange fashion, allies of the rats. It was as if they desired them to flourish, to justify their own secret fears, the cruelties they inflicted one on another. "It is not we who are vicious," they said. "It is the rats who force us to be so. It is not we who throw our brothers into hellholes and Bedlams. It is the fault of the rats who infect them and force us to destroy them to protect ourselves." So the rat catcher might be an honourable servant on paper, but in the end the burghers were unwilling to pay him. If they would not pay, then they must learn the same rude lesson that the Pied Piper had taught the citizens of Hamelin town: the hills would open up and swallow their children, so that they would never be seen again.

It was an operation worthy of Proteus, godlike in its simplicity, enormous in its consequences. The blueprint had been prepared long ago as a strategic exercise. The means were at his disposal. Each of the four vials in his cigar case contained cultures that could be multiplied indefinitely. They would produce enough toxin to contaminate a dozen major cities. All Spada needed—and it was implanted in him now by surgical procedure—was the courage and the conviction to carry out the design. As he flew through the starlit darkness over the Atlantic, he contemplated the reasons which had brought him to this millennial decision.

Most people were at heart well meaning but, in action, hypocrites. They would weep tears of blood over a child killed in the street. They would accept, without a pang, the deaths of hundreds of thousands from malnutrition. The loss of a lifeboat was an epic tragedy; tribal genocide was a paragraph hastily read, lightly dismissed. Sixty dead in a train crash was a disaster; six million dead in the camps and gas ovens was a historical statistic. The charitable would airlift a thousand tons of food to the victims of an earthquake; they would not raise voice or hand in defense of twenty thousand swept into the oblivion of the disappeared dissidents.

They did not understand, they said. The world with its political traffic was too complicated. Was it, hell! . . . Now they would learn how brutally simple it could be. And if they damned him for a fanatic, why did they kowtow to a dictator with an army at his back, or an arms peddler crying havoc in the name of trade? The strongest weapon in the tyrants' armoury was fear. Now he would turn the weapon against them—not in single combat, but by a universal revulsion.

He would hang over them the threat of a creeping death and dare them to ignore it. He would proclaim a simple, brutal fiat: "Open your jails and your Fun Palaces; let the prisoners out into the light; or I, John Spada, who have nothing now to lose, will turn your cities, one by one, into cemeteries."

From the moment he landed in London, he began to cover his tracks. Once through immigration and customs, he crossed to Terminal 2 and, using the name of Erwin Hengst, bought himself a ticket to Zurich. From Zurich he flew to Rome, entered the republic on Hengst's passport, rented a car at the airport desk and drove straight to Uncle Andrea's villa in Frascati.

The old man and Aunt Lisa gave him an emotional reception. He had to relive with them every detail of the events since Easter Day, but there was a kind of therapy in the telling. These were the *anziani*, the elders of the tribe, his links with the past, his most proper counsellors and comforters. With these two, at least he could tell the truth and they would judge him, not by codex and commandment, but by the precedents of a long and violent history. Because he was family they would protect him from pursuivants and inquisitors; they would give him safe sleeping, help him on secret journeys and, at the end, plead for his merciful judgment by an understanding Deity.

When the long tale was done, Aunt Lisa dried her eyes and bustled out to order dinner and impose a silence on the staff. Signor Giovanni was not here. He never had been. He was stricken with grief and must be left in peace. Uncle Andrea took his arm and led him out to walk on the terrace and watch the sunset.

Spada took an envelope from his pocket and handed it to the old man.

"This is how I have disposed my affairs, Uncle. Maury Feldman has the necessary instructions and authorities. When I die, he will take over the Proteus files from safe-deposit and administer the organization as I have done in the past."

Uncle Andrea gripped his arm and steered him to the stone balustrade, from where they could look down on the fall of the vineyards and the olive groves towards the Tiber. Uncle Andrea said gravely, "You are too young to talk of dying, Giovanni; and you are not too old to found another family. You cannot spend the rest of your life in mourning."

"The mourning is over, Uncle. I am going around the world to make contact with our Proteus people and set up an information network for our publications. I am travelling with a woman, a longtime friend. She's waiting for me now in the city."

"You should have brought her here."

"No, Uncle. This is she and me. It has nothing to do with family."

"In that case"—Uncle Andrea was obviously relieved—"better you enjoy each other away from the tribe. . . . But tell me, if you have a woman, why all this talk of dying?"

"It's an exercise." Spada tried to make a joke of it. "I want to get used to the idea, so that no one can ever frighten me with it again."

"It's not a good thought to take to bed with a woman." Uncle Andrea grinned mischievously. "It could have disastrous consequences. Now, nephew . . . !" Suddenly he was brusque and demanding, the old one jealous of his rights. "You have said much

302

and told nothing. What are you going to do with your life from now on?"

"Gamble with it," said John Spada.

"For what stakes?"

"One moment, one single moment in history, when the whole world will stop and listen and understand the lunacy that afflicts it."

"And you will be the man who tells them?"

"Yes."

"Can you shout so loud?"

"I can."

"What if the world rejects what you say?"

"A lot of people will die."

"And you will be their executioner?"

"Yes."

"You talk of lunacy. Are you sure you are sane, Giovanni?"

"I believe I am. I am reasoning here with you."

"Are you using Proteus people for this?"

"Yes. There are some who believe that benevolence is enough. There are others, like me, who believe that the time has come to fight. These will be my doomsday men."

"You have no right to command them to such a work!"

"I have never commanded them, Uncle. They have always been free to say yea or nay to any project."

"I will not join you, Giovanni."

"I would not ask you, Uncle, just as I did not ask Maury Feldman."

"But what you propose still involves the rest of us."

"It has always been like that, Uncle. Long ago we set down a principle for all our Proteus family.

Brothers may disagree, but they are brothers still. In a war they may be forced to fight each other, but the family goes on."

"I understand why you prepare yourself for death," said Uncle Andrea somberly. "Even I, who love you, might find it necessary to kill you."

"I would probably bless you for the kindness." Spada put his arm around the old man's shoulders and embraced him. "We've never quarreled, you and I; let's not start now. I am out to fight the butchers. You disapprove of what I do; that's your right. At least remember that my life is on the line. . . ."

"I know, Giovanni. I know." Uncle Andrea was distressed. "But I have seen a lot of dead, and young men drove tanks over their graves without a thought."

"The dying is not the tragedy, Uncle. It's the forgetting. So I shall give the world a moment to remember . . . *Ma noi due . . . almeno noi dobbiamo fare la pace*, eh? . . . At least we two should make peace. I have to leave early in the morning."

"Will you still lay your flowers in the Fosse Ardeatine?"

"Yes."

"And what will you tell the dead? That they will soon have more company?"

"That we are still in battle against the tyrants—and there is still a Spada among the partisans!"

The old man shivered. Spada drew him close to warm him.

"It's nothing," said Uncle Andrea brusquely. "I always feel cold when the sun goes down."

"It's like a dream," said Kitty Cowan. "A beautiful, quiet dream . . ."

They were standing in the temple garden of Ryoanji, looking over a sea of white sand that rippled like waves around the dark rocks planted centuries ago by the great Soami. The sun was high, the shadows of the sand furrows sharp, the rocks emphatic yet tranquil as the dreaming of the Lord Buddha.

John Spada was silent for a long moment, then he responded. "This is where it all comes together: no argument, no distraction, just tranquillity."

"When you talked about it in Tokyo, with all that bustle and neon, I thought it would be sad and empty."

"The man who first showed it to me is dead now." John Spada was caught in reverie. "His name was Takeshi Saito. He had lived a strange, violent life, first as a soldier in the Sino-Japanese War, then as a kind of muscleman for a big protection gang in Tokyo. After that he became a Zen monk."

"How? Why?"

"He would never tell me exactly. The most he would say was that one day he walked into a silence. . . . After a while I realized that, truly, no other explanation was necessary. I met him for the first time when some Japanese colleagues brought me here on a sightseeing tour. Takeshi showed us around. He and I got on well together. I was intrigued by the enormous calm that surrounded him. He, I think, saw in me something of his old, restless self. After that, whenever I came to Japan I would call on him. Once or twice I stayed in the monastery overnight. Anyway, it was Takeshi who explained the garden to me. He said, 'The sand moves because it is still; the rocks speak because they are silent . . .'"

305

"I'm glad you brought me here." said Kitty Cowan softly. "I've never seen you so relaxed."

"I haven't quite stopped yet."

Kitty Cowan was puzzled by the cryptic remark. "Stopped what?"

"I was thinking of something else Takeshi used to say. 'A man does not arrive until he stops travelling.'"

"Arrive where?"

"At a place which is no place, in a time which is no time." Spada smiled at her puzzlement. "It's a Zen riddle. You worry at it because it seems ridiculous. Then if you are lucky, there comes a moment that is called *satori* when you see that it is not ridiculous at all, but profoundly and simply true. . . . There's another garden here. It's much easier to understand."

He turned her gently away from the stark, still sand garden, led her back through the temple and out into a park of cedars and maples and rock pools. fringed with azaleas and rhododendrons. He sat her on a bench with a great stone lantern beside it and showed her the golden carp cruising the calm water below. He asked quietly: "Have you enjoyed your picnic. Kitty Cowan?"

"Oh God! Every hour of every day and every night."

"Even with Erwin Hengst?"

"Because of Erwin Hengst. . . . That was funny. At first I hated the whole idea, because the name was German, because I'd agreed to come with big John Spada, not with some—I don't know—some actor playing a role I didn't understand. I wondered why you didn't take me to all the places I'd heard you and Anna talk about: the Grand Canal, the Hermitage in Leningrad, the Acropolis, the Taj Ma-

306

hal, the famous hotels . . . I was disappointed, but I thought, well, you didn't want to share with me the past you'd had with Anna. Then I realized you didn't want to lodge in places where you were known and that you were meeting people who didn't want to be seen there either. So I settled down to make the best of it . . ." She broke off.

Spada prompted her gently, "And then?"

"Then I understood how private and special an experience you were offering me, how much of yourself you were opening to me. Erwin Hengst was a dreamer, a kind of poet. . . . Remember that day on Torcello when we sat in the old basilica holding hands and staring up at that marvellous mosaic of the Madonna? We were there nearly half an hour, all alone, hardly saying a word. . . . And at night we lay in bed listening to the frogs and the night birds, while you told me stories of the old doges and the traders of the Adriatic. They were like the fairy tales I read when I was a child. That was when the magic started to work, and it's gone on working ever since. Samarkand, Bangkok, Singapore, Sydney —those lovely days on the Reef island . . . and now this! I feel as if I've lived a whole lifetime in a few weeks. Me, Kitty Cowan from Brooklyn!"

"And now," said John Spada gravely, "it's almost time to go home."

"I was afraid of that." Her eyes filled up with tears. She groped for a handkerchief and blew her nose violently. "Damn! Damn! Damn! I promised myself I wouldn't do this. And now I'm spoiling it all."

"No!" John Spada took out his own handkerchief and wiped the tears from her cheeks. "I'm not feeling so happy myself; but I want you to know that I've enjoyed the picnic as much as you have. I'm glad you liked Erwin Hengst."

"I love the silly Kraut."

"He loves you too, Kitty. That's funny. Having another name made it easy to be in love."

"But what's going to happen to him now?"

"Better you don't ask. girl. because when you go back you'll be questioned, and you're not a very good liar. You had a nice romance with a German guy. You kissed goodbye and came home. *Basta!* It was great while it lasted and a lady's got a right to her privacy. If they start to press harder, you spit in their eye."

"I can't bear not knowing what's going to happen to you."

"In the end you'll know. I promise."

"And you think I can let it go at that?"

"You must!" There was a ring of steel in his voice. "That's the one thing I demand of you."

"What about all those people you wouldn't let me meet . . . do they know more than I do?"

"Yes, but you will be under greater threat. Please, girl! Trust me!"

"All right. But will you answer me one question?"

"I'd like to hear it first."

"What really happened about Mike Santos? When I showed you the report of his death in the *Herald Tribune*, you said you didn't want to talk about it. Fine! I was a good girl and I didn't want to spoil our picnic; but now I have to know. What if I meet his wife again. . . ?"

"She's buried her dead," said John Spada. "Let him stay buried."

"He was our man, John . . ."

308

"No! He was never our man. You remember that great speech he made about his peasant ancestors who tasted the earth to tell whether it was sweet or sour? I think everything tasted sour to Mike Santos except his own ambition. He could be happy only at the top; he would stop at nothing to stay there. He conspired to kill Anna and Teresa and Rodo. I was next on his list. He used the money he got paid to buy his first block of shares in Spada Consolidated. After that he could have built up his holdings, year by year, until he held the balance of power."

"That's horrible! . . ." Kitty gaped at him in amazement.

"Horrible, but true."

"Then who killed him?"

"I had him killed," said John Spada. "It can't be proved. I doubt anyone will try very hard."

"And how does John Spada feel about it?"

"He feels nothing at all. He's a dead man already. That's why Erwin Hengst brought you on your picnic."

"Thanks for telling me." Kitty drew him to her and kissed him on the lips. "It makes things easier in a way. I loved John Spada too, you see. It's not every girl who gets two big bites at the cherry. Thanks, my love. I think we should leave now. I'm ready to go home."

"Before we go," said John Spada. "In all this, Maury Feldman is clean; so don't tell him anything."

"I wouldn't have anyway. I've forgotten everything except the fairy tales—and the loving!"

As they walked back through the woodlands, a small, chill wind stirred among the leaves and ruffled the surface of the lily ponds. It was still high summer, but soon it would be autumn, which the Japanese call "the time of maples-in-flame."

The day after Kitty Cowan left Tokyo, John Spada began the last rites of his private existence. He made a package of all his personal documents—passport, credit cards, checkbook—sealed it and dispatched it by registered airmail to Maury Feldman. He went through his clothes, rejected every garment with a New York label and retained only those which he had bought on the Continent. He went to the American Consulate and filed an application for a visitor's visa for Erwin Hengst. Then he took a taxi to Nihonbashi, where, in a small, old-fashioned teahouse, he sat two hours over a lunch with a graduate bacteriologist from Tokyo University.

After lunch he went to a printmaker in Yoshiwara, who delivered to him a package of handmade paper. headed with a woodblock symbol of the fish in a box. From the printmaker he went to an elderly calligrapher who undertook to inscribe for him, in Romaji, a handwritten document whose contents were written in English so the old man could not understand. In the evening. alone and lonely, Spada went to a noisy nightclub. At two in the morning, weary of the clatter, he went back to his hotel and wrote a letter to Kurt Deskau at his private address in Munich.

My dear Kurt,

I am sure you will understand why I have not written to you sooner. I have been like an earthquake victim, stunned and shocked, struggling to hold on to my sanity. I am grateful

310

for your concern over my safety and for the friendship that prompts it. However, I must tell you that I am now nearly at the end of the road which leads to the place where my last battle will be fought. I am calm in the knowledge that I shall probably not survive it; but at least I shall have given an open testament— made one final stand against a creeping iniquity.

You ask me about the documents of Erwin Hengst. I have one more use for them. Then I shall post them back to you before any questions, embarrassing to you, can be asked about them.

What more can I say? I send you a last salute from a man standing on the edge of the world and looking into nowhere. I have no regrets, and only one small hope: that what I do now will demonstrate the inevitable consequence of man's violence against his fellows.

Affectionate greetings and my heartfelt thanks,

John Spada

He put down the pen and sat a long time staring at the signature. It was the last time he would use it on any document, the last affirmation that John Spada was numbered among the living.

11

<><><><><><><><><><><><><><><><><><><><><><><><><>

The first annual session of the United Nations General Assembly was scheduled for the third Tuesday in September. One week before that date a sealed package was delivered to the mail room of the United Nations. It was marked "Personal and Urgent" and addressed to the Secretary-General. The customary security check revealed that the package contained a letter, a bulky schedule in typescript and a small box padded with cotton wool, in which were two sealed glass capsules, one containing a liquid, the other a small quantity of white crystalline powder. The capsules were sent out immediately for laboratory testing. The Chief of Security personally delivered the letter and the schedule into the hands of the Secretary-General. At eight o'clock in the evening he read it aloud to his senior colleagues in the Secretariat:

"The symbol which heads this paper represents Proteus, shepherd of the creatures of the sea, custodian of knowledge, the elusive god of many shapes. It is also the symbol of the organization of which I am the founder and which, like Proteus, functions in many places and in many disguises.

"When you read this letter for the first time, you will be tempted to say: 'This is the work of a madman.' I beg you, do not yield to the temptation. As you will see, it contains no proposition to which you and your colleagues do not subscribe, no demand which the United Nations organization has not made, over and over again: the liberation of prisoners of conscience, the abolition of torture, the restoration of the rights of free speech, free assembly, fair trial, the right to enjoy life, liberty and the pursuit of happiness.

"That you have made these demands is a matter of history. That you have been unable to enforce them is a matter of universal regret. However, now that they are enforceable, I beg you and your colleagues, in the name of humanity, not to abrogate them.

"With this letter you will receive two glass vials. The liquid in one vial is a live culture of Botulinus Type A. The powder is Botulinus toxin, a deadly poison. Any competent bacteriologist will inform you that both the culture and the toxin can be produced quickly under elementary laboratory conditions and that quite small amounts can contaminate the water supplies of any large city.

"My organization, which exists in all the major countries, possesses cultures, toxin and laboratory facilities and is, therefore, in a position to create, throughout the world, a serial biological disaster, against which there is no adequate remedy.

"At this moment, I know, the familiar

313

words will spring to your mind: hijack, blackmail, terrorism. I beg you to reflect on another word: sanction. I am placing in your hands, Mr. Secretary-General, the one power you have never had: the power to impose a decision of the United Nations by sanction, by penalty without redress. If you are not prepared to use this power, then I shall use it, and continue to use it, until my and your legitimate demands are met.

"With this letter I send you a schedule, necessarily incomplete, of those places of detention where men and women are confined, interrogated, tortured, in defiance of every principle of humanity. I send you lists of prisoners, again incomplete, because secrecy is the weapon of all tyrants. I request and require that these places of detention be opened, their inmates released, and dispersed to their homes within twenty-one days of this date, and that their release and dispersal be supervised and confirmed by observers from international agencies appointed by the United Nations.

"I further request and require that this demand be made known at the first meeting of the United Nations General Assembly and that the Assembly invite me, on the next day, to plead it before the members.

"If and when the prisoners are released, I undertake that all supplies of the cultures and the toxin in the hands of the Proteus organization will be destroyed forthwith. I shall, immediately afterwards, give myself into the custody of that country of which I am a citizen and accept, without contest, all the penalties of its law. If the demand is not met, the serial disaster will begin; and you must be in no doubt of its magnitude and its continuity.

"Let me now make a disclosure. I belong to no party, either of the left or the right. I have no affiliation to national causes, only to the cause of those who cannot speak because they are deprived of the right to do so. I have no personal ambition. Once I am in custody I shall have no human future; but this I am happy to accept in order to accomplish what I have set out to do.

"Immediately after the first session of the General Assembly, I shall telephone your office to hear the decision. If the decision is affirmative, the Assembly must guarantee my immunity from arrest within the confines of the U.N. building. If the decision is negative, then there is nothing more to be said. Action will follow as certainly as night follows day.

"I am, my dear Secretary-General,
                    With profound respect,
                         Yours sincerely,
                              Proteus"

The Secretary-General put down the letter and looked around the circle of his senior colleagues. They were silent and grim. He addressed himself to the Chief of Security.

"Colonel Malin? Can you sum up for us, please?"

"First, the simple facts. You will remember that this is a preliminary investigation, carried out by U.N. security staff. The Secretary-General desired that we should not involve outside agencies unless and until it was deemed necessary to do so." Colonel Malin was a Fleming, dour and direct. "The package was posted in New York. The letter is written on hand-made Japanese paper, and the symbol is a wood-block print. The schedule of persons in detention is typed on an I.B.M. golf-ball machine. The type style is called 'letter gothic.' The paper is a standard bond, available anywhere in the United States. The vials contain exactly what is described in the letter— live botulinus culture and crystalline botulinus toxin . . . I submitted the culture and the toxin to the chief bacteriologist at Bellevue Hospital. He confirms sub-stantially what is contained in the letter. The culture is Botulinus Type A. The toxin is lethal. The threat is real. The letter itself is written in an old-fashioned calligraphy, such as was practiced by engrossers of legal documents. Certain of the embellishments are characteristic of Japanese calligraphers writing in Roman cursive. It could have been done by a Japa-nese, in Japan, or it may have been designed to lead us to that conclusion. The information on political prisoners is accurate and more detailed than that possessed by either Amnesty or the Red Cross. We have not had time to cover all organiza-tions dealing with this sort of information. The tone of the letter is carefully apolitical. The style is that of a highly literate man. . . . I think we must take the threat very seriously indeed. . . . If I may be permitted one more observation . . . It is clear that this Proteus is aware of how the United Nations organization functions. He writes formally to the Secretary-General, who is obliged to bring the matter to the attention of the General Assembly, which alone can consent to his appearance in this place—as it did to the appearance of Yasser Arafat. . . ."

"So, gentlemen." The Secretary-General faced the small, silent assembly. "A letter of demand from a literate and intelligent man, representing an organization of unknown dimension and backed by an authentic threat of serial disaster . . . How do we respond?"

"They will respond," said the Scarecrow Man, "by strict adherence to protocol. The Secretary-General will refer the matter to the heads of delegations to the General Assembly. They will advise their respective governments and seek instruction. The Chief of Security will confer with the New York Police Department, which has jurisdiction in criminal matters over the U.N. area. They in turn will most probably refer to the F.B.I., who will seek information from the C.I.A. and other U.S. intelligence agencies."

"And then," said John Spada, "the trail will lead to me. And every police agency in the world will be wanting to have a little chat."

"That's the way you arranged it." The Scarecrow Man shrugged. "This game of terror is more than half theater."

They were sitting in the sunshine in Washington Square, two nondescript fellows dressed in slacks and sweat shirts, playing checkers. Spada's hair was cropped *en brosse*. He wore a three-day growth of stubble, a pair of sunglasses and a surgical shoe which threw his walk out of kilter and forced him to use a cane. His lodging was two blocks away, in a sleazy transient hotel, where he was registered as Erwin Hengst. To be lodged so badly was, as the Scarecrow Man pointed out, an unnecessary act of masochism; but Spada's reasoning was simple. No

317

one would expect him to step so far out of character. He could move freely and sleep soundly; and besides, there was a certain satisfaction in the exercise: a lone wolf learning the lessons of survival in an environment of total indifference.

The Scarecrow Man jumped two of his pieces and crowned a black checker. He said placidly, "Suppose the General Assembly agrees to your demand and offers you immunity inside the U.N. How will you get there? Outside, remember, you will be arrested on sight."

"It seems to me," said John Spada, "they won't dare to publicize the affair before the General Assembly either debates it or reaches a consensus without debate. They'll do everything possible to avoid a panic. If they consent to receive me under immunity, I'll land by helicopter, within the precincts of the United Nations area."

"And from that moment you're in a trap. As soon as you try to leave the area you'll be arrested."

"But you and all our other people will still be free. That's the core of the situation. I shall no longer be necessary."

"You expect to be killed?"

"They have to get rid of me," said John Spada. "My own people or someone else. If they bring me to trial, the whole affair becomes public again."

"Have you thought," asked the Scarecrow Man, "that they may prefer to keep you alive and put you under interrogation? You've got a lot to tell them —and in the end you'll tell it all."

"I've thought of that too." Spada closed a box trap around the Scarecrow Man's crowned piece. "I remember what they did to Rodo and Teresa. So I've taken precautions. I carry a cyanide capsule always."

"It was necessary to be sure." The Scarecrow Man nodded approval. "I have no intention of joining you in the roll call of martyrs."

"I didn't expect it." Spada grinned.

"Have you also thought," asked the Scarecrow Man, "that they will never believe that you can or will withdraw the threat?"

"Why not?"

"Once you open Pandora's box, all the plagues fly out. No one can ever put them back again. This is the kind of threat that can be repeated indefinitely. The name of Proteus can be put to all manner of massacres. . . . For myself, I don't care. I believe man is a self-doomed species. I am simply interested to know how far you have thought through the proposition."

"According to the legend," said Spada quietly, "the one thing left in Pandora's box was Hope. It's my hope that once the horror is visible, men will recoil from it. . . . If not, then of course you're right. We're a self-doomed species."

"You contradict yourself, my friend." The Scarecrow Man gave him a wintry smile. "You accept your own execution as inevitable. You carry a death pill to protect yourself against the torturers. What kind of hope is that?"

"Not much, I agree. It's Hobson's choice: a clean exit or a long slavery."

"Like all zealots, my dear Spada, you miss the point. You make a choice too trenchant for normal folk. When Moses led the Israelites out of servitude, were they grateful? Never! They cried for the onions and the fleshpots of Egypt. Freedom was a luxury they could neither understand nor afford."

"So why are you sitting here with me now?"

"You pay very well," said the Scarecrow Man, "and besides, it's like watching a big game at the casino. I know you can't beat the bank, but I'm fascinated to see how close you'll get to it."

The machinery of power began to turn, slowly at first, faster and faster as the hours ticked away. The President of the United States called the Premier of the U.S.S.R. on the hot line, to establish, first and foremost, that each nation was as vulnerable as the other and that this was not a trick to cover some military demarche. Each promised to keep the other informed by a daily personal call. There were similar conversations with other heads of state in Europe, in the Middle East and the Orient.

It was the British Prime Minister who first uttered the definition which became the keynote of all their later discussions: "This Proteus, whoever he is, wants us to play Russian roulette."

The President of the United States embroidered the definition in the first discussions at the White House, where a briefing had to be framed for the U.S. Ambassador to the United Nations.

". . . We are exposed, gentlemen, to an intolerable gamble. We have to face, not a single catastrophe, like the loss of an aircraft full of people, but an almost unending cycle of biological invasions. We all know the scenario. Proteus knows that we know it. So he puts the pistol on the table and invites us to fire it at our own head or his own. He is, in an absolute sense, invulnerable, because he has no fear of what we may do to him, while what he can do to us is horrible to contemplate. . . . First question. Have we any idea who Proteus is and what is the size and nature of his organization?"

"About the size and nature of the organization, we know nothing." It was the Director of the F.B.I. who answered. "Proteus claims that it exists in many places and in many disguises. I'd accept that he's telling the truth. About the man himself, well . . ." He laid a pair of photostats on the table. "This is the symbol which appears on Proteus' letterhead. This other is a copy of a card found in the wallet of a German terrorist, Gebhardt Semmler, who allegedly committed suicide in Amsterdam."

"So, on the face of it, we're dealing with an existing terrorist organization?"

"On the face of it, Mr. President, possibly. However, look at the photostats again. How would you describe the symbol in words?"

"Well . . . it's a fish, inside an upturned box."

"Exactly! A fish in a box."

"But it isn't a box." Secretary Hendrick objected. "The incomplete square is an antique form of the letter *P*. The initial encloses the fish. Proteus is the protector of sea creatures. It's very ingenious."

"And irrelevant." The Director was tart. "Come back to the President's description: a fish in a box."

"And where does that take us?"

"Back to a jailbreak in Argentina. A man called Rodolfo Vallenilla was sprung. We know that Spada organized the operation. A code message was passed to him before the breakout. The text was: 'a fish in a box.'"

"My God! That means . . ."

"Please!" The Director cut him off with a peremptory gesture. He held up a copy of the schedule of prisoners and detention areas. "This list was prepared by a publishing house, recently founded in New York, to call attention to the plight of prisoners of conscience and the activities of repressive regimes. They collate information from existing organizations like Amnesty and the Red Cross and supplement it from their own sources—which, judging by the document, must be very accurate. The publishing house is called Poseidon Press . . ."

"So make your point, please!" The President was becoming testy.

"Three points, Mr. President." The Director was urbane as ever. "One: Rodolfo Vallenilla was the son-in-law of John Spada. Two: Gebhardt Semmler murdered Hugo von Kalbach, the German philosopher. John Spada was an eyewitness to the murder and was in Amsterdam at the time of Semmler's alleged suicide. Three: the Poseidon Press was founded by John Spada. Poseidon was the sea god who endowed Proteus with his powers. The fish in the box connects all these facts. . . . Think of what happened to Spada's family—and to his successor in the business. They were all murdered. What have you got now?"

"Motive," said Secretary Hendrick. "A rich and powerful man driven to desperation."

"And a mess of circumstantial evidence which you'll never sustain in court," said the President dryly. "But stay with it. The idea makes sense. Where is Spada now?"

"We don't know, Mr. President. We have a date on which he arrived in England and filed an immigration card. After that, no trace."

"What about Interpol?"

"A problem, Mr. President. It could be embarrassing for the Administration if we suggest that a U.S. citizen is holding the world to ransom."

"It could be a goddamn disaster." The President was emphatic. "For God's sake, play this one close to your chest. . . ."

"There's one way to close the whole investigation." Secretary Hendrick was equally emphatic.

"Let's hear it," said the President.

"Proteus wants to reveal himself, wants to speak, wants to surrender. Why not let him do just that?"

The Director stared at him in disbelief.

"And let a terrorist dictate ransom terms on the floor of United Nations?"

"It's been done before. Yasser Arafat stood there with a gun on his hip and addressed the General Assembly. Proteus is obviously aware of the precedent."

"He also poses a greater threat than Arafat." The President got up and began pacing restlessly. "You see, I'm in sympathy with Proteus. He is pleading a cause that I've been urging ever since I came to office. In that, he's a friend and not an enemy. However, I cannot even appear to approve the criminal means he has adopted. So here's the bottom line. How do we vote on the question in the U.N.? How do we lobby our friends to vote?"

"I think the question is premature, Mr. President." The Director challenged him boldly. "Today's Wednesday. We've still got a week before the General Assembly convenes. At least give us time to . . ."

"To do what? Arrest a man you can't find? Question a suspect who'll be out on a writ of habeas corpus before you can blink? Force him to make good his threat? You, Mr. Secretary! What's your answer?"

"Suppose, Mr. President—just suppose—this demand for an open hearing were not made under duress, would you be disposed to vote in favour of it?"

"I just might."

"Would the Russians, the Chinese, the Brazilians, the Argentines, the Chileans, the South Africans?"

"Hell, no!" The President leaned forward, covering his face with his cupped hands, and sat for a few moments, silent and absorbed. Then he faced them again. "Every country in the world is faced with a challenge to its sovereignty and security. However"—he pieced out the words slowly and carefully—"these are relative words. Not all sovereignties are wholly legitimate, as we have good cause to know because we've had a hand in some ramshackle arrangements. Not in all states does the security include the security of the subject. So balance these relatives against the absolute: that if we refuse Proteus' demand, hundreds of thousands, possibly millions, may die in a serial catastrophe. How do I decide?"

"How do you decide, Mr. President, if one successful blackmail leads to others copying this first episode?"

The Director of the F.B.I. sat back and waited while the President digested his challenge. The reply, when it came, was mild but curiously final, like the last stroke of midnight chimed by a mantel clock.

"I have to decide, gentlemen, on the basis of that which is, not that which may be. Proteus has preempted us. I say we vote for him to speak. We lobby our friends in the Assembly to vote with us."

"And if the vote fails?"

"Then there is nothing to prevent this—this black death."

Out of the silence that followed, Hendrick asked shakily: "Something else has to be faced, Mr. President. What about the press?"

"That's a decision for the United Nations. For my part, I am in favor of disclosure. The people have the right to know. Maybe they'll have more to tell us than we have to tell them."

On the Friday evening, Maury Feldman received a telephone call at his apartment. The caller identified himself as Mr. Mullet and requested an urgent meeting to discuss a contract. At ten o'clock Maury Feldman sat with John Spada in a grimy cellar bar on Bleecker Street. His opening remark was an expression of disgust.

"My God! You look like a bum!"

Spada chuckled. "I'm learning how the other half lives. Did you get the package I sent you from Tokyo?"

"Yes. It's in my safe."

"How's Kitty?"

"Fine. Except she's had visitors, as I have. The New York police and the F.B.I. are very interested in your whereabouts."

"Did they say why?"

"No. Care to tell me?"

"That's why I got you down here."

Maury Feldman heard him out in silence. Then he sat a long moment staring into the dregs of his liquor. Finally he shook his head, as if to clear away the last cobwebs of a nightmare. He said somberly, "You're a dead man, John."

"The certificate isn't signed yet, Maury. The General Assembly doesn't meet till Tuesday. The patient is still alive and living in hope."

"What hope?"

"That the water will part and God's people will march dry-shod into the Promised Land."

"As I remember, Moses never got there."

"But he still delivered the law—graven on the tablets."

"And no man knows where he's buried. What do you want from me, lover?"

Spada unbuttoned his shirt and took off the gold chain with the Proteus key on the end of it. He laid it in Feldman's palm.

"It's yours now, Maury."

"After this, what am I supposed to do with it? When we first set up the organization it was to build bridges of benevolence. Now you've blown them all!"

"Do you really believe that, Maury?"

"For Christ's sake, John! Can't you see . . ."

"I'll tell you what I see and what you know! Comes a time when benevolence is not enough. Comes a time when you stand on the crags of Masada and say: 'You've pushed us far enough. Here we stand and die.' And maybe, just maybe, you don't die and the legions fall back in retreat. The man who blew up the King David Hotel is now the Prime Minister of Israel. That's history, Maury! If you die, you're a criminal, and they plow your land with salt. If you survive, you're a hero and a statesman. Don't fail me now, Maury."

"I don't know what the hell you want."

"My day in court. And I want you there with me."

"If they give it to you . . ."

"If they don't, then all bets are off. You don't have me as a client anymore. You walk away clean."

"While you bring down the plague on innocent people!"

"Half your taxes are paying for a new holocaust, Maury, and you're voting for bigger and better bonfires every year! Don't go soft on me now, please!"

"Soft! I think I'm going crazy! Besides, what can I do?"

"What does any good lawyer do? Mediate, interpret, plead! . . . And don't tell me we have no case! Remember Yad Vashem and all the millions who died because there was no one to plead their cause and because the fight began too late."

"I have to think about it."

"Fine! I'll call you after the vote in the General Assembly."

"I wish to God I could explain you to myself!"

"It's simple enough, Maury. I'm a stripped-down man. I've got nothing to lose except my life. . . . Let's go, eh?"

He paid the check. They stood up and walked out into the chill autumn air. At the corner they shook hands and parted. Maury Feldman stood on the curb and watched him walk away, limping like Jacob after his wrestle with the angel. He felt very near to tears, not knowing whether he loved or hated him.

The first disclosure was made, according to protocol, by the Secretary-General to a plenary conference

327

of correspondents accredited to the United Nations. The conference took place at nine in the morning, New York time, on the Monday before the third Tuesday in September. The date had been decided to give time for at least a preliminary test of world opinion before the vote in the General Assembly. The Secretary-General's announcement was sedulously calm. Each correspondent received a copy of the letter of demand, the schedule of camps and inmates, a photograph of the vials containing the lethal material.

The Secretary-General deposed briefly: "Ladies and gentlemen! The documents in your hands speak for themselves. The material has been inspected by experts and has been identified as a culture and a toxin, capable of wide dissemination and lethal results. Faced with this threat, all delegates to the United Nations have been instructed by their governments to vote in the General Assembly, which will commence at ten tomorrow morning. The purpose of this session is to hear the views of all member nations and to determine, by vote, whether the person who calls himself Proteus shall be admitted to address the Assembly or whether we shall refuse to receive him—with all the consequences that may entail. I have only brief comments to make. We accept the threat as genuine and not a hoax. We believe that Proteus has the means to carry it out. His identity is suspected; but, in default of final proof, we cannot at this moment publish it. We do not know, nor can we speculate on, the location or the method of disseminating the lethal material."

They were normally restless and aggressive. Now they were quiet and abashed. The news had taken them unawares. Their usual tactics were now trivial and tasteless.

The first question came from the Tass man: "This Proteus, whose identity is known but may not be stated, is he an American citizen?"

"No comment."

"Sir. Do you have any reaction from the major powers?"

"None that I can disclose. Only their delegates are briefed to speak on their behalf."

"Sir . . ." The woman from U.P. raised a respectful hand. "What would be the death toll from a biological contamination of the water supply of a city like New York?"

"I have no figures, madam. I am told it would constitute a major catastrophe."

The man from the *Washington Post* asked: "What measures are being taken to track down this Proteus and his associates and locate the toxic material?"

"These measures are under the jurisdiction of the governments concerned. I can give you no details because I do not have them. One presumes all are committed to a maximum effort."

"What is your own disposition, sir? Would you invite a blackmailer onto the floor of the Assembly?"

"My own disposition? I have none that is relevant in this crisis."

"Have you any comment on the situation?"

"I have a question." The Secretary-General was suddenly hard as granite. "A question which you may feel disposed to put to your readers and viewers. If you sit where we shall sit very soon, how would you choose? Would you treat with the blackmailer or thrust him into confinement while you watch men and cities perish? . . . You must excuse me now. I know no more than I have told you. I cannot guess beyond the next two days."

Everywhere the authorities had expected a panic. There was none. It was as if mankind were satiated with horror, drunk and numb after an orgy of violent images thrust at it hour after hour without respite. There was no place to hide. There was no board on which they could read the odds for or against their personal survival. There was no enemy to provoke their fury—not even Proteus himself, because the very magnitude of his challenge touched some chord of elation, of desperate sympathy, deep within them. The issues of good and evil were too closely entwined to distinguish them clearly. There was no appeal to the law because the law was plainly impotent against this thunderbolt intervention in human affairs.

The one image which stuck in everyone's mind was the metaphor of Russian roulette—the pistol with one bullet and five empty chambers, passed from hand to hand at a drunken party. Click! . . . The hammer strikes an empty chamber. Thank God I'm still alive. Click! Click! Click! . . . Thank God they are still alive. Bang! . . . He's dead! Well, it was his own fault, poor clown! People shouldn't play with loaded guns. It was only afterwards, and much too late, that anyone dared to ask: "What were we doing there, anyway? How did we arrive at that moment of lunacy? Why didn't someone stop us before we got too drunk to reason?"

After the first welter of sensational headlines and hastily prepared commentary, a tone of cool, if desperate, sanity began to make itself heard. The end proposed by Proteus was good. It was not beyond human accomplishment. It had been urged for years by wise and compassionate people—yea, by us, too, of the Fourth Estate. If our urgings went unheard, it was because . . . and here the reasonings became diffuse and contradictory, a mélange of the philosophy of law, the sovereignty of states, commercial considerations, political expediencies.

Still, if the end was good, could not a good means be found to attain it? Proteus was wrong to hold the world to ransom like a highwayman. . . . They had not dropped the emotive words: terrorist, blackmail, hijack; but at least, in response either to instinct or directive, they had begun to introduce qualifications that admitted some possible goodwill. No editor was prepared to admit that his hand was being guided; but when anyone fished out photographs of victims of random epidemics and said, "Let's print those. Maybe that will stop the bastard," there was a howl of protest . . . "What do you want? Mobs inside the United Nations . . ."

In the end, it was the fear of the hostile mobs that swayed the vote. At three in the afternoon, by a narrow majority, the General Assembly voted that: "In the hope of a speedy removal of a monstrous threat to humanity, we agree to invite the person called Proteus, under guarantees of immunity, to address members of this Assembly in an extraordinary session and to permit full news coverage of the occasion by all the media."

At five, John Spada telephoned the Secretary-General and received news of the decision. At ten the next morning, he landed by helicopter within the precincts of the U.N. and was escorted with Maury Feldman to the Secretary-General's office. Those who saw him remarked that, trimmed, barbered and dressed in a five-hundred-dollar suit, he made a most unlikely terrorist. To which one cynical wit answered: "Don't you know all undertakers are well dressed?"

The Secretary-General was polite, if less than cordial.

"You will both be accommodated in the building until all this is over. Your immunity is guaranteed, but all the time you are here you will be restricted to your own quarters. The press and possibly some delegates will wish to see you."

"No, sir!" John Spada refused flatly. "I go on the record once and once only, in the Assembly itself. I shall make my speech, respond to delegates' questions if they have any, then return to my quarters to await the outcome. I hope you will not have me on your hands too long."

"I hope so too, Mr. Spada." He said it like a prayer. "In the event that the outcome is favourable, I presume you will wish to contact your—er—associates."

"That will not be necessary, sir. They are instructed how to act in either event. The only danger is that if any country—and I mean *any* country—imposes a blackout on news, my colleagues will be out of communication. In that case they will distribute the contaminants to a fixed time schedule.'"

"My God!"

"It must have occurred to you, sir, that certain governments would attempt to black out or edit the news, as indeed they have done these last few days.

It would be wise to tell them what will happen if they do it tomorrow."

"But you are setting them up for judgment by their own populace; they will not accept that."

"Then they will accept the consequence."

The Secretary-General looked at Maury Feldman, who shrugged helplessly.

"I'm sorry. This is Spada's brief, not mine."

"A question, sir." Spada addressed the Secretary-General. "In the event that consent is given to my demands, are your observers ready to move? Remember the commencement date for release is a fixed feast, not a movable one."

"But surely, some flexibility . . ."

"No, sir. I am familiar with the tactics used in dealing with terrorist groups—delay, discussion, new terms, new conditions. This situation precludes them."

"You must have very good nerves, Mr. Spada."

"I assure you, sir, that I have. May I ask a service of you? I need a secretary to type up the final draft of my speech and run off copies for distribution."

"That can be arranged. Is there anything else?"

"One matter only. I have instructed Mr. Feldman here to draw a deed dedicating a part of my personal fortune, estimated at some ten million dollars, to a trust fund to be administered by the United Nations. This fund will be used for the rehabilitation of released prisoners and their families. I shall sign the deed after the amnesty has begun."

"And if there is no amnesty?"

"Then I fear the money will have little value. It's a curious commodity: an expression of confidence in the human condition. Once that confidence goes, you might just as well use it to light your pipe. . . ."

"Do you believe in God, Mr. Spada?"

"At the moment, sir, God is absent from me. I have prayed to find him again in this place."

"I pray with you, Mr. Spada," said the Secretary-General. "The absence has been too long already."

In the great chamber of the General Assembly, John Spada faced the delegates of the nations, the press of the world, the privileged audience of the potent who filled the public galleries. They were silent, grim-faced, clearly hostile to this interloper in their midst. They had not come to hear testimony but to look on the man who was to give it, to measure his strength, his resolution, his nerve as a gambler. So be it then. He himself must prove them: whether they would know a truth when they heard it, stand for or against a right when they saw it plain. But he must look beyond them, speak over them, to the world outside, where his image and his words would reach hundreds of millions who, even if they could not enforce them yet, would make their own judgments on the witness he was about to give.

The Secretary-General stood to the rostrum. His introduction was brief and bleak.

". . . We are here under duress and under protest. The man who will address you has no right to be in this place. Nevertheless, we have granted him immunity, guaranteed his security, while he is among us. In a forum held to ransom, we will grant him a free hearing. Ladies and gentlemen, this is the man who calls himself Proteus . . . Mr. John Spada."

As he stepped down from the rostrum they applauded him. When John Spada took his place, the applause died instantly to an eerie silence. Spada arranged his papers on the lectern, adjusted the microphone and began to speak, calmly and persuasively.

". . . It is true that you are here under duress; but you are here, in comfort, in your own place, free to come and go at will, to debate openly, to eat well, to demand immunities in your persons and your houses. There are others, tens of thousands of others, in prisons, in detention camps, in torture rooms, in psychiatric institutions, who are not free, whose simplest human rights have been abrogated. It is for them that I have come to speak. It is for them that I have, temporarily and very mildly, abridged your very great freedom. I remind you that, in a public document, I have permanently surrendered my own . . ."

They had expected something else—threats, exhortations, a tirade perhaps. They were not disarmed yet, but yes, they would listen. He began now to reason with them.

"I stand before you, one man, alone. You are many. Behind you there is the serried might of nations, great and small, their wealth, their armies, navies, air forces, their police, civil and secret. You have, in short, a mandate of enormous potency. I, it would appear, have none.

"I claim that I have. It is a mandate from the silent to speak for them, from the imprisoned to plead for them, from the tortured to proclaim their wrongs, from the dead to write at least a decent epitaph. This is the meaning of the name I assumed: Proteus, the shepherd of those who live in an alien element; Proteus of the many shapes. When you look at me I want you to see many other shapes and faces: the schoolgirl raped and bleeding on a table, a great scholar reduced by drugs to mumbling lunacy, a journalist beaten to a bloody pulp, a long line of detainees, inadequately fed, inadequately clothed, working in sub-zero weather. . . . You ask who gave me my mandate. They did. The hands that first offered it to me were the hands of my own daughter, tortured to extremity in Argentina. Then my wife, my daughter and my daughter's husband were murdered . . . What more motive is needed for the action I have taken? . . . Is your own patent of authority so sound? Should you not accept mine, as I do yours, de facto, and ask, not how it was come by, but what use, good or bad, is made of it?

"I will not insult you with any of the catchwords of politics: the right, the left, the center, capitalist, communist, revolutionary, deviationist, dissident . . . You have heard them all, too many times, in this place and elsewhere. These are labels, hung on mannequins. I will use other words: man, woman, child; and I will show you what was done to this man, that woman, their child." He sensed their restiveness and he challenged them sharply: "You are bored— or embarrassed? You know it already? Then why have you not risen in revolt against it? You did not do it? Of course not! There are always vicars, deputies, surrogates to do the filthy work and leave you free in conscience afterwards. You will sit! You will be silent! You will listen! . . ."

He read the catalogue, country by country, figure by figure, detail by sordid detail, until he had cowed them again into silence. Then he tossed the papers on the floor of the chamber with a gesture of contempt.

"Challenge it, if you dare! Refute it, if you can! Prove me a liar. I would welcome it! . . . You cannot. You know it. So what do you do? You say: we are delegates only, puppet voices, puppet figures. Blame our masters, not us. I blame them—dear loving God, how I blame them! But I blame you too, because you hide behind their skirts like lapdogs, whimpering at their anger. And this is why I threaten you, put you under duress: to show you that for every monster there is a mirror image, for every terror there is a response of terror, throughout all ages of ages. Amen!"

His voice was a thunder rolling through the domed chamber. After the thunder came a silence, and after the silence a passionate plea.

"Look! Listen! Take heed, I beg you! These are your brothers and sisters! Their blood is your blood, crying, not for vengeance, but for an end of this long iniquity. What are you? Savages dancing around the fire, chanting while your victims burn? Medieval inquisitors wrenching irrelevances from dying men? If you are, then the terror which I hold over you is less than you deserve. If you are not, then, in the name of whatever gods you worship, make an end of this monstrosity! Remember, time runs out!"

He stood for one silent moment, dominating them, waiting for the questions they dared not ask. Then

337

he walked out of the chamber to the room they had provided for him, threw himself on the bed and lay like a cataleptic, staring at the white ceiling.

A long time later, a long lifetime later, Maury Feldman came and sat on the edge of the bed, patted his head and said quietly, "Brother, little brother, you did well."

"Did it all go out?"

"Here and in Europe, yes, it all went out. What they did with it in other places, how they edited it— too early to know."

"What's the reaction?"

"Among the delegates? They're sobered—and impressed."

"The press?"

"They say they've got the speech of the century."

"Which means what?"

"What it always means, Johnny boy. The man's great; now let's cut his tripes out and see what's written inside his gut. . . . How do you feel?"

"Empty."

"You'd have made a great advocate."

"From you, that's high praise. What will they do now?"

"What they always do: confer, confabulate, in the end, dilute."

"Can they?"

"Sure they can. All they have to do is put a 'but' at the end of every sentence: 'A noble plea, but . . . A splendid piece of rhetoric, but . . . An impressive summary of evidence, but . . .'"

"But what, Maury?"

"But they can't let you get away with it—no way, no how!"

"What can they say? It's all in the record. What can they do?"

"Wear you down. There's fourteen days before the amnesty has to begin. That's a long time. They'll make you sweat every hour of it."

"Stay around! Please, Maury!"

"Sure; but sometimes I have to sleep, go to the can, make phone calls. That's when they'll come at you. Can you take it?"

"I have to take it. Did you call Kitty?"

"Yes. She's coming to see you."

"How does she feel?"

"Proud. Disturbed about some things, but proud, yes."

"I'd love a drink."

"I'll try to find you a bottle. I mistrust the bar service."

"Do you think they'd try to poison me?"

"No, but I'd like to break the seals myself."

"Thanks, Maury."

"Thank you. You almost restored my faith in human nature, but I still wouldn't gamble too much on it. Let me go find that bottle."

His next visitor was the Secretary-General, polite as always, but this time much more cordial.

"My compliments, Mr. Spada. I have heard many fine speeches in my time; yours was the most moving."

"Thank you, sir. Now can you tell me what it has achieved?"

"Too early for that, Mr. Spada. It's not the reaction in the chamber that counts but the delayed one, when the delegates write their cables and respond to their inquisitors at home. . . . I will tell you something though: I hope with all my heart your bluff works."

Again Spada felt the cold fingers of fear tightening around his heart. He waited until the spasm had passed and then said, "It was not, is not, a bluff."

"I had hoped it was. You did much tonight, Mr. Spada, more than we have been able to do in ten years on this issue. We could hold the good you have won for us. I should hate to see it lost by—by untimely action."

"Not untimely; timed to the second, in fact. Don't deceive yourself. Don't let your colleagues betray you into illusion."

"I see." The Secretary-General was immediately formal. "Well, rest easy, Mr. Spada. We shall do what we can. Mr. Feldman tells me Ms. Kitty Cowan would like to visit you. I've arranged for her immediate admission."

"Thank you."

"One other matter. Ambassador Kolchak from Washington would like to see you. May I send him in?"

"Do you know what he wants?"

"I have not asked him."

"Send him in then."

Anatoly Kolchak and Maury Feldman arrived at the same moment. Spada made the introductions. Maury Feldman poured the drinks. Kolchak opened the play in his studious style.

"You were very impressive tonight, Mr. Spada."

"Thank you, Mr. Ambassador."

"I'll drink to that," said Maury Feldman. "But tell me something, Mr. Ambassador: was Mr. Spada's address televised in Moscow?"

"Most of it, yes."

"What do you mean, most of it?"

Anatoly Kolchak had his answer ready.

"The schedule of crimes and victims was edited out, as it was, I believe, in other places. Instead, there was what we call a 'dialectical analysis of the occasion.' I didn't see it, obviously, so I can't tell you how good it was. However, the rest of the transmission was intact."

"How many people saw it?"

"I don't know," said Anatoly Kolchak. "I would guess everyone who has a television set. Of course, we must not forget the vast radio audience. The excised portions were made available to a more select group: the Presidium, the K.G.B., our monitors in Moscow. I'll probably have their assessments tomorrow."

John Spada lay back on the bed and clasped his hands behind his head.

"I hope they get their sums right."

"I'm sure they will," said Anatoly Kolchak evenly. "The mathematics are not complicated. We have a population of between two hundred and fifty and two hundred and eighty million people. An estimate has been made that in a city of half a million contaminated by botulinus, we might expect a ten percent casualty rate before control measures become effective. That makes .003 or .004 percent of the population. Multiply it by ten, twenty, it is still a minimal figure, Mr. Spada. Compared with our wartime losses, our predicted losses in the event of a new war, it is—how do you say it?—peanuts!"

"And if your wife, or your son, were one of the peanuts?"

"It would break my heart," said Anatoly Kolchak. "But states have no heart, only people. I tell you this, not to mock you, simply to show you the odds against which you gamble. I happen to believe you are right, so I am doing my best . . . I fear it may not be enough."

"Then tell your people this, Mr. Ambassador. In Russia, six cities will be hit in sequence! Moscow will be one of them!"

"I believe you. In Moscow they may not. But thank you for telling me." He finished his drink at a gulp and walked out.

Maury Feldman said dryly, "There goes an honest man."

"So are they all, all honourable men!"

"Not all, Johnny boy! There are some right royal bastards, and you're going to meet some of them very soon."

That night, although he was brutally tired, he slept shallowly, his dreams haunted by debates and arguments of which the thread always eluded him. In the morning he rose early and forced himself to do fifteen minutes of floor exercises; then, bathed, shaved and dressed, he knocked on Maury Feldman's door. Maury was pouring coffee for two very formal fellows who looked like lawyers practicing to be judges. Maury presented them casually.

"Mr. Adams, Mr. Jewison . . . My client, John Spada. These gentlemen are attached to the U.S. delegation here. They wanted to talk to you. Wisely they decided to see me first."

"Mind if I have some coffee?"

"Help yourself. I'll call for some more."

Spada settled himself in a corner of the settee and asked: "Well, gentlemen, what can I do for you?"

"We'd like to ask you some questions."

"Forget the questions," said Feldman. "I'd have to advise him not to answer them. We'll probably get further if you tell Mr. Spada what you've just been telling me."

"Any way you want it." Mr. Adams was surprisingly relaxed. "You're probably aware, Mr. Spada, that the U.N. is jealous of its independence and its immunities. There would be much resentment if U.S. agencies began intruding on its premises or its business. We're accredited here, so we're functioning as, shall we say, intermediaries. We'd like to discuss your offer to surrender yourself at the end of these proceedings."

"Yes?"

"You realize what that surrender entails?"

"Of course. I'll be arrested."

"You are probably also aware that, pending your trial on criminal charges, you would be held in custody without bail."

"That's probable but not certain," said Maury Feldman. "Since we cannot preempt legal decisions."

"We also cannot preempt certain risks to Mr. Spada while he is in custody. The word is already around that quite a lot of people want him dead, and prisons are notoriously unsafe places for unpopular people. So . . . we'd suggest there is the basis of a deal."

"What sort of deal?"

"The kind that's been made before with cooperative subjects: an arranged escape, a new identity, the chance to begin a new life elsewhere."

"Amnesty, in fact," said Feldman dryly.

"Yes, you could call it that."

"And what kind of cooperation would be expected of me?"

"Names and places. Where the toxins are made, who's handling them . . . that sort of thing."

"In short, a sellout," said John Spada. "Let me ask you a question, Mr. Adams. Why would you amnesty a self-confessed criminal rather than hundreds and thousands of innocent people who are at present in confinement?"

"Because," said Mr. Adams, "there are hundreds of thousands of other innocent people whom you threaten with a painful and miserable death if your demands are not met."

"So meet the demands and the threat is removed. Amnesty can be given at the stroke of a pen. Why wait for the avenging angel to write it in blood?"

Adams gave him a long, searching look and asked: "Is that how you see yourself, Mr. Spada— as an avenging angel?"

"No, Mr. Adams. I've simply changed the balance of power a little. I've introduced enough authority to make possible a negotiation which no one would have considered before."

"So you would negotiate?" Mr. Adams was a fraction too eager.

Before Spada had a chance to answer, Maury Feldman cut in: "What the hell do you think this is all about? Spada's not peddling chestnuts. He's not trying to make himself King or Pope. He's demanding a human right for those who have been deprived of it. He says simply, if you don't give back the right, he'll try to force you to do it, and he has the means at hand. Now that's one side of the negotiating table. There has to be a response from the other: yes, no or maybe!"

"Fair enough, Counsellor. It gives me a small something to go back with, but I need more. Where are the supplies of toxin made and located, Mr. Spada?"

"No dice!" Spada shook his head. "I stand where I stood at the beginning. You give me live bodies; I'll give you the toxin."

"Before we finish," said Mr. Adams quietly, "understand this! We're the only people who can offer you half a chance of staying alive. You think about that, Mr. Spada."

"I have thought about it, Mr. Adams. I wish I could say it was important to me. It isn't. Besides"—he added a final wry comment—"you forget the Proteus story: you have to hold the god and bind him before he disgorges his secrets. Just when you think you have him, he changes shape. . . ."

Mr. Adams opened his mouth to reply, but Maury Feldman silenced him with a gesture.

"It seems to me, Mr. Adams, that you're on the wrong track. You object—and rightly—to the fact that my client is holding a threat over the nations. But you yourself are holding a similar threat over him. Isn't that precisely what has brought us to this pass? There cannot be one law for the state and another for the individual citizen."

Mr. Adams had the grace to concede the point. He shrugged resignedly.

"That's the name of the game, isn't it? It always has been. It always will be."

"If you believe that," said John Spada, "why should you care how many people die? The planet's overpopulated anyway."

"I guess it's a question of scale." For the first time Mr. Jewison found voice. "It's in the Bible, isn't it? It is expedient that one man should die for the people."

"I've already volunteered," said John Spada. "All you have to do is pick up the contract."

12

<><><><><><><><><><><><><><><><><><><><><><><><><><

In the afternoon the Secretary-General came to
see them. He looked strained and tired. He explained
himself with care and gravity.

". . . Mr. Spada, we are now at a critical moment. We need your cooperation to get us through it.
The General Assembly has appointed a special committee to deal with this situation. The committee con-
sists of delegates from the United States, the Soviet
Union, France, Italy, Brazil, Japan, China, Sweden
and Saudi Arabia. At its first meeting this morning
the committee raised three principal issues. First: If a
bargain is struck, both parties must be able to
guarantee performance. There is considerable doubt
as to whether you can offer an adequate guarantee.
Second: How can the member nations be sure that
your public communications to your members mean
what they say? Third: Your offer to surrender your
own person is deemed inadequate without the surrender of other key personnel in your organization.
In sum, your letter indicated a contrived threat. How
can we be sure that the threat will not be repeated

on another occasion, in respect of other issues like arms limitation or a Middle East peace treaty?"

There was a moment's silence before Maury Feldman said quietly, "It's a proper question, John. I think you should try to answer it. After all, recent terrorist history is not encouraging. One successful blackmail has always led to other attempts."

"I'm aware of that." Spada nodded a sober agreement. "I have been from the beginning. So in selecting members of the Proteus organization to carry out this operation I was careful to choose only those who would hold rigidly to the orders laid down."

"And what were those orders, Mr. Spada?" The Secretary-General was intent as a judge in court.

"The first and most important was that they would accept as authentic only a personal appearance by me on television—not a press message, not a recorded radio message, but solely a visual appearance, where they could see my face, my gestures, and hear my voice issuing from my own lips. The second was that the words I spoke would bear exactly the meaning which they carried in a dictionary—no more, no less. For those who do not understand English a prearranged gesture will carry the meaning. The third was that, in the event of a bargain being made, they would deposit all supplies of cultures and toxins in an appropriate place and inform the local police by an anonymous telephone call where they could be found. Finally, if an agreement was not reached, or if I failed to appear and say the appropriate words, they would disseminate the toxins in agreed areas on a series of fixed dates. . . . I trust I have made myself clear?"

"Very clear, Mr. Spada. But since the cultures are

easy to reproduce, there is no guarantee against a repetition."

"There can't be," said Spada flatly. "The bacillus is of common occurrence. You can dig it up in garden soil and start the whole process again. Anyone with the necessary skills can do that."

"Are you prepared to nominate the first targets?"

"No."

"Are any others of your personnel prepared to surrender themselves?"

"No."

"Are they aware of your offer to surrender your own person?"

"Yes."

"Are they aware of the danger to themselves if you are submitted to protracted interrogation?"

"That possibility has been fully considered and appropriate provisions have been made. You must be very clear on this; you must convey it accurately to the committee. Everything depends upon my final appearance in the General Assembly and its authentic transmission on television. It could happen, you see, that if one country decides to censor the program, that country would be struck while others were relieved of the threat."

"Suppose for any reason—illness or accident or even a breakdown of communications—you failed to appear?"

"Then the operation would proceed automatically. That's another thing you must impress on your colleagues. They must keep me alive and sane."

"Do you really believe they would do otherwise, Mr. Spada?"

"I have good reason to know that they would."

Spada's tone was cold as a winter wind. "This is the age of the assassins, and I am its perfect product—man reduced to zero in the ledgers of the state. . . . Is there anything else?"

"One matter only. Are you prepared to have Mr. Feldman negotiate on your behalf? I fear you may be too harsh an advocate in your own cause."

"That's why I'm here," said Maury Feldman. "I hope we can agree before we all hit zero."

"I have a request to make," said John Spada. "You are allowing Ms. Cowan to visit me. I appreciate the kindness. I should also like a visit from my confessor."

"Your confessor?" The Secretary-General stared at him in surprise.

Spada shrugged and smiled. "Is it so surprising? I am—or I was—a professing Christian. I am also very close to the end. I should like to dispose myself accordingly."

"It seems a reasonable request."

"It might help us all," said Maury Feldman. "I'll get in touch with him and bring him here—with your permission, of course, Mr. Secretary-General."

"I'll write an admission card for you." The Secretary-General stood up. "Our security precautions are very strict now. May I have his name, please?"

"Father Pavel . . . The Reverend Father Pavel. He's retired from parish duties and is now living privately. But I'd like him spared any embarrassment."

"There will be no embarrassment," said the Secretary-General firmly. "We could use a little godliness in this place. I take it you'll hold yourself at our disposal, Mr. Feldman? There's a great deal of work to be done."

"And little time to do it," said Maury Feldman.

"Blame your client for that," said the Secretary-General, and he walked out without another word.

When the door closed behind him, Maury Feldman exploded into low-toned anger. "For God's sake, John! What game are you playing now? The Scarecrow Man here! It's idiocy!"

"It's a private matter," said John Spada flatly. "I want him to collect a debt."

"If I were Lunarcharsky, I'd be a thousand miles away from here."

"But you're not," said Spada wearily. "He's got ice water in his veins and a stone where his heart should be. He'll feel quite at home here."

Next day Kitty Cowan came to see him. He was shocked at her appearance. She looked pinched and pale. There were lines of strain at the corners of her mouth. When he kissed her and put his arms around her she burst into tears. It took him a long time to soothe her.

Then she said, "I'm sorry. It's just seeing big John Spada locked up in here like a prisoner."

"I'm fine, Kitty. The liquor's good, the food's adequate and I'm playing poker for high stakes! How are you?"

"I'm lost. I don't seem to understand anything anymore. When I saw you on television I thought: 'Look at him! That's a real mensch. That's the man I love!' Then when I heard what people were saying, when I read what terrible things this germ thing can

351

do . . . I couldn't believe it was you who were threatening to use it. . . ." She fumbled in her purse and brought out a folded newspaper clipping. "Read that!"

Spada shrugged and scanned the familiar facts: the ease of procurement; the infinitesimal dosage that would kill a normal man; the symptoms of dizziness, nausea, double vision, the cranial involvement that presaged death; the high mortality rate of at least 50 percent of infected cases; the limited availability of antitoxin; the difficulty of policing water supplies. He folded the paper and handed it back.

"It's a pretty accurate report."

"And you could inflict that suffering on innocent people—even on babes in arms?"

"If necessary, yes."

"I don't believe it!"

"It doesn't matter what you believe. It's what they believe in cabinets and chanceries and in the U.N. Assembly chamber. They're trying to persuade themselves I'm bluffing, but I'm not."

"I don't know what to say." Suddenly she was trembling. She leaned against the table edge to steady herself. "We've been friends. We've been lovers. I still wake in the night and imagine you're there. . . . Now, suddenly, I'm staring at an executioner with an axe in his hand! . . . For God's sake! There must be some alternative, some compromise."

"Then they have to bring it to me. The moment they believe I'm weakening they'll bore in like jackals and tear me to bits. You've been around long enough to know how the power game works."

"Oh yes! But suddenly it turns out I know nothing at all! Do you think Anna or Rodo or Teresa would have wanted you to do this? Would they have let you do it?"

"I don't know, and they're not here to ask."

"But I'm here and I'm asking. Why? Why?"

"Sit down!" Suddenly he was harsh and peremptory. She obeyed, cautiously, like a child with an angry parent. Spada reached out to stroke her hair. She drew back as if afraid of his touch. "You ask why? Because this is a rigged game. The only way you can play it is with guns on the table and eyes in the back of your head. Even you, my love—you're a kind of enemy, because you distract me, you soften me. I can't afford that. The moment my attention wanders, they'll be in for the kill. . . . But if I can stand the pressure long enough, they'll be the ones to crack, because none of them is as absolute as I am. They've all got monitors—the press, their cabinets, people who want their jobs, the voters. I see you cringe from me as though I'm some kind of monster. Why don't you try again to see me as I was on the floor of the chamber, hear me as I spoke then? That was a truth. That was John Spada telling it. . . . I love you, girl. I don't want to go out with you hating me; but if I must, so be it!"

"I can never hate you, John." She reached out a tentative hand to make contact with him again. "It's just that it's all too big for me—too complicated and confusing."

"Then keep it simple. Listen! What they did to Teresa and Rodo was an act of hate. They like to debase people, humiliate them, dehumanize them. At least there's still love in what I do. I'm hanging on to that—but if I lose it, that's the end. Without love, a human being is just a paper football that kids

353

kick to pieces in an alley. Please, for your own sake, try to hold on to that one thought. . . ."

For all his indifference to it, the threat to his life was real. Now there were guards posted at each end of the corridor outside his room. His food was specially prepared. The liquor they served him was brought in bottles with the seals intact. His request, relayed through Maury Feldman, to be allowed to take some exercise in the precincts of the building was refused by the Secretary-General.

". . . They're scared," Maury Feldman explained wearily. "And I don't blame them. There's a lot of steam building up, even among the delegates and the staff. I talk to them as much as I can, and the full meaning of the situation is just beginning to dawn on them. All this crap they're talking about shades of odds and tolerable risks doesn't mean much if you're thinking about wives and families in a possible contamination area."

"How is it"—Spada gave him a sidelong grin—"you've never asked me where the toxins are and how they'll be disseminated?"

"Simple prudence, lover! If anyone thought I had half an idea, I'd be just as vulnerable as you are. I have no, repeat no, desire at all to find myself sweating under the lights in some dank cellar. As a matter of fact, I've been very plain with everyone: I don't know; I don't want to know; I've never asked you to tell me, period."

"What's your best judgment on where we stand now?"

"For the moment, everyone's stalled on the old

354

threadbare proposition that no government can, or should, bow to a threat of terror. That's balls, of course! They've bowed before; they'll bow again—to Arabs, Japanese, Germans—even to the oil sheikhs who have another kind of blackmail. But they've got to hang up the window dressing first, hold the citizens' trust, keep order in the streets. They're scared. Every damned intelligence service in the world is scouring the streets and the cellars for your cultures and your people. Airport security is doubled. They're holding people for hours at customs and immigration checkpoints. International travel is a nightmare just now. . . . So they're hurting; but who's going to make the first move and talk amnesty? The wisest thing you ever did was to get yourself immunity in this place. Otherwise they'd have you strapped down with electrodes up your backside! And that could still happen, make no mistake!"

"Why so?"

"Because one of the phrases I hear is 'an outlaw under the protection of the law.' Another is 'murder by protocol.' If they gain too wide a currency, you could be hauled out of here with a sack over your head. So far the Secretary-General is holding firm, but he's only human."

"I promised I'd surrender myself."

"They need that like a cold in the head, lover! This is black theater now. They need an act to top yours on the program. So far they haven't found it, but when they do . . ." He left the sentence unfinished and began sketching an indecent triptych on a sapphic theme. "I warned you, didn't I? This is royal tennis, played by right royal bastards."

"Oh Christ! Pour me a drink, will you?"

"Pour it yourself. I'm your attorney, not your butler!"

John Spada gaped at him for a moment and then burst into laughter. Maury Feldman gave him a slow, sardonic grin.

"I can be wittier than that if it helps."

Spada spluttered and gurgled and wiped his streaming eyes.

"Man. Oh, man! They really are getting to me, aren't they? They'll be using you next."

He poured two drinks and handed one to Maury Feldman. They drank deeply and in silence.

Feldman put down his glass and said flatly, "They are using me, John."

"What?"

"Sure. Why do they let me stay? Why am I free to wander about and talk to the delegates and the newsmen and the hired help? They figure that, when the day of reason dawns, I'll be here, Feldman the Wise, the Plato of Park Avenue, to write the settlement."

"And you will?"

"Yes."

"When will that bright day dawn?"

"Whenever you say, John."

Spada stared at him in disbelief. "Not you too?"

"Me too," said Maury Feldman. "The madness has gone on long enough."

He thrust a hand into his breast pocket and brought out two handwritten pages. He handed them to Spada and said, "Those are my suggestions. Study them and tell me what you think."

"Who else has seen these?" Spada was suddenly wary and black-tempered.

"You're the first."

"I hope to Christ I can believe you."

"If you can't"—Feldman was ice-cold—"get yourself another attorney."

"I beg your pardon. I had no right to say that."

"The subject is under stress and therefore has diminished responsibility. But straighten up now, soldier, and think! That's a good document. We might just get away with it."

Maury Feldman's written opinion was simple and concise.

Against the assembled nations, their vast aggregates of population and resources, your power is inadequate and temporary. The damage you may inflict on them is horrible but tolerable. On the other hand, the damage they would suffer by abrogating their authority to a biological blackmail would be intolerable to them.

My conclusion is that they will compromise and that you must compromise. They will not surrender their sovereignties. You will have to surrender your toxins. They will trade bodies for that. They will not trade reputations. You will have to capitulate first, not they.

As to the terms, I believe we could settle as follows: the nations would agree to release, on a given date, a limited number of detainees. Before that date you would publicly remove the threat and surrender or destroy the toxins. There is an inherent difficulty here. Since the culture and the toxin can be reproduced indefinitely, your guarantee of their destruction is of little value. However, we'll argue that at the time.

The merits of this proposal are, first, a moral and a factual victory for you, in that a substantial number of prisoners would regain their liberty; second, a face-saving operation for governments who, good or bad, have to continue to govern; third, a deterrent for any other persons or organizations which might try to organize a similar blackmail in the future.

Conclusion: an all-or-nothing stance only gets you more misery; a compromise gets you some amnesties."

"It's zero!" Spada exploded. "No guarantees, a token gesture, and I disarm myself. No way!"

"Amend it then! Improve it!" Maury Feldman was exasperated. "But don't throw it in the trash can. It's a starting point."

"O.K. Let's talk figures. Let's say one contamination of a large city equals fifty thousand dead. How many live bodies will they give me? One for one? Pro rata by population? Next, how can I believe their promises?"

"By the same token, why should they believe yours?"

"Right! So it's cash on the barrel head. The observers cable that the bodies are at the railhead. We tell them where the toxins can be picked up."

"In that case, how do you disjoin the two operations in the public mind? The nations have to win. You have to lose."

"And the only way I can contact my people is by

way of television. I have to deliver the message in person."

"So the viewers watch you eat crow." Feldman shrugged. "I guess it's not half as bad as dying of botulism."

"Let's get back to guarantees."

"I wouldn't if I were you," said Feldman somberly. "You've compromised yourself too far. Remember that piece in your letter about a continuing biological threat. You think they're going to forget that? This is a tough brief to plead, lover. Don't have any illusions about it. Well . . . what's the decision? Do I start peddling the idea or not?"

"Start peddling," said John Spada. "But never let them forget we've still got the toxins."

On the Saturday afternoon, when the U.N. was reduced to a skeleton operation, Maury Feldman brought the Scarecrow Man to see him. There was a macabre comedy in the spectacle of Lunarcharsky, dressed in clerical black, looking for all the world like a shabby curé out of a continental fiction. By some trick of makeup he had managed to transform himself so that even a close-up photograph would not identify him. He carried a battered breviary. The end of a frayed stole dangled from his coat pocket. Even his diction had a special unctuous quality.

His first words were: "I understand you wanted to make your confession, my son. Are we private enough here?"

"You're private," said Feldman curtly. "It's the first thing I established with the Secretary-General. The room is swept for electronic bugs every day. I'll leave you two to your religious exercise!"

When he had gone, the Scarecrow Man surveyed Spada like a museum specimen and then nodded approval.

"Not bad! You're wearing well enough. How is it going?"

"It's rough. It'll get rougher. What's the climate like outside?"

"Changeable," said the Scarecrow Man. "It depends on the company you keep. . . . On the issue of the prisoners, there's sympathy and some understanding. But when you talk about toxins in the water, there's pure anger. I'd say you could get yourself torn limb from limb before you walked a hundred yards on Broadway. . . ."

"But if we win?"

"The betting is you'll break. What did you want to see me about?"

"My two friends in Argentina. Major O'Higgins and the President. I promised a day of reckoning. I want you to see that it's arranged."

"It will be a pleasure. Do we send them an engraved invitation?"

"No. Let them get the news at the judgment seat."

"Spoken like a true Christian. Does your own judgment bother you?"

"Yes," said John Spada. "It bothers me. Before it comes I hope to prepare a speech for the defense."

"It might be a good idea," said the Scarecrow Man. "I can't speak for the Almighty because I don't believe He exists. However, it could be a useful document for posterity—provided there are any left to read it."

Maury Feldman's first brief document had been favourably received. It was seen as "a first ray of hope, a possible ground of negotiation," which, as Feldman put it, was like swinging a carrot in front of the donkey while someone found a stick to beat him on the rump.

"What happens now?" asked John Spada.

"Hell! You've drawn contracts yourself! You've sweated people with drafts and redrafts. Just imagine it's you sitting out there in a polyglot committee, where each member has to report to the big boys at home. They've still got a week before deadline. You can count on them to make the most of it. Why don't you relax and catch up on your reading?"

"I have been," said Spada with a grin. He held up a paperback copy of Machiavelli's *The Prince*. "Years since I've read it. It's instructive, if not encouraging. . . . There's something I want to get straight between us."

"I thought we always had been straight with each other."

"We have. I want to keep it that way."

"Go ahead."

"Are you sure we'll get a compromise?"

"I believe we will. I can't be sure."

"Suppose we don't?"

"Then the final decision rests with you."

"I decide to disseminate the toxin. Where do you stand then?"

"I am not here," said Feldman gravely. "I walk away. I am a servant of the law. I defend my clients under the law. I cannot, I will not, cooperate with them in the commission of a crime."

"Nor would I ask you to do it. But your regard is

important to me, Maury. More important than you know. During the war you killed, you blew up barracks and houses. People died. . . . When you come finally to judge me, remember that.

"There's another question."

"Make it an easy one."

"I wish I could. Is a state less guilty than an individual? Is it beyond attainder because there is no court before which it can be tried? Is there no redress against its monstrosities?"

"None—except the bloodbath. That's why I draw dirty pictures. They distract me from the dirtiest one of all—what man inflicts on his own offspring. Anything else?"

"Just this. When and if we get a settlement and you bring it to me to sign, you know you can guarantee my performance; can you guarantee theirs?"

Feldman's answer, for all the irony with which he pronounced it, was touched with the pathos of despair.

"I'm an attorney. I draw very good documents. God makes men. I've never felt able to guarantee His handiwork. Sad, isn't it?"

As the days and the nights passed, in his room in the great building, the sadness grew in John Spada. They were really sweating him now, sending him reams of papers: conditions, exclusions, addenda, interpretations, extra clauses, sub-clauses and cross-references that made his eyes water and his head swim.

Maury Feldman was with him less and less now because he was called to this committee and that sub-committee, with interpreters, with Embassy lawyers, clerks and drafters of legal jargon. Each time he came, stubble-cheeked and weary, there was a new summary to be prepared, a new decision to be made against the inexorable fidget of the hand across the clock face. They were sweating him, too, and he confessed it in a final burst of vehemence.

"First it's the numbers. Russia agrees one, then withdraws because the Argentine won't give more. The Chileans want the Cubans to concede as many as they do. The South Africans and the Koreans are ganged up against the East Germans and the Czechs. You'd think it was cattle they were trading, not human beings. Then it's the observers: who's acceptable and who isn't. Some want the Red Cross. Some will take Amnesty. The Iranians won't have religious groups. The British want a clean distinction between prisoners of conscience and political terrorists. . . . Then there's the time factor, and the delivery points, and where the released people are to be housed, and how to ensure they won't be pulled back when the crisis is over . . . It's a bloody madhouse! They all say much more time is needed."

"I wondered when they'd get to that." Spada was grim. "It's the technique, isn't it? Push back the deadline. Once they're over that, the first crisis is past. They can breathe freely and think up new ways to stall against the second deadline. This time, Maury, they're not going to do it."

"I've told them, John. I think they believe it. I've suggested a way out. If you buy it, I'll try to fight it through."

"Let's hear it." Spada waved a hand at the mess of papers around them. "Anything would sound good after this dreck!"

363

"Before I start," said Feldman cautiously, "remember the big stumbling block. They insist that we disjoin the two events. The threat must be removed first; then the amnesty can take place. Clear?"

"Clear, but . . ."

"Forget the buts. Just listen! The deadline is noon, Tuesday, New York time. Now here's the proposal. Between now and then we feed the press the usual routine: hopeful negotiations, settlement near, all that. Your people are on notice and waiting for the final television transmission. At nine A.M., New York time, you go on the air with a statement. Goodwill has been shown. Humanity has been displayed. In view of this you surrender your position. You call on your people to make known the location of the toxin. Twenty-four hours later the first token groups are released. One hundred prisoners from each country. The observers are already on hand to supervise their reception. Meantime, the negotiations for larger numbers go on."

"And all that's in the statement?"

"All of it. A public commitment has been made. Even if they stall later, it's a start."

"Why can't the two things be done simultaneously?"

"Sovereignty, for Christ's sake! We've been over it a hundred times!"

"Who writes the broadcast statement?"

"You do; but they'll have to agree it."

"O.K., let's try it for size. But I reserve my position until I see the final terms."

"Good. I'll take it back to them now."

"Stay and have some dinner with me first."

"No, thanks. I've lost my appetite. They're carrion birds out there."

"Tell them I'm not dead yet."

He was very near dead and he knew it. They had him backed against a wall, and their swords were pricking at his throat. Once they had him disarmed, the game was over; and the token releases, even if they took place, would be the last and only gain—low-category inmates, washed out and empty, whom the jailers would gladly send back to the charity of the world. Their promises were worthless. He had seen too many documents not to know that they were hedged and qualified to extinction. Before you could extract a meaning, let alone an enforceable judgment, you could litigate for ten years and feed an army of lawyers on the way.

Mercy? Anatoly Kolchak had said it, straight and plain: men had hearts; Russians, Americans, Chileans, Chinese, they all had hearts; but states, nations, juntas, they had none. They were idols with hollow bellies, filled with the charred bones of children. By some strange trick of memory he had a picture of Rudolf Hess, an old, broken madman, sitting in Spandau prison, denied the most minimal mercy, while others, a thousand times more guilty, waxed fat in freedom. This was statecraft. This was politics. This was the power game pushed to its ultimate, obscene absurdity.

In spite of Maury Feldman's hopes they wrangled for another three days over the wording of his surrender document. They would have no more sermons, they said, no more propaganda for a lost cause. He had agreed to disjoin the threat from the act of grace; they would not permit him to rejoin them. His case had been stated once. He might state, briefly, the issue upon which it had failed; if he attempted to elaborate it, he would be cut off the air.

Then they came up with a new demand. He must reveal the names of his accomplices as well as the location of the toxin. On this point he was adamant. He would not betray his friends. He could not change the agreed communication arrangements, since this would indicate to his collaborators that he was acting under duress. This was take-it-or-leave-it time. They took it and hated him. Their hatred was the last justification for what he intended to do. He signed the document at seven in the evening on the day before the deadline.

Maury Feldman stuffed the document in his briefcase and fished out a brown envelope. He said, "I didn't mention this before. I never thought I'd win it. It's a new passport with a new name. You're free to go wherever it will take you, as long as you can stay alive. . . . Our people agreed because they don't want the sweat of bringing you to public trial and having the whole debate on their hands again."

Spada held the document in his hands for a moment, then passed it back. His voice was unsteady. "Thanks, Maury—thanks for everything. But I can't accept it. If I do, it will be seen that I've sold out, that I've made a bad deal to save my own skin. No way I'll submit to that indignity."

"It's your life, lover," said Maury Feldman. "I can't say I disagree."

"I've got something for you, Maury. I'd like you to read it and show it to Kitty. It's what I'd hoped I could say tomorrow. Still, there's no one who will understand it better than you."

He put his arms around Feldman and they embraced in the old Latin way. For the first time since their friendship began, Maury's control cracked. Characteristically he cursed himself.

"Christ! The Jews and the Italians—we must be the greatest wailers in the world!"

"Relax!" said Spada with a grin. "You're getting paid for the tears as well!"

"This time there's no fee." Maury refused to be comforted.

"Come on! All this work . . ."

"Call it the coin of the tribute," said Maury Feldman. "I owe it to you. I'm sorry we lost the case. See you tomorrow in court."

It was perhaps an hour later when Anatoly Kolchak came in, solicitous and urbane as ever. Yes, he would enjoy a drink. Now that the great, windy debate was over, he would like to spend a few moments with a friend.

"John . . ." It was the first time he had ever used the Christian name. "I had to come. I had to pay a respect."

"Thank you, Anatoly."

"To say something also. You have not lost. You have gained more than you will ever know. I wish it had been a full triumph, but I am a servant of what is. Perhaps my children will enjoy what can be."

"I'll drink to that."

"How do you feel?"

"Empty."

"I shall be in the gallery tomorrow. I should like you to know you will have a friend."

"I'll remember it . . . Tell me, Anatoly, will they keep their promises?"

"They will seem to keep them," said Anatoly Kolchak. "That's the game, isn't it?"

"Yes, that's the game."

"Where will you go afterwards?"

"I haven't thought of it."

"You cannot always be a fugitive with a false passport. So if I can help . . . some small republic perhaps, where the people are too ignorant to read, too simple to care about anything but the rain and the maize crop. Something can be arranged."

"It won't be necessary. Thanks, my friend."

"For nothing. Try to get a good night's sleep. Tomorrow will be bad; but, like love affairs and financial scandals, it will be a nine-day wonder."

"I know. That's the problem. People have such short memories."

"If they hadn't," said Anatoly Kolchak, "a political career would mean a first-class ticket to a death cell."

In the great chamber they were all assembled again, not grim this time, not fearful, as they had been before, but quietly exultant, waiting for the epilogue in which good would triumph over evil, order over chaos, the art of the possible over the impossible dream.

This time there was no introduction from the Secretary-General. The murmurs died as John Spada advanced to the rostrum alone with a single sheet of paper in his hand. He laid it on the lectern, smoothed it against the wood and read from it in a dead, level voice.

"I say what it is agreed that I say, not what I myself believe. One man, alone, I entered into contest with the nations of the world, with the forces of law and established order, to plead a human cause. I backed the plea with a threat, because the forces of law and established order also hold threats over us all. My cause, the cause of the silent, has been lost.

"It is lost upon a fundamental issue: whether the individual is more important than the mass, the sovereignty of a nation less important than the liberty of the people who live within its boundaries. You, the nations, have decided against me. Whether the people have so decided, I do not know, because I have not heard them speak.

"I am promised that, as an act of grace, some categories of prisoners will be released in all countries. This is a good thing, but it is not enough. The shame still lies upon you. You have yet to endure the scorn of your children. For myself, I have no more to say.

"The following message is for my friends and collaborators . . . 'Proteus to the fishes, capitulate! Proteus to the fishes, capitulate! Proteus to the fishes, capitulate!' I go now to join the silent."

The cameraman held on him. They had been told that the last gesture was an integral part of the script. Spada raised his left hand to his lips. Then he lifted the water glass from the rostrum and drank. He put down the glass. They saw his face contort in a rictus of agony; then, in full view of the delegates of a hundred and forty-nine nations, he collapsed.

In his apartment on Park Avenue, Maury Feldman read aloud the last testament of John Spada:

"... On this, the eve of my exit from the world, I find myself very calm. This is strange, because, in spite of all, I am still a believer and I am convinced that there must be some kind of casting up of accounts, some judgment upon our deeds and misdeeds. I know that I am not guiltless. I do not ask that anything I have done be condoned or excused. At the same time, I am aware that there was a terrible, inevitable logic to this situation. The exercise of power was habitual to me. I was educated not to suffer but to act. The act once performed, I was committed to its consequence, however long, however drastic.

"From my youngest years, the Christian ethic was proposed to me: forgive your enemies, bless those who curse you, pray for your persecutors. I assented to it as a formal creed; but the truth is that I was never able to consent to it absolutely or apply it in my own life. I wonder—as I have wondered many times—what would have happened had I been able to accept the violation of my daughter with resignation, leaving redress to an unseen God? I do not know. I think if I had been the victim I could have forgiven the violator. But as the witness, the vicarious sufferer? God help me! I still cannot believe there is enough grace in the world for that kind of submission. If we cannot invoke the law in defense of the innocent, what is left but the code of retaliation?

370

"So I fought back! I killed. I threatened to kill. I walked the long road to the edge of the world and saw that it came to a dead end. One more step and I would be whirling in a void. So I drew back, not from cowardice, but simply because I saw that the final act was a pointless massacre of innocents. Yet even as I retracted, I knew that others would not. I knew, as certainly as I know that summer follows spring, that some mad general, some desperate committee would one day pull the plug and flush mankind into nowhere. My gamble was that mankind, seeing the imminent horror, would reject it in a universal revulsion. The gamble has failed.

"Even so, I want it known, at least to my friends, that my suicide is not an act of despair. It is—I wish it to be—a religious act, a donation to my friends, whom I know I could betray under torture. . . . And let no one think that torture is some kind of medieval monstrosity, with hooded inquisitors and red-hot pokers. We have that, too, but in our enlightened age it is an unnecessary sadism. Deprive any man of light and sound and tactile reference, you will reduce him in days to total insanity. Feed him psychotropic drugs and you will do it sooner. And even we, the free, the enlightened and the civilized, practice these brutalities. I do not believe that any of us is obliged, by any morality, to submit to this ultimate debasement.

"So I go. I go grateful for the love I have been given, the light I have once seen—yes, even the fight I have lost. I ask you to keep our Proteus people together—the benevolent and the combative. Both are needed. Neither can survive without the other. The tyrants must hear the growling in the forest. Their victims must hear

the singing in the darkness. Ciao, Maury! Ciao,
Kitty! Give my love to Uncle Andrea and see
that he gets a copy of what I have written. John
Spada will die; but Proteus is still unchained
and—who knows how many fish there are in the
sea? . . ."

Maury Feldman laid down the manuscript. He
picked up the book of the Speech of Truth, fumbled
for the page and intoned the Kaddish prayer:

"God, full of mercy, who dwellest on high, cause
the soul of John Spada, which has gone to its rest,
to find repose in the wings of the Schechinah, among
the souls of the holy, pure as the firmament of the
skies, for they have offered charity for the memory
of his soul; for the sake of this, hide him in the
mystery of thy wings forever and bind up his soul in
the bond of life; may the Lord be his inheritance;
and may he repose in peace in his resting place . . ."

"Requiescat," said Uncle Andrea. "Thank you for
your friendship to my nephew."

Maury Feldman pinched out the Shivah candle
and said in his edgy way, "I loved him. I'll miss him.
He had so much goddam style. . . . And he's right. He
didn't fail altogether. Proteus is still unchained!"

"Like all myths, it's man-made," said Uncle
Andrea moodily. "And it has a flaw in it. Proteus is
the shepherd of the sea creatures. But even in his
kingdom, the big fish still eat the little fish, and they'll
go on doing it for ever and ever. . . ."

"Amen!" said Kitty Cowan in her brusque fashion.
"I'm tired—and I'm scared of the dark. Which of
you gentlemen is going to walk me home?"

"I will," said Uncle Andrea. "I'd like to keep you
in the family, Caterina!"

372

MORRIS WEST ON *PROTEUS*

Mr. West was born in Australia, where he studied and lived with the Christian Brothers and graduated from the University of Melbourne. Prior to World War II he taught in New South Wales and Tasmania. During the war Mr. West served with the Australian Imperial Forces, specializing in cryptology. After a stint as a writer, director and producer of radio programs, he turned to writing books and plays and has become known for his theological thrillers dealing with contemporary events. The results were a succession of international bestsellers including *The Devil's Advocate, The Shoes of the Fisherman, The Ambassador, The Salamander, Daughter of Silence* and *The Navigator.*

In his latest novel, *Proteus,* already an international bestseller, Mr. West deals with the subject of terrorism. He states, "Having lived in Rome with my family for seven years before leaving there, I was aware of the rise of terrorist groups—Baader-Meinhof in Germany, the Red Brigades in Italy, the Palestinian hijackers. And so I wondered what would be my own response to terrorism?"

It was further brought home to him when West was asked to return to Rome and work on a motion picture. He said, "Although I had always lived modestly in Rome and kept a low profile, I wondered if I accepted the job and returned there, was there a possibility of being kidnapped? And when my Italian lawyer advised how much it would take to insure me (the premium was $50,000 for a one million dollar policy) I decided not to take the assignment. Besides, kidnappers do not provide guarantees of returning their victims in one piece. It was that sort of experience that underscored the questions that I dramatize in *Proteus.*"

In Mr. West's words, *Proteus* is about "the irretrievable positions to which man commits himself. There is no salvation for man from the bloody, pragmatic terror of today's politics. Terror produces counterterror; the cycle completes itself as we have seen in Iran."

He adds, "We are all familiar with the phenomena, the things that happen: assassination, hijacking, bombing, the violence practiced by police, by security men, by professional torturers. It is our response which is in question. How far can we go? What morality applies? I have written not an answer but a riddle: If I act not, I become their slave."

Mr. West currently lives with his family in Surrey, England, where his four children are going to school.